With Stars in My Eyes:
My Adventures in British Fandom

is published on behalf of

Noreascon 4

for their
Guest of Honour
Peter Weston

With Stars in My Eyes:
My Adventures in British Fandom

by

Peter Weston

The NESFA Press
Post Office Box 809
Framingham, MA 01701
U.S.A.
2004

International Standard Book Number
1-886778-55-8

FIRST EDITION

September 2004

Acknowledgements

Parts of this book have appeared elsewhere in an earlier form:

Chapter 1 first appeared in Rob Jackson's *Maya* 11, July 1976, and also in Dick Smith & Leah Zeldes Smith's fanthology *Contact*, October 2001.
Chapter 2 first appeared in Rich & Nicki Lynch's *Mimosa* 30, August 2003,
Chapter 3 first appeared in Mark Plummer & Claire Brialey's *Banana Wings* 19, March 2004
Small portions of Chapters 8 & 9 first appeared in *Maya* 12/13, January 1977
A small portion of Chapter 17 first appeared in *Science Fiction Monthly*, June 1975
Portions of Chapter 18 first appeared in *Maya* 9, November 1975, and *Maya* 15, 1978
Portions of Chapter 19 first appeared in *Maya* 8, July 1975, & *Maya* 9, November 1975, and a section was reprinted in the fanthology *Easter Wine*, edited by Claire Brialey & Mark Plummer and produced for Seacon '03, the 2003 British Easter convention.
A portion of Chapter 20 first appeared in *Maya* 15, 1978, and other portions in *Progress Report* 1 of Interaction, the 63rd World SF Convention, August 2003, and in *Progress Report* 4 of Noreascon, the 62nd World SF Convention, July 2003.
Appendix 2 first appeared in the *Programme Book* of Helicon 2, the 2002 British Easter convention, edited by Claire Brialey & Mark Plummer.

Special thanks are due to a number of individuals without whose help this story could not have been written. I used four major sources of information: First, Greg Pickersgill, who made so much old fanzine material available for research, and gave a great deal of useful advice and encouragement in the early stages of the book's evolution. For a full background of British fandom at the time I was indebted to Rob Hansen's invaluable guide *Then*, and Rob similarly provided a number of rare items. Bill Burns unearthed valuable photographs, and his vast eFanzines web-site proved very useful, while Dave Langford's web-site proved a gateway to many riches, particularly to my 1975 TAFF Report for *SF Monthly*, which I had completely forgotten ever writing. Dave's computer-brain cross-indexed file of *Ansible* also helped me to compile my final round-up of "Where Are They Now?" Contact details for all of the above are provided in Appendix 1.
I want to thank Joe Siclari, for getting the project started, and Tony Lewis, for safeguarding it through to completion. Quotations, advice, material help

and moral support were given variously by Brian Aldiss, Ron Bennett, Vernon Brown, Malcolm Edwards, Steve Green, Harry Harrison, Dicky Howett, Edward James, John Jarrold, Dave Langford, Jim Linwood, Darroll Pardoe, Rog Peyton, Martin Pitt, Mark Plummer, Chris Priest, David Pringle, David Redd, Peter Roberts, Bob Rickard, Doreen Rogers, Tom Shippey, Ken Slater, Andrew Stephenson, Mike Turner, Gerry Webb, and Kevin Williams.

Particular help in finding photographs came from Dave Barber, Harry Bell, Bill Burns, Tony Edwards, Rob Hansen, Dicky Howett, Rob Jackson, Jim Linwood, Ina Shorrock, and Kevin Williams. New cartoons were kindly provided by Jim Barker, who cleverly turned various points of my text into absolute works of art, and earlier cartoons from Harry Bell, Mike Higgs, Dicky Howett, and Steve Green are reprinted with their permission from the original sources shown.

Finally, three people stand out for very special mention. First, Cliff Teague, without whose pluck, determination, and audacity none of this would have happened. Second, Rog Peyton, who was in at the very beginning, who has stuck with it through all these years, and with whom I have never yet had a seriously cross word, despite our slightly different attitudes towards fanzine fandom and certain science fiction writers. Finally, of course, my wife Eileen, who wasn't put off by my peculiar hobby back in 1967, who has participated enthusiastically in my fannish adventures ever since, and who last year endured through the hundreds of hours I spent at the computer, with hardly a word of complaint.

Peter Weston
April 2004

Art Credits

Previously published drawings

Melting Pot, Ivor Latto, from *Zenith Speculation,* 1965, page 127

Melting Pot, Pam Yates, from *Zenith Speculation,* 1966, page 143

Thirdmancon Programme Book cover, 1969, Ivor Latto, page 171

Robot, Jack Gaughan, from *Speculation,* 1969, page 176

Worcestercon Programme Book, 1971, Vincent Di Fate, page 197

Seacon logo—adopted April 1977, Harry Bell, page 263

Previously published cartoons

Harry Bell, from *Maya* 8, 1975, page 24

Mike Higgs, from *Link* 1, 1964, page 76

Dicky Howett, from *Con* 1, 1965, page 99

Dicky Howett, from *Padlock,* 1965, page 105

Dicky Howett, from *Wrinkled Shrew* 5, 1976, page 178

Harry Bell, from *Maya* 9, 1976, page 242

Jim Barker, from *Maya* 15, 1976, page 246

Harry Bell, from *Maya* 8, 1975, page 248

Harry Bell, from *Maya* 9, 1976, page 254

Harry Bell, from *Maya* 9, 1976, page 242

Jim Barker, from *Maya* 15, 1976, page 246

Jim Barker, from *Maya* 15, 1976, page 269

Steve Green, from *Prolapse* 2, 1983, page 281, page 282

All other cartoons are by Jim Barker and were commissioned for this book.

Covers

Zenith 1, Mike Higgs

Zenith 2, Mike Higgs

Zenith 3, Arthur Thomson

Zenith 4, Arthur Thomson

Zenith 5, Eddie Jones

Zenith 6, Eddie Jones

Zenith Speculation 7, Brian McCabe

Zenith Speculation 8, Arthur Thomson

Zenith Speculation 9, Eddie Jones

Zenith Speculation 10, Jim Cawthorn

Zenith Speculation 11, Joseph Zajackowski

Zenith Speculation 12, Jim Groves

Zenith Speculation 13, Ken McIntyre

Speculation 14, Riccardo Leveghi

Speculation 15, Pam Yates

Speculation 16, Bob Rickard

Speculation 17, Bob Rickard

Speculation 18, Riccardo Leveghi

Speculation 19, Bob Rickard

Speculation 20, Bob Rickard

Speculation 21, Jack Gaughan

Speculation 22, Eddie Jones

Speculation 23, Pam Yates

Speculation 24, Ivor Latto

Speculation 25, Dick Bergeron

Speculation 26, Ivor Latto

Speculation 27, Bob Rickard

Speculation 28, Ivor Latto

Speculation 29, Vincent Di Fate

Speculation 30, Bob Rickard

Speculation 31, photograph

Speculation 32, photograph

Speculation 33, Andrew Stephenson

Contents

With Stars in My Eyes:
My Adventures in British Fandom

Preface
by
Peter Weston

"What's it all about, really," writes fan-critic Mark Plummer, "all those stages on the road from pink slips in Birmingham to fannish celebrity?"

What indeed but a journey of discovery on a road leading first, to the junk-shops of post-war England in search of old science fiction magazines, then onwards in a quest for the Perfect Fanzine, and ultimately for the Perfect Convention.

Peter Weston will now happily settle for the perfect Room Party, but he can tell stories about his travels through the great years of British fandom, about old fans and new, professionals and publishers. Why did Harry Harrison throw a meat pie at Brian Aldiss? Who locked Charles Platt in the wardrobe? Why did Michael Moorcock flee for the station? Who forgot to introduce Arthur C. Clarke?

He charts the end of the old, cosy British fandom of the early '60s and describes the newcomers who eventually became the movers and shapers of the later era. Peter meets the young Terry Pratchett, and describes the trials and tribulations of producing his own magazine *Speculation* for ten years, during which time it chronicled the birth of the much-hyped "New Wave" and its head-on collision with the "Old School" of SF writers. He explores fannish legends, reveals hilarious convention incidents, and explains what it is really like to edit an original anthology series. Peter describes his quest for the coveted Hugo, his travels to conventions in Washington and Florida, and culminates with the success of Seacon '79, the first of the modern British World SF conventions.

11

Introduction

Appropriately, this book begins—and ends—with a quotation from Brian Aldiss, who figures so prominently in a good many chapters.

"I'm glad to hear you are writing an autobiography," he said, when I first told him about the project. For, as Brian advised from his own recent experience, "I found it enjoyable; it's a bit like being psychoanalysed, because once you get going you remember things previously quite hidden in the mists of drink and time."

He was absolutely right. Although I thought it would be easy when Joe Siclari first broached the idea at the 2003 Boskone; all I needed to do was look up the five "Slice of Life" columns I wrote in the mid-seventies for Rob Jackson's fanzine *Maya,* and simply link them together with a bit of new material to fill in the gaps. Nothing to it!

"How many words will that make?" asked Joe, sceptically.

"Oh, about twenty-five thousand," I guessed, wondering if that would be too long.

"No good," he responded, looking worried in the way he does so well. "I'll need fifty thousand, minimum."

I reeled back, aghast. I couldn't do that much! Why, I could hardly remember anything about those early days. Even the *Maya* columns were a distant memory, the fanzines buried somewhere beneath the debris of thirty years. Where to begin?

Back from Boston, I dug out those columns and found out how to scan them with OCR, thanks to help from my technical expert, Ben Wheeler. Then I sat and thought about the earliest installment, "The Little Pink Slip," still the best piece I ever wrote, which described my first meeting with Cliff Teague and the other "Ancient Brummies." There was more juice to be squeezed from that lemon, I realised; it needed a prequel, about the five frustrating years during which I scoured the back-streets of Birmingham for science fiction and didn't know anyone else who read the stuff. And a sequel—what happened to Cliff and the others from Charlie's front room?

The memories started to seep back. I e-mailed some of my old pals and asked for their recollections of days past, people like Rog Peyton, Doreen Rogers, Ken Slater, Ron Bennett. They responded—Rog, bless him, had just been given a box of old fanzines from Rod Milner, undisturbed for nearly forty years, an absolute treasure-trove, with the programme book from the 1964 Peterborough convention along with Rod's (unused) badge, some issues of the Brum-group fanzine, *Brumble,* several of Archie Mercer's *Vectors,* and other rarities.

I asked Greg Pickersgill for more fanzines from the period—Charles Platt's *Beyond,* Ken Cheslin's *Les Spinge,* and obscure titles like *Tensor* and *Chaos.* Greg had nearly everything, squirreled neatly away in his "Memory Hole" collection, an incredible repository of material which he stores in his tiny terraced house in a remote corner of Wales, all catalogued and listed on his web-site. It's amazing how much detail I was able to find in convention reports and letter-columns, supplemented by personal stories as they came in—with particularly good stuff from Chris Priest and Jim Linwood, to name but two.

I re-read Rob Hansen's *Then,* a painstaking history of British fandom from the earliest beginnings up to 1980—accessible on Rob's web-site—and Rob was able to help with a couple of fanzine titles like Ivor Latto's *Fankle,* which even Greg didn't have. Rob also let me browse through Ethel Lindsay's photo-album, though there didn't seem to be many images from the mid-sixties. Few of us had cameras in those days! That was another problem, until I was fortunate enough to contact two fans from the period, Dave Barber and Dicky Howett, both of whom had marvellous bits of old film footage stored away, from which I was able to extract stills of personalities like Terry Pratchett and Michael Moorcock, back when they still walked amongst us! Later, Kevin Williams unearthed an equally valuable cache of previously unseen images from Seacon '79, including a picture of our Tower of Beercans to the Moon.

Slowly, it all started to come together as I embarked on a voyage of discovery into my own forgotten past. At first I had only the haziest recollections of my first convention, the people I met, the things we did. Even my own fanzine,

Speculation, was a dim memory, although I once thought of almost nothing else for a period of nearly ten years. Yet, as Brian Aldiss had predicted, when I began to do the research, started to read the fanzines and correspond with old chums—Mike Turner, Edward James, Darroll Pardoe—the memories came back in a flood. It turned out that I had actually forgotten very little, deep down those early experiences were still there, perhaps because they made such a vivid impression at the time. They mattered, they gave meaning to my life. So I was able to recall those function rooms at the "Bull" in Peterborough, the sea-front at Great Yarmouth, the squalor of the London Sci-con. Conversations, too; the first words Malcolm Edwards said to me in 1970, my last encounter with Charles Platt in Buxton, Andy Porter's midnight greeting at JFK in 1974.

For six months I worked away industriously, averaging a chapter per month. In June I suddenly had to go to New Zealand for a family emergency and bought a laptop—with more technical help from Ben—so that I could continue during what was expected to be a protracted stay-over. In the end I was back within ten days, but even so, portions of chapters 8 & 9 were written on aeroplanes and in hotel rooms in Auckland and Brisbane. The laptop came on holidays with us to Brittany and Florida (to my wife Eileen's considerable disgust) but as winter approached I began to panic; by the beginning of December when I visited Greg and Catherine in Haverfordwest, I was still only up to 1967!

From then onwards (with only a brief respite for Christmas), I did almost nothing else but write, producing a chapter per week through January and early February, and managed to deliver the complete book at Boskone 41. It wasn't the fifty thousand words that Joe had requested but more than twice as much. I hadn't realised I had so much to say—and with another six months I could have added a further 30,000 words, perish the thought!

I've attempted to describe the various incidents exactly as they happened, resisting the urge to second-guess my earlier self by assuming knowledge I couldn't possibly have had at the time. Where the temptation for hindsight has been too strong I have put such details into footnotes. Otherwise, I have tried to be scrupulously honest throughout, telling the story of an earnest young man with stars in his eyes, who fell in love with science fiction at an early age and who spent most of his time and money for many years upon a quest for something he could probably have only hazily defined, the idea that the loose entity we call science fiction *fandom,* for all its faults, is something special and something uniquely worthwhile.

Peter Weston, April 2004

(Once this book appears, there will doubtless be a chorus of "that's not right," and "you didn't mention...," and I will of course be very interested in these comments, which might one day be incorporated into a subsequent re-issue. E-mail me at: pr.weston@btinternet.com).

The Little Pink Slip
Chapter 1

What would it be like, I wondered, to meet somebody else who was interested in science fiction? People I could talk to, others like myself, who might perhaps have a few books I hadn't already read?

It was January 1963, a dark, wet Tuesday evening, and I had travelled for over an hour on draughty Corporation buses from Northfield, right across to the other side of the city. Now I walked down Hunters Road, Erdington, in a mood of some apprehension. Two weeks earlier, I had found a little slip of pink paper in an old magazine at the Rag Market; "Are you interested in SF?" it asked. "Join the Erdington Science Fiction Circle."

After years of solitary reading it was my first indication that others like me existed, and I badly needed something like this. Since moving out to the council estate I had lost my old pals, and at nineteen you don't easily make new friendships, particularly when you'd rather spend Saturday afternoons hunting for old *Galaxy* and *Astounding* magazines than going to football matches. I knew too that I had gone about as far as I could on my own. After five years of hanging around the market every week I'd nearly given up hope of finding *Galaxy* numbers 5, 6, 7, 36, and 52, issues I desperately needed to complete my index of authors and story titles.

The houses were tall, redbrick Victorian, set back from the road behind protective privet and overgrown front gardens, with a railway cutting on the

15

right-hand side. In the dark I stumbled up several paths until I found number 35, a big, detached house, the first one as the road turned away from the railway. My finger hovered for a moment before I pushed the bell button. This was the turning-point, the moment of no return.

The door opened to reveal a shadowy figure.

"I'm Cliff Teague. Quick, come in before she catches us!"

I followed him inside, into a dismal hall. Cold floor tiles in the intricate little diamond patterns of red, buff, and ochre that had been all the rage seventy years earlier. Smells of clothes washing and cabbage cooking, a general air of dimness and gloom.

"In here," said my host furtively, opening a door into the front room. I went inside and was transfixed! Books! More books than I had ever seen in my life outside the public libraries! Shelves of them, all along one long wall, round the corner, up and over the fireplace, down the other side. And all science fiction! My hold on reality blurred for a moment. Cliff said something to me, and no doubt I said something to him. But my fingers itched to get at all those books!

Books...and all science fiction

Vaguely I noticed we were in a large, bare room, which contained two unmade beds, some crockery, and a few sticks of broken down furniture. And two other people.

"This is Rog," said Cliff. "And this is Dave Casey."

Rog was fair haired and stocky, and in his business suit seemed very confident and several years older than me. Dave looked younger, big and lolloping in a thick sweater. I noticed he had a huge blackhead on the end of his nose and I wondered why he didn't squeeze it.

"Have you read the *Foundation* series?" said Rog. "Fantastic, isn't it? What have you got to trade? I'll swap two paperbacks for SFBC hardcovers. Here's my wants list. Now…"

Those little blue and red ones, could they be Ace Doubles? I marvelled, because for years I had read about them in Schuyler Miller's column but had never actually seen them before. Cliff had things I had never even heard of. All those magazines! Not just the cherished *Astounding* and *Galaxy* (with a start, I realised he had those missing five issues) but others, with names like *Startling, Super Science, Planet Stories,* and lots more. Paperbacks, too. Hundreds of them. And hardcovers. Where had he got all those books? But Cliff was still talking to me.

"Oh yes," he said proudly. "I want to get four copies of everything. The American paperback and hardcover, and the British PB and hardback. The covers are different, you see."

Strange chap! I didn't care about the covers; I just wanted to *read* them! I looked at him more closely. Cliff was thin and wiry, with a pale, pinched face and a dusting of freckles around the bridge of his nose and upper cheekbones. He had a mop of untidy, curly hair and deep brown eyes, which shone with excitement when he talked about His Collection.

Rog had met Cliff two years earlier, when he'd been looking in vain for a new paperback title (*The 27th Day,* by John Mantley). Having tried everywhere else in the city, Rog had rushed around to the bookstall on Birmingham's New Street Station, just before closing time. No, they did not have it either, and he was turning away when the young lad behind the counter asked him, "Do you read much science fiction?" It was Cliff.

That night the two of them talked to nine o'clock, and arranged to get together on Sunday at Cliff's place. Rog thought he had a huge collection—192 books—until he saw that Cliff already had over 300. Together, they decided to form a club, the Birmingham Science Fiction Group, and to hold regular meetings. They'd been slowly building it up ever since, bringing in recruits like Dave Casey, and Jack Pickering, who at 26 was a bit older than the others, although he soon gave up science fiction in favour of collecting Victorian pop bottles.

Every Tuesday they met in Cliff's room, occasions enlivened by an unpredictable landlady forever likely to rage and rant about "not having strangers in her house," or by the presence of the International Socialist who shared the room and who would sometimes come in and lie on his bed or cook a rough supper on the gas ring. Dimly, I realised this wasn't exactly what I had expected.

"Care for a game of chess?" asked Dave shyly, taking a miniature set out of his pocket. But I had spotted a copy of Damon Knight's *In Search of Wonder* on the mantelpiece, and was reverently turning its pages. A whole book about Science Fiction! I started to read "The Jagged Blade," the chapter on James Blish. I had found what I was looking for. I had been deprived too long.

That night I borrowed Jack Vance's *Big Planet,* the Ace Double with the wonderful Emsh cover, and started to read it on the long bus journey home. I was totally captivated; Vance was one of my favourites anyway, from his occasional short stories in the magazines, but this was terrific. Even better, it was backed with another short novel, *Slaves of the Klau.* Suddenly I had access to books I had only dreamed about. A whole new world had opened up!

At the next meeting, I met other members. Mike Higgs had been one of Cliff's earliest recruits, enlisted while working in a newsagent's shop. He had a long face with dark, intense eyes, tight-curled hair, and unlike the rest of us, he had a long-time girlfriend, Cynthia (who later came along to a few meetings). He was already starting to sell some artwork professionally and was interested in fandom at least partly because of the opportunities it seemed to offer to do illustrations. Mike was fascinated by the pulp-magazine character "The Shadow," and had a strong interest in comics and graphic novels.

Darroll Pardoe had come to us from the former Stourbridge fandom, dark-haired with an infectious grin, our resident boffin, who visited us during vacations from his Chemistry course at Cambridge. For many years Darroll's chief claim to fame was his entry in *Who's Who in Fandom*, that he "had read *Lord of the Rings* seven times." Then there was Oliver Harvey from the back streets of Aston, a poor, inner suburb. Ollie was small and pale with a thick shock of black hair that was already starting to recede, glasses, and a thin beak of a nose. He was keen enough, came to every meeting, but didn't say much and would totally clam up in the presence of strangers. Finally, we had Rod Milner, a rather sardonic, worldly-wise character whom Rog had befriended when Rod started to work in the paperback department of Hudson's, the city's biggest bookshop.

Just a week or two earlier Cliff had managed to pull something of a masterstroke by getting the club mentioned in the local weekly newspaper. He had contacted a sympathetic reporter, Tony Ventris-Field, who had made the "Erdington SF Circle" his front-page story in the first 1963 issue. (The BSFG changed its name especially for the occasion, since he was only allowed to write about local organisations and events.) Living on the other side of the city, of course, I hadn't seen the paper but it brought in some other recruits, in particular Charlie Winstone, who came along just a few weeks after I did.

Charlie's house was close by, so when Cliff had a massive row with his landlady a few months later we moved a half mile down the hill and began to meet in his front room. Charlie seemed much older than the rest of us, although he was only 31, and tragically, he was a hunchbacked dwarf. At first, I had a little trouble adjusting to this, but soon didn't give it a thought.

Charlie lived with his widowed mother and brothers, John and Harry, in a gloomy Victorian villa, perched high up above George Road, Erdington, behind an overgrown front garden. If we should want to use the toilet, we had to get a torch, stumble in the dark down twenty or so treacherous steps, out the front gate, along the pavement and under the house through a dank, cobwebbed passage that was really Lovecraftian. At the rear, we would climb back up another flight of stone steps and edge gingerly past an enormous mad dog, leaping and snarling at the end of its chain, to a cold and spider-infested outdoor lavatory. Usually we tried to hold our liquid, which seemed the safest option!

The front room itself was jammed with a broken down sofa and armchairs to match, together with a respectable collection of books. Not as many as Cliff had, of course—nobody had as many books as Cliff—but hundreds of volumes nonetheless. We developed a routine. Every Tuesday evening we would crowd around the gas-fire in the parlour and after displaying our latest acquisitions would commence a board game. Usually we played "Risk," but Charlie and his brothers had almost every board game you could imagine. We paid sixpence in "dues," and had a collection to pay for the little cakes and tea, which his mother brought in at half time.

Life was good. They told me about Ken Slater's catalogues and I filled the holes in my magazine collection. I told them about "Pick-A-Book" and we put together a collective order for twelve titles. They introduced me to Richard Witter's F&SF Book Co. on Staten Island and I started to buy Scribners' Heinlein juveniles. We got up to as many as three meetings per week, seeing Cliff on Sunday and sometimes visiting Rog's house in up-market Quinton, a "good" area, although his father didn't really approve. "It's a mug's game," Fred Peyton said. "Getting into science fiction fandom is like digging a big hole, jumping in, and pulling the sides down on top of yourself." My mother had similar advice. "All this science fiction will turn your brain," she prophesised darkly.

Cliff moved in with his mother after the authorities gave her a tiny, reconditioned back-house (number 1/299 Heath Street, near to Winson Green Prison), and on Sunday afternoons we used to meet there for our traditional fare of pineapple and melted ice cream (they didn't have a refrigerator). You see, Cliff's early life had been difficult. He had never had a father, and his mother had been institutionalised. A bright boy, but lonely, he had spent his childhood in various care-homes and with foster parents. He didn't have very much in life except for his books. No wonder they meant so much to him.

I had been deprived, but only of science fiction. Cliff was my first experience of meeting someone who had been *really* deprived, of a home life, a family, everything we take for granted. Oh, I had lived in rough areas of Birmingham for most of my life, but I was far better off than poor old Cliff. And what about Charlie, physically forever apart? What dark shadow was hovering over Dave Casey? (Eventually, he withdraw from the world and became a recluse.) Rog and I began to wonder, what was *our* problem?

But at least we were all trying to make our way in the world. Rog was a trainee at a firm of quantity surveyors, while I was in the final months at school, doing A-Level Sciences and starting to think about getting a job. Dave worked in a brass foundry and Charlie was employed by the Electricity Board. Cliff led a more haphazard existence, and though he claimed to be working at the station bookstall, I could never quite understand how he managed to spend so much time roaming around with his battered cardboard suitcase, looking for science fiction. For Cliff could smell SF at a half mile radius. He seemed to have visited every junk-shop and bookseller in the city, and he'd found incredible bargains such as the Scribner's juvenile edition of *Have Spacesuit, Will Travel*, at a time when American books were completely unavailable in the U.K.

Here's an example. A few months after we met, I turned up early for a meeting to find Cliff flourishing his latest acquisition, a paperback edition of Jack Vance's *The Dying Earth* from a new publisher called Lancer. I went wild; this was his legendary first novel, long out of print and totally unavailable, and now Cliff had found it, just like that. I simply had to have the book! Where did he get it? Cliff told me that he had bought it that very afternoon in an obscure newspaper shop a few miles away and yes, he thought they might have another copy. Immediately, I shot off, literally running to the 'bus stop to get there before the shop closed, returning an hour later, triumphant, with the precious volume. That book meant a lot to me, but I think Cliff was more interested in the cover painting. To him it was strictly routine, just one more title for the Collection.

He had the most amazing talent for "gettin," and he would buy books and sell books to get whatever he needed. Cliff never borrowed money from us, but every week, somehow, he had managed to acquire a few dozen more books. He travelled all over the area and had started to hitchhike down to London, going around the bookshops during the day and living rough at night. He once told an incredible tale about finding an abandoned sack of potatoes in a vegetable market and frying them up in a squat for a bunch of hippies.

Jim Linwood commented, "When he came to Kingdon Road he used to be terribly spoiled by Marion and Nell Golding, who took pity on the little ragamuffin boy from Brum. He always came with a hit list of jumble sales around Ladbroke Grove where he was sure he could pick up complete runs of *Weird Tales* or *Amazing Stories* for nothing, or even be paid to take them away.

"I recall we were once walking through the mean streets of Paddington one Saturday morning, chatting with Dick Ellingsworth, and Cliff vanished in mid-sentence leaving Dick and me alone for several minutes, trying to figure out which rag-and-bone shop he'd disappeared into. He eventually emerged from one with an enraged look, snarling, 'They haven't got anything!' "

One of his trips was a Turning Point. In mid-1963, Cliff heard about the Friday evening meetings that Ella Parker was holding for the SF Club of London at the time. He had found her address in a magazine, so he hitched down with the idea of dropping in on the meeting. He got to Canterbury Road, only to find the house was empty and boarded-up; unbeknown to Cliff, Ella had been re-housed in a nearby tower block of flats. Undeterred, however, he broke in and found several fanzines, which had arrived after Ella's departure. They were *Inside* from Jon White, and *New Frontiers* from Norm Metcalf. (Both were half size, litho-printed, and were entirely about science fiction, and when Cliff gave them to me back in Birmingham they were to have a tremendous influence on my own fanac. I promptly subscribed to both, 10/- each, which was a lot of money in those days, and never heard a word from either.)

Cliff admired the wall of one room that, so he told us, had been inscribed with the signatures of visiting fans, and he settled down to sleep rough in an upstairs bedroom. However, in the small hours, he heard the sound of heavy footsteps coming up the stairs, and panic-stricken he hid behind a door as a tramp came into the room. Cliff darted out and away, and wandered around Kilburn, spending the rest of the night in a public convenience. Early next morning he slipped into a cafeteria and went around eating the left over toast from the tables of people who had finished their breakfast, before starting his long journey home.

He was an incredible character, no doubt about it. One Sunday afternoon we visited his mother's house and found him looking dazed, his room a shambles. Cliff had put up shelves all around the walls, and because the room was too small, he had taken down his bed and rolled up the mattress, only letting it down at night. He slept

Jim Barker

Buried alive in science fiction

on a heap of books, surrounded on all sides by books, and early that morning his shelves had collapsed while he was still asleep, bringing the lot down on top of him. What a way to go, we thought, *buried alive* in science fiction!

Good old Cliff was courageous, generous with his friends, and good company. If it hadn't been for his little pink slip, I might never have found the local group; if it hadn't been for his enterprise we might not have learned of the bigger world of fandom outside our little circle. For very shortly after I joined the Group he told us about some sort of "convention" to be held in Peterborough over Easter, 1963. It all sounded very far away and forbidding and we took no notice, except for Cliff, who hitchhiked there and freeloaded for the weekend. He slept in a broom cupboard, frightening the life out of the cleaning woman next morning who thought she had found a dead body! Back he came with a rucksack of books—including an autographed copy of *Stormbringer* from Mike Moorcock, of which he was particularly proud.

We were impressed, this sounded good. So when Cliff told us there was going to be a second Peterborough convention the following year, we decided to go along. Under the mistaken impression that we needed to be members of the British Science Fiction Association in order to attend, eight of us joined the BSFA, to make it "official." This would prove to be our collective breakthrough into national fandom and it would sow the seeds for the eventual destruction of the local group.

But another time bomb was ticking. I had only seen the two fanzines Cliff had brought back from London, until one night we were visited by our local BNF, Ken Cheslin from the town of Stourbridge, about 15 miles west of the city. Ken had been in fandom for *ages,* ever since 1959, and he had been running a group which had attracted people like Dave Hale and Darroll Pardoe. He had lost his right hand a few years earlier through some sort of terrible industrial accident, and had spent part of his compensation on a Gestetner duplicator and the rest on science fiction. He lived with relatives and seemed to manage well enough, driving a specially adapted mini-van. Ken had contacts all over the place, and lots of books—not as many as Cliff had, of course, nobody had as many books as Cliff—and he was well into fanzine fandom.

Ken pushed his fanzines at us in a peculiarly off-hand manner, without much explanation. *Envoy* seemed to be an "OMPA-zine," whatever that was, with unfunny cartoons about "Olaf the Viking" and lines of print that wandered across the pages, changing colour from muddy red to green-black along the way. *Hyphen* was another one of Ken's fanzines, done entirely on green paper, although when he opened it there was another cover underneath, with the improbable title of *Les Spinge.* "He's a Stourbridge fan," Ken said, chuckling, "Leslie P. Hinge." It was obviously some sort of in-group joke that I didn't understand.

In fact I didn't understand any of it. All this, together with Ken's erratic grammar and spelling, meant that I couldn't relate to his fanzines at all. But they showed me that quite ordinary people could bring out a magazine, while *Inside* and *New Frontiers* had given me a goal I could comprehend. They, together with Damon Knight's *In Search of Wonder* (which I re-read over and over, and eventually begged off Cliff), made me want to put out my own fanzine, which would, naturally, be entirely about science fiction.

The idea grew in my mind through the late summer. I was working by then, and when I discovered the company had a duplicating machine I started to nag at the others in the group to write something. The first issue of *Zenith* appeared in October 1963, just before my twentieth birthday. It was half sized, spirit duplicated in purple ink, and only ran to 35 copies. But through an incredible coincidence, that same week another neofan called Charles Platt produced *his* first issue, also half sized and equally purple. Henceforth our names would be uneasily linked.

On the Threshold
Chapter 2

When I was a little boy, I was fascinated with the Moon and the stars, which in those days you could see quite clearly from even the middle of a big city. Later, when I was growing up, I read a library book that told you how "easy" it was to make a simple telescope of your own. Begging a set of lenses from a neighbourhood optician, I installed them in a cardboard tube, but found the net increase in magnification hardly worth the trouble.

Then I saw a newspaper advertisement from an Army & Navy surplus dealer which offered a war-surplus telescope for the princely sum of £7.10s.0d (a lot, for a twelve-year-old in 1955). I agreed to pay for it out of my pocket money in 26 weekly instalments, and it came by post in a large box, a magnificent brass monster with leather carrying-case, all of three feet long when fully extended. Later, I bought a tripod from the same surplus dealer. This was more like it! It was a "terrestrial" telescope, of course, and didn't give the inverted image of a true astronomical instrument, but that suited me just fine. I pointed it at the Moon and for the first time saw the round dish of Mare Crisium, the dark crater of Plato and the peculiar, raised-up appearance of *Palus Somnli*. And the tiny, bright crescent of Venus just after sunset in the early evening sky.

However, it's amazing how suspicious the local neighbourhood becomes when they know you have a telescope. No one would have cared if I'd tied tin cans to cats' tails or ridden noisy motorbikes up and down the street in the rather poor district where I grew up. But because of my telescope I came in for much abuse. I used to take it to a communal back yard with a halfway reasonable view of the sky, set up on a convenient dustbin, and peer at the constellations until invariably being told to "clear off." One man even threatened to set his dog on me, and he didn't even live around there!

To see the Pleiades from a coalshed roof

How much spice this added to the thrill of discovery! To see the Pleiades from a coalshed roof,[1] Orion's Belt on a winter night, and Jupiter's moons from my bedroom window, this was the real thing, pure undiluted sense of wonder.

I found Fred Hoyle's magnificent *Frontiers of Astronomy* in the local library, a thick book absolutely overflowing with his controversial theories about the "steady state" Universe, how the heavy elements were made in supernovae, and the origins of the Solar System. I borrowed Cecilia Payne-Gaposhkin's splendid book *Stars in the Making,* and struggled to understand her explanation of the Cepheid Variable method of measuring stellar distances.

Yes, Astronomy made a lasting impression on my soul and after my brief, abortive attempt to organise a group at school the Physics teacher told me about the Birmingham Astronomy Group. They met in a cellar at the University's city-centre faculty, an elegant Gothic building, and for a time I was their youngest member. Unfortunately, through a combination of extreme youth and diffidence I didn't get very much out of the BAG. Nobody spoke to me at their meetings, and they seemed to be totally occupied with grinding a 21-inch mirror, a project they had already been working on for the six years since the group had been formed.

---

[1] This phrase appeared in my first *Maya* column, and I was immensely pleased when at the next convention Bob Shaw complimented me on it. "To see the Pleiades from a coalshed roof," he mused, "I like that, it's poetic."

Well, I wasn't too enthusiastic about this since I had already spent many hours in the school basement in an unsuccessful attempt to grind my own 8-inch mirror. I'd seen enough carborundum powder and jeweller's rouge to last a lifetime, thank you, so within the year I had drifted away from the Group. (They continued to grind away for many more years before finally selling their unfinished mirror to someone else. If only they had possessed a working telescope, it might have been different.)

However, two things about the group had excited my attention. First, I'd overheard some of the younger and more enterprising members talking about making their own rockets. This was more like it! After all, I knew a lot about rockets, ever since I'd begged my mother to take me to see *Rocketship XM* (remember the pink sky?) and then *Destination Moon* back when I was a little lad in 1950. And there was a tattered heap of coverless "Yank magazines" in a box on the floor in the Group's library containing parts of something called the "Lensman" series. At the time, I didn't take much notice, but these battered magazines gave me my first bemused sight of adult science fiction.

I flirted briefly and spectacularly with rocketry, beginning as we all do with smoking mixtures of weed killer and sugar, and then switching to permanganate and magnesium powder. I put a rocket or two onto neighbours' roofs, fiddled around with electrical ignition and launching ramps, messed with ammonium nitrate (no solid residues but it can blow up quite spontaneously and is absolutely lethal), then went on to zinc-&-sulphur, which was supposedly safer although quite hard to ignite. Giving up on cardboard tubes, I persuaded a friend's dad to weld a primitive nozzle onto a piece of steel pipe, though fortunately I never actually tried to use it, because it would probably have blown up in my face!

To my amazement, I discovered that rocketry was an approved hobby in the United States. I spent some time in the reading room of the wonderful old Reference Library in Chamberlain Square and managed to get hold of a couple of American rocketry magazines. They were full of useful information. Apparently, in America there were thousands of enthusiasts who could buy kits and build rockets perfectly legally, and societies who launched them from obliging Army bases. I even got into occasional correspondence with one of them, the "Allen Park Rocket Society" in Michigan. They seemed to live in a different world.[2]

Because things were very different in Britain. The Fireworks Act of 1888 threatened severe punishment for anyone who messed around with bangers.

---

[2] At exactly the same time, as I found out much, much later, Homer Hickam and his chums were launching their first rockets in Coalville, West Virginia, going through exactly the same steps as I did, although with a bit more encouragement from local authorities. Yes, I was a "Rocket Boy"!

No distinction was made between fireworks and scientific research, which is the reason why the poor old British Interplanetary Society could never do anything practical, the way that Oberth, von Braun and Goddard did in more reasonable countries. I felt this restriction was a bit old-fashioned, and wrote a letter to the Air Ministry asking permission to fire my rockets from the disused Spitfire airfield at Castle Bromwich. They didn't answer, but passed my letter to a senior officer at the Birmingham central police station, who politely asked me to come and see him at his office.

He was very nice and gave me a cup of tea. Diplomatically, he didn't actually *forbid* me from making rockets. He knew he couldn't make it stick, not when I'd already discovered the wide range of interesting propellants which could be made from simple household ingredients (largely thanks to Arthur Mee's splendid book in the local library, *1001 Things a Boy Can Do,* long since withdrawn on safety grounds). Instead, he showed me a cupboard full of shrapnel, and an album of photographs of what had happened to previous experimenters. So effective was this persuasion that I never made another missile. Very soon afterwards, I learned that one of my heroes at the BAG had lost most of one hand through an accident on the launching pad.

Nothing was left for me but to investigate the British Interplanetary Society, in those days residing at 12 Bessborough Gardens, near the Thames. I used to write to them every few months asking for "details," and they would sent me big envelopes full of publicity blurbs for books, information about lectures, even sample copies of publications. In the 'thirties the BIS must have been an exciting crowd, and some of them (like Arthur C. Clarke and Eric Frank Russell) were science fiction fans, but after having been forbidden to experiment they had retreated into the realms of theory. As early as 1939 they had prepared a detail design for a Moon-project, using clusters of solid-fuel rockets; it wouldn't have worked, of course, but it was a revolutionary idea.

By my time, however, the BIS had become "respectable," a professional society with nothing much for me. I wanted to dream about the stars but all they offered was a forbidding printed *Journal,* rich in the realms of higher math with papers having titles like "Specific Impulse Ratios of Fuel Configurations Using Dimethylhydrazine."

Until one day they sent me another magazine, *Spaceflight,* something they had recently started that was intended to be a bit more "accessible" to the general public. This had less maths, although it still had no real "bite," no editorial personality, and was very much a scissors-&-paste compendium of launchings and hardware data. For in the real world things had started to happen. With the launch of *Sputnik 1* on October 4th, 1957, just before I was fourteen, the Space Race had begun. Suddenly the newspapers were full of headlines like "Beware The Red Moon!" (An allusion drawn straight from "Dan Dare" in *The Eagle,* that favourite comic of all British schoolboys.)

Wheels started to go round in my head. While I hadn't taken much notice of the old magazines at the Astronomy Group, an advert in *Spaceflight* for the (British) Science Fiction Book Club prompted me to send away for my first adult hardcover title, the *Robert Heinlein Omnibus*. The book consisted of two volumes of something called the "Future History," bound together under one cover. Now, I'd never heard of this Heinlein chap before, or his Future History, but it was certainly an eye-opener, though a bit dated, of course—even by 1957, it was pretty clear he'd got some details wrong. But I was intrigued by the idea of developing a consistent track for future events and by his casual, matter-of-fact treatment of new ideas, particularly in the second volume. I was hooked, and immediately sent off to join the Club.

Then I remembered I had seen some science fiction magazines while looking for *Superman* comics in a junk-shop, just down the road. These shops were on almost every corner in the inner city, a hangover from wartime shortages and rationing, full of beat-up old prams, old clothes, household oddments and usually stacks of second-hand books and magazines. I went and rummaged around, and bought several magazines at 6d per copy.

The first one I opened was called *Astounding,* dated October 1956, with a cover story illustrating something titled "Critical Difference," by Murray Leinster. I was tremendously impressed, because here was a complete future world with an entirely new technology, not just space travel with regular rockets, but with landing grids, force fields, and a way of drawing power from the ionosphere. It all sounded pretty convincing to me, with a very clever solution to the disaster facing Leinster's colony planet. I was hooked!

Leinster's name must have registered, because almost immediately afterwards I acquired the September 1957 issue with his "Ribbon in the Sky," which from the title and cover illustration I thought might be a direct sequel. Unfortunately, it was a great disappointment. In the first story Leinster had built the entire plot around a problem (the onset of an Ice Age) and an ingenious scientific gimmick with which his hero solved it (increase solar radiation by putting a cloud of reflective metallic ions into low orbit). The second story was a much more ordinary, good-guys-vs.-bad-guys situation with the clever idea relegated to being a mere backdrop. However, there were compensations, because the issue also contained "Among Thieves," a very satisfying story by Poul Anderson, along with A. Bertram Chandler's "Drift," and a clever piece of space-opera by Randall Garrett.

Next day I went out and bought another magazine, *Galaxy,* undated, but numbered "Volume 3, No.1." It had a cover showing the launch of a massive spaceship, illustrating Willy Ley's article, "Space Travel by 1960?" and a number of short, snappy stories, which I enjoyed very much. I quickly hunted out another issue, this one with a cartoon cover showing "Galaxy's 2nd Birthday," with the stories "Halo," by Hal Clement, "A Little Oil," by Eric Frank Russell, and "Baby Is Three," by Theodore Sturgeon (though I was a bit baffled by this last one).

I started to go round the neighbourhood, buying every issue I could find of *Galaxy* and *Astounding*, and other magazines, too. *If* quickly became a favourite, with those wonderful covers by Ken Fagg on the first dozen issues, none of them having anything to do with the stories inside. The first one I found showed a robot on a sort of flying saucer diving into the Sun, and it contained a brilliant story, "The Custodian," by William Tenn. Great stuff!

Science fiction hit me hard. By the end of 1957 I was addicted, every Saturday morning taking the 'bus into the city to the Rag Market. This was an indoor market in a Victorian redbrick building with cast-iron pillars, glass roof, and cobblestone floor. It contained rows and rows of stalls where you could buy almost anything—cheap clothing and fabrics (hence the "Rag" in the name), household odds-&-ends, toys, china, and of course piles of sec- ond-hand comics, books and magazines. I used to get there early and wait outside with the growing crowd until 1.00 p.m., when they rang a bell and opened the gates. The crowd would surge forward, and in they rushed, old ladies, mothers with children, men with shopping bags, literally running in their eagerness for bargains. I would be in the front row, of course, heading at full speed for the best stalls, firmly convinced that other people were trying to beat me to those precious science fiction magazines!

At first it was easy. I bought a pile every week, usually starting to read them on the 'bus on the way home. I only had my pocket money so had to be a bit choosy, and at first I didn't buy magazines containing parts of serials because I only wanted issues that could be read right through at a sitting. I wasn't too keen, either, on the homegrown British magazines. The stories in *New Worlds* didn't compare with my American favourites, so I tended to buy issues at random, read them, and trade them away the following week. I was more impressed with *Authentic,* which under the editorship of someone called Ted Tubb had started to look really good, but it ceased publication in October 1957, just when I was getting started. The larger-sized *Nebula* seemed a bit anaemic and lacked personality, but I half-heartedly collected a full run of the 40-odd issues, until it, too, stopped in 1959.

Those older issues of *Astounding* were not very satisfying either, the very thin, large-sized jobs with the crudely painted covers and no editorial features. Eventually I came to understand that all the magazines I had been collecting were British Reprint Editions and that *Astounding* in particular had a compli- cated history. Because of paper shortages during the war it had been reduced to a mere 64 pages, a stripped-down shadow of the American pulp, shorn of features like book reviews and letter-column, with stories omitted and covers switched around. While the American *ASF* had gone to digest-size in 1943, the British publisher, Atlas, carried on with their 64-page large-size editions for another ten years, because of continued economic difficulties or maybe through sheer inertia. They left out a great deal! And even when the British edition finally went to digest-size in 1953, it was still edited down to 128 pages rather than 160, as was the British edition of *Galaxy*. We British readers were being short-changed without even realising it![3]

I subscribed to both *Galaxy* and *Astounding* from their June 1958 issues. Or rather, put in a standing order with the local newsagent for both magazines. They came out as regularly as clockwork on the nineteenth day of the month, Sundays excepted, and at their peak, both apparently sold over 25,000 copies per issue. No wonder they were piled high in every junk-shop in the land! In early 1959 Atlas brought out a British edition of *F&SF*, also cut to 128 pages, and naturally I added that to my list.

My collection slowly grew more complete, and things became more difficult; now I was looking for specific issues. The first four numbers of *Galaxy* were easy, but 5, 6, & 7 were like gold dust, nowhere to be found. (The British publishers, Thorpe & Porter, had probably reduced their print-run after seeing disappointing returns from the first four issues!) What I was actually doing was playing the statistical odds, hoping that if I looked often enough the missing issues would come to light. But it was a slow and frustrating business. Sometimes I would come home without having found anything at all. I started to wonder if there was any other way. Where did the stallholders get their stock? Was there some place I didn't know about, a sort of Magazine Central, where they topped up their supplies? I struck up a conversation with "old Lil," my best source, to try and find out where she went on weekdays, but she only muttered something about "other markets" and I was no wiser. I started to have dreams about finding a shop with walls lined with science fiction magazines. I was getting desperate!

There were paperbacks, of course, just a few titles. Pan had done Arthur Clarke's *Prelude to Space* and *Earthlight* and a few other titles. Panther was really only just getting started, in 1959 taking on a little-known American

---

[3] Bizarrely, for reasons not understood, Atlas had the covers of their British editions (*ASF* and *F&SF*) re-painted by local artists, copying them more-or-less exactly from the American originals. There appears to have been no legal or technical reason for this (*Galaxy* used U.S. cover art) and I have speculated elsewhere that maybe the reason was something as ridiculous as the Atlas managing director having an unemployed artist son-in-law! The U.S. fan Curt Phillips has told how Kelly Freas was extremely upset when he discovered his work was being copied in this way, not having suspected the practice existed. Sometimes, if a cover painting was too complex, as with Freas' September 1955 cover for "Gift of Gab," Atlas made a complete substitution—a cover from a back number, or a reworked interior illustration on one occasion. Dave Wood has now constructed an entire web-site to compare these covers, which can be accessed through Bill Burns' site, www.efanzines.com.

author called Isaac Asimov with *The Currents of Space*. Market-leader was Corgi, with those tiny, green-spined editions. I used to send up for their leaflets and news releases and eagerly anticipated the day in July 1958 that *The Sands of Mars* came out. I bought it on the way to school and had half-finished it by the time I got home. Corgi followed up with *Expedition to Earth,* and then Russell's *Three to Conquer.* They were doing one book per month, and their backlist mentioned *City and the Stars,* although it was out-of-print. To my elation, however, I found a sun-faded copy in the window of a particularly decrepit shop, battered but intact. It was absolutely mind-blowing!

I was also into the public library system, although our local branch library was very strict about letting "children" into the Adult Section. They colour-coded your card to show you were under 16, and they wouldn't let you take out an "adult" book with a junior card. I got around this by getting my mother to register for a card, and used that, but you were still only allowed one fiction book (white card) and one non-fiction title (red card) at a time. That library wasn't much good, anyway. I found *Starman Jones* in the children's section, the only Heinlein juvenile to appear in the U.K. in the fifties, and, quite by chance (by looking for titles with giveaway words in them like "Moon" or "Space"), J. T. McIntosh's *World Out of Mind,* a novel that I enjoyed tremendously at the time, but there was very little else.

At the Central Library I found an oddly-titled collection, *Space, Time and Nathaniel,* by someone named Brian Aldiss, with a number of stories that really stuck in my mind. However, the big breakthrough came when I discovered that libraries in other suburbs were much better stocked. In particular, five miles up the road was Yardley & Sheldon, which had *two entire shelves* full of science fiction anthologies! The word "anthology" was a new concept to me, a sort of magazine in hardcovers, and I went at them furiously. They were British editions of American titles, generally abridged (as I discovered later), and of mixed quality, but I devoured Bleiler & Dikty, Groff Conklin, August Derleth and so on (and wondered why the editors all seemed to have such funny names). Because I was only allowed to take out one book at a time I used to hide others until my next visit, concealing them behind the gloomy racks of technical volumes, which looked as if they hadn't been disturbed since time began.

Until one day, shock horror! Those two shelves had been emptied, cleared-out completely. And I hadn't read more than half of them! Stunned, I asked the woman at the desk what had happened.

"They're out of date," she said severely; "they've been withdrawn from circulation."

"But I wanted to read them," I protested, making no impression on her whatsoever. "If they've been withdrawn, can I buy them?"

"Of course not!" she replied, shocked and affronted. "They have to be *burnt.*"

She was only following the rules, and it was not until some years later that public libraries abandoned this system and started to sell off unwanted stock, something you might have thought would have been an obvious thing to do from the start. Libraries didn't give you very much encouragement in those days.

However, by this time I had got stuck into the reader's departments of the magazines. There was no letter column in *Galaxy* and only the occasional short "Brass Tacks" in *Astounding,* but that magazine did sometimes have Schuyler Miller's excellent book reviews in "The Reference Library," and I used to drool over all those American titles which weren't available in Britain. In particular, I liked the look of the new paperback publisher, Ballantine Books, and their excellent list, with books like *Brain Wave, Search the Sky,* and *The Human Angle.*

I wrote a letter, addressed to "Ballantine Books, New York," asking if I could buy their books by post. They replied, bless them, by airmail with a super foldout catalogue of science fiction titles, all at 35¢ each. I carefully selected six, which was about all I could afford, added on postage, and calculated that I needed to send $2.75 in payment. This was about £1-2-0d in old money. How to do it? I went along to the local Post Office, and asked about an International Money Order. They looked doubtful. "You'll need a Permit," they said, "so fill in this form."

The form wanted all sorts of information about my age, address, occupation (and for all I remember, shoe size), with an ominous section headed, "Reason for requiring Order." I wrote innocently "to buy science fiction books" and handed it in to the counter.

"Right," they said, "we'll have to send this off to London for permission. You should hear from the Ministry in two or three weeks."

It seemed like a case of bureaucracy gone mad. However, the rationale was that after the war, Britain was extremely hard up and the government wanted to stop money going out of the country, so they instituted something called "Exchange Control." Anyone who wanted to buy something from overseas had to have a jolly good reason. This is why bookshops couldn't import American titles, and magazines like *Galaxy* and *Astounding* had to be reprinted in this country.

Apparently, some clerk, somewhere in London, thought that "buying science fiction books" was a sufficiently good enough reason to allow Britain's precious foreign exchange reserves to be depleted, because my permit form was returned, duly signed and stamped, and I took it back to the Post Office, bought my money order and sent it off with great excitement.

Good old Ballantine! They must have felt sorry for this poor kid in England because they rushed my order by airmail. A treasure chest of science fiction, all with superb Richard Powers covers. There was *Far and Away* from

Anthony Boucher; *Caviar* by Theodore Sturgeon; *The Frozen Year* by James Blish; *Man of Earth* by Algis Budrys and best of all, two collections from Arthur C. Clarke, *Reach for Tomorrow* and *Tales from the White Hart*. I still have most of them to this day.

I wasn't so successful with the Doubleday Science Fiction Book Club, which advertised "Take Any Three for a Dollar!" on magazine back-covers, showing huge, hardcover books like the "Foundation" trilogy and *Treasury of Science Fiction*. But in the small print, it said "Good for USA and Canada only," and they meant it! Begging letters did no good. "Copyright reasons," they replied politely, "preclude us from accepting foreign members." There was no way for me to get my hands on American hardbacks. Or was there?

In "The Reference Library" I had read about a scheme called "Pick-A-Book," operated by Martin Greenberg from an address in Hicksville, New York. "Write for free illustrated catalogue," they said, so I did, thoughtfully enclosing some American stamps (from a stamp dealer) for return postage. Marty Greenberg duly sent a fabulous catalogue crammed full of wonderful titles from Gnome Press, Fantasy Press, and Avalon. "Three titles for $4.00, six for $7.50, or ten for $12.00," was the offer but I could only afford to buy three books. I selected them carefully (the Avalon *Big Planet, The Seedling Stars,* and the Fantasy Press *Deep Space*), and sent off the money order. By then—1962—things were starting to loosen up and a permit was no longer required, though it took several months until the parcel arrived by sea-mail. It was worth waiting for.

However, in all this activity, I had somehow missed the plot. How could I possibly have failed to notice the existence of science fiction *fandom* for so long? True, the BREs were pretty well eviscerated; I subsequently found that in U.S. editions of *Astounding* "The Reference Library" usually consisted of quite a long preamble before the reviews, with mentions of World Science Fiction Conventions, *SF Times,* and so on. Not so with our reprint editions, where the book review column was obviously looked upon as expendable boilerplate to be trimmed to size, with almost all references to fan activities ruthlessly expunged.

Even so, the British *Nebula* had carried a column titled "Fanorama" by someone named Willis, and I'm pretty sure it would also have run the occasional advertisement for Ken Slater's Fantast dealership. I just can't understand how I failed to investigate them. And by ignoring *New Worlds* I'd missed reference to the nascent BSFA, and worst of all I didn't know about Brumcon, which took place in Birmingham's Imperial Hotel over Easter weekend, 1959.

Just think of it; while I was hanging around the market stalls on Saturday afternoon, a whole convention was taking place no more than a quarter-mile away. With professional writers like Ted Tubb, James White and Ken Bulmer and 40 or 50 other people, with fans and dealers and more science fiction books and magazines than I'd ever seen! I could have completed my *Galaxy* collection at a stroke and saved four years of hanging around the Rag Market. Instead of messing around with permits and Pick-A-Book, I could simply have gone onto Ken Slater's mailing list![4]

I was *ready* for fandom, needed fandom, but just didn't find the right door. It was not until the beginning of 1963 that I came across the famous little pink slip in one of those Rag Market acquisitions, "Are you interested in science fiction?" it began. "Join the Erdington SF Circle."

Finally, I had made Contact, four years late.

---

[4] This was the con, too, at which Ken Cheslin and his pals walked in and got so wildly enthusiastic about fandom that they began their local group in Stourbridge. I might have met them, become part of all that. I would have been a contemporary of people like Jim Linwood and Dick Ellingsworth, would have been around for Inchmery fandom and *Aporrheta*, and the golden years of *Hyphen, Ooopsla!* and *Void*. I might have joined the infant BSFA in 1959, have started a fanzine, and would have been well into fandom by the time the "New Wave" came along.

Recruiting Station
Chapter 3

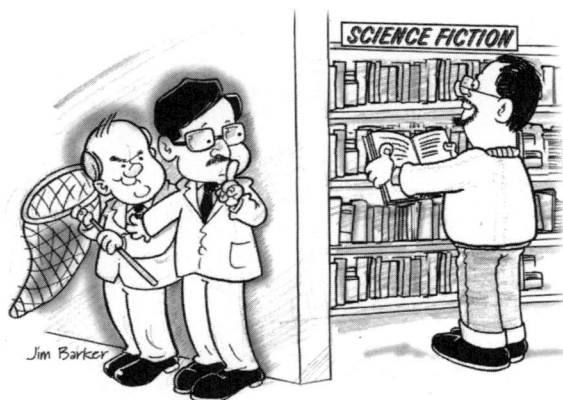

On the lookout for anyone interested in science fiction

Recruiting had always been important to Cliff and Rog as they tried to expand their little club, and I was the first of a wave of newcomers in early 1963. Oliver Harvey came aboard soon after, when he found a card Rod Milner had put into a paperback in Hudsons Bookshop, as did Edward James, a dark-haired, smartly dressed schoolboy from upper crust Solihull. Hudsons was a great asset for the group and some of us would hang around in there most weekends, on the lookout for anyone who might seem particularly interested in the science fiction section.

34

That's how we caught Mike "The Beard" Turner one Saturday in July. Mike was another youngster, almost hyper-enthusiastic and already sporting the bright orange beard that gave him his nickname. He swiftly discovered a mutual interest with Dave Casey in railways and train spotting, and coincidentally, soon afterwards bumped into Darroll Pardoe on some remote station platform, at a time when Darroll was trying to fulfil his ambition to travel every mile of Britain's rail network.

It helped to have two members on Hudson's payroll, Cliff down in the despatch basement busily mailing boxes of books to himself, and Rod behind the counter handing out recruiting cards to anyone who bought a few SF titles. Jokingly, I wondered what if one day someone asked if *we'd* like to join *their* science fiction club? Rog said it would never happen. Cliff took me more seriously, and explained that years ago there *had* been another group before ours came along.

On his travels Cliff had met a chap called Bert Barton, who had founded a group as long ago as 1949. They used to hold meetings in a local pub, and the really keen members had occasionally visited the famous "White Horse" in London, to meet authors like Arthur C. Clarke, John Wyndham, and their like. Strangely, the group didn't seem to have made any contact with national fandom and it had faded away by about 1955, leaving almost no trace.[1]

We were determined *we* would be more successful, and gradually we did find more members, such as genial Martin Pitt, who saw a notice Charlie Winstone had placed in the *Evening Despatch*. Martin was also studying chemistry and so got on particularly well with Darroll and with Mike Beard. "Mike was a useful contact," said Martin. "He scrounged odd bits of unwanted equipment from where he worked in the chemistry dept at Birmingham University so that I could carry out dangerous experiments at home."

Then there was schoolteacher Geoff Winterman, who had moved to Birmingham from Cheltenham, where he had previously been involved with the famous (but short-lived) Cheltenham Circle. "I was a bit aggrieved when I first turned up," Geoff recalled, "because Peter Mabey asked me where I lived, and when I said 'Dean Drive' they all started laughing, and I didn't understand the joke." This rang particularly true for me, since my address was "Porlock Crescent" and I was already heartily sick of Archie Mercer's witticisms about "the person from Porlock."

I tried to help, and had another brush with the Public Library system when I innocently took in a postcard and asked if they would display it on the vast expanse of empty pin-board just inside the entrance hall. The librarian was

---

[1] Many years later, the widow of another member, Alf Dean, brought an exquisite, hand-painted lapel badge into Rog's Andromeda bookshop, the only remaining evidence the early group had ever existed.

shocked; "That's reserved for important notices," she said, "not for advertisements from private individuals."

Undeterred by this rebuff I tried a more covert approach, taking SF titles from the shelves and slipping our little invitation cards between the pages. However, I must have been careless and gradually realised I was being shadowed. A large, official-looking man was watching me with great suspicion. He knew I was up to *something*, but he couldn't quite work out what. Ripping out illustrations, maybe? Writing dirty messages? Whatever it was, he was determined to catch me at it. All I could do was to put on a great show of innocence, nonchalantly flipping through books, grinning like an idiot, almost whistling a happy tune before scuttling out of the building. Libraries really didn't give you much encouragement in those days!

I had already found one new member in the person of Beryl Henley, after putting a notice in the *Newsletter* of the Science Fiction Book Club, a concertina-like single-column strip of paper, listing forthcoming books and items of general interest. By the time Beryl answered I had already met Cliff, so I was keen to see her and tell her all about it. She lived in Crabb's Cross, an unlikely-sounding district on the far side of Redditch, a small town about fifteen miles south of Birmingham, famous for "needles, fish-hooks, and springs." It wasn't actually that far from my home, but without a car, it was a difficult journey. In March 1963, I went over by Midland Red bus one Sunday afternoon and found Beryl's little pre-fab at "The Fearnings," where she gave me tea and introduced me to her husband and two young sons.

Beryl was small, with short-cut black hair and a pixie grin. She was seventeen years older than me but full of life and enthusiasm. She'd driven Army lorries as a Wren, was actively involved with the "Redditch Revellers," a local dramatics group, and she'd fallen for just about every oddball idea going, including reincarnation, Charles Fort, and most notably Scientology. Beryl loved John Campbell's psionics, Eric Frank Russell's *Great World Mysteries* and Algis Budrys's story "The Real People," in which most of the World's inhabitants are automatons. I think she was a bit bored by domestic life, and was looking for something more exciting.

Of course, Beryl was an absolute natural for science fiction fandom, and although there was no way she could get to our Tuesday evening sessions we agreed to meet again, somehow, and I caught my 'bus home feeling very pleased with myself. We continued to write to each other, and later that year Beryl joined our mass-enrolment into the BSFA. That put her in touch with fandom, in particular with Archie Mercer, and with several other newcomers, notably Mary Reed in Banbury. Both Mary and Beryl came to Birmingham for a special Sunday meeting at Cliff's house and got on like the proverbial house on fire. The meeting was also notable because for the first time two local girls came along. As Mike Turner recalls:

"Their names were Margaret Burton and Janet Mills, and I have an idea they were recruited by Cliff, who met them in the Public Library, where they worked. I remember looking at Margaret and Janet sitting at the table, and then looking around at the meagre surroundings of 1/299's downstairs room and thinking, 'They'll never be back.' Somehow it seemed too squalid a place and the girls too fresh and bright for there to be a connection."

Despite all this apparent success, the Brum group was still a small and fragile entity and sometimes things would go wrong. One Tuesday in late Autumn only Cliff, Ollie and I turned up at Charlie's house for "the meeting that never was." We were bored, and I said something like, "We've got to get more members into this club."

"Good idea," Ollie responded, "but what're you going to do, run round the streets asking people if they read science fiction?"

"No," said Cliff. "No need for that. I've got a few names in my book that I've been meaning to look up for ages."

We turned to him in amazement. I mean, how did Cliff *always* know someone? And why hadn't he told us about these people before? Still, we considered the addresses, which all seemed to be in the Yardley/Sheldon area, and the three of us decided we would investigate them that very night. Charlie wisely decided to give it a miss.

We had to catch three different buses on our long, miserable journey from Erdington across half the city, but somehow we arrived in the right neighbourhood and began to look for the first address. By now it must have been well after 9.00 p.m., it was dark and very cold, and we wandered around for ages before finding the house, a run-down bungalow next to a large garage, out of which bounded a large black dog that promptly went for Cliff. Quick thinking as ever, he fended it off with a paperback of *Rogue Queen* he happened to have in his pocket (a terrible way to treat a rare book, Ollie and I thought), and rang the door-bell.

A woman appeared at the door and regarded the three of us with suspicion as we stood there on her

A particularly bedraggled and incompetent bunch of Jehovah's Witnesses

doorstep in dark overcoats, clutching books in our hands. She probably thought we were a particularly bedraggled and incompetent bunch of Jehovah's Witnesses or something like that, but Cliff hastened to explain in his incomparable way, "Science fiction group... We... books... your son?..."

"In there," she said dismissively, and disappeared into the house.

We shuffled into the front room and met our prospective new member, a 14-year-old lad who put down his comic and eventually produced an ancient copy of Murray Leinster's *Talents Incorporated* as his only credentials. It was clear we were on a loser here, so Ollie gave him *War with the Gizmos* (which he'd been reading on the bus and had just abandoned in disgust) and we made our excuses and went back into the night.

The next address wasn't too far and we walked along briskly to keep warm, arriving at a much better-looking residence. This time I took the lead and enquired politely (of the supposed mother) if we could speak to her son, who read science fiction. She was very pleasant but said that he wasn't there at the moment. Encouraged now, I produced my trump card, a purple-inked *Zenith,* and asked her to give it to him when he came back. "Certainly," said his mother, "he should be home on leave some time in June."

The third one had married and left home. By now we were getting a bit discouraged, but we made one last attempt and knocked on our final door. Even Cliff, though, couldn't find a ready answer to our prospect's retort, "Oh, I got rid of all that science fiction stuff years ago. I breed budgies, now." So much for his "names"! And Ollie hadn't said a word the whole time.

Still, it was only a week or two later that Ollie and I tried again. This time we were looking for science fiction rather than for recruits. Both of us were keen to build up our collections and we had been getting a bit fed-up with Cliff's apparently effortless conquests, the way he would turn up at meetings with yet another rare title or pile of paperbacks, and tell us about the great times he'd had in London. He was a bit secretive when it came to the actual details, and the only person he had ever taken along on his scavenging trips was Mike "Beard."

Ollie and I arranged to meet one Saturday at ten o'clock outside a second-hand bookshop I'd seen on the Washwood Heath Road, and go on from there. Needless to say, the shop had been cleared out years ago. It was just too visible, we needed to go further afield. "What about Wolverhampton?" I said. It was about twenty miles away, and I'd never heard Cliff mention going there. Back we went into the city centre, and boarded a train at Snow Hill.

Despite being so close, Wolverhampton is a completely alien place which no inhabitant of Birmingham ever visits, and *vice versa*. The architecture is different, the people speak differently, and naturally we didn't have a clue where to go. Ollie and I wandered about this strange twin city, looking for bookshops, a market, anywhere we might find some science fiction. All in vain because we only found one shop, which had nothing but a few very battered British editions. Glumly we caught the return train. It was then I had my wonderful idea. "Ollie," I said, "it's still early. Let's go down to London."

We bought cheap day-return tickets; this was quite an adventure! Ollie had never been to London and I had only visited a couple of times, but this time I knew exactly where to go because I had seen an advertisement in *New Worlds*. We would call at the Fantasy Book Centre, run by Les Flood at Sicilian Avenue, an alleged Emporium of all things science fictional.

It was probably mid-afternoon when we arrived at Paddington and after a short tube journey we found our destination, a pedestrian arcade cutting diagonally across a corner block just off Southampton Row. It had entrance pillars in a sort of yellow tile or stone that did give it a vaguely Mediterranean air, if you ignored the bitterly cold wind swirling round your ankles. But the ground floor was a disappointment. I suppose it's hard to make a living in the West End just by selling science fiction, so the shop was stocked with jazz records. An indifferent youth directed us downstairs into a small room that seemed almost like an Aladdin's Cave.

Except for the prices, that is. Books a-plenty, yes, on shelves around the walls but almost all were hardcovers rather than paperbacks or magazines, and any "bargains" must have been snapped up years before. They were so expensive! There were some nice U.S. titles at what seemed like astronomical prices, and British editions, mostly in "mint" condition but at almost full cover price. I picked up a recent Gollancz title and a review slip fell out. I felt vaguely irritated because this wasn't quite what I'd expected. So we bought nothing, and emerged onto the pavement feeling a bit let-down. It was getting dark.

"Never mind." I said, "Cliff gave me a telephone number, someone he met on his last trip. Cliff said he is a really Big Name Fan, in with all the London group, and he said to get in touch if any of us were ever in the area and he'd show us a great time. His name is Gerry Webb." Ollie brightened visibly at this news, and we found a telephone box and dialled the number. A female voice answered, whom I took to be Gerry's mother but was probably his girlfriend, Anne Keylock. She was terribly sorry, but Gerry had gone to Sweden to let off rockets. Could she put us in touch with anyone else? How about Gerry's best friend, Langdon Jones?

Anne gave us the number and I called Langdon Jones, whom I had never heard of, though he had already produced a fanzine, *Tensor*. I didn't actually say, "A fan in need is a fan indeed," but poor old Lang got the message and very kindly (but foolishly) invited us to come and see him. He gave us his address and told us to take the tube to Ealing. Now, not knowing London, we failed to appreciate that Ealing is about as far as you can go on the Underground, a long way out, and there are actually *three* tube stations in the area, Ealing Common, North Ealing, and Ealing Broadway, all on different lines.

Naturally we went to the wrong one and had to back-track, change lines and try again, and by the time we emerged from the deserted station it was completely dark. We walked along the main road, asking passers-by for directions. Ollie had gone very quiet.

We finally found Lang's house and knocked on the door. He gamely invited us up to his bedroom, where we sat on the bed in the freezing cold and stared at each other. I thought he looked a bit foreign, Spanish or something, with a dark complexion and swept-back black hair, and I was fascinated by his eyebrows, which met in the middle. He didn't know what to do with us, so he made small talk, telling us about his job at Woolworth's. Ollie was now totally silent, his usual reaction to strangers. Lang then told us what a great time they had at meetings of the SF Club of London, although for some reason this didn't cheer me up. Eventually, and to his great relief, we said goodbye, and in gloomy silence began the long, slow, journey home. Somehow, Cliff always seemed to do better when he went on *his* adventures!

In the end I didn't actually need to go very far to improve my collection. One night at the Brum group I started to talk to Ron Haycock, another of Cliff's early contacts, who worked as a warehouseman and lived with his parents in Hall Green. He only came once or twice to meetings and somehow I felt his heart wasn't really in it. However, I was immediately interested when he told me that he had a lot of U.S. editions of *Astounding*. Ever since I'd discovered the inadequacies of my BREs I'd wanted to replace them, and Ron said he had a full run from 1953 onwards. Did he want to sell them? No, not really. But he might be willing to swap them. What for? Oh, hardcover editions, he said vaguely.

Well, this suited me very well because I was now starting to get regular review copies from Faber, Gollancz, and one or two other publishers. Ron didn't seem to care what books he took, by which authors, and I used to go around to his house every couple of weeks, swapping at the rate of about three magazines per book. I was delighted; these were the full, uncut editions, in excellent condition. The only mystery was, how had they come into Ron's possession? He didn't show any sign of ever having read them. Had he really gone to all the trouble to buy them from America? He certainly never seemed to appreciate their value.

I was very proud of my new *Astounding*s. The covers were so much brighter, the paintings more detailed, with lots of interior illustrations, features, and stories missed from the BREs. I discussed them with Lawrence Terry, yet another of Cliff's discoveries, a peripheral member of the group, though he never came to our meetings. He was the only one who lived near me, in a terraced cottage in Northfield. Lawrence was tall, thin, with a mousey little moustache and pebble-glasses, and he always wore a long, grey raincoat, tightly belted. In later years I thought, "Frank Spencer."[2]

Lawrence had a three-wheeler car, an evil little two-stroke contraption with uncomfortable seats, a flapping canvas top and something called a "crash" gearbox which worked in exactly the way it sounded. One Sunday we went over to Redditch to see Beryl Henley, and I endured one of the most painful journeys of my life as we ground slowly and noisily along the road like a giant lawnmower, trailing a cloud of blue smoke.

Still, I thought, Lawrence was a bit strange but he meant well, so I was happy to oblige when he asked if he could borrow a few issues of my *Astoundings*. He gave me a list of about twenty, ones he hadn't been able to get, he explained, and he wanted to catch up on his reading. Like an idiot I sorted out my nice, clean copies, took them over to Lawrence's house and picked them up two or three weeks later. Except when I looked at them I found my nice, clean copies had somehow turned into very battered, dog-eared copies. Lawrence had decided to upgrade his collection at my expense. I had been robbed!

Furious, I stormed over to his house and demanded the return of my magazines. Lawrence looked at me blandly through his thick lenses and denied any offence. I must have been mistaken. Those *were* my magazines. I stormed around his kitchen, swearing and shouting. I don't know what I said. Lawrence's wife came into the room and demanded to know what was going on. I told her, she looked very pointedly at Lawrence, and he crept upstairs and came down with my *Astoundings*. I checked they were all there, and left the house. I don't think I ever saw him again.

Finally, there was Graham Hall and his friend Dick Richardson, who had just joined the BSFA. Graham lived just a few miles away in Kings Norton, so I arranged to visit him one Saturday afternoon at the beginning of 1964, setting off in happy anticipation of bringing another recruit into the fold. Only, it didn't work out that way.

Graham had dark, greasy-looking hair hanging over his collar, a weak chin, and a good line in glowers. He was waiting for me with Dick Richardson, who was tall and blonde, hardly spoke, and appeared to be his "yes-man." We were immediately at odds. Everything I said made things worse. We seemed to have nothing in common. He didn't like Heinlein, he said scornfully. I said that I wasn't very keen on dark fantasy. We talked about fanzines and I showed him *Zenith* but he wasn't impressed. And he certainly didn't want to join the Brum group. After an hour or so, he was literally *snarling* at me, and I thought I had better leave.

I went home feeling a bit depressed, not knowing what had gone wrong, but mentally shrugged my shoulders; you can't win them all. Graham, how-

---

[2] An idiot character played by Michael Crawford in the British TV comedy series *Some Mothers Do 'Ave 'Em*. He always wore a long, tightly belted raincoat (and beret; I never saw Lawrence wearing a beret, but on him it would have looked about right).

ever, was a nasty piece of work and began a feud, for no more reason than that. He started to make nasty cracks about me in the fanzines, keeping this up for years, and I often wondered what I had said that had upset him so much. I was vaguely relieved to see a throwaway comment Charles Platt made a year or so later in *Spinge,* "Graham Hall…a master of the art of not only losing friends, but ensuring he doesn't make any by mistake. A rare gift."

Still, what did these tribulations and disappointments matter? Because by now I was deeply involved in fanzine publishing, and that was where the real excitement was happening!

"Pubbing My Ish"
Chapter 4

Rog Peyton was horrified when I showed him the first purple issue of *Zenith*. It was a mess, the result of some really bad decisions. "Why didn't you use stencils?" he asked. The answer was that I had no idea what a wax stencil was, had never even *seen* a Gestetner.

Things could so easily have been different. Several months earlier Ken Cheslin had invited us over to Stourbridge for a Saturday session to run off an issue of *Les Spinge*. I had never been there before, had no idea where he lived, so Rog suggested we should meet outside "The Kings Head" pub at 9.30 a.m., to catch the 'bus. I was really looking forward to it and arrived early, and waited, walking up and down outside the pub for nearly an hour, wondering what had gone wrong. No Rog, and I went home, bitterly disappointed. Only at the next meeting when we asked each other, "Where were *you*?" did it turn out there were actually two pubs in the area, the "Kings *Head*" on the Hagley Road, where Rog had waited for me, and the "Kings *Arms*" in Harborne, a mile away, where I had waited for him.

What a shame! If I had seen Ken's Gestetner in action, I would never have considered using anything else. It would have been great to be in Ken's den as he ran off pages, talking about *Spinge*, about fandom in general. Maybe he would have showed me a few of the current fanzines, giving me a better idea of what fannish fandom was about. Perhaps I might have got to know Ken a bit better, more than I ever actually managed to do, but unfortunately, it didn't happen that way.

So to me, a "duplicator" meant the little Banda in the office of the metallurgical laboratory at Fisher & Ludlow, where I had started work a few months earlier. Fortunately, the secretary was a young chap only a little older than I was (the manager didn't want to employ women; he thought they would only cause trouble). His name was Brian MacDonald and he had learned to type in the army when he did his National Service. He even read a bit of science fiction, though mostly Charles Eric Maine, and he indulged me in my madness and let me steal office supplies.

The Banda was a primitive affair. You typed a stiff paper "master" with special carbon paper behind it, face-up, to create a reverse copy. Then you attached the master to a drum and turned the handle, rotating it past a sponge strip soaked in spirit, moistening the carbon so that some went onto the pages as you fed them through, one sheet at a time. And onto fingers, clothes, and everywhere else! It gave a virulent purple imprint for the first few sheets, swiftly fading away into illegibility, with a print-run of about 50 before becoming unreadable. Americans call it "ditto."

I started taking masters home and typed away furiously at night all through September, bringing them back in my briefcase the next morning so I could run them off in my lunchtime, to much ribaldry from the other young men in the lab. And, being over-ambitious, I promptly made things much more difficult for myself than they need have been. Heavily under the influence of the immaculate, half-size *Inside* and *New Frontiers,* I decided to copy their format, which meant my printed sheets had to be folded in half and stapled in the centre.

Before I could start typing I had to get all my material together and work out how much room each piece would take, sorting out page numbers so they would be in the right order when folded. Then I had to put the masters horizontally into my poor little portable typewriter (which was completely unequal to the task) and type two "pages" per sheet. It made very small pages, especially with a clumsy Pica typeface (10 characters per inch), and if you go too near the edges of the master (which of course I did), you get slippage, bits that don't reproduce, blotches and smears. I had also clumsily tried to justify right-hand margins, another unnecessary chore. Oh, it was a mess all right. Thank goodness, I only printed 35 copies!

Although in a way, it *was* an achievement of sorts. The group had no real idea of what was needed, but they responded to my nagging, and did just about what might have been expected. Rog handed in a checklist of Digit Books and an article about Poul Anderson. Beryl Henley gave me a poem. Charlie Winstone submitted a bland little piece on "SF landscaping," and I wrote a rave review of Jack Vance's *Big Planet* and an editorial declaring, "We are determined to get into the world of deep-dyed fandom." Cliff, of course, did nothing. The written word wasn't his scene.

Then came the decision I had been putting off for weeks. What to call it? I was paralysed with indecision. Suddenly, every potential title seemed to be either silly or pretentious. I toyed with misguided ideas like *Mercia Calling*, before settling on Charlie Winstone's suggestion of *Nadir*. It seemed an unusual sort of word, and I lettered up a master before realising that nadir actually meant the very lowest point, which would leave me open to obvious ridicule. Panicking, now, I went for the exact opposite, the highest point, and called it *Zenith* instead (not knowing this had been one of the most famous British fanzine titles of an earlier epoch).

Mike Higgs, or "Mik" as he signed himself, did the illustrations, and they weren't bad if your taste ran to cartoon figures of dinosaurs and evil Overlords. However, I had another failure of nerve with the cover. I could have used a full-page cartoon from Mike or Brian MacDonald's sketch of a Titan missile launch. Either would have been at least eye-catching, but instead I put Brian's rocket on the inside cover and Mike's cartoon on the back page. The front cover itself was blank apart from a small purple BEM in the bottom right corner.

Having produced the fanzine, I didn't know what to do with it except to give copies to group members. This was probably just as well, although I see from their kind letters in the following issue that I must somehow have sent *Zenith* to a few well-known fans like Archie Mercer and Roy Kay. Somehow, they both found encouraging things to say, tactfully overlooking the worst aspects of the minor disaster that had landed on their doormats. Someone put me in touch with veteran fan Harry Turner in Cheshire, who sent me a nice letter forgiving me for using his title. It wasn't a very good way to get started, and I would probably have done better to have simply sent out postcards saying, "Here I am, can I join your game?" The trouble was that I hadn't even seen the BSFA's journal, *Vector,* and I was working in a total vacuum.

The first issue had to be regarded as a bit of a "trial run," and I quickly began work on Number Two. This time Rog took me firmly in hand, bringing me into the Surveyors' office where he worked and demonstrating how to use a Gestetner. I was a bit frightened of the thing at first sight, so black and inky with all those knobs and levers and the sinister "swishing" sound the rollers made as you turned the handle. I was impressed by the quality of reproduc-

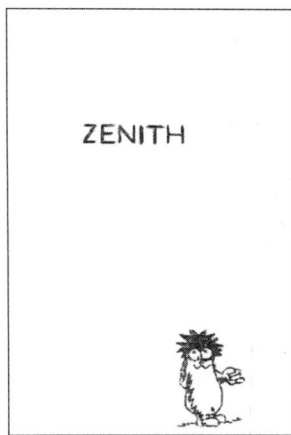

tion and promptly bought a box of stencils. This time *Zenith* would be a normal, quarto-size (8 inches x 10 inches) fanzine.

Typing was much easier with full-size pages, as long as I periodically cleared the wax out of the typewriter keys with an old toothbrush, although I still tried to justify the right-side margins. I left gaps in various places for "Mik" to illustrate, and he proved a dab hand at drawing titles and filler-illos on stencil with stylus and texturing plates. But a minor technological revolution was looming with this issue.

By now I was now doing a 3-month stint at the College of Advanced Technology (later to become Aston University) on a block-release scheme from my company. This was convenient because it allowed me to ingratiate myself into the secretarial office, where they let me use their excellent Gestetner 320 at lunchtimes. And a kindly soul told me about *electro-stencilling*, a wonderful high-tech process that would scan a page and burn it onto a stencil, avoiding all that messy hand cutting. The college had a machine in their photographic department and charged students a concessionary price of only 1/6d. This was more like it!

Mike had already done me a cover, a full-page illo on wax stencil, but I was worried because he had put in no less than *four* naked women! I thought this might be the wrong "image," it might get me into trouble, so I asked him for something a bit more "classy," and he came up with a very nice ink drawing of a rocket zipping over a Roman bust on a pedestal. I was delighted, and took it straight into the college for my very first electro-stencil. The man in charge let me watch as he clipped my artwork to a long cylinder, and put a blank stencil on the other end. He switched the machine on, the drum revolved, and a sensor started to travel slowly across the original, while with a strong smell of burning, a parallel cutting head sparked its way along the stencil. The result was jet-black, like a foolscap sheet of slightly shiny carbon paper, with the image showing faintly where the top layer had been burnt away.

The cover was the last thing needed, and Rog and I decided to make a hard push to get the issue out in the second weekend of December. I packed all the pages I had already printed into a couple of large suitcases, along with the final stencils and paper, and met Rog at his office on the Saturday morning. We were alone in the office and we worked all day, uninterrupted. Just before we came to print the cover, however, we realised that I'd forgotten to put a title above Mike's drawing, so Rog lettered it freehand on a wax stencil, making his famous observation that "the good thing about *Zenith* is that it's all straight lines," which was a fair point under the circumstances.

We thought about putting the cover through twice, printing picture and title separately, but instead decided to try *splicing* the two together. That meant cutting Mike's drawing from the black sheet and fitting it into a slightly smaller hole in the wax stencil, painting around the edges with copious quantities of

red, sweet-smelling correcting fluid. It held together, somehow, and I was thrilled when the first
copies came off the machine, particularly when
we found some pale green paper in the office. It
made the cover look very effective and, yes, even
"classy," with Mike's original, more lurid artwork
tucked away on the inside back cover.

2 ZENITH

As the hours went by, I started to worry. This
time I had thought a bit more about distribution, and, ambitiously, had decided to send *Zenith* to every member of the British Science Fiction Association, all 180 of them. I typed address
labels and by some piece of skulduggery, Cliff Teague ran a pile of mailing
wrappers through the franking machine at Hudson's bookshop. They had to
be in the post by a certain time that very night or the pre-dated franks would
be invalid.

We finished printing and started collating. Putting together that many 40-
page copies was a slow business, and then they had to be stapled together. It
was starting to get dark outside. Panicking now, we rolled up each copy in a
wrapper, glued it down, put on a label, and threw them into my suitcases. We
dragged the heavy cases through the darkened streets to the Central Post Office with just minutes to spare—I think the deadline was probably seven
o'clock—where we handed them over the counter. Exhausted, we caught our
separate 'buses and went home.

Zenith 2 might have looked more attractive, but in content it was no improvement. It had four stories, by Beryl, Ollie Harvey, Rod Milner, and Jack
Pickering, all terrible. Our reporter friend Tony Ventris-Field provided a boring little article about "Astro-Philately" and Rog did a checklist on Pan Books.
I wrote two pages about Future Histories (a preamble, really, for material I
hoped to get in future issues), and a "complete" listing of Jack Vance story-
titles. There were three or four pages of book reviews, an uptight little editorial, and a few short excerpts from letters. Not many comment-hooks there!

Maybe this was why the response was so poor. It wasn't a good idea to post
it just before Christmas, and I suppose it didn't help to have to fight those
tightly rolled pages before trying to read them (surely the very *worst* way to
mail a fanzine!). I had also made a fundamental mistake in supposing the
BSFA was fandom. It wasn't, and I suspect many members would have never
dreamed of writing a letter of comment, let alone anything more substantial.
The lettercolumn in the following issue showed the dismal result. I received
only nine letters, from Archie Mercer and Roy Kay, once again being tactful,
and from Alan Dodd and Terry Jeeves, two other fans noted for encouraging
ugly ducklings. Then there were letters from Charles Platt and Chris Priest,

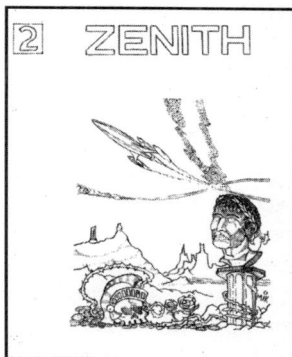

two fellow newcomers. Chris was very complimentary, particularly about Mike's cover, which was kind of him. Charles, however, sent a very long and picky letter, which irritated me immensely.

He was highly disparaging about everything in the issue, not missing the smallest detail, even querying an innocent little "Mik" filler illustration, asking, "Why is the man in the illo a eunuch?" I thought Charles was being very over-critical but I didn't know quite how to handle his letter. I could either have ignored it, or published it complete, without comment, letting others judge for themselves whether or not he was being entirely fair. Foolishly, I cut it to pieces and used just odd fragments, which didn't achieve anything and certainly didn't please Charles.

However, I was greatly cheered by the response from a few "big names." Harry Harrison wrote a nice postcard from Denmark and Arthur Thomson (ATom) sent me some artwork. Best of all, Ted Tubb sent me a short story. What a thrill when I opened the envelope! Just those few kind words made all the difference and encouraged me to start thinking about a third issue. After all, I had announced that *Zenith* would appear bimonthly, and I wanted to keep to this schedule.

By early 1964, my parents might have wondered if I had been taken over by space-aliens. Not that they were familiar with the concept, but surely they must have noticed they hardly saw me any more. Each morning I left early for the long journey across the city to my job, returning after 6.00 p.m. to read my post, eat dinner and then rush upstairs to my bedroom to answer letters and type stencils. Except for the middle of the month when *Galaxy* and *Astounding* came out, and Tuesdays when I came home at midnight, on the last 'bus after a Brum Group meeting.

In the early New Year, I somehow managed to put out another fanzine, which I called *Nadir,* (Charlie Winstone's original suggestion). It was a poor little thing of only ten pages, hastily typed onto Banda masters, and duplicated and collated by Charlie because I didn't want any more leg pulling from the lads in the lab where I worked. I thought *Nadir* could be a home for various things that didn't fit *Zenith,* it would run more fannishly slanted articles, and in the editorial hoped the fanzine would develop a "more easy-going, peaceful character." It was crude but oddly, it *was* interesting.

The first item was by one of Charlie's brothers, John Winstone, a non-fan, in which he tried to describe how disconcerting it was for him when our crowd descended upon the house (perhaps it was no coincidence that around this time Charlie cut back meetings to once per fortnight, to our considerable dismay). John's piece would have benefited from being longer, as would the final item by Ken Cheslin, poking mild fun at the antics of the "Brummies," as he called us. However, the best thing was a laconic little article by Ollie Harvey, the silent man of the Group, in which he described our abortive recruiting mission of a few months earlier.

Since then my situation had changed completely. No longer the complete outsider, I was now writing to fans all over the country, getting occasional subscriptions, and fanzines from other newcomers, like Charles Platt's *Points of View,* Roy Kay's *Chaos,* Langdon Jones's *Tensor,* and *Alien* from the Manchester Group. Their editors were almost as inexperienced as I was, but in the white-hot flame of discovery I was oblivious, busily exchanging letters, making friends and exploring this whole exciting new world which had so suddenly opened-up.

Then came the January *Les Spinge,* which changed everything. In his editorial Ken Cheslin mused, "...fandom seems very quiet just now. Nothing much happening, no new talking point. Gee, what's happened to everybody?" and then, presciently, he asked, "I wonder what's brewing?.... pardon me while I pop out and dig myself a fallout shelter." It was ironic that Ken hadn't noticed the new fandom which was stirring under his very nose, and the fannish calm was about to be shattered with a vengeance.

The trouble all began in that same issue of *Spinge,* with Jim Linwood's famous review of the "New Wave" fanzines, as he called them, *Zenith* and *Points of View.* It hit me very hard. The first I knew about it was when I turned up at a meeting of the BSFG and Cliff Teague rushed up excitedly and said that *Zenith* had been given "a real slamming." In his usual way he had been first to get his hands on *Spinge,* and so I read the review under the worst possible circumstances, with the others standing around feeding my paranoia that this was an "attack" by the older fans.

Jim was deliberately nasty in a few places and got some of his facts wrong, but he was almost entirely correct in his conclusion: "...only *Zenith* will improve and learn from mistakes because the editor doesn't take himself too seriously, but with Charles Platt, who does, I predict disillusionment after a few more issues." The worst thing about the review was the way Jim lumped us both together in his column, and henceforward in most people's minds, whereas actually we had almost nothing in common.

Much later Jim Linwood said, "The item caused repercussions totally beyond its merits as a piece of criticism: I was deploring the fact that two amateur magazines had prozine pretensions and their editors seemed totally unaware of the usual ground rules for fanzines. This was a period when fanzine reviews were supposed to be complimentary and supportive and I'd decided to break with tradition and write humorous, sarcastic columns to counter this."

He was absolutely right; we *were* totally unaware of those rules! Because no one had explained them to us, neither of us understood what was going on, and we were both convinced that the fannish "Establishment" had just declared war. For Charles it confirmed his preconceived opinions, and he fired the opening shots in what became a battle against perceived fannish wisdom. For me, it caused a retreat *away* from fandom at just the time I should have been embracing it. As I commented a few years later, "my first two issues of

Zenith were exactly the sort of thing every young (neo)fan thinks of putting out on first discovering fandom. Normally, they quickly pass through this stage when they learn something of what it's all about from Older and Wiser heads who have done it all before."

But where *were* these O&W heads? British fandom was so run-down it was at an all-time low, with very few fanzines around from older fans apart from Ethel Lindsay's *Scottishe*, Ron Bennett's *Skyrack*, Terry Jeeves' *Erg*, and the occasional *Les Spinge*. We waited in eager anticipation when Alan Dodd announced he was working on a new issue of *Camber* and were tremendously disappointed when we actually saw it. There wasn't anything else.

Soon, I discovered the situation was nearly as bad in America. Every major title seemed to have folded just before I came on the scene; *Cry, Void, Psychotic, Shaggy, Xero, VoM, Oopsla!, Quandry*, all gone, and while *Warhoon* was still technically alive, I didn't see an issue before it finally folded in early 1965. This was the time of the Great Fannish Desert, and about the only U.S. fanzine still going strong appeared to be *Yandro*.

Since I hadn't seen any good examples of fannish fanzines, the Linwood review caused me to harden my attitudes, strait-jacketing myself into something I called "formality," under the impression I had to hammer out all personality from a magazine dealing with something as sacred as science fiction. I also had some misguided advice from a man with the *Birmingham Mail* who had fleeting contact with our group at the time, and he lectured me about journalism, how one should never use the first person pronoun. The result was that I began writing pompous sentences like, "The Editor's aversion to many of the average 'fannish' types of article or story makes *Zenith* into a magazine that attempts to avoid fannish contents and concentrate on SF as its field."

This was completely the *wrong* response! I didn't understand that Jim wasn't part of any fannish "Establishment," indeed he still considered himself one of the young London insurgents. I should have asked for advice from someone who had been around a bit longer, asked to borrow a few *real* fanzines. After all, I didn't *want* to fight established fandom, I thought it was pretty wonderful. All I wanted was to get more into it, become accepted. Ken Cheslin could certainly have helped a lot more than he did. As our local BNF he might have taught me a lot, but he was uncommunicative, seemed to regard me with suspicion, perhaps thought I had deliberately let him down by not turning up for that duplicating session. As it was, I accidentally embarked upon a difficult and lonely path. Rob Hansen said as much in his historical round-up in *Then*:

"Weston was setting the course that British fandom would follow through much of the sixties. Where the fannish zines were produced by those who, though SF readers, regarded fandom as an end in and of itself, the sercon zines tended to be produced by those who regarded themselves as fans in the more general sense, who perhaps saw fandom as a sort of cheering section for the professionals and a possible gateway for becoming pros themselves. In choosing the latter road Weston ensured that things would be very different than they had been."

Determinedly, I pressed on with a third issue, this time using electro-stencils from the start. Somehow, the subtitle "Science fiction" had attached itself to the cover logo. Taken literally, this implied *Zenith* actually *was* a magazine of fiction, which wasn't my intention at all. Rather, it was a bit of woolly and imprecise marketing. What I meant of course, was "a magazine *about* science fiction," but this mistake left me wide open to criticism. Graham Hall, for instance, seemed to deliberately misunderstand, saying in a letter to *Les Spinge,* "I like a 'zine that sets out a policy and sticks to it; when it raves madly about being an attempted copy of a prozine, like *Zenith,* and then goes out of its way to be a fanzine, it leaves me cold."

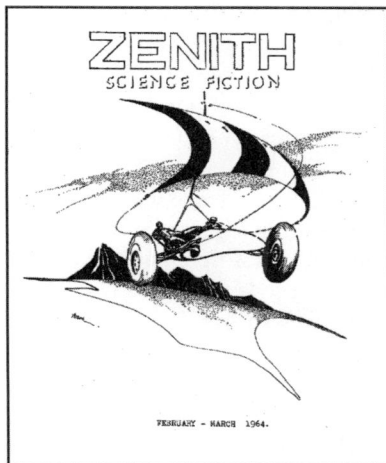

ZENITH
SCIENCE FICTION

FEBRUARY - MARCH 1964.

The cover for Issue 3 was even more magnificent than before, a dramatic ATom sand-yacht, printed on lovely orange paper. It was a shame that Mike Higgs had already submitted a prospective cover illustration and once again I unkindly bumped him to the back. He had done an effective set of pen-portraits of leading professional SF authors, which was actually much more relevant to *Zenith*'s supposed subject matter than sand yachting! He was very patient, however, and continued to supply ink drawings and headings which I would paste onto a foolscap sheet, get the stencil cut, and splice the bits into the appropriate places. Although at only 1/6d each I could afford to go to town with full-page electro-stencils, running a photograph of a Titan missile launch from the Martin Company in Denver, and a still from the very first *Dr Who* TV serial, supplied by the BBC Publicity Office. I even had pictures of more bloody space stamps!

This pointed to a fundamental problem, in that I was still relying on material from local group members and it just wasn't good enough. Probably the best thing in the issue was Rog Peyton's publisher survey, this time on Panther Books, and much longer and more thoughtful than before. However, while I wasn't the slightest bit interested in Astro-Philately, Charlie Winstone had written another four pages on the subject, which I felt obliged to run, failing to understand that a fanzine is not a newspaper, which has to fill its pages with *something.* Rather than use boring "fillers" it would have been better—and certainly cheaper—to have produced a smaller, more punchy issue. I had to learn that if an article didn't interest me, then it probably wouldn't interest anyone else, either.

I was quite proud of my own contribution to the issue, an article on the foibles of John W. Campbell, until Canadian critic Leland Sapiro completely demolished me by writing in a subsequent letter, "*that* Campbell was interested in Dianetics, the Dean Drive, etc, is common knowledge. What we wish to know is *why*—and about this you say nothing." Good point, I thought, and promptly wrote back and asked Leland for *his* theory of what made Campbell tick.

Ted Tubb's story was the highlight of the issue, and I was very proud of it. Ted began with a preamble in which he outlined his method of generating a plot—take a simple, mundane action and ask questions, "Who? Where? Why?" This is exactly what Ted had done ("Mark Kelmore lit a cigarette...") and the result was short, slick and instructive, but it *wasn't science fiction,* as Archie Mercer reproached me in a subsequent letter. I should have tried to bracket the story with an introduction and conclusion that applied the lesson to SF; maybe I could even have asked Ted himself to write a bit more?

Production this time was even more intensive. My period at college had finished and I couldn't get at their machine, so instead Rog and I decided to run off the entire 40-page issue over the first weekend in February, all 300 copies of it, using the Gestetner in his office. The first (Saturday) session went smoothly and we collated batches of pages as we went along, leaving them spread all around the office to dry. Next morning I turned up with two heavy suitcases of paper and waited outside for ages, but Rog didn't appear. I wondered what had gone wrong. Was he ill? What would happen when his boss arrived on Monday to find hundreds of half-collated fanzines on the desks, the floor, and every available flat surface? When he realised that strangers had been in the office, using his equipment? What would he say to Rog? What about my fanzine!

Waiting for Rog!

Rog's parents didn't have a telephone at home, and after two hours of standing around on the pavement I decided there was no alternative but to go out to Quinton on the 'bus, dragging the heavy suitcases the whole way. Meanwhile, of course, Rog had woken late after a party the night before, had rushed into the city, and was by now at the office, wondering what had happened to me. It was a complete comedy of errors, but I wasn't too amused when I arrived back an hour and a half later. We worked until very late that day!

Three hundred copies were far too many, since I didn't have anywhere near that many subscribers. I started to send them out to prospects, using Ron Bennett's *Skyrack* Directory as a mailing list. For the first time I sent some copies to the United States, as a result receiving a long air-mail letter from Al Lewis in Los Angeles. This was a tremendous stroke of luck for me, since I had actually sent the issue to Ron Ellik, who'd been TAFF-winner in 1963, but Ron shared an apartment with Al, who was more interested in "that sercon stuff." Al Lewis knew his way around American fandom and he sent me a whole list of useful addresses, which included people like Fritz Leiber, Poul Anderson, Damon Knight, and—yes!—Jack Vance. I fired off a fan letter straight away, saying how much I liked his books and explaining how difficult it was to get them (none had been published in Britain), and to my delight Jack sent me a signed copy of the Avalon edition of *The Languages of Pao*. What a nice man, I thought.

It was probably the performance at Rog's office, thatmade me decide I needed my own duplicator, and on impulse, I walked into the Roneo showroom on New Street in March 1964, and signed a hire-purchase agreement to buy a model 360 machine. It was another big mistake in lots of ways, and it would have been much more sensible to buy a decent typewriter instead. I didn't really *need* a duplicator, since I could probably have carried on with Rog's help, or maybe Ken Cheslin would have let me use his, if I had asked. Why go for a new machine I couldn't really afford, instead of something cheaper, second-hand? Most of all I should *never* have bought a Roneo!

The Roneo had a metal drum full of ink, the top half of which was finely perforated, and the whole thing covered with an absorbent cotton blanket. As the drum rotated, centrifugal force threw ink at the perforations, through the blanket, and through the stencil. That's the theory, anyway. In practice, I found it very difficult to control the intensity of inking, leading to a disappointingly "patchy" effect when I started to run off my stencils. The main reason for choosing a Roneo was because colour changes were very easy—you simply changed the drum. I bought an extra (blue) drum and they kindly loaned me a red drum "on trial" for a few weeks. It also helped that the Roneo was smaller, a bit more portable than a Gestetner and easier to move around. That was important because this machine was going to do a lot of travelling!

So now, I could use colour. I had also made another technical breakthrough; while waiting at a 'bus-stop with Mike Higgs he had explained about Letraset and Zippertone, which he'd been using in his artwork for some time. They were a revelation to me, and I could immediately see their potential as a way to do my own headings.

I started to run off *Zenith* 4 immediately. Arthur Thomson had sent me another dramatic cover illustration, and I tried running it in blue ink on light blue paper. Yes, it looked good, so I ran the *Zenith* logo in red. These new colour drums were great! I printed several large pieces of interior artwork, including reprints of some delicate work by Virgil Finlay, though I couldn't get the inking quite right. For the first time I also featured a few pieces of artwork from Eddie Jones which stood out for its sheer professionalism. The contents showed a small improvement because at last I was starting to get material from outside the Birmingham group. Alan Dodd contributed an article on aliens in science fiction, the Irish John Berry provided a short story, and North-East fan Phil Harbottle had written a very competent article on pulp-era illustrators.

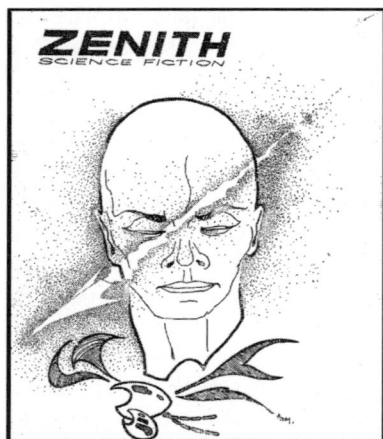

Unfortunately, all of this was still essentially "filler." The real substance of the issue came from Rog Peyton with his survey of Corgi Books, Beryl Henley (who had taken over the book reviews), and Rod Milner, who analysed sales figures for various SF titles from his personal experience in Hudsons bookshop. The surprise item, my first big scoop, was an original piece from the author H. Beam Piper about his future history series. I liked Piper's work and had written him a fan letter in which I had tried to organise his stories in chronological order. He sent me a very kind reply, putting me right on some details I had missed, together with a chart of his "history" over the next few thousand years. Sadly, I didn't exploit this opportunity to the full, choosing to withhold the letter (now lost) and using only the chart. Even so, it was quite a triumph!

However, by this time it felt as if I was walking some kind of tightrope. After the Linwood review, it felt that on one side a gallery of older fans were shaking their heads in silent disapproval, a feeling reinforced by comments in the lettercolumn of the next *Spinge*. Dick Ellingsworth, a London fan I didn't know, said, "I agree with Linwood ...*Zenith* & *Beyond* are definitely the two least-admired fanzines in my book." Ron Bennett (who with his *Skyrack Newsletter* was about the most influential fan around) said in a peculiar letter which was *probably* intended to be ironic, but didn't read that way at the time, "I was especially glad to see Jim jump on *Zenith* in this way."

Later, Jim Linwood commented, "The review in *Spinge* was just my opinion and in no way a consensus view of the fannish status-quo at that time. I had been equally critical of friends like Moorcock and Pat Kearney as well as older fen like Ella (perhaps more verbally than in print). There wasn't a group of fans who were opposed to new blood, quite the opposite: Vince Clarke, Archie Mercer and Ron Bennett had been very supportive to me and others when we entered fandom, while Ella and I had written to new BSFA members to get them actively involved. Ron wrote encouraging reviews of *Zenith* and *Beyond* in *Skyrack* which were far more representative of the fannish establishment than mine. In fact, I was never part of the fannish in-crowd or ever wanted to be."

There was no doubt about the criticism I was getting from the *other* side, from fellow New Wavers like Charles Platt, Graham Hall and their pals. I probably took too much notice of them, trying to minimise their target by stripping all traces of personality from the magazine. Fanzine reviews went, replaced by a mere listing, and I stopped writing anything myself apart from a brief editorial which made statements like, "I have quite deliberately modelled *Zenith* after the professional science fiction magazines," and "*Zenith* will leave alone those things exclusively fannish." Worst of all, I said, "a large letter-column is not really wanted," which is likely to take the all-time prize as the single most stupid thing ever written by a fanzine editor!

Work was interrupted before I could finish the issue. Everything went on "hold" for a while, because at Easter I was going to my first convention.

Easter Brummies
Chapter 5

Charles Platt had driven up from Letchworth the day before the convention, in his temperamental old car, to my home on the council estate in Northfield. It was the first time we had met, and I thought how young he looked. Charles was about my height, pale-complexioned, with a long, sensitive face and light, tousled hair. We seemed to hit it off pretty well, although he was a little shocked that my parents, brother, sister and I lived in such a small house with just three bedrooms and one downstairs room.

I kept my collection in two bookcases balanced one on top of the other, in the 18 inches at the bottom of the bed, with my paperwork in boxes under the bed, and to cut stencils I sat on the edge of the bed with my portable typewriter balanced on my knees. Not an ideal arrangement, and to make matters worse I had recently bought the Roneo duplicator. Charles later commented, "God knows how he manages to produce his fanzines, he's so short of space."

He was going to spend the night on the settee, but first Charles wanted to meet Cliff Teague, so in the evening we battled through the city traffic to the even tinier back house where he lived with his mother. Charles was probably a bit taken aback, although he only noted, "Cliff's collection has got so much out of hand I doubt if he is really aware of what is in it. Boxes of magazines and piles of fanzines litter the floor and help to support his bed…"

Early next morning, Friday 27th March, we set out for Peterborough. Charles had a 1951 Vauxhall F-Type Victor, a hulking brute of a car, finished in light green with brown rust stains at the bottoms of the doors, but it went well enough and we made a fair speed. It was a long journey on country roads through such places as Market Harborough, Corby, and Oundle, although Charles was good company and we chattered away happily about our fanzines and our expectations for the convention. As we finally approached the town, I started to get an odd feeling, as if every other car on the road was going to the same destination, and I scrutinised their occupants, wondering, if they, too, were science fiction fans.

We arrived at The Bull Hotel, just around the corner from Peterborough's famous Cathedral. It was quite a small hotel, more like a large pub, and it was hosting the convention for the second year running. This time it was being chaired by Bridgewater fan Tony Walsh, with help by fans from all over the country. Ken Slater, the bookseller, did hotel liaison, with programme handled by his pal Dave Barber, with help from Ethel Lindsay, and George Locke and Arthur Thomson were responsible for publications. The convention book was a bit rudimentary, however, omitting such basic details as date, location, or that Ted Tubb was Guest of Honour. This also appeared to be "The Con With No Name," since book, badge, and backdrop called it, clumsily, "The British Science Fiction Association Peterborough Convention." (Just imagine how the committee must have smitten their collective foreheads when, a month *after* it was all over, London fan Jim Groves thought of the clever title "Repetercon" for his report in *Vector*.)

In many ways, the two Peterborough conventions were a watershed, the last gasp of the old-style cons run by a unified fandom as a sort of giant house party. They didn't need to impress anyone and didn't have to cater for minority interests because by-and-large they were gatherings of old friends. However, the same "New Wave" which had hit the fanzines was about to sweep through the cosy world of the convention-goers.

The seeds of change had actually been planted a year earlier by Ken Slater when he was con Chairman. He said, "I knew there were a lot more people reading the rubbish out there, who actively sought after it. They were not fans in the intense sense of the word, but from my viewpoint if they read fantasy and SF, they belonged. At Bullcon we set a target that was about fifty more than the 'normal' attendance outside London, I think. GoH was No.1, Chairman was No.150, and we tried to fill the gap between the figures. I don't recall just how many we had in the end, but it was well above target."

This brought in lots of newcomers, people like Roy Kay, Gerry Webb, and Langdon Jones, who had immediately blended in, and some like Charles Partington, Harry Nadler, and other members of the Manchester Delta group, who hadn't—not quite. With their interest in films, supernatural, and horror they were the first media sub-group, and in some ways they were more out-of-step with the older fans than anyone. They were friendly with the Liverpool group, however, participated enthusiastically in the Fancy Dress, and they weren't out to change anything. Now, in 1964, some rather more vocal newcomers were arriving on the scene.

Of course, Charles and I knew none of this when we walked into the hotel. My first reaction was one of dismay; who *were* all these people? Most of them were at least ten years older than me and they seemed to know each other very well, the men in sports jackets and suits, and the women—the very few women—in day-dresses. Cautiously we signed in at reception, at seven shillings and sixpence per night, and we were given keys, each attached to a heavy, grey metal tag the size of a small postcard with a serrated edge that would have made a good knuckle-duster.

I found my room, came down and registered, and received a large paper badge with my name typed on it. I looked around anxiously for the rest of the Birmingham contingent. The group had come in force, Rog Peyton and Ed James arriving by early train, sharing a copy of Edmond Hamilton's *Star Kings* between them, along with Charlie Winstone, who was away from home for the first time. Mike Higgs worked on Fridays so he came on a later train with girlfriend Cynthia and Mike "The Beard" Turner. As Mike Higgs remembers, "We had to change at Leicester and wait on a cold and draughty platform. The station-master took pity on us and opened up the waiting room where Cynth and I huddled around a coal-fire, while Mike Beard disappeared into the mist, happily train-spotting." The return fare was two pounds, six shillings and sixpence, so, being penniless as usual, Cliff hitchhiked to Peterborough.

Archie Mercer noticed this influx. In *Les Spinge* 13, he said, "The hotel seemed to be overrun with Brummies. 'Easter Brummies,' I dubbed them. For every ten new faces one saw, fifteen belonged to Brummies." He then went on to describe the newcomers:

"Pete Weston is young, serious, and slightly vague," he said, which I suppose was about right. "Rog Peyton, the BSFA's new Editor, is slightly older, and exudes an air of quiet competence. Charlie Winstone is small and obliging. Mike Higgs, the cartoonist 'Mik,' swears he was drawing that way before he even *heard* of Arthur Thomson. Cynthia, his girlfriend, has a lovely smile. Mike Turner is just old enough to have grown his first beard, and Ed James is capable of talking but seldom admits it. I'm sure there were more but one tends to lose count. And some of the best ones, so I hear, didn't turn up at all."

He meant Beryl Henley, who hadn't seriously considered leaving her family for the weekend. And Darroll Pardoe, who'd joined the con but was coming up to his finals at Cambridge and had wisely decided to concentrate on that. Geoff Winterman, Oliver Harvey, and Rod Milner had taken supporting memberships but hadn't felt sufficiently motivated to come along. Archie also credits two girls as members of the Birmingham group, although Mary Reed came from Banbury, and Julia Stone from Chipping Norton. "Both girls had got hold of the notion that the way to spend a convention is by going for three whole nights without sleep," he said.

Archie himself wasn't quite what I had expected. After corresponding with him for nearly six months, I thought he must surely be one of the biggest BNFs around. He had been BSFA Treasurer for the first three years and was currently editing *Vector*. He seemed to specialise in befriending neofans and really was very good at it, encouraging people hovering on the edge of fandom. His letters were little gems, erudite, full of puns and wordplay, and they had given me a mental picture of a refined, Oscar Wilde-like aesthete, a master of witty repartee.

In reality, he was nothing like that at all. He was a big man, tall, well-built, with a shock of black hair and thick black moustache and beard, wearing his standard kit: a grey-green open-neck shirt, grey-green V-neck pullover, baggy grey trousers and open-toe leather sandals. Archie loved puns and word play but disappointingly, he wasn't a very good conversationalist, and this made talking to him rather difficult. I thought he was probably quite a shy man who found the forced conviviality of the convention a bit hard to handle.

Early on I saw Langdon Jones in the bar, having a fine time with some of his London friends. He didn't appear to recognise me from our unfortunate meeting the previous autumn, and for some reason I didn't want to remind him. Then I met Roy Kay, a quiet, unassuming young man from Birkenhead who had his own fanzine, *Chaos*. He was slim, with a slightly pockmarked complexion and a lock of blond hair, which drooped over his forehead. He didn't seem to know many people either, so we started to drift around together.

I started talking to Doreen Parker, an attractive blonde woman a few years older than I was, and her friend, Daphne Sewell. They both lived locally, and the previous year Doreen had found out about Bullcon from the pages of *New Worlds*, just a week before Easter. "Come along anyway," Ken Slater had advised, and she had, meeting Mack Reynolds and becoming truly hooked on fandom. Then I met Chris Priest for the first time, with whom I had been exchanging letters furiously since the previous November. Doreen thought we looked like "identical twin undertakers, both tall and thin with glasses, dressed in dark suits with dark ties and short-back-&-sides haircuts."

Chris recollects, "It was my first con and made an impression on me. I wonder how it would seem now, in the light of hindsight? Probably like a big room party, compared with some of the huge cons we have these days. The hum and sway. Quotecards. Meeting Terry Pratchett, who in those days was still at school and had a shock of black frizzy hair. Ted Tubb's GoH speech, which I have often quoted as the ideal GoH speech on which all others should be modelled. Leigh Brackett and Edmond Hamilton. A movie, *The Day the*

Earth Caught Fire, shown on a portable screen with a noisy projector. Another, *Metropolis,* with people shouting "funny" dialogue. Lots more small fragments like that.

"My main disappointment was that there weren't more famous writers there. I had hoped to meet Wyndham, Christopher, Aldiss, Brunner, Ballard, Clarke, etc. Instead, it was a bit low-key, as far as pros went. Of course, I realize now that Wyndham, Christopher, and Ballard never went to cons (although I did glimpse Wyndham the following year, when he dropped in at the Worldcon for a few minutes), Aldiss was away in Yugoslavia, and Brunner was on his ban-the-bomb march. But in 1964 I had just started to write, it was a deadly secret, but I was desperate to meet other writers, pick up tips, and so on. And I particularly remember coming across Rog Peyton in full flight, enthusiastically applauding or condemning one SF writer after another."

That certainly sounds like Rog. He had arrived early and Ken Cheslin had immediately introduced him to special guests Edmond Hamilton and his wife Leigh Brackett, and he just went on from there. I was much more diffident, staying well in the background, observing the proceedings with a certain fascination. Rog definitely had the right idea, the thing to do was to plunge in and meet people. Most of them were genuinely pleased to see newcomers, as Langdon Jones had found with his own first experience the previous year: "As a neofan I had expected to be a sort of social outcast. However this wasn't so at all."

We were all a little bit frightened of Ken Slater, another big man, who had a penetrating stare and fierce eyebrows. Ken ran the book-room with his attractive, red-headed wife Joyce—as the only dealer he *was* the book-room— and I went predictably wild over his tables. He was already a bit of a legend because of his Operation Fantast, which had kept British fandom alive almost single-handed during the immediate post-war years, but we soon found his brusque manner actually disguised a very kind heart.

Roy Kay and I wandered around all afternoon with some of the other Brummies. Ed James fell in with another schoolboy named Terry Pratchett, who impressed us greatly because he had already sold a story to John Carnell's *Science Fantasy.* He said that Carnell had accepted it when he was only thirteen, although it wasn't published until after his fifteenth birthday!

Terry comments now, "Easter was early that year and it was bitterly cold. I think I was simply overawed by it all. It was not, as I recall, hugely packed with pros, just fans in ties and suits. Bliss was it in that dawn to be alive, unless you'd bought one of Mr Burgess's pork pies."

I saw several people whose names I recognised, like Arthur Thomson, who had sent me that wonderful cover for the third *Zenith.* He looked so *worried,* like a cost accountant whose sums wouldn't add up! Ethel Lindsay appeared, a tiny Scottish woman with a warm smile like everyone's favourite teacher, who ran two fanzines *Scottishe,* and *Haverings.* Strangely, though, I didn't see much of my new pal, Charles Platt, who seemed to have gone off with a circle of his own friends, people like Peter White, Dick Howett and Dave Busby.

After the *Spinge* review, I kept well clear of Jim Linwood, thinking he had declared himself an "enemy" and wouldn't want to talk to me. I didn't understand that in fandom, one bad review isn't necessarily reason to fall out, and I was imagining feelings of hostility that were not really there. Maybe if Jim had taken the initiative it would have broken the ice, but as it was, the opportunity was lost, a chance to meet people who could so easily have been my natural contemporaries. Jim and his friends had mostly entered fandom in 1959–61 and were the immediately-previous fan-generation, the Kingdon Road set, Dick Ellingsworth and his attractive girlfriend Diane ("Nell") Goulding, Alan Rispin, and Marion Lansdale, all living in a house in Kingdon Road, West Hampstead, and hosting many others like Barry Bayley, Mike Moorcock, and occasionally Cliff Teague on his travels. Later, I discovered that Jim and Marion had only got married that Thursday, and the convention was part of their honeymoon.

In the bar I met Ron Bennett, whose *Skyrack* newsletter was already proving indispensable and who appeared to know everybody. He was thin, with heavy-rimmed glasses, moustache, and jet-black hair, with a good line of patter, seemingly able to crack a witticism at an instant's notice. We suspected him of being the originator of the quote-cards that were now appearing, tucked into picture frames, on tables, everywhere! I also met Eddie Jones, who somehow didn't *look* like my idea of an artist; he was a smallish man, slightly plump and pink-cheeked with a little ginger moustache, but he had no airs and graces, had already sent me a few headings for *Zenith,* and very kindly offered to do some more art if I wanted.

At eight o'clock, we filed upstairs for the start of the programme in the con-hall. This was dominated by a huge, painted backdrop held up on poles, an intricate, 12-foot tableau of some sort of undersea scene, with papier-mâché rocks and an old sea-trunk with a rounded lid. Many years later Ken Slater explained the rationale:

"We 'themed' the two Peterborough cons on books by the Guest of Honour. For Repetercon we based the backdrop on Ted Tubb's *City of No Return.* We had lots of fun painting it on big sheets of that grey paper intended for carpet underlay, which came in rolls about 10 foot long. We did it in the yard behind my shop in Norfolk Street, using tempera colour, and bottles of wine as aids. Dave Barber was involved, and a local semi-fan named Mark Ashby who was a pretty fair artist."

A man with short-cropped hair stood up and welcomed everyone to the convention. This was the chairman, Tony Walsh, and I thought how much he resembled David Frost. He was followed by a Meet the Notables session conducted by Ethel Lindsay, although unfortunately it didn't mean much to me.

Tony introduced Walter Willis, the columnist from the old *Nebula*, and James White—ah, he'd written "Sector General." Bob and Sadie Shaw?—never heard of them! Little did I realise that Irish fandom was here in force. And I was petrified when they asked me to stand up to be introduced as editor of one of the new fanzines!

The next item was Memory Man, in which the audience was invited to ask Ken Slater "snap" questions on any SF subject. It was a good idea in principle, but unfortunately, there *weren't* any questions, apart from Doreen wanting to know some fine details of the plot of *The Puppet Masters*. After that, however, things started to warm up, as London fan Charles Smith (also attending his first convention) described in *Spinge*:

"Strange sounds were issuing from the con-hall; it was the 'Bellyflops,' billed as 'fandom's own R & B in the key of E,' with Mike Moorcock on guitar, Dick 'Wrists' Ellingsworth on bongos, Norman Shorrock on second guitar, and Alan Rispin making peculiar noises with a harmonica. Every now and then the particular number they were playing (good oldies like 'Jungle Man' and 'Oh, Didn't He Ramble') would collapse into chaos, and Mike would turn and shout, 'Norman!!,' or 'Wouldn't it be better if we all played the same tune?'

"Somehow the concert degenerated into a wrestling match between Max ('The French Fiend') Jakubowski and Pat ('Mauler') Kearney, to the accompaniment of Norman still playing guitar to 'Aava Naguela [*sic*],' not having realised they'd finished all that. There was a superb, improvised commentary by Mike Moorcock which he kept up for at least half-an-hour, non-stop."

Jim Linwood continues, "Mike acted like a demented referee, with an improvised shtick about 'Good wholesome family entertainment' (wrestling was prime-time TV Saturday viewing then), as opposed to the 'degenerate prose' of William Burroughs. Pat Kearney actually got a severe beating from Max Jakubowski."

Michael Moorcock had just gained control of *New Worlds,* and he came to Peterborough like a young god, tall and well built, in a wide-brimmed hat with his guitar slung over his shoulder. He wore a smart dark suit, white shirt and tie, with golden hair and a neatly trimmed beard and moustache exactly like that sported by John Brunner in later years. He was bursting with personality and I regarded him with awe. Later, Mike invited Lang Jones and a crowd of others back to his room and continued in fine form until five in the morning, drinking, playing guitar with accompaniment from radiator pipes and kazoo, and revising the Bible. Sadly, I missed the fun, not having heard about room parties, and had gone to bed soon after the bar closed.

Saturday morning, and the programme started with a fan-panel chaired by Ron Bennett with Wally Weber from Seattle, the TAFF representative that year. He didn't say much. But what exactly *was* TAFF? Neither Roy nor I had much idea. Fortunately, a little later someone came by and explained that it was a way to send Arthur Thomson to America to meet all his friends. This seemed fair enough since ATom had been good to me, so we signed up and paid five shillings.

In the afternoon Ted Tubb gave his Guest of Honour speech, about which Dick Howettt later commented, "It had us all hypnotised. That chap definitely had a way with words. At the time I thought Ted Tubb would make a very effective salesman, so it came as no surprise when a few months later I caught sight of him in a large department store where he was energetically flogging 'Sharpo,' the miracle kitchen knife, to an enthralled crowd of shoppers."

Some time during the day we heard that a reporter from the local paper had turned up, but as Walt Willis remarked approvingly, "it was all right, no-one was talking to him." And at the first opportunity, chairman Tony Walsh issued a Public Warning to avoid him at all costs, so the reporter sat alone in the bar, writing his piece out of his head. "No doubt it was just as accurate as any other newspaper report of a convention," said Willis philosophically.

The Fancy Dress Party that evening was amazing; I had never seen anything like it before. In came a mutant with four eyes and goodness-knows how many arms, followed by a superb BEM from the pages of Brian Aldiss' *Bow Down to Nul*, both costumes coming from the Manchester group. Then followed Fafhrd and the Grey Mouser, and chairman Tony Walsh staggered on inside an eight-foot silver "rocket," so solid that it stood up by itself when untenanted. The best outfit that night was worn by Eddie, who swaggered around in bonnet and cloak as "The Original Kelly Freas," looking uncannily like one of the swashbuckling Freas characters from *Astounding*.

Everyone was in a jolly mood as the party broke up into informality, thanks to Norman Shorrock, an affable member of the Liverpool Group, who had supplied an incredible quantity of his famous home-brewed punch. Various things then started to happen. Ron Bennett assembled a brag school on the landing, with Tony Walsh, Dave Barber, and a tough-looking Yorkshireman with a loud voice and a mass of curly hair. In the deserted con-hall, Ken Slater and a few pals sat around the old sea chest, trying to work out a proper constitution for TAFF. Upstairs, Mike Moorcock and some of the other Londoners hosted a room party with an impressive selection of drink, while a splinter group went up onto the roof, and at midnight, a large, portly man in a suit came around with a cardboard suitcase, hawking his wares in a sonorous voice, "Pies anyone? Pork pies?" It was Brian Burgess, already a fannish legend.

Meanwhile, something "pretty traumatic" was happening to Walt Willis, as he later described in his column in *Quark 8*:

"I was standing in the corridor about 1.00 a.m. on Easter Sunday when some young men came along and started to sell copies of the sixth issue of a fanzine called *Alien* which I had never seen before. Madeleine counter-attacked by producing a copy of *Hyphen* 34 and trying to sell them a subscription.

"'What is it?' asked one of them.

"'It's called *Hyphen*,' said the other. 'You remember, that green thing we saw downstairs.'

"'But it's dated September. Is it still being published? Why isn't she selling the current issue?'

"'This is the current issue,' said Madeleine weakly.

'Huh, that's not very good, is it?'

"Slowly and painfully, I leaped to her defence. 'Maybe after you've published 34 issues you won't be monthly either?' I suggested.

"'Maybe not,' the young faned shrugged, 'but we're doing all right.'

"Reinforcements arrived, in the shape of Bob Shaw.

"'Anything in it?' he asked, watching me leaf through *Alien*.

"'There is some amateur science fiction,' I said, trying to keep all trace of emotion from my voice, 'and a page of cartoons called "Laffs." '

"Bob shuddered. However, quite unconscious of this damning indictment, the neofan nodded and turned away. It was abruptly clear to me that he was not a neofan at all; he was a BNF in another fandom. What did that make me and my friends? What had we done?"

Walt had met Harry Nadler and Chuck Partington from the Manchester group. Contrary to his impression, they weren't really that influential themselves, but they were a symptom of the "generation gap" that had suddenly opened in British fandom. Willis continued:

"...at the annual general meeting of the BSFA it was quite clear what we had done. After the folding of *Nebula,* British fandom had been worried at the complete absence of channels of recruitment. Deliberately and in cold blood, they had started a sercon organisation, sacrificing valuable fanning time to publish an official organ, full of reviews of science fiction; in this bait was a hook consisting of reviews of, and reprints from fanzines.

"The policy had been spectacularly successful, because the membership of the BSFA was now in the hundreds and scores of them were here at Peterborough. The only trouble was that while they seemed to have eaten the bait and grown fat on it, they had ignored the hook.

"The situation was starkly illuminated at that meeting, after one of the founder members had remarked casually and unguardedly that the purpose of the BSFA was to recruit new members to fandom. A storm of protest made it clear that this was not the purpose of the BSFA at all. Fandom as we knew it was to them a useless excrescence, our fanzines incomprehensible and irrelevant. *They* were fandom."

Rog, Charlie, and I were oblivious to these undercurrents as next morning we trooped dutifully into the con-hall for the sixth Annual General Meeting of the British Science Fiction Association. We assumed this was the important bit, that the BSFA was in charge of things, and we didn't know that really, it was all a bit of a bluff. Conventions were said to be held "under the auspices of the BSFA," which actually meant, well, nothing very much at all, apart from the formality of "awarding" the con to each successive year's committee.

The AGM itself was poorly attended because it began at 10.00 a.m. and many people were still comatose from the night before. It was conducted by the fierce Yorkshireman with the loud voice, who turned out to be Phil Rogers, outgoing Chairman of the BSFA. As I had now discovered from the programme book, he was also standing for TAFF that year in competition with Arthur Thomson.[1]

Phil was brusque and efficient, the business was scant, and committee reports were minimal. It started out as a tame affair, but then the occasion was enlivened by Ted Tubb in true messianic mood. A tall, broad-shouldered man with horn-rimmed glasses, swept-back grey hair, and a sardonic expression, Ted had been one of the founders of the Association. Now he argued loudly and passionately that people really *ought* to join the BSFA, the organisation needed to pull itself together, put on a bit of a show, get out there, and find more members! When Secretary Gill Adams inconveniently pointed out to Ted that he wasn't actually a member *himself*, he proceeded to re-join the Association there and then with a great show of theatre, and appealed for others to do the same. "Free drinks tonight for all new members!" he pleaded earnestly.

Charles Platt put his hand up and made some serious and constructive suggestions. "What about starting a 'Round Robin,' " he asked. "What about helping beginners to produce their own fanzines?" Yes, and yes again, was the reply. If you want to do it, go right ahead with our blessing.

However, as Walt Willis reported, real trouble broke out when the actual *purpose* of the BSFA was inadvertently questioned. The depth of misunderstanding was made clear by the reaction of another newcomer, North-East fan Phil Harbottle: "When Ella Parker said that the purpose of the BSFA was to recruit for fandom, I nearly fell off my chair I was so surprised. Surely, the BSFA stands for the advancement and recognition of SF, British SF in particular, and is only indirectly connected to fandom? One was given the impression that the BSFA is being run as a sufferance sideline by the fans."[2]

Next was the election of officers. We didn't know it, but these positions were not exactly sought-after. Roy Kay explained how the system usually

---

[1] Appearances can be deceptive! Foolishly, I was frightened of Phil for several more years before discovering that beneath the fierce appearance he was the gentlest and kindest of men!

[2] "Well, yes, that's right" might have been the reaction from some of the veterans. Really, there wasn't any doubt about the BSFA's purpose. As Ina Shorrock recalls, "At the last Kettering con we were down to forty. It looked as if fandom was going to die out if we didn't do something."

worked: "At the AGM, committee members are picked by an astonishing process, with last year's mob pointing at people in the audience, who hadn't had a post before, and asking, begging, bullying them to take the job. Any job. Just to fill up the hole." (*Beyond* 4)

This year was different. Incredibly, there were *volunteers!* Ken Cheslin had agreed to be Chairman, and he had talked some of the Birmingham group into joining him. Rog hadn't needed much persuasion—he had wanted to edit a fanzine anyway, and he'd volunteered to be Publications Officer as soon as Archie Mercer had announced he was standing down, back in November. Ken had persuaded Charlie Winstone to be Treasurer, and Rod Milner to take over as Secretary from Max Jakubowski, with Roy Kay becoming Vice-Chairman. This meant all the executive officers would now be in Birmingham.

Then came the site-selection meeting, and to everyone's surprise some poor fools actually *wanted* to put on the Easter convention. Absolutely unheard of! The usual procedure was to argue round and round in circles until somebody weakened and agreed to take on the job. Now there were two competing bids for 1965, while Dave Barber was asking for a commitment for 1966—two whole years away—for his bid for Great Yarmouth. (There was no precedent for looking so far ahead, so the meeting gave a lukewarm endorsement of his plan, saying well, yes, maybe it would be all right, if something else didn't come up in the meantime.)

The real excitement came with the two bids for next year. Ken Cheslin was bidding for Brumcon 2, while Ron Bennett proposed a return to Harrogate, scene of his successful 1962 Ronvention. On the surface, this seemed reasonable enough, but was there perhaps rather more to this situation than met the eye? Why should Ron bid for another convention so soon after he had "done his turn" only two years earlier, when another offer was already on the table? Were some fans unhappy with the whole idea of Ken and a bunch of newcomers taking the convention to Birmingham, so some of them hastily put together an impromptu "spoiler"?

Because Ken didn't exactly inspire much confidence with his presentation. He said that he expected attendance next Easter to be low because London was hosting the Worldcon in August, but this would suit him because Birmingham was a bad town as far as hotels were concerned and he would find it easier to hold a small convention rather than a large one. It was hardly an exciting prospect, and Harrogate might easily have won if poor old Ron Bennett hadn't lost his voice the previous day and so couldn't rally support with his usual conviction. A decision had to be made, and this is where the BSFA's nominal authority suddenly became important, because it turned out that only paid-up members could vote, and of course it was mostly the younger, "keen" types who'd come to the AGM rather than the more blasé older fans still asleep upstairs. Even so, Birmingham won by just one vote, 27/26.

Do the numbers and you will see the vote must have been almost a straight "old fan" vs. "new fan" split. Most of the younger element would have backed Brumcon, but a good majority of "older" fans must have wanted to go back to Harrogate. So was there a forgotten power-struggle here, right at this critical juncture for British fandom? Feelings must have been running high because the next morning a large notice mysteriously appeared on the hotel notice board. "Let's go to Harrogate anyway," it said. But now even Ron Bennett himself isn't sure what happened: "Can't think why I should have wanted to put it on, but the clue that my bid might well have been a last minute 'panic' effort is the fact that I had no GoH or committee lined up."

What would have happened if the vote had gone the other way? Would Harrogate have been one final "house party," the last gasp of the previous generation? Might it have been better for the Birmingham fans if they hadn't been pitched so quickly and so deeply into organising activities when they were still such relative newcomers? For immediately after the vote, Chairman Ken announced that his Guest of Honour would be Harry Harrison, with a committee comprising Rog Peyton, Charlie Winstone, and Mike Higgs. They were going to be *busy* Easter Brummies!

But he didn't include *me,* not in the BSFA committee, nor with the Brumcon. I felt hurt and rejected. Ken Cheslin simply hadn't asked me to take part in either project, even though I would have loved to have been involved. Afterwards I put a brave face on it because I had *Zenith* to keep me busy, but it rankled, and I felt excluded. I suspected more than ever that Ken Cheslin had never really accepted me.

In the afternoon the Delta group showed a half-dozen of their 8mm films, with titles such as *I was a Teenage Birdman, Conquest in Space, Son of Godzilla,* and so on. Their lampoon of *Frankenstein* was the best, but *Birdman* was funny, and the Manchester chaps had generally put in a tremendous amount of effort in making miniature sets and costumes, and with their animation techniques. The audience went wild and promptly decided to give one-third of any convention profits to the group so that they could make a full-length feature film for the 1965 London Worldcon.

I thought the films were great fun, but Charles Platt was less enthusiastic. "The main reason [they] were so well thought of was that the majority of the audience had never seen any serious amateur films before," he said. "They did not deserve the praise that was showered upon them. Judged by the standards of serious amateur film-making they were not very good, nor was there any real attempt to make them serious SF; they were either humorous monster or serious monster films." Privately, Charles decided to make his own film for the Worldcon, to show them how it *should* be done.[3]

The rest of the day fled past, and Rog and I had our evening meal in the hotel, probably because the local Wimpy bar closed on Sunday. It was here the drizzle of quote-cards reached blizzard proportions, with card after card making the rounds of the dining room. *"Pass the grasshoppers,"* said one, and *"Help I am a prisoner in a fanzine factory."* I was particularly taken with the one, *"I have just won TAFF. Please send three more 'Joan-the-Wads'—signed, P.R.."* [4]

And soon, too soon, came the final event of the convention, as described by Charles Smith:

"Things began to happen in the con-hall. The doors were held tight, and through the glass dim figures wearing strange garb could be seen, moving about inside. Eventually we were told that we were about to witness a Hum-and-Sway ceremony, the first for ten years. Only people with glasses were allowed inside. We were instructed to sit on the floor in a great circle. A well-oiled Ted Tubb was issuing instructions, and the Cup Bearers, Eddie Jones and Norman Shorrock, were dispensing an innocuous-looking liquid from great vats. I took one sip and discovered this was the genuine Shorrock home-brewed damson gin."

Charles Platt was similarly impressed by the originality and appeal of the occasion:

"In the dim glow from one ceiling light the audience hummed and swayed in a circle about the mysterious gowned figures of Moorcock, Tubb, and Ken Bulmer, until at the sound of Moorock's kazoo they were commanded to drink. At the climax of the ceremony a 'young and virginal girl' (Diane Goulding) was brought forth, laid on the floor, slain with one stroke of a sword to her heart, and then was resurrected through the psychic power of renewed humming-and-swaying." The effect was slightly spoiled when Mike Moorcock fell noisily over a table but otherwise the event went with a real swing. It certainly convinced Langdon Jones, who claimed to be "in a state of Enlightenment" (although the Shorrock home-brew may have had something to do with it) and for a long time afterwards wandered around wild-eyed, shouting, "I believe! I believe!"

Strangely, Bob Shaw seemed to take it rather too seriously, and said, "Irish Fandom refused to join in. Several people we know well were in it and had a

---

[3] Dick Howett said, "The film was supposed to be a superior effort called *The Cardboard Man*, which was going to compete with the Delta Group's Worldcon film project. Like most Platty things it never came to much. This is not to be confused with the film Chris Priest and I began, concerning the travels and development of a fan. We began shooting on the road to Brum, then at Rog Peyton's party and at Brumcon. The film is mentioned in Rob Hansen's fan history as being 'lost.' Demonstrably Not So, although all that remains is a bit of 16mm negative."

[4] "Joan-the-Wad" was a figurine of a "Cornish pisky," regularly advertised in the pages of all the British SF magazines and supposed to bring good luck to the purchaser.

great time, so it seems that one must be able to have a good time messing around on the fringes of mass hypnosis. But, this being so, why does the affair have to be invested with an air of childish unpleasantness by tricks like fake sacrifices? ...rather unappetising undertones were present. What's it all in aid of?"

And that was the convention. I hadn't been entirely sure what

A young and virginal girl was brought forth

was going on for most of the time, but I had enjoyed the weekend immensely. So, apparently, had almost everyone else, for it prompted a record number of con-reports.

Langdon Jones said that "it was a very fannish convention. 1964 saw the return of some things which had seemed to have been gone for ever: Quotecards, and the kind of fannishness that the hum & sway ceremony typified. One of my great regrets is that I came into fandom too late to experience the kind of activity that was going on in the late fifties, and I can only hope that this convention was an indication of a return to this happy state. I think that part of the fannish atmosphere was due to the deliberate under-programming, for which the organisers are to be congratulated." He then continued with a prescient comment, "There was a strong sercon element at this con, which was large enough to be disturbing, to me at least. I mean 'science-fiction-is-all' types. Maybe if things keep their present directions we shall see a split between the two groups?"

Because one voice dissented from the general praise, and that was Charles Platt, who was considerably more critical. For instance, the Friday night extravaganza seemed to have passed him by completely, and he reported only that after the question-and-answer session, "It all broke up and people were left to themselves for the rest of the evening, all right for older fans reunited with their companions, but discouraging and boring for newcomers who could find little to do."

Similarly, he remarked disapprovingly about the events of the Saturday night:

"Cliques gathered in the downstairs lounge, parties started in various rooms, drunkards roamed the corridors, and rooms were broken into by a phantom inebriate with a master key. While neofans grumbled morosely about the lack of organisation and the lack of SF interest in older fans, the older ones smoked pipes and played cards on the landing and in the lounge. Michael Moorcock, assisted as always by his London group of hangers-on, spent the evening crooning and bellowing into a microphone, revising the Bible, climbing over the roofs and generally making a nuisance of himself.

"The parties were fun… yes. But there was a continual feeling that the fun was a trifle unnatural or forced. I wonder how many people enter fandom as an escape; correspondence can so easily and successfully disguise the social outcast or introvert, enabling him to become whatever sort of person he pleases, until his correspondents meet him—and so often find that the person they have been writing to is not what his letters sounded like at all. Consequently, it is hardly surprising that the social atmosphere was 'forced' on Saturday night, with natural introverts trying hard to be extroverts. There was a slight feeling of 'Why am I staying up for this?', and indeed the main reason was, 'because everyone else is.' "

Charles' report is important, because he was to become the leader among the Young Turks who would set about changing British fandom forever. As Walt Willis commented, "it gives a vivid mental picture of the reaction of a serious-minded and intelligent newcomer to his first convention, and I found it quite fascinating… not least in its resemblance to my own first convention report. There is the same ambivalent attitude of being in, but not of, the convention, and the same almost defensive readiness to attack what seems to be established authority."

Archie Mercer made similar remarks: "I'm not quite sure how to deal with your convention report. You sound as if you're walking round with a perpetual chip—or rather, about half a tree—on your shoulder. I never wrote a report of *my* first convention—though it would have been even less favourable to its subjects, had it been written. Nor on my second, nor yet on my third—which was the first one I really *enjoyed*." (Letter, *Beyond* 6)

Charles didn't seem to have enjoyed the convention very much. He also managed to annoy Michael Moorcock, who afterwards wrote a tart letter, "Even allowing for your evidently poor state of mind at Peterborough, your report abounds with inaccuracies and is extremely offensive, both to myself and my friends. I have no group of 'hangers-on' from London, or anywhere else. I do have a number of friends, some of whom come from London, whose company I enjoy and whose friendship I value to the extent that I was deeply shocked and made extremely angry to find them described as 'hangers-on.'

"Your report notes also that the 'fun' seemed unnatural or forced. Again it is obvious that this impression was entirely subjective, produced by the writer's own state of mind. This impression is not shared by the people who were actually enjoying themselves instead of hanging about on the sidelines with a dour expression."

Mike ended his letter with some good advice, "I think the reforming spirit that *Beyond* and its contemporary fanzines are encouraging is a good sign. However, there's no need to make yourself unpopular while doing it.... As it is, you're diffusing your energies by starting these little vendettas here and there and this could easily end—it's happened before—with your turning your back on fandom... At the moment *Beyond* has rather a shrill note. Try to give it a firm one."

There is another side to the somewhat sanctimonious attitude Charles adopted towards the Saturday night festivities. For instance Lang Jones commented, "Platt's party was rather wild, with the bed moved out into the corridor," while Charles Smith noted, "Someone came rushing by me screaming that Charles Platt had been sick, as if this was great news..." Walt Willis wrote, "Some of them [the new fans] seemed to spend the days sneering at us for not being serious and constructive like them, and the nights running up and down the corridors drunk, shouting and banging at our doors." Finally, Ken Cheslin in *Spinge* 13 said, "Charles Platt running down a corridor, screaming blue murder at 3.00 a.m., is not conducive to the image of a serious and constructive editor of a New Wave fanzine."

In his supposedly critical report, Charles was actually boasting about his own escapades: *he* was one of the "drunkards" who roamed the corridors. Nothing particularly wrong with that, of course, apart from the hypocrisy involved, but he was also the "phantom inebriate with a master key" who broke into various bedrooms, which was not quite so funny if it happened to be *your* room he broke into.

Apparently, Peter White approached Jim Linwood the next morning and with much mirth enquired if he had found anything unusual about the state of his bed the previous night. When Jim expressed bewilderment, Peter said something to the effect of "Ohmigod we did the wrong room," and scooted off at high speed to inform Charles that they'd accidentally "apple-pied" someone else in error. Was this the reason why Alan Rispin, normally the gentlest of souls, "nearly throttled" Charles Platt early that morning? We may never know!

On Monday, the hotel emptied rapidly. Charles had to break a window to get into his temperamental old car before driving back to London with Chris Priest and Peter White. I walked to the railway station with Rog, Charlie and the other group members for our long journey home. Somehow, we didn't seem to have talked much about science fiction, but I'd had a wonderful time anyway. I also now had a girlfriend, Mary Reed from Banbury, who had cosied up to me in the con-hall late on the Sunday evening. This would complicate life enormously, but first, I had a fanzine to get out.

Post-Convention Depression
Chapter 6

The long train journey from Peterborough took most of the day and I didn't get home until quite late on Monday evening. My parents were only vaguely curious about how it had gone, so I went to bed to catch up on some sleep. But while I was desperately tired I couldn't settle, my brain still too full of it all, replaying images of Ted Tubb at the Hum-&-Sway, Mike Moorcock and the wrestling match, Ken Slater and his books, the Fancy Dress, the room parties, the excitement of meeting new people, so many other experiences.

Grey morning came, and with it the bleak realisation that I was back in my own bed, back in the council house, back in Northfield, and the excitement was well and truly over. Now it was real life once more, drab and boring, and I had to go back to my detested job in the metallurgical laboratory. As I travelled across the city that morning, I resolved not to tell anyone about the weekend because they wouldn't understand and I'd already had enough leg pulling about my crazy hobby. But it was hard to keep it all to myself, when I desperately wanted to talk about the con with Rog and the others, compare notes, discuss what we'd seen and done. We didn't have a telephone at home, there wasn't a Brum Group meeting for another week, and I began to realise that the next convention was a whole *year* away, an absolute eternity!

I started to feel deeply depressed. And worried; had I made the most of it? After all, I hadn't dared speak to any of the professionals, had exchanged only a few embarrassed words with Walt Willis, who I now understood to be a sort of father figure to fandom. Rog had done a lot better because he had been confident while I was shy and diffident, waiting for others to make the first move. They probably thought I was standoffish, that I didn't want to be friends.

The one bright spot on the horizon was Mary Reed. I'd had a few girl-friends at school but this was different, Mary was a fan, and I was anxious to see her again. I wrote her a long letter, suggesting I should come down to Banbury the following weekend, though I had no idea how I was going to get there. Then there was nothing for it but to get on with *Zenith;* the fourth issue was nearly finished anyway, and at least it took my mind off the convention. So I hauled out my new Roneo from the bottom of the bed, set it up at the top of the stairs (the only place with enough room) and glumly started to run off the final pages.

However, I was cheered up immensely on Saturday morning when out of the blue I received a letter from Walt Willis, unsolicited and dated 2nd April. He said, "I've been thinking over our all-too-brief conversation during the Convention, when you flattered me by remembering the columns I used to do for *Nebula.* Would you like me to do a fanzine review column for *Zenith?*"

"Yes!" Although if I had been *really* true to the editorial I had printed just a few days earlier ("*Zenith* will leave alone those things exclusively fannish…") I would have politely rejected Walt's kind offer. Fortunately, I was not quite that stupid and wrote back gratefully, without for a moment wondering why a writer of his stature should want to contribute to a fanzine from a new and very callow editor. Considerably encouraged by this unexpected good fortune, I collated the fourth issue over the weekend and posted it out on Monday.

The following evening I went straight from work to Charlie Winstone's house for the Brum group meeting. I was the first one into his front room, followed quickly by Rog Peyton. I told him about the Willis column but it didn't mean much to him. Rog just wanted to talk about the con, and he was just as depressed as I had been a few days earlier. "What a fantastic weekend!" he said, "but now I feel so down. I can't go a whole year until the next convention!"

Charlie agreed, for him the con had been a real adventure, but he, too, felt miserable now it was over. Suddenly the Brum group wasn't enough, somehow the fun had gone out of it, and the familiar faces seemed stale and unexciting. Cliff's arrival with a stack of *Amazing Stories* didn't help matters. He seemed strangely unaffected by the general malaise, but he had just come back from another visit to London, and the thrill of the hunt had probably already taken his mind off the previous week's convention.

Mike Beard bounced in, even more enthusiastically than usual, having just turned seventeen. No, he had no complaints, he'd had a fine time, bought lots of books from Ken Slater. Then Mike Higgs arrived in his sheepskin jacket, calm and self-possessed as ever. It wasn't quite his thing, he thought, and Cynthia hadn't been too enthusiastic, but he was more worried about his involvement in next year's Brumcon. What exactly had he let himself in for?

I gave out the new *Zenith* while Charlie and Rog started to talk about their new positions on the BSFA committee. Rog was anxious to get on with his first issue of *Vector*, and was worried about how to get it printed; could he use my new Roneo machine? We discussed how to transport it over to his house, neither of us having a car. Somewhere in there, Dave Casey and Ollie came into the room. They hadn't been to the convention so Rog and Cliff started to tell them about all the people they'd met—Edmond Hamilton and Leigh Brackett, Mike Moorcock and Ted Tubb, and all the rest of the crowd. Dave was quieter than usual, didn't make his usual jokes, and I think he felt a bit out of it. Eventually Charlie got out the Risk board, but we couldn't concentrate on the game, something had changed.

That Saturday morning I set out for Banbury on the Midland Red long-distance bus service. As it trundled through Kenilworth in the bright spring sunshine, I watched the normal people tidying gardens and washing cars outside their houses and thought, "I bet they don't read science fiction!" We went through Warwick, where I had my first sight of the ancient castle, then past the RAF base at Gaydon with a couple of Vulcan V-bombers at the far end of the runway. We passed the Army camp at Kineton, up steep, historic Edge Hill with its Civil War battlefield and the stubby old church at the top, built in the golden Banbury ironstone that now started to predominate in the buildings along the way. Almost there, now, and I started to get nervous.

Mary met me at the bus stop and we had something to eat in a café, and then walked around the town talking about this and that, but largely about fandom and the convention. The time passed quickly, we went to the cinema,

Jump in the back, mate!

and then back to the house where she lived with her mother and stepfather. Since the last 'bus back to Birmingham departed at a ridiculously early time Mary had assured me I could stay overnight, if I didn't mind sleeping on their settee. Unfortunately, she had failed to explain this to her stepfather, who had just come back from the Working Men's Club. He had only one word to say about the situation, which was "Out!"

There I was, thrown out into the dark night of a strange town. It was well past eleven, the 'buses had stopped, the trains had stopped, and I had nowhere to go. The only thing I could think of was to try and hitch-hike home. I'd never done it in my life but Cliff seemed to travel the country that way, so it was worth a try. Fortunately Mary's house was just off the main road, so I walked to a straight bit and stood there under a streetlight, a forlorn figure with my little Woolworth's suitcase. Hesitantly I stuck out my thumb.

Within a half-minute, a white Transit van stopped beside me. The driver wound his window down. "Where're you going?" he asked. "Birmingham?— we're going as far as Warwick, jump in the back, mate."

I opened the sliding door in the back of the van to find ten or twelve girls in party dresses, sitting on cushions. They had been to a dance in Banbury and were now going home.

"Oh, a nice young man," they giggled, as I climbed in to join them.

"Thank you, God!" I thought, and "if this is hitch-hiking, I'll do it every weekend!"

It was twenty miles to Warwick and it must have taken the slow van three-quarters of an hour but the time seemed to pass in an instant. The rest of the journey was easy enough, and I stumbled into the house in the small hours, elated!

After that first trip, I had to make some decisions. If I was going to see Mary every weekend it would mean much less time for fan-activity and something would have to go. Not *Zenith,* of course, so it would have to be little *Nadir,* my "fun" title. At the very next group meeting I talked Charlie Winstone into taking it on, which wasn't really difficult because he'd already caught the publishing bug. I had already stencilled a weird little story by Rod Milner, a short article by Mike Higgs and a cover by Terry Jeeves. I handed the lot over to Charlie, and he published his first issue soon after.

For a second weekend I went down to Banbury, this time hitchhiking both ways with no incident (and, alas, no sign of the white Transit van). The following week was going to be more difficult because Mary and I were spending Saturday night at Beryl Henley's house at Crabbs Cross, in Redditch. Beryl wasn't the problem, we got on well, and I had been delighted when she had invited us to the last night of a show at the local theatre. Beryl had written the script of something called "Revellers out West," and had the female lead as "Little Passion Flower," the unwed and somewhat ancient daughter of "Big Chief Hole-in-the-Head."

It all sounded great fun, until I discovered that Graham Hall and his friend Dick Richardson had invited themselves along. Our paths hadn't crossed since our unfortunate meeting the previous autumn, but Graham had been

Little Passion Flower

muttering in the undergrowth and I didn't relish the thought of a weekend in his company. I wanted to get out of it, although it was awkward, since I had already accepted Beryl's invitation and didn't want to let Mary down. In the end the evening was as just difficult as I'd thought it would be, Graham and Dick playing up to Mary and Beryl, cutting me out, making little digs and being generally unpleasant. I felt very isolated and took refuge with Beryl's husband, Bob, a quiet, home-loving man who seemed bemused by the whole affair.

The show itself was hilarious, and at the end of the last act, Beryl was presented with several large bouquets. Finally the producer held up a box. "This is for Beryl," he announced mysteriously. "I was asked to keep it until last." Somewhat nervously she opened it, to find two tins of herring roes and a tin of crab-meat, all wired up together and wrapped in the shape of another bouquet. And a card with the message: "A Bouquet of Roes-es and Things from a Distant Admirer." Beryl remembered a postcard she had received from Bristol, which had said, "Crossed any good Crabbs lately?" and all became clear.

"Mercer, You fredlike *fool!*" she howled.

Still, the weekend hadn't done a lot for my fairly fragile self-confidence. I started to wonder if I was doing something wrong, because Graham Hall had obviously hated me on sight, Ken Cheslin was distant and had excluded me from his committees, and apart from Doreen Parker, I hadn't made any new friends at the convention, the way Ed James had done with Terry Pratchett. Why, I had even failed to get on with people I'd been corresponding with for months—Charles Platt and Chris Priest, for instance, who had been very offhand, while their friend Peter White had seemed quite dismissive.

Very much later Chris Priest gave me his perspective on events, which would have been a great comfort if he'd told me at the time:

"What you have to bear in mind is that I was closely allied with Charles, and rather more influenced by him than was good for me. I'm embarrassed now to remember how aware I was of perceived tribalism: the Alien lot from

Manchester, the Brummies, and so on. Platt was so sneery about people like you and Chuck Partington and everyone else that a lot of negative impressions overlay what I realize now are the more true personal memories.

"He was so relentlessly negative, so quick to sneer, so hostile to people enjoying themselves that I couldn't see past it. It was my first con too: I knew almost nobody but Charles, so tended to stay with him. I didn't care for his friends. Peter White was a supercilious twat who endlessly irritated me and made me feel small. Graham Hall described him as only wanting to become an airline pilot so he could look down on everyone at once.

"I think if left to myself I would have rubbed along pretty happily with everyone and by the Saturday evening would have made friends with a lot of people I didn't in fact get friendly with until a long time afterwards. To take a quick example, Charles seemed to loathe Ron Bennett on sight, and made endless derogatory comments about him. It took me years to get past this... not because I agreed with Charles, or was influenced by him, but because I simply felt a barrier of hostility had been set up. Another example is Jim Linwood, whom Charles was extremely negative about, but when I finally met Jim a few years later he turned out to be a friendly, clever guy. So Charles wasted a lot of time.

"When we were driving back from Peterborough in Charles's car with Peter White, we were tearing down the A1 at high speed and caught up with a brewery van. Charles pointed it out, and said in his best sneering voice, 'You can tell the driver's not a fan.' I asked why that was, and Charles said, 'Because he spells "beer" without the "h."' I didn't know what he was talking about, so Charles explained, and needless to say, the explanation was highly coloured by his sarcastic views of fannish fans. I thought to myself that it sounded like a mildly funny, harmless in-joke but Charles was so terminally scathing about that sort of thing that I kept mum."

Still, on the surface my own relations with Charles seemed amicable enough, and it was about this time that he asked me to take part in his pet project, PaDS, the BSFA's Publishing and Distributing Service. The plan was to encourage more people to produce fanzines, even if they didn't have access to a duplicator, or even a typewriter, by getting volunteers to do the work for them. PaDS would supply many copies as were required, circulating the titles in a quarterly bundle, and acting as the BSFA's very own APA (Amateur Publishing Association).

It all struck me as a bit misguided because I thought the whole point was to get involved in doing the work yourself, and surely, most fans ought to be able to find a way to pub their ish if they used a little initiative? And of course, PaDS was the absolute kiss of death for OMPA, Britain's existing APA, draining off the newcomers it so desperately needed. Not that I was exactly a newcomer any more and neither was Charles, but he wanted us both to put a magazine into the first bundle to get PaDS off to a flying start. So, only a month after dropping *Nadir* I found myself working on a new title, which I decided to call *Nexus*, "something that ties or binds," according to the dictionary. Well, that seemed appropriate.

I also needed to get on with another issue of *Zenith*. The bimonthly schedule was remorseless, and the weekends in Banbury were drastically cutting down on my time. Suddenly, however, my fanzine was to have an unexpected impact on my mundane life. For nine months I had been employed as an industrial chemist, hated it, and desperately wanted something more interesting. While looking through the local paper in late April I saw a classified ad for a "Technical Writer" at the Birmingham Small Arms Group, to prepare catalogues, manuals and sales leaflets for their small engine company in Redditch. Well, I thought, this sounded more my sort of thing, and I knew how to get there after having visited Beryl a few times, so I applied for the position. For the interview, I took along a couple of issues of *Zenith,* and although there were several other candidates the interviewer was impressed and I got the job!

Delighted, I went back to my fanzines with renewed enthusiasm. *Zenith* took the most work because there were books to send out for review, articles to get illustrated, more pages, more need for caution. *Nexus,* on the other hand, was great fun. It almost assembled itself, from material submitted for *Zenith* but which I thought wasn't quite right, "not serious enough," or "too chatty." The first issue had an article from Beryl defending John Campbell's ideas about dianetics and psi, a piece from BSFA member Joe Patrizio on the "right-wing" philosophy in H. Beam Piper's stories, a long review by Archie Mercer of an amusing early Panther title, and a free-style editorial rant about the criticism I was getting about *Zenith*. I typed the lot at one sitting (a *long* sitting!) and produced it well before the deadline; but then I needed to, because Rog Peyton was having the Roneo for his first issue of *Vector.*

He hadn't wasted any time, completing stencils for a 34-page issue in not much more than a month. It was everything the BSFA's journal should be, with book reviews and a long lettercolumn from members. There was an article by Dick Howett and a rather bland report on Repetercon by Jim Groves, complete with three pages of blurry electro-stencilled photographs. In an item about PaDS, my friend Doreen Parker announced that she was willing to type stencils for those in need. She must have had time on her hands, I thought!

And another feature was the Dr Peristyle column, in which the pseudonymous Doctor answered questions in a very school-masterly way.[1]

---

[1] His identity attracted much speculation at the time, but was a well-guarded secret until many years later. We all thought it was Archie Mercer under a pseudonym, and were surprised when it was revealed to be Brian Aldiss, at the time President of the BSFA.

Rog persuaded a mundane friend to drive over the hill from Quinton to collect my Roneo, which fortunately folded up into a fairly compact package, and while he had the machine, I was able to catch up on the various fanzines that appeared in quick succession at the start of May. There was Charles Platt's *Beyond* 5 with his controversial con report, and *Hyphen* 35, the first issue I'd seen. Biggest of all was the two-volume issue of *Les Spinge,* with its multiple convention reports and a letter from Leon Collins which served to inflame the "new wave" controversy:

"Into fandom have suddenly bounced several highly talented and enthusiastic youngsters. They have said, 'away with all this talk of subjects fans know nothing about,' and have started a revival of fanzines that are serious and constructive.... They want to write about science fiction and hear other fans' opinions of it. Amazed by the following these youngsters have, the 'fannish' fans make vicious attacks on them with undertones of sour jealousy...."

I took the letter at face value, although thinking it rather overstated the case. Later, I assumed Charles Platt was using one of his many alter egos to buttress his own opinions. However, in fact "Leon" was a fake, a name used in *Spinge* to stir things up, as Jim Linwood later explained:

"Leon Collins? You've probably guessed that 'he' was a LS house name, I wrote some of his letters and I suspect Colin Freeman was also involved, although Dave (Hale) never let on."

I started my new job at BSA at the beginning of June, and finished *Zenith* 5 in the same week. This one had an eye-catching cover that really was gorgeous, litho-printed on white card, possibly the best-looking cover ever seen on *any* fanzine, anywhere. It would never have come about but for the help of Charles Platt, who after six months had given up his Economics course at Cambridge in disgust, enrolling instead at the London School of Printing. Charles had offered to get a cover litho-printed for me, keeping the costs down by doing most of the work himself. All I had to do was provide the original artwork.

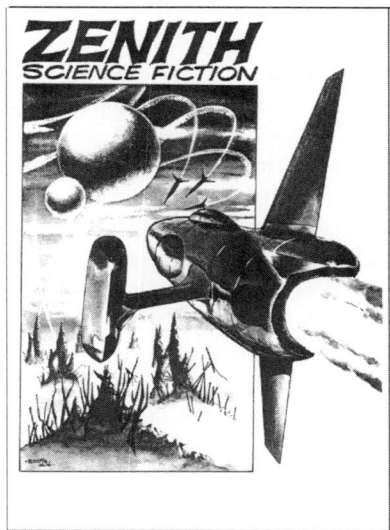

The opportunity had been too good to miss, so I wrote to Eddie Jones and explained what was on offer. Cunningly, or so I thought, I also approached a couple of publishers, inviting them to advertise on the back cover for the sum of £5-0-0d., which would pay for the whole thing.[2] Four Square accepted and I was delighted, but then two days later Corgi Books also wrote back and agreed to take the same space, which necessitated some rather less cunning explanations to explain an embarrassing situation!

Eddie sent a magnificent painting that took my breath away, and Four Square Books were as good as gold in sending their back-cover copy, which advertised *Beachheads in Space*. But trouble started as soon as I sent it off to Charles. "I told you we needed *line* artwork," he wrote vexedly. "These are half-tones which will require cutting-out and screening, and it's going to cost a lot more." I didn't really understand what he was saying but it sounded bad. "How much extra?" I wrote anxiously, but he wasn't able to answer. The dialogue continued, me getting more and more worried, Charles getting more and more snappy as the problems multiplied.

The end result was that I did get my covers, but I was annoyed at having to pay considerably more than the five pounds I'd charged Four Square, which was a serious blow when I was already struggling to pay for the fanzine out of my very low wages, a situation aggravated by the monthly payments to Roneo. Charles, on the other hand, was aggrieved because I hadn't been suitably grateful for all the trouble he had taken on my behalf.

Eddie supplied interior artwork, too, with highly professional headings for most of the articles and columns, which I reproduced in blue and red (having hung on to that "loaned" colour drum). It was the best-looking issue yet, and at 50 pages and 300 copies, it was also the biggest, spoilt only by the terrible, uneven Pica typeface from my rapidly deteriorating portable typewriter.

Unfortunately the contents were still very mixed, with another terrible story, and more filler in the shape of a pseudo-science article on "The Nasapods," which Charlie Winstone had submitted and I hadn't had sense to decline. However, this time there was a good, solid piece from Chris Priest on the state of the professional magazines in 1963, and an equally strong survey of Four Square Books from Rog Peyton. (Even though, as John-Henri Holmberg remarked in amused correspondence afterwards, no professional magazine would have been so rude to a publisher who had been so generous with advertising!)

In the final article, "The Life of Sector General," Edward James meticulously catalogued the aliens in James White's series of stories and explained his classification system, with illustrations by Eddie Jones, who provided six superb sketches of various alien life forms, fitted into the text at suitable points. The quality of this work made me realise just how good an artist Eddie was,

---

[2] This doesn't seem very much now, so to put it into context consider that the average price of a Gollancz hardback then was just fifteen shillings, so my cover would have cost about as much as seven books. At today's inflated book prices of around fifteen *pounds* each, it equates to about £100.00 for the ad, which sounds much more sensible.

and how fortunate we were that he was willing to devote so much of his time to fanzines. However, the issue was really dominated by three columns. Beryl Henley had eight pages of book reviews, in which she started to develop an idiosyncratic style of her own. Terry Jeeves appeared for the first time with his highly trenchant magazine reviews, a feature revived from earlier issues of *Vector*. The big surprise, of course, was the revival of Walt Willis' "Fanorama."

Willis had decided to try to reach out to the new fans, to do something that had been needed six months earlier. In Rob Hansen's words, "…Willis, realising that something needed to be done to heal the growing generational rift in British fandom, decided to fight a final rearguard action for the type of fandom he had known in the fifties." It was a brave effort, more so than we appreciated. It would have been so much easier for Willis to keep his head down, to have stayed with his old friends and ignored the upstarts.

He must have deliberated long and hard over his tactics. While I had been making vaguely disapproving noises about "fannishness," it was clear that Charles Platt was by far the most vociferous critic among the "New Wavers." So Walt probably reasoned that while *Zenith* was a pretty sercon fanzine it did at least seem to be fairly regular and widely distributed, and by giving me the column, he automatically got me "on side." It also allowed Willis to tackle Charles' *Beyond* as his first subject for review.

Unfortunately, I don't think he took sufficient account of the rivalry which was already developing between the two camps. It must have really annoyed Charles for me to get a prize like "Fanorama," and perhaps Willis might have done better to put his head all the way into the lion's mouth, as it were, by offering his column to Charles himself. For despite its muddled beginnings, *Beyond* was already rapidly evolving into a fanzine with a lot of personality, and the column would have been a much better fit there than in the more stilted *Zenith*. What's more, it might have enabled Walt to begin a personal dialogue with Charles, which would have been highly beneficial.

As it was, Walt's first instalment in *Zenith* was entirely devoted to a review of *Beyond,* issue number five (the one with the Repetercon report). It was a courtly, intelligent and sympathetic analysis at which no one could possibly take offence, or so I thought, and his final paragraph was particularly charming:

"…older fans at the moment have to choose between feigning interest, or keeping quiet, and unfortunately this latter reaction is sometimes mistaken for hostility. Whereas older fans cordially welcome fanzines like this, recognising them as essential for the continuation of fandom; it is just that having published them themselves for years they are surfeited with science fiction and talk of science fiction, and view these reincarnations of their former selves with a mixture of nostalgia and guilt. Not patronisingly, like students who have graduated, but like pensioners who have already done their part in the propagation of the species."

Sadly, it made things worse, not better. Those looking for trouble succeeded in finding it, and one of my correspondents (unnamed, but probably Graham Hall) called the column "a personal attack on Charles Platt," which was very far from the truth. Although Charles himself appeared perfectly happy with the review (in *Beyond* 6 he called it "well-written, balanced and intelligent," and "the fairest and most perceptive criticism yet"), the Willis column was a ticking time bomb, just waiting to explode in my face. That aside, this issue was a long way removed from the little purple combozine of only nine months before, and I was quite proud of it.

On the first weekend in June, I went along with other BSFG members to a Sunday afternoon party in Stourbridge, hosted by one of Ken Cheslin's neighbours, and took a copy of my new issue to show around. I was pleased with the Willis column, but particularly proud of the superb cover. Our host didn't know much about fanzines but he was clearly impressed with Eddie's painting and said so loudly to Ken. "If you'd taken advertising, you could have had covers like this," he said. Ken only grimaced and shook his head gloomily. "It isn't fannish," he replied.

He was right, of course, it wasn't. But Ken didn't appreciate how fast my attitudes to fandom were changing.

Revelations!
Chapter 7

June was a busy time! I started my new job at BSA at the beginning of the month, published the fifth issue of *Zenith* on the first weekend, received *Nexus* in the initial PaDS bundle on the second weekend, and on Sunday 27th, Mary's birthday, we announced our engagement.

A couple of weeks later there was another engagement, this time between Cliff Teague and his girl-friend Lesta Holmes, on his 22nd birthday. Cliff had become involved with Lesta when he called on her brother, Kris, and stayed overnight at the big old house in Hall Green where they both lived with their parents. Kris was an SF fan, and amazingly, he had been at Peterborough, although he must have been *very* shy and retiring because I don't think we noticed him at the time. You couldn't possibly overlook Lesta, who was a blonde bombshell, a tall, powerful girl who decided she liked the look of Cliff and (literally) swept him off his feet!

Most of the group attended their Sunday afternoon engagement party. We were genuinely pleased for Cliff. We thought he was finally getting himself together, now he had a regular job at Hudsons, and Lesta, with whom he soon moved in. He was ecstatically happy, so much so that he started to skip group meetings, something unthinkable a few months earlier. Unfortunately, it didn't last long. Quite suddenly, Lesta fell in love with an ambulance driver and the romance was over. Cliff was devastated and fell into a mood of deep depression, was almost suicidal, and even threatened at one stage to get rid of his collection! The group rallied around to try to cheer him up, but he stopped coming to Charlie's house for months, and was never quite the same again.

Meanwhile, fandom continued to roll along. Chris Priest produced his first issue of *Con,* in which he tried to bridge the imagined gap between "fannish" and "sercon" camps. Arthur Thomson won TAFF, to no-one's great surprise, although by a surprisingly small margin in British votes. Yet another Birmingham fanzine appeared in the form of Mike Higgs' *Shudder,* while Ken Cheslin put out an extremely scruffy-looking *Brumble,* the first issue of a combined fanzine and progress report on next year's Brumcon. And after only three months as BSFA Secretary, Rod Milner resigned, handing the job over to Graham Bullock, another SF enthusiast he had met in Hudsons Bookshop.

I continued to work hard on *Zenith,* but soon discovered I wasn't the only one who wanted to produce a magazine about science fiction. First, my Canadian correspondent Leland Sapiro surprised me in July with his revival of the former *Inside,* transplanted from New York to Saskatchewan, and with title changed to *Riverside Quarterly.* It was a handsome, half-size offset magazine with artwork by Charles Schneeman and Jim Cawthorn, an article by the writer Kris Neville, and Sapiro's own piece, "The Faustus Tradition in Science Fiction." Strangely, this new competitor didn't upset me as much as it might have, because, despite the attractive production, it all seemed a bit *boring!*

Much more worrying was *SF Horizons,* which came out in the following month. Unknown to me, publisher Tom Boardman had collected subscriptions for his new critical magazine at the first Peterborough convention, and eighteen months later the first issue appeared, with Brian Aldiss and Harry Harrison as co-editors.

Professionally typeset and printed, and saddle-stitched in book-size format, *SF Horizons* was like a grown-up brother of fanzines like *RQ.* It contained Harry Harrison's speech from the 1963 con, along with a three-way recorded discussion between Brian Aldiss, Kingsley Amis and C. S. Lewis. There was an article by Geoff Doherty (a teacher who attended several conventions around this time), and—best of all—Brian's long demolition of Jack Williamson's novel *The Legion of Time.* This was very much in the same style as Damon Knight's *In Search of Wonder,* although I felt vaguely disappointed that Brian had not chosen a more recent, more interesting target for his essay.

This might have been a good time for me to stop and take stock, and maybe even change direction, since there was no way I could hope to compete with *SFH* for serious critical material. After all, I now knew there were other ways of doing a fanzine. Two titles had been particularly instructive; the first being *Tensor,* from Langdon Jones, and the other was Roy Kay's *Chaos,* both somewhat scrappy but full of personality, showing how easy it really was to get into fandom. They simply wrote about their everyday lives, Lang Jones describing his tribulations as a musician in a regiment of the Guards, his tail-less cat, and his mother's efforts to get him to tidy up his room. Roy told us about life as a window-dresser in a department store, and about enrolling in a correspondence course on "How to Be a Writer." Simple stuff, really, with no pretensions, but it was interesting and amusing and people liked it.

Jim Linwood wrote to Roy Kay, "There seem to be two kinds of 'zines published by young fans; ones with immaculate production and lousy material, and those with lousy production and excellent material. *Chaos* is in the latter category."

As it was however, the very excellence of *SF Horizons* served to insulate me from any real feelings of having been beaten at my own game. It was so clearly in a different league that I regarded it as being more like a rather thin book, something similar to James Blish's *The Issue at Hand,* also published around this time.

Then I received *Quark,* undated and unnumbered, a slim American fanzine from Tom Perry of Omaha, Nebraska. It was a revelation, witty, topical, full of personality, and it continued Walt Willis' re-entry into active fandom with a revival of his column "The Harp That Once or Twice" from the defunct *Warhoon.* I wrote to Tom immediately to express appreciation, and we became regular correspondents. I liked his style, his humour, the sheer *readability* of *Quark.* It was a real eye-opener, right enough, but I was about to experience an even more cosmic revelation.

Al Lewis and I had been trading books and magazines from the time we began writing to each other. He wanted Moorcock's *New Worlds* and its companion, *SF Impulse,* while I was anxious to get the American editions of *Galaxy,* particularly the first two years' issues, which were never reprinted in Britain. Every few months Al would raid his local bookshops and send me a parcel of twenty or thirty magazines. However, he must have felt that I needed to complete my fannish education, because in August he also sent me a copy of Walt Willis' and Bob Shaw's classic parable, *The Enchanted Duplicator.*

To say I was completely knocked out would be an understatement. I had enjoyed my first *Hyphen* and I was aware of Willis' reputation as a fan-writer. But *TED* was just so *clever,* so apt, yet it rang so true! As I read about Jophan travelling through the Canyon of Criticism, I thought "Yes, that's right, that's me!" and I realised that what I had needed, all along, was a good, reliable Shield of Umor. The fan with the Kollectinbug on his back was Cliff, surely, and the Circle of Lassitude was a perfect description of the Brum group! But I worried, was the Sercon City *really* where I wanted to spend the rest of my days?

It was a true masterpiece, and yet it was something of which I had only been vaguely aware. It ought to be required reading for every new fanzine editor. Why wasn't it more generally available? My copy was from the second edition, number 133 out of 150, published in 1962 by California fan Ted Johnstone, with illos cut directly on-stencil by Eddie Jones, and it was already out-of-print. "A reprint," I thought, "What a fine, fannish project that would be." With illustrations by Arthur Thomson, of course, who was the natural artist for something like this. But Arthur was in the United States on his TAFF trip, attending the 1964 Worldcon in Los Angeles. It would have to wait until he came back, and anyway, I still had my fanzines to get out.

However, that month I saw *Envoy*, Ken Cheslin's OMPAzine, in which he ranted about the fannish New Wave. He said, "I quote from my personal contacts and experience when I say that many of them are as intense as a German fan-group could wish for, true-blue Gernsbackians, appalled by fanzines because they expect fanzines to be about SF. ALL about SF. They are intolerant of older fans, and [the editors of] the sercon 'zines *Zenith* and *Beyond* excrete on our type of fandom. Sometimes this results in very amusing situations, not the least of which is when one of these militant sercon types gets bitten by the fannish bug."

So there it was in black and white, Ken Cheslin's opinion of me, comments that were not true when I began *Zenith*, even less accurate a year later, which Ken would have realised if he had bothered to talk to me, or had looked at *Nexus*. It seemed so unfair, to damn me for being sercon and then double damning me for getting interested in more fannish ideas. I wondered why he was so hostile when he could have helped so much.

Undeterred, I pressed on, and *Zenith* 6 appeared in September. While not the best-looking issue, it was probably the most readable so far, and Jim Linwood dutifully commented in *Spinge:*

ZENITH

"The new wave's wonderzine, and a vast improvement on its humble beginning. It has all the major faults ironed out yet is still vaguely disappointing after the excellent Number five."

Well, it *was* a bit drab. I had intended to have a good selection of interior illos but the man at Aston University refused to do any more electro-stencils because he discovered I had left the college more than six months earlier. By looking through the *Exchange & Mart*, I found a commercial firm that would do it, but they were so much more expensive, at 15/- per sheet rather than 1/6d, that I economised and omitted most of the artwork. The issue *did* have another Eddie Jones cover, although it was an early, 1955 drawing given to me by Alan Dodd, and duplicated because I couldn't afford to have it printed this time. I ran the "Zenith" title in blue, and the inadequacies of the Roneo caused it to be heavily over-inked. This, combined with poor layout, messy typing, and absence of illustrations, made the issue look scruffy in a way that previous numbers never had.

Despite Jim Linwood's comments, the standard of contents had taken a major leap forward. There were five original items, the most interesting being a follow-up on my earlier piece about John W. Campbell. As I had hoped, Leland Sapiro had responded with some opinions on Campbell's motivations, and my American friend, Al Lewis, had added a few observations of his own. This was genuinely new, speculative material. Somewhat less successful was an article on Colin Kapp, co-authored by Ed James and his new pal Terry Pratchett, which unfortunately confined itself almost entirely to a list of plot-summaries of a dozen or so of Kapp's short stories, none of which had any particular merit![1]

There was an article by "Ray Peters" (a thinly-disguised editorial alias), which gave similar treatment to three fairly worthless stories by Algis Budrys, and a letter from Poul Anderson on his Future History, to which I had appended a Bibliography from a 1955 issue of *Startling Stories*. The final piece was one of Rog Peyton's workmanlike reviews of British publishers, this time covering Penguin Books.

The true heart of the issue was in the departments. In Fanorama, Walt Willis performed an instructive dissection of two fanzines, one from "old" fandom (*The Scarr*) and one "new" (*Alien*), while in her book reviews Beryl Henley planted a few more land mines. The most outspoken item was Terry Jeeves's column in which he continued to blast the professional magazines. He was already in trouble with William F. Temple, and Terry now tempted fate by commenting on the story "Goodbye Miranda" by Michael Moorcock, saying, "which is just what it is, if you add the words 'and bull.' " Elsewhere, under the heading "The Society for the Abolition of Cordwainer Smith," Terry explained why he didn't much care for Smith's work. ("He uses words, colour and movement to cover up his lack of a story and plot.")

The two final pieces were really only fillers, a bland little Arthur C. Clarke reprint from 1938 (wished on me by Phil Harbottle) and a "story" from Fritz Leiber that was actually an advertisement from *Scientific American*. I had fallen into the trap of trying to get Big Names into my fanzine without much regard for whether their contributions had any real merit, something over which I would get a lot of criticism. Still, this did get me into regular correspondence

---

[1] In 2001 this was advertised on e-Bay as an "incredibly rare item for Terry Pratchett fans," and the issue fetched over $200 in consequence!

with Fritz, whom I greatly admired, and he kindly sent me an advance copy of *The Wanderer,* his new novel from Ballantine. It wasn't a bad issue, with four good pages of letters from people like Lloyd Biggle, Al Lewis, Alex Eisenstein and Dave Hale, and the best part of 20,000 words of reasonably intelligent material. I looked forward eagerly to reactions from the readers.

In November came another, even more impressive issue of *Quark,* this one with Willis' anguished report of the Peterborough convention. After describing his experience in meeting a party of neofans and the storm that had arisen at the AGM over the disputed origins of the BSFA, Walt went on to conclude:

"Somehow I felt there was something sciencefictional about the whole situation, and suddenly I realised what it was. We were in Basic SF Plot No.8, the Pygmalion/Frankenstein Group, the variation in which a scientist creates an intelligent race in the laboratory and finds it has created a cosmology in which he has no part. There is of course no reason why it should end as it usually does in science fiction, in the destruction of either side; in fact, assimilation is rapidly proceeding. But meanwhile I thought you deserved this devious explanation of a phenomenon so fantastic as that of somebody called Phil Rogers getting only four less votes from England as a TAFF candidate than Arthur Thomson."

Well, Willis was wrong on a few things there, as even I could tell. He didn't seem to know Phil Rogers and implied that he was one of the "new wavers," whereas in fact he was an old-time convention fan, popular with his friends in Liverpool and the North of England, who had obviously rallied around to give him their support. If the newcomers had voted for anyone in the 1964 TAFF race it would have been for ATom, who we all knew and liked. The rest of the column was amusing in the way it captured the feelings of the established fans at Repetercon, their mistaken belief that the newcomers were involved in a fandom that didn't include them. No one was quite prepared for the reaction it drew from Ron Bennett in his December *Skyrack* Newsletter:

"A disturbing tone is present in Walt Willis' column, in which Walt writes about the Peterborough Convention, mentioning a meeting between himself and the Delta boys from Salford. Well, certainly, they may not have been in fandom for long, they may not have been fed on fannish lore like Courtney's boat and so on, but is this so terrible? Perhaps to Walt it is, since he appears to consider it a major calamity that Phil Rogers gained only four U.K. votes fewer then did Arthur Thomson in the recent TAFF campaign. Whilst we can well dismiss Walt's rather narrow view of all this, in the same column he expresses the opinion—as if it were fact—that the BSFA was formed because fandom had been worried about the 'complete absence of channels of recruitment' after the prozine *Nebula* had folded.

"There are two points to consider here. First, *Nebula,* with its excellent Willis fan column, was by no means the all-important recruiting agent that it is made out to be in the *Harp,* though no one can deny that it did recruit and recruit well. And secondly, the foundation of the BSFA was not linked with the demise of *Nebula.* The BSFA was formed at Easter, 1958, and *Nebula* folded in June 1959. It is sad that one who can rise to such heights in humorous writing should be satisfied with the snide, and with being funny at the expense of others."

Ron's comments revealed a surprising degree of animosity to the man who for so long had been considered the supreme fannish personality, and Willis was stung to respond in his next Fanorama column in *Zenith* 7 (December 1964):

"I wrote in an American fanzine about meeting the new British fandom in Peterborough, and poked fun at the discomfiture of us old has-been BNFs. To my utter incredulity, Ron Bennett reported to British fandom that I had been 'snide.' Naturally, I was quite overwhelmed at the revelation of this new and unsuspected facet of my genius—in seventeen years of fandom nobody had ever called me 'snide' before—but after searching vainly for those hidden subtleties in what I actually wrote, I was forced to the reluctant conclusion that Ron's judgment revealed more about himself than about me.

"I remembered that a year or so ago he had said something else peculiar, something about 'Irish fandom's air of wry superiority.' At the time, we all thought this was one of his more obscure jokes, but it looks as if he actually meant it, and now I wouldn't be surprised to hear that he reads aloud everything I write with a sneering expression and a John Brunner accent. No wonder he gets the wrong impression, because anyone thinking of giving public readings from my works should do so in a rather diffident Belfast brogue, to a rhythmic accompaniment of knees knocking in a cold attic. It would never fill Carnegie Hall."

That was the lesser part of Walt's column. He used most of his space for a long review of the first issue of Beryl Henley's fanzine, *Link.* Now, this was an odd fanzine in many ways, intensely personal, with Beryl writing about her life and her theories, reprinting one of Mary Reed's "mad" letters, and the script of a "play" by "Ringo Fakespeare," with some poems, and a very peculiar piece by Mary's friend, "Haggis Campbell." Even though I knew Beryl pretty well by now, I freely admitted I couldn't make very much of it.

Walt Willis, however, was more conscientious and tried a little harder, as he reported in his column. After an amusing and self-deprecating opening, cleverly structured around a mock-Dr Johnson quotation, he continued;

"Beryl, you will remember, wrote an article about reincarnation, and I said in this column that I had always thought of it as a crackpot idea. Subsequently in a letter somewhere Beryl defined fandom as a place where being called a crackpot could make you feel ten feet tall. Well, good for her, I thought. And good for us, I added; here we have a likeable girl who is a good sport, can write well, has a sense of humour, and doesn't take criticism of her work as a personal affront. You don't get people like that coming into fandom every day. She is my very favourite ten-foot-tall crackpot."

And then he continued:

"So it was with pleasant expectations that I started to read *Link,* especially as it was billed as a humorous fanzine. Unfortunately, as far as I was concerned it seemed to have one defect which was quite serious for such a publication. It wasn't funny. It has all the superficial attributes of humour. The style is informal, it deals with interesting people in potentially amusing situations, and it even has the characteristics of the best type of fannish humour—wild logic, allusiveness, running gags, wordplay, and an element of fantasy. What we have here, I concluded, is the raw material of humour. It is an interesting lode, but it has just been dug up and left there in a heap."

Willis went on with an analysis of how humour should work, taking a couple of lines of dialogue from Beryl's report on "Revellers Out West," the amateur dramatics production in which she'd been involved. He tried to explain what was wrong with a particular pun ("Pore soles!"), and by extension, with the whole report. The whole thing is a careful, kind, and perceptive review, ending with the comment, "Beryl's answers are not silly. Indeed, they show a sensitivity and ability to handle words which make one realise that the first draft we have just been reading may be one for a very good humorous fanzine indeed."

Fair enough, you might think. Personally, I regarded the column as a minor masterpiece; elegant, witty, and putting forward a reasoned argument in an entertaining and constructive way. However, the Fanorama column had been a ticking time bomb all along, and now the explosion was imminent, as subsequent reactions would demonstrate.

With this issue, *Zenith* took off! It's clear from the lettercolumn that the previous number had touched some sort of nerve in the collective consciousness of fandom, with 13 pages of good letters, from people like Charlie Brown, Fritz Leiber, Harry Warner, Charles Platt and Scottish fan Ivor Latto, among many others. The highlight, however, was a fascinating, 4-page diatribe from Michael Moorcock that gave considerable insight into his own attitudes towards science fiction, as well as making a declaration of war. He took particular umbrage at Terry Jeeves' review of his story in the previous issue:

"Jeeves is thick, thick, THICK," he declared, "and the only way I can think of getting some sense into him at this late stage is to challenge him to a few rounds of fisticuffs." It was great knockabout stuff for the fans!

The covers were again offset-printed; I had discovered the local Rank Xerox copy-centre would run paper plates quickly and cheaply without all the fuss Charles Platt had encountered. Corgi Books took the back-cover space, entering into the spirit of things with an amusing advertisement that paid very

nicely for the front cover. This came
from a new artist, Brian McCabe, who
illustrated Charles Platt's article on
Philip Jose Farmer. He also did several
interior illos from Farmer stories, including a beautiful scene from "Mother"
done in a painstakingly intricate technique reminiscent of Virgil Finlay. Elsewhere in the issue, Brian provided some
free-flowing artwork more like that of
Roy Krenkel. Both styles were equally
impressive, and only much later did I
discover he was only sixteen years old at
the time.

Charles Platt's article looked at four
of Farmer's books without coming to any very definite conclusions. There
were two other original pieces, with American fan John Boston writing about
Edgar Pangborn, and Ivor Latto reviewing the novel *Hadrian VII*. All three
were oddly unsatisfying; competent but somehow lacking bite, instantly for-
gettable, unlike Terry Jeeves' column, which under the title "Brickbats & Roses"
continued to stir things up with his magazine reviews. Not so either, with an
odd little piece by "W. T. Webb," an occasional writer for Carnell's *New Worlds,*
who had offered to try his hand at reviewing.

This worked out rather badly. I had been anxious to give some special
attention to Fritz Leiber's *The Wanderer,* having by now received my advance
copy, and I thought that Bill Webb, as a professional, might be just the person
to do it justice. The result was a minor disaster. The reviewer took violent
exception to the novel, saying, "much of it reads like the erotic wishful thinking of a dirty old man." And, "It seems as repulsive as the deeds of ugly per-
verts in a smelly urinal." It was an extreme reaction, and the book deserved a
lot better. Once again a bit of editorial discretion would have been in order,
but I didn't know quite what to do, couldn't ask anyone else to look at the
book since I didn't have another copy, so in the end went ahead and printed
the review anyway. This must have been very hurtful to Fritz Leiber, who was
obviously proud of his new brainchild, which, despite Bill Webb's opinion,
went on to win the Hugo for that year.

Significantly, for the first time the cover and contents page logo used a
new sub-title; now it would be "Zenith *Speculation*." It was easily the best
issue yet, though it *did* get a bit out of hand so far as size was concerned, at 66
pages plus covers. Mike Moorcock's letter had arrived right at the last minute,
as had Al Lewis's very solid, 7-page review of the newly-published *Farnham's
Freehold.* Both were clearly too good to hold over, so I shuffled things around

and stretched the issue from the intended 50 pages. It would have been easier(and a lot cheaper) to lighten ship by throwing out Alan Dodd's piece on Robert Bloch, and maybe Joe Patrizio's commentary on *Starship Troopers,* which had carried over from the discussions in *Nexus.* Neither were exactly filler, but they didn't really add much.

Life was much easier in *Nexus,* with a second issue in December in which correspondents like Joe Patrizio and Chris Priest argued about H. Beam Piper, about Beryl's various theories, about my complaints about criticism. The issue ran to 24 effortless pages, and it made me wonder again if I was on the wrong track with *Zenith.* As I remarked in the editorial, "my enthusiasm is behind *Nexus.* It is much more fun to write articles for myself rather than wait for others to oblige." This issue went out with the second PaDS mailing, and also with the 42nd OMPA bundle.

However, it was time I did some socialising. Chris Priest had repeatedly invited me to come along to one of the Friday-evening meetings of the SF Club of London, held at Ella Parker's flat in Kilburn. In early December I decided to take him up on it, booked a day's holiday from work and set off, using my new expertise at hitch-hiking because I was very hard-up. Chris, thinking I was coming by train, had suggested we should meet at Holborn Station at 5.30 p.m.

Well, when you hitchhike you *can't* keep to a definite timetable. A succession of drivers took me by an incredibly circuitous route and I ended up in Hoddesdon, Alan Dodd territory, miles away from central London. I found a call-box and tried to get Chris at his office, but missed him by five minutes since he had left early (to meet me). I caught a bus into central London, and was by this time several hours late, so rather than wasting any more time I made my way directly to Ella's. Chris, of course, had been standing with his friend Dick Howett in the cold, draughty station forecourt for over two hours, and when they finally arrived, they were not best pleased to see me there ahead of them. It was one of those horrible muddles, wretched at the time and funny afterwards; so much so that the very next day we decided to do a one-shot fanzine.

Chris typed up a stencil entitled "My Side of It," and as soon as I arrived home I wrote my own account of the disaster and ran them off, back-to-back, on a single sheet of foolscap. It was a very minor episode but for some reason Ethel Lindsay gave our one-shot a very good review in *Haverings,* inspiring a highly enthusiastic letter from Chris in which he attempted to work out the philosophy of egoboo:

"I don't believe egoboo is the actual *receipt* of acclaim, but the expectation of it. I get more egoboo out of typing *Con* stencils than I do out of reading reviews of it—even good ones. When I write a story, I get terrific egoboo out of reading and re-reading it, much more than I do when I read comments on it in a fanzine. Like the one-shot. I wrote that the afternoon after I dropped you at Paddington. I went out that evening to a party and I sat in a corner all night just wallowing in egoboo, and at this point I hadn't even sent it up to you.

"Then there's unexpected egoboo, like Ethel's review. I read *Haver* when it came in, not suspecting she'd reviewed [the one-shot]. I was halfway through the review before I realised she was talking about *me!* Wham! A great fix of egoboo that lasted about a week."

That meeting in Ella's flat turned out to be the penultimate one, because the following week she ended her long series of Friday night sessions with a huge party, attended by Cliff Teague and notables from far and wide. This was the notorious occasion when Ella ticked off Charles Platt for jumping on her new sofa, a charge he strenuously denied. The following day Chris, Dick Howett and Charles Platt drove up to Birmingham (picking up Cliff along the way, who had not been very fortunate in hitching a lift) for a party at Rog Peyton's house. Sadly, I missed it; I had gone down to Banbury in the hope of persuading Mary to come back for the party, without success. It was a pity, because everyone had a great time, as Chris described in *Con:*

"Beryl Henley was there, round-faced, red-nosed and terrific fun; Gray Hall, looking a bit yobbish in a funny hat; Ken Cheslin with a headache; Archie Mercer, arm around Beryl; Daphne Sewell, petite and delectable; Mike Higgs, looking haggard; Charles Platt, being cynical; Ed James, looking uncomfortable on a settee primarily occupied by three other people.

"The high spot for me came at about 9.30. Ken Cheslin was standing next to me, hands behind him, back to the fireplace. He looked sideways at me. 'Who're you?' he said. 'Chris Priest,' I said. He looked at me again. 'Oh,' he finally said, 'you're more prepossessing than I thought.'

"I went away to find out what 'prepossessing' meant. When I did, I was flattered. Thinking about it afterwards, in the sanity of home surroundings, I decided I had been complimented in the short-term but had definitely been insulted on a longer basis. What *had* he thought I looked like? And why?"

Rog was doing a good job with the BSFA's *Vector,* bringing it out at regular two-monthly intervals, improving it and introducing new contributors. Just after the party, however, Charles Platt announced his intention of standing against him for Publications Officer, a contest that would be voted upon at the AGM at Brumcon. Suddenly, two strong candidates were fighting for what had previously been the most unwanted job in fandom!

Why did Charles stand for office? He'd had a busy year himself, putting out *Beyond* at quarterly intervals. From a very wrong-footed start it had evolved very quickly, had found its voice and by this time was actually a considerably better fanzine than *Zenith.* Charles was always more articulate, more ready to express an opinion, and if he had taken over *Vector* he could have made it into a livelier and more controversial journal. Much more in doubt is whether Charles would have had the patience to have stuck at it for a whole year, when he was already starting to tire of fandom and becoming more interested in professional writing.

One might also have wondered about the number of people Charles would have upset along the way. From the beginning he'd been quick to make enemies, sometimes for no apparent reason, which was reflected in a little quotation buried in the Eavesdroppings column of the February 1965 issue of *Hyphen:* "Funny how you can just say 'contentious little ****' and every English fan knows who you mean."

There is the well-known incident when Charles called in to see Midlands fan Jim England, on his travels around the country during the previous summer. Charles described the friendly way he had been received, how Jim's wife had kindly cooked his lunch, and then later, Jim had driven him on to his next port of call. However, he also commented that "Our talk was enlivened by the fact that Mr England was under the impression that my name was Peter White. We talked about Charles Platt—his egotism, his big-headedness, his stupidity. "You'd hardly think he was only 19, the way he carries on,' said 30-odd years' old Mr England. Sadly I was forced to agree with him."

I thought this was a pretty underhand sort of trick. I mean, how would you feel if someone did it to you? To me it seemed a negation of decent behaviour to enter someone's house, lie to their face for hours on end, accept their hospitality under false pretences and then betray them. In some cultures it might be regarded as a blood-insult. And why? Jim England wasn't an enemy, he had written some encouraging letters to the early *Beyond*. He was just an easy target, someone to play a cruel trick upon. Charles reported this incident himself in the January *Les Spinge,* and to his credit Ken Cheslin was particularly scathing and didn't want to print details of the stunt, only being over-ruled by Dave Hale. It certainly showed a very unpleasant side to Charles' personality.[2]

So Charles Platt's candidature was always going to divide loyalties, and Graham Hall provoked a great deal of resentment, at least in the Brum group, with an inaccurate and highly partisan flier which he circulated in support of

---

[2] This was the "black" issue of *Spinge,* probably the largest single issue of any British fanzine, before or since. It came in at 108 pages, plus black card covers printed in white ink. It was so enormous that no stapler could penetrate its bulk, and Ken Cheslin resorted to the use of an electric drill to make holes in the assembled stack before securing it together with metal filing clips. The sheer size made collating a fearsome task, and it took Ken and Dave Hale several months to get the issue out. From a reader's point of view, it was equally impossible, far too much to read, difficult to comment upon. All in all, it was the ultimate fulfilment of the "Bigger & Better" syndrome!

his friend. Rod Milner and Ken Cheslin prepared a counter-blast in reply, but all this exacerbated the bad feeling that was rapidly growing between Charles and the Birmingham fans.

My third issue of *Nexus* appeared in February, thirty pages composed almost entirely of letters, including a picky one from Charles Platt and a highly flattering note from an American, Seth Johnson, who congratulated me on having created a "focal point fanzine." Not that it was anything of the sort, but I had taken a few ideas from Tom Perry, including the liberal use of interlineations, and it *was* very easy to read. I had also found an answer to my lack of time by asking Doreen Parker to type the stencils, which she did quickly and efficiently, although repeating one of the interlineations several times in the process. Doreen was so good that I asked if she would also cut stencils for my new edition of *The Enchanted Duplicator*. I sent Doreen a photostat copy, and she agreed to bring the completed stencils to the Easter Brumcon, and Arthur Thomson could take it from there.

The eighth issue of *Zenith* appeared in March 1965, and was much slimmer, at only 32 pages, with a bold ATom front cover on blue card, backed with Faber & Faber's advertisement for Brian Aldiss' *Earthworks*. Inside, printed in red, were two spectacular headings by long-time fan Harry Turner for the columns "Fanorama" and "Brickbats & Roses." There was no other art because space was too precious, even though (at last) the entire issue had been typed in readable and economical Elite, done by the simple expedient of my staying behind after work at Redditch to type all the stencils on the office machine.

The contents came together easily and naturally. Chris Priest wrote on the "New Wave Prozines," Robert Bloch had a short item (a letter, really) on Alan Dodd's piece in the previous issue, and—a real scoop—Fritz Leiber had generously forgiven me for Bill Webb's review of *The Wanderer,* and now wrote at length about the way in which he'd created his novel. There were more brickbats (and not many roses) from Terry Jeeves, reviews from Beryl Henley, and twelve pages of good letters. Everyone had something different to say about the previous issue. On Bill Webb's review, Archie Mercer very sensibly observed, "although I know that books can hardly be allocated according to the pre-set taste of the reviewer *every* time, I do wish that *The Wanderer* could have been entrusted to someone capable of deriving more from it than Webb seems to have done."

Al Lewis's analysis of *Farnham's Freehold* attracted more comment. Peter White said, "this is the philosophy of Goldwater and of Heinlein too. It is the philosophy that has transformed the USA into the greatest threat to civilisation that exists today." Longer and less extreme letters followed from my American correspondents, with Tom Perry speculating on Heinlein's motives, "I think he decided to exploit racism as Goldwater propaganda, and I think it quite possible he deceived himself as to what its true message was; the book's symbolism seems to run wild, suggesting that Heinlein told himself it 'really' meant something else."

Brian Aldiss made an appearance in *Zenith* for the first time, in splendid form:

"… although you devote overmuch space to that arch lowbrow Heinlein, you more than recompense your readers by the thrilling spectacle of Moorcock and Jeeves bleeding and dying for their beliefs. The spectacle is the more thrilling since their attitudes are perfectly worthy in both cases… Moorcock is, or thinks he is, looking ahead; Jeeves is, but does not know he is, looking back. …And so, for the first time, we have a genuine controversy in science fiction that hinges on style, rather than content. Good old science fiction, always years behind the times!"[3]

Ivor Latto said, "Beryl's review of *The Ethical Engineer* was first-rate as far as it went. But here we have a novel which is written around just as distasteful a premise as *Starship Troopers,* and she doesn't touch on the fact that the book is based on a theme which is as questionable as anything Heinlein has ever done." He concluded, "I haven't the energy to find which Campbell editorial this came from." But most of the letters were about the previous issue's instalment of "Fanorama" and Willis' review of *Link*. Archie led the pack, saying mildly:

"At first Walt's meandering around the subject of *Link* seemed generally fair. At second sight I'm not so sure. For one thing he seems to be taking something of a patronising air towards the whole female sex. When he made that 'could-it-be-Dr-Johnson' quote I fully expected him to go on to cite the apparently genuine Johnsonism about the woman preaching in church, which, he claimed, resembled a dog walking on its hind legs in that it wasn't the quality of the performance that mattered but the fact that it was being done at all. I'd have been very interested to see how Walt would have treated *Link* had Beryl been a man.

"In any case I think he's missing the main point about Beryl. This isn't, of course, exactly his fault in that he hasn't had the pleasure of meeting her yet, and doesn't (I understand) even correspond with her. But Beryl's crackpottery

---

[3] In my fifth anniversary issue, I suggested this was the first shot in the entire New Wave vs Old School argument in science fiction circles, which rumbled on in *Zenith* for the next four years!

is of a very special kind that doesn't leave her disappointed when she finds that other people tend not to see things quite her way."

However, Archie's remarks were followed by a personal letter from Beryl to Walt Willis (with a copy for publication in *Zenith*), which promptly proved him wrong:

"When I heard that 'Fanorama' dealt almost exclusively with *Link* I alternated between being terrified and elated. Well, I told myself, even if he pans it to hell-an'-gone, at least we'll get some clever and constructive criticism.

"I was keenly disappointed. Not because you found *Link* unfunny; a sense of humour, as you said, is a subjective thing. Not because you referred to it as 'an interesting lode which has just been dug up and left there in a heap.' I accept that assessment without rancour. No, my disappointment was threefold, a steam-hammer to crack a very small chestnut? Walt, it sounds more like a man digging for gold in a field of buttercups. Why search for hidden significances, which were never intended to be there anyway? I'm a Midlander, I speak with a Brummie accent, and I wrote 'pore' because that's the way I pronounce the word. That's *all*, I assure you!

"Second, anyone who had not read *Link* before reading 'Fanorama' would probably assume that it was a solo job. It wasn't. And third, no wonder that serious poetry usually sends you into 'a sort of coma;...shows she can write very well when she works at it.' But as far as poetry is concerned I *don't* work at it. I don't write poetry, it happens to me.

"Anyway, thank you for the nice things you said. I stress this is not intended as a letter of self-defence, I'm not protesting against your criticisms. It's just that I expected so much more from the doyen of fanzine reviewers. You're not *quite* as mute as if your soul were dead, but this certainly isn't the kind of music I'd anticipated hearing from my position as a supplicant outside Tara's walls."

Walt clearly was taken aback by this reaction, and rather than reviewing a particular fanzine this time he devoted 'Fanorama' to a more general discussion:

"Faced with a communications breakdown as serious as this, it seems to me that I had better say something about the purpose of this column. It's easy to write reviews that are all kindness, if you don't mind wasting everyone's time; and it's easy to write honest reviews, if you don't care about people's feelings, but it's hard to be both honest and kind. Unfortunately, I *do* care about people's feelings, and I have been brooding quite a bit recently about Beryl Henley, whose indignant letter you'll find elsewhere in this issue.

"Despite the sleep I've lost over Beryl's letter I still can't think of any answer I could give her that wasn't in the original review. For instance, I explained that I analysed the passage in question (not just two words) because I thought it was unfair to criticise technique without giving an example, and that I chose that particular passage because I could be sure she thought it was funny. And Beryl's description of how she writes poetry—inspiration, followed by revision and polishing—is exactly the way I suggest she should write humour. That's what I said.

"...I've offered Beryl a deal whereby we each promise to read *Link* and its review eight months from now, and the one who admits he or she was wrong buys the other a drink at the London Worldcon. I hope by then I'll have progressed with Beryl to the status I had with Chuch Harris during our most violent altercations, when I used to sign my letters, 'Your best friend and most savage critic...alternately'."

I should have left it there, I really should. Unfortunately, in the same issue I printed an unpleasant letter from Charles Platt. Why? Partly because I was excited by the developing "controversy," but also because I was fed up with Charles' continual sniping and thought it would serve him right to let him show himself up. This turned out to be my biggest-ever mistake.

Charles said:

"Not long ago, and this you are welcome to print, I received a touching letter from good old Walt, saying how much he resented his reputation, how he enjoyed meeting neos at the con who treated him as an equal, how he wished he could start again under a pseudonym. Behind this falsest of false modesties, however, I see the man has pathetically blatant delusions of grandeur. The superior, talking-down, aren't-I-fabulous first paragraph of 'Fanorama' is simply nauseating. No-one but a famous millionaire author can get away with pseudo-pseudo-muck like this.

"In addition to being an Authority on fanzines (a pretty microscopic field, but no doubt he's proud of it) Willis is an expert on humour, it seems. Well, after all, many people in Britain and the USA—perhaps even more than 500— know about the legendary wit of Willis. So I was on the edge of my chair during his brilliant dissection of the least important piece of Beryl's fanzine. With skill and scalding sarcasm that left me breathless (with fury) Willis expertly tells us what is wrong with an ad-lib line in a fannish description of a slapstick comedy. And then, with a casual inference, Willis uses this to damn Beryl, the whole magazine, and all the other contributors in it. Can the inane high-handedness of this inflated-headed bigot be believed?"

Several more paragraphs followed in the same vein, but the damage was done. For the sake of a little excitement I had allowed Charles to hurt Walt Willis, a man I admired immensely.

Rog Peyton made exactly the same mistake. Just before the Birmingham convention he put out one more issue of *Vector* (possibly his last) that was notable for Charles Platt's review of Brian Aldiss' new novel, *Earthworks*. Charles had always been an acerbic reviewer but this time he really let fly:

"The plot is bad, the writing is inconsistent and laughably expanded to fill the space, the book is a formless mess.... Don't buy this book. Don't use a book token on it. Don't expend the energy to walk down and get it from your public library. If you're given a copy, don't open it. It's just not worth the trouble."

Brian was not amused and Rog had to apologise. Even Charles was taken aback when he received *Vector,* and he too wrote to Brian Aldiss and apologised. However, all these incidents, one after the other, had a cumulative effect. In just three months, relationships had deteriorated alarmingly between the Birmingham fans and Platt and his allies, and this would lead to further trouble at the Brumcon.

"As soon as I received *Vector* and read the review I had done of his novel, I sent a letter to Brian Aldiss apologising"

Brumcon Blues
Chapter 8

"It didn't take a great deal of insight to realise that the convention was fraught with internecine strife waging between Charles Platt and the Birmingham group," wrote Ivor Latto in his fanzine *Fankle*. "Charles acted as a sort of one-man demolition squad upon the morale of the Birmingham fans, who looked decidedly nervous most of the time. By contrast their persecutor acted with the careless abandon of one on the verge of gafiation. I just hung around, trying to avoid being spattered with blood."

Charles Platt came to Birmingham in a bad mood and a stubbly beard. During the preceding months he had succeeded in falling out with just about everyone but his closest supporters, and he was determined to find fault with everything about the Brumcon, or "Bumcon," as he insisted on calling it. The city, the hotel, the committee (Charles had a particular dislike of Ken Cheslin), the programme, everything was wrong. He said, "In the *Brumbles,* ha-ha Higgs cartoons (gosh, those funny badges!) and illegible maps with North 45 degrees off vertical, all contributed to a spirit of mad despair and hopelessness."

It had been pretty clear all along that Brumcon 2 was going to have its problems, though I'm not sure if the organisers ever realised quite what they were up against. But with the London Worldcon only six months away it was clear that many people couldn't afford both events and would be likely to give

Easter a miss. Besides that, the Brumcon bid had not been very popular, strongly contested at Peterborough and winning by only one vote with overtones of the "old fan vs. new fan" schism.

Chairman Ken Cheslin hadn't been inspiring, when in his platform statement he said, "Birmingham is a bad town so far as conventions are concerned." He had been equally negative in his progress reports, saying things like, "I'm sorry but we misjudged the support we could expect," and, "to those of you who come I believe we can promise a fairly decent convention." Ken was never one to talk things up, and a few days before the convention only 67 people had booked at the Midland Hotel in central Birmingham, a painfully low number when compared to the previous year, taking probably only a quarter of the hotel's rooms.

That figure doesn't tell the whole story, of course. Some of the local fans went home at night, like impoverished students Mike Turner and Edward James (along with the equally youthful and hard-up Terry Pratchett, who stayed with Ed in Solihull). Others, like Cliff and Charles Platt, freeloaded, sleeping on the floors of more affluent friends.

Why did Ken Cheslin chose the walnut-and-chrome vastness of the Midland? It was too large, too expensive and it had pretensions of grandeur compared with the friendlier Imperial just across the road. Ken himself said, "The manager seems a good deal posher than the ones we usually get and I was worried about his attitude towards fans running around late and the inevitable noise." And Charles Platt commented, "The Midland is typical of the worst type of large provincial hotel; they have not, as yet, learned that a hotel is run to please the guests rather than to please itself. Everywhere there were porters and attendants and officious under-managers, scowling and mumbling and looking with offensive disapproval at the con-goers."

The convention was using the "Jersey Suite" on the first floor, with the main hall and an adjacent room for art-show and books, manned by the indispensable Ken Slater with his wife Joyce, despite her ill health. Another room served as a general area for sitting around, with fanzines and various fliers on the tables, but there was no bar. For drinks we would have to go downstairs to the main hotel bar. It closed to the public at 10.30 p.m., and while as residents we could theoretically be served until midnight or more, the prices were high and the staff not too happy with this idea.

Chairman Ken appears to have made most of the decisions affecting Brumcon, and he also took the posts of Secretary and Treasurer. That left Charlie Winstone with programme and Rog Peyton with Publications—although once again, Ken did his own Progress Reports. Most of the local group hadn't been involved at all, until the Sunday afternoon before the convention when we were asked to turn up at Mike Higgs' house to assemble Programme books, make badges and help him paint the backdrop. Unfortunately, faced with an extremely large, extremely blank sheet of heavy paper pinned to his kitchen wall, Mike developed an artistic block.

For several hours he stood there deep in thought, occasionally scribbling and discarding ideas until he suddenly attacked the sheet in a creative frenzy worthy of Rolf Harris himself. Cliff was persuaded to sit cross-legged on the floor as a model for the mighty, demon-like figure that slowly took shape under Mike's busy charcoal-stick. Everyone was given a paint-brush and a section to work on, and labours continued until late that night…and the next…until the backdrop was finally rolled up and transported to the hotel on Thursday evening in the butcher's van that Mike drove for his day job. After a few more hours of frantic activity it was finally finished and hung on the back wall of the main hall. There it loomed, a menacing demon figure in black against a purple and yellow background, and none of us for one moment paused to consider whether it was really appropriate for a *science fiction* convention.

Easter was late this year, and the sun was shining brightly as I checked in about two-thirty on Friday 16th April, meeting Doreen Parker on the stairs. She had arrived even earlier and was off again in her car, taking Archie Mercer out to Beryl's house to transport her in from Redditch. "I've finished your stencils for *The Enchanted Duplicator*," she said. "They're in my room and I'll bring them down later."

The Midland wasn't a particularly welcoming sort of hotel, with a gloomy reception area furnished with padded, purple velvet benches behind a revolving wooden door, which led out into the busy traffic of New Street. I hung around in there for most of the afternoon, anxiously looking out for familiar faces. Sure enough, along came good old Roy Kay, down from Birkenhead on the afternoon train, and Dick Howett from London, carrying a big, black projector case. Mary Reed appeared with her pal Julia Stone, and after a hasty greeting they vanished into the depths of the hotel, not to be seen again for some hours. Suddenly I was startled by a loud "Ta-ta-ta-tarrara!" and looked back to see Mike Moorcock running down the stairs with his pal Langdon Jones, who was wearing a large, floppy Cavalier hat, both of them playing imaginary trombones. The London extroverts had obviously arrived early!

Registration began at 6.30, and at 8.00, Phil Rogers officially opened the convention. Ted Tubb introduced Harry Harrison as Guest of Honour, and as he appeared in front of the 10-foot-high black demon figure of the backdrop, Brian Aldiss shouted, "You're casting a long shadow today, Harry!" Then, after a few more words, that was it, and all we had for the rest of the evening was *Forbidden Planet,* screened by Dick Howett with his army-surplus projector. "I provided my ancient, 16mm L516 projector," he said. "They used them in camps to entertain the troops during WWII. During feature films, it got very hot and gave quite a dim picture, coupled with pathetically weak optical sound. Still, it was free."

It's always difficult to get a convention under way, and Repetercon had experienced the same problem, but showing the film may have been a bit of a mistake. People who haven't seen each other for twelve months generally want to do something rather more sociable than sit in the dark for a couple of hours on the first night. I certainly didn't want to, neither did Rog Peyton, and I'm pretty sure Ken Cheslin didn't either. Unfortunately, this divided the audience, and it didn't provide a very welcoming introduction for first-timers like Scottish fan Ivor Latto.

Ivor had entered fandom in 1963 through the BSFA, contributing intelligent, well-written letters to *Vector* and then to *Zenith, Beyond,* and other titles. Even better, he was a highly talented artist with a beautiful neatness of line and puckish sense of humour. He lived in Glasgow and was an architect, and while no one had ever met him, he was hardly a complete newcomer, a "nobody." Unfortunately, after travelling all day on the train and arriving too late to register, his first night was not a success:

"I made my entrance at the start of the film show…and a hideous experience it was too; when I walked in the lights were on and fifty pairs of accusing eyes greeted my appearance…with fifty minds all too obviously thinking, 'who the Hell's *this?*' I shuffled nervously to the very back of the hall and took a chair in the most inconspicuous spot I could find. I'd never felt so alone in my life, not since starting at a new school.

"I tried to identify some of the people I had been corresponding with; I thought I recognised Mike Moorcock (I didn't, it was Peter Day), I thought I spotted Chris Priest (Pete Weston), and then I saw someone who could have been Pete Weston (Bob Little), but I was too confused to follow it up…just as well, too. While I was anxiously speculating, Dick Howett (whom I *instantly* spotted) started off *Forbidden Planet* and I was stuck there in the dark until it had finished, half-watching it and half-wondering what the devil to do when the lights went up again. When they did, with superb indecision I hung around nervously while everyone split into pally groups and disappeared. I tried to register but it was too late, and finally, utterly fed-up, I went off to get a drink.

"Even in the hotel lounge the fans were split up into isolated little bunches, and I joined a rather harmless-looking gentleman drinking tea in a corner. By curious chance he turned out to be only the third Scot at the con, Mr David Marwick from Edinburgh, and even more confused than I was, being almost completely innocent of all knowledge of fandom. I left his company (having seen him shock Brian Burgess by bluntly asking him *why* he was compiling his mammoth bibliography of British prozines) and went to bed. So Friday was a bit of a dead loss."

Ivor was partly to blame for his own misery, of course. I would have been delighted to meet him, as would Chris Priest, Rog Peyton, and any number of others. We had gone into the bar as soon as the film started, which is where

Ivor should have gone and where he would easily have found us, if he had only asked around. Agreed, a convention needs to make it easy for newcomers on the first night, but they, too, need to make *some* effort besides sitting in a corner. Ivor seems to have been chronically shy and retiring.

Which was certainly not true of Beryl Henley, whose Friday-night experience can hardly have been more different, "…a whirling kaleidoscope of faces known and unknown, voices, laughter, song… a jumble of numbers on various doors…bottles, books, fanzines, badges…." This was Beryl's first convention, and she hit the ground running. As Archie wrote, "there were so many people she wanted to meet, people who had until then been only signatures at the bottoms of letters, Mike Moorcock, Lang Jones, Terry Pratchett, Frank Herbert and Roy Kay. Later that evening she was hauled-off to a room party held in Norman Weedall's room. Norman himself wasn't there, of course. Eddie Jones was, though, and so were Ted Tubb and Ken McIntyre."

And what did Charles Platt think of it so far? With heavy sarcasm he reported, "Excited by the prospect of watching *Forbidden Planet,* half the audience seized the opportunity of leaving the hall. Since attendance anyway was so miserably small the result was that twenty or so fans wandered aimlessly through the endless corridors and sat around in the fanzine room, while twenty-five others sat hypnotised in the darkened con-hall. No doubt about it, Friday was certainly a mad raving scene, we all stayed up until 11.00, or even midnight, having a wild time that is impossible to imagine."

Well, he was partly right, it wasn't a wild night, rather more of a quiet get-together in the upstairs lounge as we checked to see who was there and who wasn't, and it was clear that some of the familiar faces hadn't made it to the Brumcon. So we had Ella Parker but not Ethel, Lang Jones but not Gerry Webb, Phil Rogers but not Ron Bennett, Jim Groves but not Jim Linwood or Dick Ellingsworth. There was a good turn-out of professionals; Harry with wife Joan, Brian Aldiss with Margaret (who looked so much like The Queen), Tom Boardman, Mike Moorcock, Ted Tubb (but not Ken Bulmer), and James White (but not Bob Shaw). Arthur Thomson hadn't come but Eddie Jones had (and he asked me if I'd like another cover painting for *Zenith*. Oh yes, I said, very much).

The Liverpool group was well represented with Norman Shorrock and his attractive wife Ina, Norman Weedall, John Roles, and Ramsey Campbell, and there was a full squad of Aliens (the Delta group) from Manchester. Some Brummies came along beside the committee—Cliff, Mike Turner, Edward James, and Darroll Pardoe, but others, people like Dave Casey, Ollie Harvey, Martin Pitt, and Rod Milner, surprisingly hadn't even bothered to join. However, I noticed that Graham Hall had arrived, wearing a silly hat, trailed by his ever-present shadow, Dick Richardson. They were going from table to table at the back of the room with Charles Platt, and strangely, it was about this time that quote-cards started to appear with unfunny messages such as "Pete Weston

1. Graham Hall; 2. Charles Platt; 3. Peter Weston; 4. Mary Reed; 5. Ivor Latto;
6. Chris Priest; 7. Beryl Henley; 8. Jim Groves; 9. Harry Harrison;
10. Rog Peyton; 11. Archie Mercer; 12. Mike Moorcock; 13. Langdon Jones

is a Pervert" and "Roger Peyton is a Homosexual."

Still, the convention was now up and running, and next morning a certain amount of jollity was in evidence during the first auction, in which Phil Rogers tried his hardest to shift huge mountains of fairly worthless magazines and paperbacks. It was another failure of imagination, especially with the amount of professional talent present. This is where the committee's lack of experience showed, because it would have been so easy to have organised a panel discussion or invited Mike Moorcock to talk about his first year editing *New Worlds,* for instance.

Fortunately, the auction was followed by a talk from Geoff Doherty (a schoolteacher friend of Brian Aldiss) which was solidly interesting although his arguments might have gone over the heads of some of the audience. However, for the afternoon, all the committee had arranged were another two full-length films. I looked around again for Mary Reed—after all, we *were* supposed to be engaged—but she was having a fine time with Graham Hall, Dick Richardson, and one or two other people I didn't particularly care for, so I left them to it and went for a walk with a new friend, Richard Gordon, the third Scotsman present.

Richard came from Buckie, a little town on the Northern coast of Scotland, and he was at Newcastle University. He was a quiet-spoken, sensible

chap just a few years younger than I was and he too had become involved
through the BSFA. He was trying to write professionally under the name "Stuart
Gordon," and had some ideas for articles for *Zenith*. We seemed to get on well
and I took Richard to see the new Bull Ring shopping centre, recently completed and at the time seeming very futuristic. Dryly, he commented that it
was just what Buckie needed.

I still hadn't met that other Scotsman, Ivor Latto, who was still doing his
very best to remain invisible. He wrote, "The next day I determined to try to
breach this fannish clique. Trouble was, I was afraid of introducing myself to
someone, and possibly being crushed, as for example, 'Hullo there, I'm Ivor
Latto,' the possible replies being, 'Yes?' or 'So?' or 'We should jump up and
down, maybe?' "

This was carrying caution and diffidence to a ridiculous extent, as Ivor
discovered when he finally did the obvious thing and registered. He was then
pleasantly surprised at the reaction: "Once I'd received my little lapel ticket
things were easier and kindly people kept coming up and saying, 'So *you're*
Ivor Latto!' " After that he started to loosen up, reporting, "I found sufficient
interest in meeting and talking to people to pass Saturday afternoon easily
enough. It was the great Saturday Night Fancy Dress Parade I really dreaded.
I was sure it would be *excruciatingly* embarrassing."

This was a very strange reaction to a bit of innocent fun. The entrants were
amusing enough, although the event was a little lost in the gaping vastness of
the main hall. Beryl Henley made her debut as "Burlington Bertie," in tramp's
costume with bowler hat and knapsack on a stick, Dick Howett carried candle
and matches as "Lest Darkness Fall," and Archie Mercer was in flowing white
cloak and flying goggles as "Pontius Pilot." The winners were all the "Mancunian
Candidates" as Beryl called them, with Peter Day and Bill Burns as "Mad
Scientist and Tame Assistant," Chuck Partington as "The Man with the Head
and Teeth," and ringleader Harry Nadler as "The Atrocious Monster with a
Gun in his Mitt" (Harry Harrison's descriptions).

Bill Burns recollects, "It was my one and only appearance in costume and
won first prize (£2-worth of books from Ken Slater) as Frankenstein's Monster, junior-size, accompanying Peter Day's mad Doctor. Harry Nadler did the
make-up, of course. It was my first con, I was 17, still at school, had no money
at all and was sleeping on the floor in Harry and Chuck's room."

Norman Shorrock made sure the occasion was lubricated with vast amounts
of his famous Dandelion Wine and quite suddenly, everybody's defences were
down. The con hall was left to its own devices and everyone headed for the
parties. I forced my way into a ridiculous crush in Jim Groves' room, where
Ted Tubb was in full flow, then wandered out with Beryl and Archie at the
rumour of a party down the corridor in Harry Harrison's room. We found a
crowd besieging Room 127, and Beryl said, "Somebody attacked the door,

which was opened by about two inches, and Brian Aldiss's voice politely invited the would-be invaders to go away, because they were filming, or summoning-up demons, or something like that."

Surprisingly, they really *were* filming in there. The Manchester group were making a film for the London Worldcon and Peter Day had scripted *Breathworld,* a spoof on Harry Harrison's *Deathworld.* In one scene, the hero is schooled by an inept instructor who manages to shoot himself in the foot with an automated weapon, and the opportunity of having Harry himself play the part of the instructor was just too good to miss. The Delta crew turned up with camera, lights, and props and shot Harry's scenes inside his hotel room, with prompting and assistance from Messrs. Aldiss, Boardman and Moorcock, and special effects scratched onto the film later.

Once the filming was over the whole thing turned into a room party, and when around midnight Charles Platt unwisely appeared on the scene, I was among the select company privileged to see him seized and stuffed into a large oak wardrobe, the door locked, and the wardrobe tipped-over, face-down. If only Harry Nadler had kept his camera running a little longer this great fannish moment might have been preserved for posterity!

Harry Harrison later explained what happened:

"Charles hadn't booked at the hotel and he'd talked Mike Moorcock into letting him sleep on Mike's floor. Then Charles came into the room party and kept whining at Mike to 'give him the key to *our* room.' Mike was unimpressed. When Charles kept on, Brian and Mike pushed him into the wardrobe and we all helped turn it face down—then sat on it. I do remember Brian, Tom Boardman and I

We shut young Charles in the wardrobe

were on it. He banged feebly to be let out. We laughed, and enjoyed it when someone managed to let loose a fart. Everything gets dim after that."

Brian offered a slightly more literary rationale:

"Charles had committed the crime of zoilism—unfair criticism. He had reviewed my short novel *Earthworks,* which he disliked. Fair enough. But at the end he said, 'Do not buy this book. Do not look at it. If you see a copy, burn it,' or words to that effect. Very Ayatollah-ish. However little one likes the book under review, that's one's own opinion; you should not instruct potential readers not to buy it. After all, the poor bugger of an author lives by his writing, however feeble it may be. So we shut young Charles in the wardrobe, Harry helping, pulled it over and danced a jig on it. Had a drop to drink? Oh, I don't think so."

Fans roamed the corridors and staircases and in the small hours the ponderous figure of Brian Burgess appeared with his little suitcase and the plangent cry, "Pies, Pork pies anyone?" This had become Brian's unique role at conventions, and he was very welcome, filling a genuine need, because there was no chance of anything else to eat from the hotel and it had been a long time since dinner. This year he was also offering bottles of milk, which were surprisingly popular.

Mike Higgs remembers, "I ended up at a rather small room party held by Ken Cheslin, with Ella Parker, Doreen Parker, James and Peggy White (her first convention), and a few others. Later on, other people joined in and we finally had a pretty crowded affair. This carried on into the small hours until only four of us were left, and Doreen, Rog, Ed James and I left Ken to dream of power and tramped off to Doreen's room, to be joined by Mike Moorcock, who came in and prolonged the conversation for another hour or so. Finally, poor old Doreen was nearly asleep so we piled out and headed for Rog's room.

"Arriving there we found someone else was already in the room. Foaming at the mouth Rog finally got in, to find his bed was occupied by none less than Charles Platt, who had cleverly used his lock-picking skills for a second year. Charles was in his pyjamas, with his friend Peter White asleep on the floor. He groaned, 'Oh God, why did it have to be you!' as Rog picked him up and slung him out bodily, throwing clothes and shoes after him as Charles and Peter dodged down the corridor to spend the rest of the night in the bathroom. Afterwards we sat talking for hours until the sun came up and the birds began to sing. Mike Moorcock signed my copies of *The Stealer of Souls* and *Stormbringer*, and then disappeared to await the start of breakfast service."

All in all, it was a pretty good Saturday night and even Ivor Latto almost managed to enjoy himself. He said:

"The feeling of rather desperate forced gaiety constantly hovered in the back of my mind, the feeling that I would enjoy this if it bloody well killed me. Throughout the con I was torn between flinging myself heart and soul into the social whirl, and reluctance to inflict my company where it might not be wanted. Take, for example, those social highlights of conventions, the room-parties; I had been heartened during that horrible Friday evening and colourless Saturday by assurances that the con would really liven-up after the Fancy Dress affair, with riotous fannish parties. Great! And my resolve was stiffened by

Simone Walsh telling me that I would have to search out what life there was…it wouldn't come to me…which seemed very sensible.

"So, about eleven o'clock someone mentioned there is a room-party raging in room twenty-something and I am boozed up enough to set out determinedly to Live It Up. Entrance into room twenty-something is like a scene from the Goon Show; rattling of the catch, suspicious stares, passwords, but finally I'm inside this den of vice, grinning sheepishly. Despite a determined effort by the occupants to guard their liquor, I slowly begin to enjoy the party, and am just getting into the swing of it all, when a flunky comes to the door and has us all flung out for creating too much noise. 'To room thirty-something,' someone cries, and all eager, I gallop off in pursuit of someone who seems to know where he's going. Unfortunately…he didn't, and the second party didn't materialise. After a few embarrassing minutes, I cut my losses and retire philosophically to bed."

Ivor seems to have suffered a lot from "embarrassment," with the result that he missed most of the fun. It's interesting to read how Archie Mercer and Beryl saw him, "A quiet, bespectacled young man with a short ginger beard, Ivor gave the impression that he wasn't quite sure if he wanted to be classed as one of 'this mad lot' or not. After reading his brilliantly funny 'Uncle Ivor's Neo-Fans' Guide' in *Beyond* 8, it's quite clear that, like it or not, Ivor *is* 'One of Us.' And we wish we'd been able to have more conversation with him."

At the Annual General Meeting of the BSFA on the Sunday morning it was announced that the Association now had a paid-up membership of 269, a good increase from the previous year. After that the meeting teetered on the edge of chaos. Endless points of order were raised and questions asked, and Chairman Ken Cheslin was completely unable to maintain order. Fortunately, Ken Slater had both the necessary loud voice and determination to keep the meeting on track, and every time it threatened to swing away from its appointed course Ken firmly steered it back again, enjoying himself enormously in the process.

Charles' faction was vociferous in their attempts to tie down the committee to a hitherto unprecedented degree, with Peter White and Graham Hall putting forward motion after motion to drop the fiction magazine *Tangent* (one of Rog's innovations), and make changes to *Vector*. As Archie Mercer noted, "One would have thought that such a matter should be left to the committee's discretion in the light of current availability of finance, equipment, and volunteer labour."

Then came the appointment of a new committee, and retiring Chairman Ken Cheslin handed over to Roy Kay, Charlie Winstone kept the Treasury, and chaos ensued over the Secretary's position. It had been contested between the incumbent, Graham Bullock, and Doreen Parker, and when votes were counted Graham had won by a narrow margin—but having had second thoughts he'd gone home on Friday night, so Doreen won after all, which I thought was a very good thing.

A similar postal ballot had been held for the contested post of Publications Officer, with the result that Rog Peyton won by 57/27 against challenger Charles Platt. This result created uproar and a renewed assault on the committee. Then Charles scented an unexpected consolation prize when Ella Parker mischievously nominated him for the vacant post of Vice-Chairman, but in a straight vote of those present the job went to the BSFA's Librarian, Joe Navin of Liverpool. Joe then stood up and said he would be unable to continue with the library, which he proposed to transfer to the custody of fellow-Liverpuddlian John Nash.

At last we came to the selection of the site for the next year's con, and mercifully there was no argument with Dave Barber's bid for Yarmouth, first proposed the year before, although we were horrified when Phil Rogers said that the hotel would require attendees to take half-board terms at £3.0.0d per day. This was very expensive, we thought. Finally, Tony Walsh stood up and to general acclamation said he would be willing to hold the 1967 con at some location in the West Country, possibly in Bath, since he and Simone would shortly be moving to Bristol.

Afterwards, Platt was scathing about the AGM. He said, "As Cheslin's total ineptitude was rubbed in our faces, Doreen Parker took over. She didn't appear to know about Standard Procedure but at least she was aware of what was going on. Cheslin, sensing dimly that his authority had been usurped, contented himself by telling people occasionally to 'shut up.' He then smiled in embarrassment." Personally, I thought Charles' comments were a bit much, considering that he had been ringleader of the group that had caused all the trouble.

Rather late in the weekend the convention suddenly came alive with Harry Harrison's Guest-of-Honour address, titled "SF Confidential." To the uninvited accompaniment of the Salvation Army brass band playing in the street below, Harry launched into an unrehearsed and hilarious "exposé" of the private and professional lives of the American SF fraternity.

"Undoubtedly Harry is one of the most entertaining speakers I have ever had the good fortune to listen to," said Chris Priest. "To listen is one thing, to watch is another. If Harry is not watched while he is speaking half the entertainment is lost. His facial expressions, his gesticulations, his posture... Anyway, Harry was concerned that British fans would be meeting American professionals for the first time at the London Worldcon, and he took it upon himself to forewarn us of some of their foibles. Few escaped, Blish, Anderson, Pohl, Campbell, Silverberg, they all came in for it."

Partway through his talk, Harry enlivened matters still further when Brian Aldiss entered the room, late back from lunch. With a great roar of "This pie is *rotten!*" Harry seized an unsold pork-pie from Brian Burgess in the front row and hurled it at Brian, narrowly missing Beryl and the reporter from the *Birmingham Post,* who observed in the next day's paper that "the pie was still nestling inside its protective cellophane wrapper (British Railways issue)." Thus are the great legends of British fandom conceived.[1]

With a great roar of "This pie is *rotten!*"

Brian explained, "The meat pie performance began in Harrogate. At the con hotel, I found that they charged twelve-and-six for a plate of pallid, thin, chicken sandwiches, on white bread. So next morning we went shopping and bought a dozen pork pies in a rather genteel shop. I believe we started selling them in rivalry with the late, great Brian Burgess, who was charging steeply for his pies. Or if not for that reason, then because we were young and foolish in those days."

Again, Harry's memories diverge a little: "What Brian says is true, except that the fans were a wee bit suspicious of pros, and wouldn't buy the sixpenny pies from us. In the end we gave them to Brian Burgess, thus starting him in business—and in a tradition."

At the end of Harry's solo act he gave the first presentation of The Harrison Award, offering the original manuscript of *The Plague from Space* to the first person who could answer the question, "Who wrote 'The Green Men of Graypec'?" Our very own Mike "The Beard" Turner won by correctly answering, "Festus Pragnell," and proudly carried off the prize.

Next followed a "Pro-Panel," upon which Harry was joined on the dais by Brian Aldiss, Ted Tubb, Michael Moorcock, Tom Boardman, and James White to answer questions from the audience. Chuck Partington asked, "Who wrote the best SF, American or British writers?" Tom Boardman opted for the Americans, while Mike Moorcock expressed a serious-sounding belief that the Russians still had a sort of Slavic sense of wonder and were therefore the best, and this caused Brian Aldiss to expound his own curious theory that science fiction regenerates every two years.

---

[1] A few months later Aldiss and Tom Boardman bombarded Harry with pies at the London Worldcon. These episodes led directly to such fannish traditions as "The Great Pork-Pie Race" and the ceremonial hurling of pies at convention miscreants, though a heretic recently proposed the substitution of taped-together volumes of fantasy trilogies. It will never catch on!

Somehow the panel turned into an auction, with Harry, Brian, Mike and Ted stoking up a frenzied atmosphere of compulsive buying. They sold the same books several times over to different bidders, hopeless rejects from the previous auction were boosted to extortionate prices, and Mike Moorcock knocked down an empty whisky bottle, allegedly autographed by famous authors, for four shillings and sixpence. When Harry Harrison finally ran out of breath and adjectives to damn the books he was selling, Brian took over in style. "I'll sign this C. S. Lewis trilogy," he said, "since the author isn't around any more to do it himself."

The madness was infectious and it was reported that an auctioned copy of *Starship Troopers* bore a "Robert Heinlein" autograph strangely reminiscent of Michael Moorcock's writing. And Ted Tubb appealed to our instincts for self-preservation as he held up a 2-inch-thick fantasy novel and assured us that paper was the best shield against gamma rays. "Protect your unborn family from harmful radiation," he solemnly advised.

I put in a bid for a piece of artwork by British artist Jim Cawthorn, and was surprised and pleased to get it for only three shillings and sixpence. Titled "Entry to Dragonsguard," it was a two-foot piece of white art-board upon which Jim had sketched a fantasy scene in what looked like blue fountain-pen ink. A real bargain, I thought, though I had no idea what I was going to do with it.

Afterwards, Archie Mercer stood to present the Doc Weir Award, an event originally scheduled for the morning session but postponed because of the non-availability of the silver goblet. Earlier in the weekend Archie had asked the hotel to lock it in their safe, only to find that the head receptionist had gone home with the key. By late afternoon the ceremony couldn't be postponed any longer, so Archie had the slightly difficult job of presenting an absent Award to an absent recipient, in this instance Terry Jeeves, who was generally thought to have been an excellent choice.

Then the convention plunged from its high to an absolute low as a tall thin man with a crewcut and red blazer stood up and talked slowly and deliberately about the Rotation Plan, which governed U.S. Worldcons, and why he thought it should be set aside. It was Dave Kyle, who had come all the way from Upper New York State to lecture us about the merits of his Syracuse bid against the opposing, and more legitimate, Tri-con.

We didn't have the slightest interest in American fan-affairs, but this year British fans were being wooed because voting for the 1966 site-selection would take place at the London Worldcon in August. However, Dave's presentation was counter-productive; he had chosen his time very badly, and all he achieved was to bore everyone rigid, and generate a lingering resentment that he had spoiled our party. Not for many years afterwards did I get past that initial impression to find Dave was really a fun person when he wasn't talking fan-politics.

The programme had scheduled a fan-panel for seven-thirty, but it never happened. After a very brief closing ceremony in the Main Hall we went next door into a party sponsored by Tri-con's George Scithers, who appeared in a very loud check-jacket and spoke at mercifully brief length. It was here I discovered he edited a fanzine called *Amra*. I had no real interest in Conan or heroic fantasy, but was so impressed by its appearance that I subscribed on the spot.

The Tri-con people had kindly donated £25 for drinks all round and the con-committee had thoughtfully spent it on a mixture of beer, sherry, gin, and a few mixers, dispensed by Ted Tubb with his usual enthusiasm. It was here that Charles Platt had several drinks too many, and while doubtless already being somewhat tired after the previous night's exertions, he now became highly emotional as well. After many adventures, which included falling off a stepladder in the convention hall and nearly braining Ivor Latto in the process, and after having put his fist through Lang Jones' door, Charles finally sank into merciful oblivion in Harry Nadler's room.

Eventually the Tri-con party broke up and fans drifted away. Just before I left, however, Doreen Parker appeared with a large black cardboard folder. "They're the stencils for *The Enchanted Duplicator,*" she said. "I wanted to make sure you had them, in case I don't see you tomorrow." I thanked Doreen for all the work she had put in and offered to get her a drink. We didn't want to stay in the fast-emptying room, however, nor go down to the gloomy and overpriced hotel bar, so we went off to find the room-parties, which began early that night.

Upstairs, the Manchester fans were running a "knurdling" tournament in their room while Charles Platt slept soundly in a corner. I gave it a try, and after I had collapsed, wheezing and spluttering helplessly on the floor, I watched new-boy Bill Burns beat reigning champion Harry Nadler by arm-walking a good six feet on empty beer-bottles. It certainly helps to be lean and wiry with good stomach muscles and no beer-belly.[2]

Mike Higgs and girlfriend Cynthia went back to his room to unload his bags, and were invited in for a drink by his next-door neighbours, Harry and Joan Harrison. Mike said:

"We sat there for a long time, talking about anything and everything. Harry had us in stitches with his conversation, and so did his wife, who was one of the liveliest people we'd met. I was delighted to learn that Harry was once a comic-strip artist and then a strip writer. He related many interesting stories from his comic-book days, and both of them expressed a certain gratitude to *Flash Gordon,* who served as bread-and-butter to Harry, in his early days. What

---

[2] Reigning World Champion Damien Warman commented at Helicon 2 that he did a lot of mountain climbing, and that knurdling "uses the same sort of muscles as when you're doing difficult traverses." So, fans, now we know how to get into training!

struck me as being pretty nice was the fact that they were interested in me and listened attentively while I rattled on about my hopes and dreams. Many pros only go on about themselves and never think about anyone else."

Looking for Mary Reed again, I investigated the sounds coming from a room along the corridor which had a hole in the door. Inside, Mary was banging a tambourine, Dick Richardson was playing a harmonica and Graham Hall (still wearing his hat) was singing "What Have They Done to the Rain." The room was festooned with a mass of cables and leads, amplifiers and speakers, with Charles Platt's electronic organ, Mike Moorcock's guitar and kazoo, bongos, and various other items of musical equipment. Intercepting one of Graham's famous scowls, I felt unwelcome and left them to it.

By this time fans were sitting on the staircases and in little groups on the floor in the corridors. The Midland's peculiar geometry was such that it appeared you could climb a flight of stairs, go round various corners, climb more stairs and then arrive back at your starting place. As Mike Turner explained, "a group of us started touring the closed loop of the corridors in the belief that there was some sort of space warp which one would encounter in the process, causing you to switch floors without noticing it."

At about 3.00 a.m. Ted Tubb decided to organise one of his pilgrimages and rounded up some of the scattered strays to form an all-male line, twenty or so strong. Taking our lead from Ted, we shuffled slowly along behind him like monks, rhythmically clinking bottles and chanting "Get back to your wives." The procession ambled along corridors, past rooms of sleeping nonfans, and gradually picked up a trail of slightly nervous under-managers, nightporters and so on, wondering what would happen next. Unfortunately, nothing did and eventually, reluctantly, we went to bed.

Next morning a blizzard was raging outside the windows and this accentuated the sense of finality, the realisation that the con was over, as fans paid their bills and departed. Belatedly I remembered the stencils Doreen had given me the night before and which I'd carelessly put down in the party room. I checked, but they weren't there, asked at the desk and was assured I would be contacted if they were found. By this time I was a bit worried but I was sure they would eventually turn up. After all, it was pretty obvious what they were and surely no harm would come to them.

Ken Cheslin said his farewells and was given a round of applause from a little group that included Archie and Beryl, the Walshes and the Shorrocks. Afterwards, Ken Cheslin reported in tones of amazement that the hotel manager had been pleased to have the convention and "we were welcome to go back, any time." Brumcon even made a small profit, with income at £160.3s.2d and expenditure of £147.17s.2d.

As Mike Higgs reflected, "maybe this hadn't been the best convention out, but it had had its moments." Most people had enjoyed it, even Ivor Latto in the end, who said, "despite the overall disillusionment which I felt once it was all over, I'm glad I went, if only to have heard Harry Harrison's speech and to have met some of the people I've been writing to for the past few months, most of whom pleasantly confirmed my hopes. Having now broken the ice, I trust that the next convention I attend will be an improvement."

Charles Platt, however, was convinced it had all been a dismal failure. He said, "The sense of hopelessness, of nothing happening, of boredom, of depression, could be felt everywhere." But as we all know a convention is what you make of it, and Charles' weekend had reflected his own state of mind. He had been surrounded by people who would have been perfectly willing to be his friends if he had only let them. Doreen Parker, for instance, commented, "I remember thinking what a handsome, pleasant young man he was, until he caused all that trouble at Birmingham."

"Happy, innocent days…," Charles said later in *Maya* 14, "…but actually they were miserable, I was suicidally depressed, and desperate attempts to have a good time just made things worse in the end."

Summer of Discontent
Chapter 9

I left Brumcon with very mixed feelings. We'd had some good moments, especially on the Sunday afternoon, but I hadn't enjoyed the convention as much as I had hoped because of Charles Platt's antics. I'd also had a blazing row with Mary Reed in the final hours of the con. I told her it might have been nice to have seen her occasionally (after all, we *were* supposed to be engaged), especially since she seemed to have spent most of her time with people like Platt and Graham Hall who had become my enemies.

The committee must have felt similarly upset. They had done their best, worked hard, yet some people had denigrated and belittled their every move. Ken Cheslin disappeared almost without trace afterwards, as did Mike Higgs, and Charlie Winstone cut back again on Brum group meetings at his house to just once per month. Only Rog seemed unaffected, pleased at having kept *Vector* and full of plans to "go litho" at the first opportunity.

Why had Charles Platt been such an all-round pain in the backside? What had motivated him to be such a wrecker, what had *he* got out of it? Much later, I asked Dick Howett (who was one of his pals at the time) what it had all been about, and he replied,

"I'm a little embarrassed to say that at the time we were eagerly waiting to see what he would do next (egging him on, really)." Naughty boys! Platt's state of mind at Brumcon hardly seemed "depressive" in the clinical sense. He affected this profile as a latter justification. I know real depressives and Platt doesn't fit. Basically, Platt just didn't like Brummies. He thought the Brum group was a bunch of hicks. His letter to me of March 1965 illustrates this,

" 'Incidentally, it looks as if I've lost the BSFA elections and Doreen Parker has too. At the last count—made Friday—the votes so far were Platt 24, Peyton 40. Graham Bullock had a similar lead as secretary, which only goes to show, seeing that he is totally unknown (as well as totally illiterate) how many friends the Brummies have after all.' He continued, '*Zenith* is pretty weak, isn't it? Since I'm packing in my fanzines and trying to go pro, that is, gafiating to some extent, I've written Weston a pretty nasty letter (though I wonder if he'll be intelligent enough to realise he's being insulted) and have indicated I don't like his fanzines very much.' "

What had happened to my poor stencils? They hadn't been handed in, to either the hotel or the convention committee. After a couple of days I had a feeling of sick certainty that they weren't going to turn up, now, and all Doreen's work had been for nothing. Someone had taken them and there wasn't going to *be* a new edition of *The Enchanted Duplicator,* not unless we started all over again.

Making me feel even worse, Walt Willis wrote, only a few days after the convention. He was clearly hurt and upset by the unpleasant letter from Charles Platt in *Zenith* 8, which I had printed alongside his own appeal to Charles' better nature. Walt's last paragraph had read,

"I would in all sincerity ask you to examine your own attitude with the intellectual honesty I believe you do possess. In particular, I ask you to consider whether you might not be projecting your own feelings of hostility into what both of us write. Does it not seem even a little bit strange, for example, that when I attempt a documented analysis of a piece of writing, you feel I am being 'bad-mannered and unkind,' but when you publicly say I have 'pathetically false delusions of grandeur' you feel this is just your 'sense of fun'?"

Walt was nearly as unhappy with Ron Bennett's comments in *Skyrack* (to which he had already replied in his "Fanorama" column). I think he had hoped for more support from older fans like Ron. I had noticed myself that there did indeed seem to be something of a reaction against Willis among British fans of the time, later confirmed by Jim Linwood, "When I came into fandom Walt was conspicuous by his absence at conventions, which provoked some sour grapes among his contemporaries, particularly as there was a feeling he cared more about American fandom. Most of my crowd couldn't understand the adulation in which he was held."

Archie Mercer inadvertently ventured onto similar ground in a letter to Tom Perry's *Quark* (undated, but from context April). He said, "Until he started his *Zenith* column Walt hadn't been doing anything in particular to keep himself in the eye of Anglo fandom. A fannish legend requires more than a name to keep it evergreen."

Tom replied to Archie at some length, "I've recently read Charles Platt's disturbing attack on Willis, and Walt's remarkably forbearing reply. I don't know who or what Platt is, but I would like to think he isn't representative of the British new wave. It may be he is no older than he sounds, and if so I may be taking ordinary adolescent rebellion too much to heart. But on the other hand wouldn't an adolescent be the first to insist he be taken seriously *despite* his age?

"It is to fandom's credit that Platt can be heard at all—in stuffier movements his resentments wouldn't be allowed to come to the surface. But at the same time there seems to be a tendency, almost a readiness, to misunderstand Walt on the part of intelligent adults like yourself. Walt has done a great deal, by example, encouragement, and helpful criticism, to improve standards in fandom; a top fanzine from the period he entered fandom seems like a typical one today. I think he is still our best writer, but now there are many that approach him, and his health has recently caused him to cut back. So now fans are beginning to realise that many things said half in jest—that Willis is Ghod, that he has Impeccable Taste, etc.—are of course not true, and they are disparaging him as if to make up for the previous excess; his faults are magnified just because it was once said, and sometimes believed, that he had none. If my impression is right it's a very sad thing, for Walt is a wonderfully talented, unusually kind, and very wise man who has contributed enormously to fandom. Platt's sneer that 'many people in Britain and the USA—perhaps *even more than 500*—know about the legendary wit of Willis' is sickening in its cruelty."

Archie was partly right, because when I entered fandom it had been six months or more before I knew anything about Walt Willis. However, that was more a reflection of my ignorance and the generally run-down state of British fandom in general than any fault of Willis. If Walt had been more active in American fandom during the previous five or six years, it was because that was where the action was. I think Walt was trying to make something of a "comeback" into British fandom in the early Sixties. He had attended Harrogate and both Peterborough conventions, put out a couple of issues of *Hyphen,* revived his "Harp" column for *Quark,* and made a brave attempt to build bridges with his "Fanorama" column in *Zenith.* All he had received in return was aggravation and upset.

Not surprisingly, Willis decided to call it a day. He told me there wouldn't be any more "Fanorama" columns, at least for a while, because he was moving, away from the famous "Oblique House" to Donaghadee on the coast. However, I knew this was the end of it, that through my stupidity I had lost my most distinguished contributor, someone I liked and admired. When I wrote again, months afterwards, Walt replied, "As for the column, I felt less and less that I had anything to say to your readership. Not only had I gone off contemporary English fandom but I no longer read contemporary science fiction."

Charles Platt was unrepentant. He wrote a mocking letter of comment (the one to which he referred in his correspondence with Dick Howett), which I *didn't* print,

"This *Zenith* is rather a pale, weak thing; even the wonderful opportunity for controversy that I presented to you in the form of the Willis business was rather played down. While on this subject, incidentally, I'd just like to say that it seems sad that someone who's been in fandom as long as Walt still takes to heart—or appears to—the overstated comments of a teenager. Moreover, he doesn't really fight back, which is always discouraging. While some of what I said was definitely sincerely meant, I overstated it (the places are obvious) in the hopes of a good, old-fashioned knock-down drag-out fight. Walt has effectively prevented this. I'm surprised he didn't add that he wrote his *Link* review during an asthma attack."

Enough! I was fed up with all the nastiness, was sick of the very sound of Charles Platt's name. I was in fandom to make friends, not enemies. My mind was finally made up by two letters which arrived in the same post at the start of May. Richard Gordon wrote from far-off Buckie, "I had another letter from Platt—this time he seems to be planning to assassinate you for some reason. He thinks he is doing you a favour by starting scandal and ill-feeling in the letter column—in the golden name of controversy. Wish I could make him out."

The other letter was from Graham Hall, taunting me about my lost stencils and pointing the finger pretty firmly in Platt's direction.[1] *That was it!* From now on, I decided I didn't want anything to do with Charles Platt. If I ignored him completely, maybe he would go away.

Meantime, I had other troubles. I had patched things up, after a fashion, with Mary Reed, but had been hitching down to Banbury almost every weekend for over twelve months, all through one miserable English winter, and I was heartily sick of it. I'd had my share of scrapes and scares, like the time I was dropped off after midnight in the empty countryside without a light in sight and had to walk for hours to the next town. Or the day I was caught in a thunderstorm, miles from anywhere, and was soaked to the skin. I had passed my driving test and wanted to buy a car, but couldn't afford it because of the burden of those continued monthly payments to Roneo. The hire-purchase agreement was costing me nearly a quarter of my monthly salary and I still had another year to go. How I wished I had never bought that stupid machine!

---

[1] A piece of sheer mischief making. Many years later Graham Hall admitted in *Maya* 14 (1977) that Charles wasn't to blame and the real culprit was his own sycophant, Dick Richardson.

Still, it was time to get together another issue of *Zenith*. By now, it was paying for itself, or rather, after each issue I would receive enough subscriptions to pay for the next one. Of course, this was storing up a lot of trouble for the future if I ever stopped and had to refund all those subs! And I had a pleasant surprise when I received a flat, white cardboard box marked "Special Delivery." Inside was a brief letter from Eddie Jones, "Here's the cover painting I promised. Hope you like it. I've worked on it non-stop for the last 48 hours." Under the tissue paper was another superb picture, in almost photographic detail. I was quite overwhelmed and rushed off a letter of thanks to Eddie, and wondered if I could tap-up Faber for another back-cover advertisement to pay the printing bill. Eddie's painting duly appeared on *Zenith*-9 as the first of my "wrap-around" covers, and it looked very good indeed.

The issue itself was a little bland after all the previous excitement. No Willis, no Platt, and just the fading embers of old arguments. I wrote an innocent little editorial extolling the recent improvements in *Galaxy* and *If* under Frederik Pohl, and my new friend Richard Gordon provided a thoughtful article on Edmund Cooper. The biggest innovation was a new way of pulling together the review section by getting Beryl Henley and Archie Mercer to perform an extended double act. Under Archie's punning title "Double Booking" they staged a running dialogue on the books being reviewed, all the more remarkable for being conducted at a 100-mile separation. They must have written a lot of letters!

And my hero, Tom Perry sent a clever little rhyme on an interlineation from a letter of Archie's, which Tom had noticed we'd accidentally repeated several times:

"After just one glance at *Zenith*, through my mind the question ran; how would Walt have treated *Link* had Beryl been a man? With repetition that perplexes Archie worries on the sexes, once in *Zenith*, twice in *Nexus*. If gallantry is patronising (in even fanzine analysing), then women are quite used to being patronised by men. And male fans find some charm in the most brummagem of fenne. A question here for Archie, to answer if he can; is he sure *he'd* be Linked to Beryl, if Beryl were a man?"

Shortly after came the incredible news that *Zenith* had been nominated to the short-list for the 1965 Fanzine Hugo Award, which would be presented at the London Worldcon at the end of August. I was tremendously pleased but quite amazed because until now the Hugo had seemed impossibly far away and nothing to do with me, something that rich and influential Americans gave to each other. Now the Awards were here on our doorstep!

Actually, I shouldn't have been so surprised since this year there were far more British members (and voters) than usual, which was naturally to my advantage. Of course, on any objective level it was ridiculous for a fanzine as new and raw as *Zenith* to be nominated for anything at all, except perhaps for staying power in the face of adversity. I didn't deserve to win, or even to be nominated. I was amazed that British fandom had not taken this golden opportunity to put forward *Hyphen,* a much more worthy candidate.

Tom Perry had actually suggested this idea in January, in reply to Ron Bennett, who had suggested *Quark* might be up for a Hugo. "I am terribly flattered and most grateful," Tom said, "but I have to dissent. *Quark* is at best an imitation *Hyphen,* and *Hyphen,* one of the oldest fanzines in existence, is long overdue for its Hugo. It has been around since 1952, setting trends and spanning fannish eras." I agreed, and thought that giving the award to *Hyphen* would have been absolutely right, and a welcome comfort to Walt Willis' battered ego.

The other candidates were both American, *Yandro* from Buck and Juanita Coulson and *Double: Bill* from Bill Bowers and Bill Mallardi. Neither of these were particularly good fanzines on any sort of absolute scale. Every issue of *Yandro* looked the same, printed on hairy yellow paper to a strict formula; a page each from the two editors, reviews, letters, and occasional articles illustrated by Juanita's on-stencil drawings. It was really a lightweight personalzine, but it had appeared monthly almost since time began. *Double: Bill* was completely different, a sprawling genzine from two recent entrants into fanzine publishing. It was more experimental, more varied, but it had rough edges both figuratively and literally, no real clout, no distinctive style of its own.

News of the nominations was a reminder that Loncon 2 was drawing nearer by the day, and now we received our hotel booking forms. The con was being held at the Mount Royal Hotel in Oxford Street, right in the middle of the West End, and rooms were incredibly expensive at £7.00 per night for bed-&-breakfast, nearly a week's wages for me. Not surprisingly, most members of the Brum group had cold feet about the expense and only Rog, Charlie and I had joined the convention. Then suddenly, we had an advance taste of sophisticated international fandom when my American pal, Al Lewis, announced his intention of arriving early in Britain in order to see some of the sights. Could we get together, he asked?

I was excited by the prospect because I regarded Al with a certain amount of awe. This was "tyrannical" Albert J. Lewis who had run LASFS with an iron hand (as opposed to the "good" Alan J. Lewis on the East Coast, neither of them to be confused with NESFA's Anthony Lewis, with whom I had also started corresponding). He lived in fabulous, fannish Sherman Oaks with TAFF-winner Ron Ellik and all those other famous American fans, and he had written some powerful material for my fanzine. Above all, he was *my* friend, the first overseas fan with whom I had really corresponded, and he was coming halfway across the world, a real "Travelling Jiant." Al would arrive in London in the last week of June and wanted to come and see us on the weekend of 27th June. Hastily I made some plans; it was Mary's birthday and she would be in Birmingham, our friend Chris Priest could drive up from London, and maybe Al could stay the night at Rog's house?

We met him on the platform at Snow Hill Station as Mary Reed described in *Crabapple* 1, "a small, brown-skinned, long crew-cutted A. J. Lewis, complete with camera and bag big enough for any amount of squirrels (Ron Ellik was known as 'the squirrel'). The only words I could think of to say on this momentous occasion were, 'Hello Al' and, 'Say hominy grits.' "

Fortunately, this was the day of the Carnival Procession so we watched over twenty floats of various shapes and sizes as they trundled through the city-centre, before finding something to eat and talking late into the evening. I was pleased to meet Al at last, and he seemed to hit it off particularly well with Rog because they were both interested in collecting and indexing and had similar tastes in science fiction.

Next morning we all piled into Chris Priest's trusty Ford Prefect and went to Dudley Zoo, a local "pleasure-spot" about ten miles west of the city. This was located in Dudley Castle, destroyed by Oliver Cromwell some three hundred years before, and the ruined limestone battlements now looked out over an uninspiring vista of smoking chimneys and built-up sprawl, stretching to the horizon in every direction. It was home to a motley collection of dispirited beasts housed in rusty cages and overgrown enclosures, and a small funfair. I thought how tin-pot and grubby it must all seem to Al, used to the sunshine and affluence of California.

However, it was at Dudley that "Dodgem Car Fandom" was born. At the bottom of the hill we found a dodgem rink that was open but completely unpatronised, and it was generally felt that this was too good an opportunity to miss. We each took a car and commenced battle, hurtling round the rink at high-speed, blue sparks flashing, slamming into each other with great gusto. Mary

Slamming into each other with great gusto

soon declared herself "bruised all over" and quit, Rog went off to look at the gaming machines and Al took photographs, but Chris and I went round and round the floor, crashing into each other and anyone else who might get in the way. Time after time, the power stopped and we would look across, nod happily, and have another turn, until finally we gave up, hot, sticky, bruised, and considerably poorer.

We walked on a little further, then Chris and I looked at each other, grinned, and ran back for one last session. Afterwards Mary told us we lost years whilst in the brightly painted cars, "battering round the floor, hunched over the wheel, teeth bared, and having a wonderful time." We talked excitedly about a dodgem-car fanzine and a trip to Battersea Funfair, but we knew it was only a daydream; it had just been a spontaneous bit of fun. And finally, to end the day, we crossed the road to a restaurant and I sampled my very first Chinese meal.

That weekend spurred me into buying a car. It had been such a slow and laborious performance to travel backwards and forwards by bus from my house to Rog's, and I was vastly impressed by the ease with which Chris had zipped up from London and conveyed us out to Dudley. I decided I really couldn't continue any longer without a car, and somehow or other I would just have to find the money to pay for it. So I looked in the newspaper and on the next Saturday morning marched into a showroom and bought a black, 1960-model 105E Ford Popular with side-valve engine, registration 944 BOM. It cost just over £200, payable in easy instalments over the next two years. I signed the papers, got the insurance and suddenly the deed was done—just like that!

It was wonderful to be motorised, and I felt very pleased with myself as I drove down to Banbury the following weekend. The rosy glow lasted until Monday morning when I went into work, found the company had been sold, and I had lost my job—just like that! My company, BSA Power Units, had been doing very well with their new designs of small industrial engines. So, in the best traditions of mid-sixties British industry, the BSA top men had sold the company to its leading competitor, who was going to close it down. There followed an anxious time while I worried about my future. Unemployment loomed as a very real prospect, and I now had to meet monthly payments on *two* hire-purchase commitments, for the Roneo and for the car. My chances of going to the Worldcon started to seem more and more remote.

Eventually I was offered another position but something altogether more tenuous, a place on the Group's management trainee scheme. This sounded good but in practice, it meant that I had no fixed abode and would be required to do all sorts of short-term jobs and projects at various sites, a sort of floating "temp" and dogsbody, until something permanent came up. It was a good thing I had my own transport, and while I would be able to draw modest expenses for petrol money, the salary was even less than the pittance I had been receiving. The only good thing about the situation was that the various offices around the BSA Group seemed to be *full* of Gestetner duplicators!

With this in mind, I decided to try to lighten ship by selling my Roneo. Fortunately, I had a likely purchaser in the shape of another new fan, Jim Grant, whom I had met a few months earlier at Brumcon. Jim had a fanzine titled *Fusion,* which he was putting through PADs, but I knew he wanted his own machine and he was particularly interested in being able to do colour-changes. I quickly wrote to him and proposed a deal, which he accepted, and I agreed to deliver the Roneo the following weekend to his home in Christ-church, on the South Coast.

Mary wanted to come along so I stopped at Banbury on the way. It was about 160 miles from Birmingham and the journey seemed interminable, on single-lane roads that didn't allow overtaking. We finally arrived and delivered the machine to Jim. He was getting a really good deal—because I was desper-ate—just £20.00 in cash, and he would pay the remaining nine instalments of the contract by sending me a postal order every month. So now, without that burden on my back, maybe I could go to the Worldcon after all.

However, my finances were still very tight, and for the first and only time in my life I decided to "freeload" in someone else's room. I suggested to Rog that I would give him a lift to the con if I could sleep on his floor, or sofa, or whatever (in the event there were two single beds). So, at the end of August, we set off down the M1, and I had my first experience of London traffic in the rush hour! Round and round Hyde Park Corner I went, desperately looking for the right exit while five lanes of cars, taxis, and London buses zipped across in front and behind me. The hotel turned out to be just along Oxford Street, on a corner, a grim, multi-storey affair, very noisy with all the traffic roaring past the ground-floor entrance, and with all facilities upstairs. It wasn't exactly welcoming and I didn't feel comfortable throughout the entire weekend.

That impression might have been highly subjective, for just like Charles Platt six months earlier I had come to a convention burdened by emotional baggage. This coloured my experience to the extent that I didn't enjoy the Worldcon at all. Certainly, there were high spots—I watched John W. Campbell on a panel, for instance, a burly man in crew cut and check jacket. I met Ted White, a young, crop-haired New York fan whose name I knew, and found he was easy to talk to and very knowledgeable. I bought a painting from Eddie—his first attempt at acrylics, he said—and was delighted to secure a couple of items in the auction, using the money from Jim Grant to buy *Fancyclopedia II* and *A Sense of FAPA,* two items which sounded as though they'd be important for my further education in fannish affairs.

On Saturday night I met Frederik Pohl, to whom I had previously sent a few issues of my fanzine. Fred was editing *Galaxy* and *If* at the time and he was extremely kind and courteous. He told me about a new Heinlein novel he had bought and was going to run in *If*. It was more like Heinlein's earlier work, he said, and the title was *The Moon Is a Harsh Mistress*. Later that night.they held a St Fantony ceremony, the first for some years, but after that we were left to our own devices in the main hall. Ivor Latto was indignant that he wasn't being "entertained," that there was nothing to do, but just then Walt Willis kindly invited me over to join him and his friends for a chat, though I suspect I was too over-awed to be very good company.

Zenith didn't win the fanzine Hugo, of course, which went to *Yandro* as expected, probably the most deserving of the contenders. That didn't bother me because I hadn't expected to win anyway, but I *was* extremely upset that my relationship with Mary had deteriorated to a point where it was preying on my mind to the exclusion of almost everything else. The Worldcon seemed to be an exact repeat of my Brumcon experience, and once again I spent half my time looking for her, hoping to share the experience together, only to find her having a good time with people like Graham Hall and her other cronies. Really, I had no reason to complain, it was just an outward sign that we had nothing much in common. However, for most of the weekend I was in a depressed and gloomy state of mind and was glad to leave in the early hours of Monday morning, dropping off Mary at Banbury and then continuing on back home (we both had to go to work the following day).

Two weeks later, I went down to Banbury for one last time and we ended our "engagement" by mutual consent. We were both too young, hadn't been suited, didn't even have the same tastes in science fiction. I turned around and drove straight back to Birmingham feeling curiously light-headed, as if a huge weight had been lifted. It had been a mistake for both of us and now it was over, and I could move forward with my life.

Back on Track
Chapter 10

The deadline for the September OMPA mailing came immediately after the London Worldcon, and I just managed to get out another *Nexus* in time. It was only a six-pager (dressed up with fancy covers), but one I had written almost entirely myself, directly onto stencil. It was also the first fanzine I did

ZENITH
SPECULATION

october 1965   2/-

on a BSA Gestetner—or rather, on several different machines as my work took me from office to office. It wasn't easy, dragging stencils and paper all round the West Midlands and printing batches of pages in lunchtimes and after hours in the evening, continually in danger of being apprehended.

I had similar problems the following month with the tenth *Zenith*, having to use no less than *seven* different typewriters to get the issue finished. For the cover I used my huge Jim Cawthorn sketch from the Brumcon auction (with his permission), reduced down to more manageable proportions by the obliging BSA photographic department. Inside, most of the earlier arguments had died down but the lead article fanned the smouldering embers of the new wave controversy, which would run and run. Under the title "The New Establishment" Irish fan Ian McAulay criticised recent science fiction and pronouncements *about* science fiction made by people like Moorcock and Ballard. Ian said, "the present situation seems to have arisen from the desire on the part of editors to be 'with it' on the cultural scene, without having to have any actual understanding of the different branches of literature."

As an unintended counter to Ian's argument, I ran a long letter from Mike Moorcock in my letter column. This now had a title of its own, "The Melting Pot," a consequence of my first few subscription issues of *Amra*. I had been impressed at the way George Scithers gave names to his various departments, such as "Scrolls," "Sherds," and so on, and with his "Centaur," drawn each issue by a different artist. I thought that in a small way I could emulate this idea, with a different heading for the letter column each time, beginning with an illustration from Ivor Latto.

Mike Moorcock poured scorn on my praise for *Galaxy* and *If*, and his letter was really quite insulting. He said, "To me the sort of thing you are enthusiastic about is sensational, juvenile, and repellent to any intelligent and literate adult who happens to pick up a book or magazine containing this sort of rubbish."

All I had said in the previous issue was that I enjoyed stories like "Becalmed in Hell" and "The Coldest Place" from new writer Larry Niven, who Fred Pohl had helped to get started in his magazines. I thought Larry's stories were fresh, interesting, and rich in idea-content. Mike Moorcock disagreed, saying, "The contents of *Worlds of Tomorrow* and its like are barely above the level of the stuff found in the *Superman* comic stable (there is, as you know, a strong overlap in the readership of both)." He concluded, "I find the quasi-poeticism of Bradbury as off-putting as the pseudo-Hemingwayesque of Anderson and Heinlein. While I am forced to print a certain proportion of both kinds (in *New Worlds*), I am constantly striving to find stories which are neither."

Well, this was strong stuff, and I thought it would make a lively lettercolumn. First, though, I decided to take a weekend off, and at Rog's suggestion we went to visit Archie Mercer in Bristol. It was a primarily a social call, although we were also going to collect some stencils and other bits and pieces Archie had found from his *Vector* days. So, one Saturday in September we set off down the A38 and by early afternoon had found our way to Archie's Worrall Road flat in Clifton, quite a nice area near Bristol Downs. The flat consisted of two rooms on the ground floor of a big old house, with a little shared kitchenette and a bathroom upstairs—with no hot water.

Archie wasn't much interested in appearances, as we knew, but it looked as if he didn't bother about his creature comforts either, leading the somewhat Spartan life of a middle-aged bachelor. He had very little furniture, probably because he had lived for many years in a caravan, and the main things in his room were the green-painted orange boxes in which he stored his books and fanzine collection, an armchair, and a table for his Gestetner. Unfortunately, Rog and I had forgotten that while Archie was undoubtedly the kindest, most genuine person in fandom he wasn't much good at casual small talk, and from his point of view we were pretty hopeless at responding to his barrage of puns and word play. So the conversation was a bit stilted.

We discussed the BSFA for ten minutes, and then for want of something else to do we started to run off some stencils for Archie's OMPAzine, *Amble,* only to find the ink tube was empty. Archie didn't have a spare, it was Saturday afternoon and the shops were shut, so that put an end to that. We wandered aimlessly around Bristol for a while and then returned to the flat for "tea." You should have seen Rog's face! He had asked Archie to "get something in" for the evening, and Archie had interpreted this to mean triple helpings of all the stuff he normally ate. "Where's the food?" demanded Rog. "This is it," answered Archie, indicating a spread of peanuts, crisps, and Kit-Kat bars. Rog was aghast. Then, since Archie didn't have a television and didn't want to go to a pub, we played Ludo before retiring, me on a narrow camp bed, Rog in the armchair. It was a long, uncomfortable night!

If we had waited a week, we could have gone to the big party that Tony and Simone Walsh threw on September 25th to launch their new Bristol & District (BAD) Group. They had moved into a house only just round the corner from Archie, so he was no longer the only science fiction fan in Bristol and would now have regular fannish company. This was only the first of many changes in Archie's life-style that autumn. First, he passed his driving test, so he could now drive something bigger than his motor scooter. Then, he moved from his little flat to a much more spacious location with rooms to spare.

Most dramatically of all, however, in early November Beryl Henley left her home in Redditch and moved in with Archie. We were surprised and a little taken aback by this, but we really shouldn't have been if we had taken more notice of the way they had been growing closer over the previous year or more. Archie and Beryl had hit it off from the very beginning, first in correspondence and then in person. It couldn't have been easy for Beryl to leave her family and she probably agonised over her decision, but it was pretty clear that she and Archie felt they were soul mates, made for each other, and in the end, that was what counted above all.[1]

Back home again, I spent a lot of time reading my acquisitions from the Worldcon auction. I enjoyed *A Sense of FAPA* immensely, a huge compendium selected from FAPA mailings and featuring work from Burbee, Laney, and other famous names, but Dick Eney's massive 200-page *Fancyclopedia II* made a greater impression. It was written in a sort of dry, laconic style and I read it from cover to cover. These two, together with *The Enchanted Duplicator* and Terry Carr's *The Wizard of Iz* (which had come through OMPA a few months earlier), made me keen to learn more about fannish history. Back at the Easter convention I'd heard about the BSFA's half-forgotten Fanzine Foundation, which was now supposedly being run by John Nash in Liverpool, and so I fired off a request to borrow some of the items I'd been reading about. Back issues of *Hyphen,* please, and Greg Calkins' *Oopsla!* What about *Space Diversions,* a defunct British fanzine that had run serious material about SF, so I had been told, something like my *Zenith?*

A week or so later I received an embarrassed reply and a couple of fanzines apparently selected at random. John explained that the Foundation wasn't really a going concern since it had been dumped in his garage six months ago by the previous custodian. He had not had time to sort it out, and in fact was quite anxious to get rid of it so he could put his car away again at nights.

This seemed a terrible state of affairs to me and I thought we should do something about it. What a great project it would be, to go through all those fanzines and catalogue them. I would have loved to have taken it on, but couldn't, not in the tiny house where I lived with my parents. Mike "The Beard" Turner had more room and was at first quite keen on the idea before he had rapid second thoughts. Eventually, Charlie Winstone came to the rescue. He was already Treasurer of the BSFA but he still produced the occasional *Nadir,* was quite interested in fanzines himself, and he agreed to store the collection in the cavernous old house he shared with his mother and brothers.

So one Saturday morning in October, the two of us set off up the M6 to the outskirts of Liverpool. The motorway was still under construction for parts of its length, so it was several hours before we arrived in the unlovely-named suburb of Garston and found the house. John opened his up-&-over garage door to reveal a mound of fanzines, spilling over in every direction. Out of curiosity I picked up one or two and looked at address labels like "Mr Arthur Weir" and "Mr Eric Jones." It seemed that the founders of the BSFA had donated their own collections, and there was obviously some pretty good

---

[1] By sad coincidence I was writing these lines on the very morning (13th October) that I heard of Beryl's death. I had only re-established contact with her a few months before. She and Archie enjoyed over thirty happy years together, almost entirely out of touch with fandom.

stuff here. I couldn't wait to get them home! Was my car big enough, I wondered? We filled the boot, and the back seat, and the shelf in the back window, and stuffed more fanzines under the front seats. In the end poor old Charlie was sitting on a heap of them, with more packed around his feet and on his lap. Then we set off on the long drive back, and in all that time John hadn't even offered us a cup of tea.

We arrived back in Birmingham in late afternoon, and both Charlie and I were too tired to unload the car, so I dropped him off and went home with my precious cargo of fanzines. This was a wonderful chance to investigate them, and I sat up late that night in the cold driver's seat outside the house, pawing through the pile by the light of a flashlight and a convenient streetlamp, occasionally coming inside to get warm and to read choice items. There was a file of *Hyphen,* issues of *Quandry, Xero, A-Bas,* all sorts of gems. I

I sat up late that night on the cold driver's seat

went into mental overdrive, an orgy of reading about people and places, cons, fan-groups, the fabulous Berkeley boys and their tower of beer cans to the moon, *Cry* and the Nameless Ones, "Willis Discovers America" and the Wheels of IF. I took out two titles that looked particularly interesting, *Aporrheta,* a British fanzine I had never heard of before, and *Void,* an American title that seemed to have a multiplicity of editors.

Next day I went back to Charlie's and with help from his brothers we slowly emptied the car, carrying armfuls of fanzines up the 20-odd steps into the house, up a gloomy staircase and into a musty back bedroom with paper peeling off the walls. No table, no shelves, and we had to drop the fanzines onto the floor in a pile, in no better order than they had been in the garage. Still, I looked forward eagerly to the job of sorting it out; maybe if I came round once or twice a week we could get it organised within a month or two. However, to my great surprise Charlie made it clear that it wasn't going to be like that at all.

He was going to look after the Foundation, in his own way and in his own time, and he didn't want any help from me. I would have to be content with an occasional browse on nights when the Brum group met at his house.

I wasn't entirely happy about the way this had worked out, but it was part of a pattern, because for some time Charlie had been cutting back on his involvement with the group. At first we had gone round every Tuesday; then, after six months or so it had become a fortnightly meeting, and after Brumcon we'd been limited to just once per month. I think his mother had put her foot down. She was fiercely protective of Charlie because of his disability, and while at first she must have been pleased that he had found some friends and an absorbing hobby, she was probably fed up with playing open house to anyone who might come by. It was understandable, but frustrating because Charlie wasn't a very organised person at the best of times and his physical condition meant he couldn't put in the sustained effort needed. It looked as if there wasn't going to be a functioning Fanzine Foundation in the foreseeable future!

That file of *Aporrheta* was fascinating and I read it from beginning to end. It was a day-by-day diary of Inchmery Fandom, a hyperactive London fan-group during the late 'fifties. It sounded such wonderful fun and it had all been happening only five or six years earlier, yet I had never heard of any of these people, Vince and Joy Clarke and their lodger, Sandy Sanderson, who seemed to have vanished without trace. How strange!

Void was a similar, chatty, immensely-readable fanzine from the other side of the Atlantic, densely packed in micro-elite type, with stories of legendary New York fans whose very names were fabulously fannish, like Bhob Stewart, Redd Boggs, and Calvin "Biff" Demmon. There were columns like "Happy Benford Chatter" and Pete Graham's "West Coast Jass," with lots of material by and about Willis, Lee Hoffman and Terry Carr. It had wonderful Steve Stiles multi-page covers, and featured work by senior editor Ted White himself, the "trenchant bludgeon"! I *faunched* to join in the fun! (a new word I'd found in *Fancyclopedia* that seemed to fit). But it was all over, dead and buried five years in the past like Inchmery Fandom. If only *Void* had come my way *before* the Worldcon, I thought, I might have been able to talk a bit more intelligently to Ted White.

Modern-day, late-1965 fandom seemed very lacking by comparison, with no fannish fanzines around apart from *Quark* (and even that hadn't been seen since before the Worldcon). As for our own little Birmingham group, it was flat and dull. It had somehow changed without our noticing, the old intimacy gone, and along with it the excitement of making new acquisitions or of dis-covering a new author. Cliff Teague hadn't been seen for months, neither had Mike Higgs, Dave Casey or Oliver Harvey. Our involvement with conven-tions and fanzines had divided the group, and Rog, Charlie and I had been so busy with our various projects that some of the original members had felt left out, uninvolved, and had drifted away.

One or two others were now appearing more often., Darroll Pardoe, for instance, who had finished at Cambridge and was now doing his PhD at Birmingham, and our other chemist, Martin Pitt, who was now submitting artwork to fanzines under the name "Santos." Then we had the phenomenon of Mike "The Beard" Turner, so single-mindedly devoting himself to science fiction that he could boast his collection "had grown to fifteen hundred items, including something like one hundred first-edition hardbacks" and he had read them all, a book every day, keeping a detailed diary of his progress. Mike had done particularly well out of cataloguing Ken Cheslin's disordered collection, Ken having agreed that he could keep any duplicates. Mike said, "My haul from the cataloguing work totalled 146 items, including dozens of rare pulps, at least one from 1926."

Mike was also responsible for getting the Birmingham Reference Library to purchase a copy of Damon Knight's *In Search of Wonder*. "I couldn't afford to buy it myself," he said, "so I applied for a loan copy at the Central Library. After some weeks they wrote back, saying not only that they didn't have it, but they had established there was not one single copy in public ownership anywhere in the UK. They asked how they could get hold of one, and I pointed them at the F&SF Book Company in Staten Island. When the book arrived, I went into their reading room on a number of successive days to read the thing— they wouldn't let me take it away under any circumstances, given that it was the only publicly-owned copy in the land!"

Rog was well into his second term as editor of *Vector,* and now he succeeded in doing something I could only dream about. He "went litho," producing the magazine in printed, half-foolscap size, which finally did away with the need for duplicating. The BSFA had rapidly been gaining members, which he thought would enable them to afford the additional expense, obviously making things a great deal easier. With a wrap-around photographic cover, his October issue was attractive, clear, and readable and yet...somehow, I thought it lacked the personal touch that came with the sweat and tears of having to run off your own pages.

I was still taking advantage of every unattended Gestetner I could find, but missed the convenience of having my own machine, especially since I still had to keep up the monthly standing orders to Roneo. Jim Grant had sent me the promised postal order for the September payment, but October passed with no sign of any money and I wrote him an anxious note. Meanwhile, my old antagonist Charles Platt sent me a letter on *Zenith* 10:

"I see you're still publishing *Zenith*. Why? Mike Moorcock has lent me his copy and I must say that it has degenerated into a pretty tatty and spineless publication. Thinner, greyer, even worse-designed and certainly more objectionable in content…which should make it a good contender for the Hugo next year, if nothing else."

Well, thank you but I wasn't taking the bait, not this time. After six months without Charles it was possible to be a bit more objective, to see that he was just looking for trouble. I didn't print his letter, but wondered again what made him tick. Much later, Jim Linwood offered his observations:

"I liked the way Charles tilted at fannish icons and questioned whether or not Willis deserved such high standing in fandom. Although he was wrong and motivated by self-promotion, I felt there was a need for such iconoclasm in the 60s. After my review of *Points of View,* I had an amicable correspondence with Charles, explaining where I thought he was going wrong. I also discovered that, although he was only slightly younger than I was, he came from a completely different social and educational background from me and most other British fans of the time.

"Charles was the first public schoolboy of my generation that I knowingly met. He told me that he had gone to a 'very progressive' school and I assumed it was Summerhill or something like it. I also got the impression that, while his family may not have been moneyed, his father was a high-flying professional."

Chris Priest said much the same thing:

"Charles came from a social background quite unlike yours or mine. I went to the local grammar school. I imagine you did, too. Charles went to one of these special private schools, where the pupils basically run the place and discipline themselves, with predictable results.

"You were never in with a chance of gaining Charles's long-term respect (although I knew there was a time when he did envy you for the quality of *Zenith*). You were always a Brummie, from the wrong sort of social background with the wrong sort of accent, endlessly reading and re-reading Heinlein, getting pally with all those ancient trufen from the old days, and so on. You were someone to mock, to sneer at, and to snigger about."

So that explained everything; private school, well-to-do parents (Charles' father was a director of Vauxhall, the General Motors subsidiary in England). Charles Platt was simply a poor little rich kid! Although that wise old bird Ethel Lindsay summed him up more simply when she said in *Scottishe* 44 that "Charles could never quite forgive fandom for starting without him."

Either way, I didn't much care any more *what* he thought. I was preoccupied with an idea that had been growing for some time at the back of my mind. I wanted to get rid of that naïve "Zenith," and adopt a new, more serious title, and it was obvious what it should be, something I'd already been using as a subheading. Yes, I thought, "Speculation" sounded about right; adult, self-descriptive, and distinctive. Unfortunately, I didn't just *do* it, then and there, but instead messed around with an unnecessarily slow and progressive name-change, inspired by the way John W. Campbell had turned *Astounding* into *Analog*.

By now, I was also getting seriously worried about Jim Grant in Christchurch. He had sent the money for the October payment, eventually, but he was now more than two months behind. I sent him more letters, imploring him to keep his promise, but there was a stony silence from the other end, and meanwhile the monthly payments to Roneo kept on being taken from my bank account. I was as hard up as ever.

Still, somehow the January issue appeared, as *Zenith Speculation,* giving equal weight to the old and the new name, with an unusual scraperboard cover-illustration by new artist Joseph Zajackowski and an interior illo by Martin Pitt. Richard Gordon contributed another of his author-appraisals, this time on Eric Frank Russell, but the controversial lead article was by Joe Patrizio, with "The Drowned Plot of J. G. Ballard." As Joe said, "It seems that whenever Ballard's name is mentioned, all reason flies, laying bare blinding emotions which cause protagonists to abandon logic and to resort to insults. Having read extremist arguments on both sides, it seems to me that a more detailed examination of Ballard's writing might be in order; if it achieves nothing else it will explain why I find him so unsatisfactory as an author."

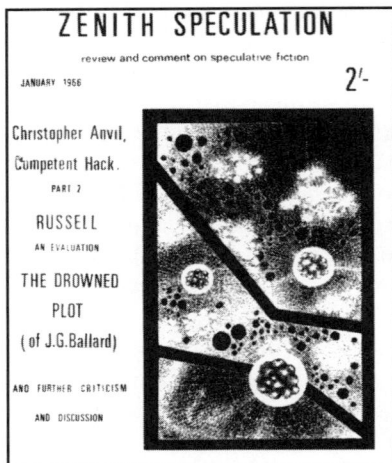

The "Melting Pot" was shorter than usual, with Ted Tubb treading cautiously, as if through a minefield, to make a few straightforward points, like, "a bad story, no matter how told, is a bad story. The rules of craftsmanship still apply and should be applied whether a story is told in the old, familiar way or in some new style." More outspokenly, and covering his back with disclaimers along the way, London fan David Piper took up the gauntlet thrown down by Mike Moorcock in the previous issue. "I doubt very much indeed whether any of his ideas regarding SF are of the remotest interest to the average fan," he wrote, "Mr Moorcock's views, like his pro- and fan-writing, seem to me to be very precious and contrived. Ballard is in my opinion an extremely minor author on an entertainment level—I quite liked *Drowned World* and enjoyed 'Terminal Beach'—but a continual re-hash of the same story, over and over again, only shows up his limitations."

I was starting to think that maybe I was getting into deep waters with these cutting-edge confrontations and was glad to get to the January meeting of the Brum group, so that I could dig deeper into the fanzine repository in the back bedroom. By now I had returned *Aporrheta* to the pile (though couldn't quite

---

ZENITH SPECULATION

review and comment on speculative fiction

JANUARY 1966   2/-

Christopher Anvil,
Competent Hack.
PART 2

RUSSELL
AN EVALUATION

THE DROWNED
PLOT
(of J.G.Ballard)

AND FURTHER CRITICISM
AND DISCUSSION

bear to let go of *Void,* not just yet, anyway) and had already worked through *Hyphen, Oopsla!* and *Quandry.* I was looking for other fabulous titles, but it was a particularly cold winter's night and though Charlie had kindly provided a small electric fire, it gave only a token of heat in the big, draughty house. I kept on my overcoat and scarf, but I was freezing and my fingers were soon numb with the cold.

Burrowing deeper into the dusty heap, I unearthed more famous names from the past, fanzines like *Shaggy, Cry,* and *Rhodomagnetic Digest,* which I had eagerly looked forward to reading. But disappointingly, they weren't as good as I had anticipated; they were only club-zines, really. I was much more taken with the few issues of Richard Bergeron's *Warhoon,* and a single *Psychotic,* which I brought down into the front room to read by the warmth of the gas-fire. I was intrigued by the quirky, stylistic tricks of Dick Geis with his "Alter-Ego" dialogues, and awed by the impeccable reproduction and superior quality of writing in *Warhoon,* which had high-powered contributors like James Blish, Damon Knight and Robert W. Lowndes. Now *that's* the way to do a fanzine, I thought.

Surprisingly, there were very few serious fanzines about science fiction. I was intensely curious to see how past editors had tackled the subject, and had been hoping for some sort of a role model, ideas, or maybe even potential reprint material. People had told me that Eric Bentcliffe's *Space Diversions* had been similar to my *Zenith,* but it wasn't, not at all. I was even more disappointed with Ed Wood's *Journal of Science Fiction,* another half-size printed fanzine that looked good but was stiff and laboured, a sort of fake-academic effort. Best by far was Dick Eney's *Speculative Review,* a slim fanzine that seemed to have printed some perceptive criticism on various stories; straightaway my eye was caught by a sharp little piece about *Rogue Moon.*

However, in late January a thick new fanzine arrived, one which almost literally set me jumping for joy. Titled *Quip,* it was *Void* re-born under a different name. Produced by Arnie Katz and Len Bailes, a new team of New York fans, *Quip* was consciously modelled after Ted White's ground-breaking example, with the same cartoon-covers featuring Qwertyuiop with his boater and cane (though drawn by artist Ross Chamberlain rather than the great Steve Stiles). *This* was something I could relate to, and I fired off an enthusiastic letter of thanks. Only a few weeks later came Terry Carr's *Lighthouse* (number thirteen), another fannish title I had thought was dead but which turned out to have been only "resting." The lights were coming on again in fandom!

Letters were coming in well after my own January issue and I had already started work on the next number of *Zenith Speculation,* but I was a bit depressed. Jim Grant had totally gone to ground, sending me just a couple of pounds in November and nothing since, while I still had to keep up regular monthly payments to Roneo. I wondered what to do, whether I could cancel the standing order and tell Roneo where to collect their machine, but was pretty sure this wouldn't wash, they'd still hold me responsible. I wrote to Jim again, threatening to come down to Christchurch and retrieve my property, but that seemed easier said than done. I had the nasty feeling that I had been taken for a fool.

My mood wasn't helped by a perceptive letter from Chris Priest, who had been through his own period of soul-searching, had decided to escape from accountancy, and was now starting to sell science fiction stories professionally. Chris said,

"You're wasting your time, Pete. You can't go on doing *Zenith* for ever. You see, in the world of SF you are well-known as a serious fan. This rather classes you in the earnest gang, who go around at conventions clasping SF books in their sweaty mitts and looking at authors with eyes full of awe. I know you're not like that really, but it does tend to be your image."

Chris's words struck home, so I was immediately receptive when Rog Peyton asked me to do a fanzine review feature for *Vector*. He had a hole to fill because he had just lost Jim Groves' "For Your Information" column, since Jim was emigrating to the United States, and "Dr Peristyle" had faded away some issues earlier. I liked the idea of trying to draw others into the fannish web, but made the big mistake of using a pen name. At the time, it seemed a great idea, because I imagined it would excite as much curiosity and as had the mysterious "Dr Peristyle." So Rog and I put our heads together and decided on some misdirection, choosing our pseudonym by combining the names of two Scottish authors who were active in the BSFA at the time, Donald Malcolm and Edward Macklin.

The first instalment appeared in *Vector* (March 1966) and was intended to be a little controversial. "A recent columnist exposed a long-held and festering belief that the BSFA was only a recruiting station," I began, "that it had no purpose other than to provide cannon-fodder for the Big Guns of Science Fiction Fandom. Now that's an extremist attitude (one not to be encouraged, semaphores the outraged committee behind the scenes), yet I'll stick out my tender neck and say that it does have some elements of truth. Like it or not, this is a dual-purpose organisation."

My title came from that first paragraph, and in "Behind the Scenes" I set out to promote fandom, saying things like "fandom is a rather wonderful labyrinth of intellectual side-streets that lead to many an intriguing discovery." I enjoyed writing the column and ended with reviews of *Lighthouse, Double: Bill,* and *Zenith* (that'll really fool 'em, I thought). It was my first attempt at structured fan writing rather than last-minute composed-on-stencil pieces for *Nexus,* and Rog and I thought the timing would be perfect, so that the Yarmouth Eastercon would be buzzing with surmise and speculation at the secret identity of the new man. Who was this mysterious, masked columnist? Who *was* "Malcolm Edwards"?

End of the Beginning
Chapter 11

Charlie didn't say a word, all the way back from Great Yarmouth. And it had started so well, as the four of us—Rog in the front seat, Darroll and Charlie in the rear—had set off on the long drive to the 1966 convention, over 180 miles due East on winding country roads. We stopped for a quick Chinese meal at Peterborough; two years earlier, I had thought that was remote. Now we were going nearly twice as far, through picturesque Wisbech, home of Ken Slater's "Fantast" bookshop, across sugar-beet fields and flat, empty fenlands that seemed to go on forever.

It was four o'clock before we eventually checked in at the Royal Hotel on the seafront at Yarmouth. We were among the first to arrive, and Rog and I had a beer in the bar, where we met Con Turner and Jim Marshall, a genial couple of old fans from the North-East who had recently published their fanzine *Gestalt*, with a newcomer, Harry Bell, who had come down with them. It was a warm afternoon and we decided to go for a stroll along the promenade, but we didn't get far because only a few hundred yards down the beach was a fun fair, which Rog insisted upon investigating. It had been ages since I had been to a fair, so naturally we had candyfloss all round, and then Rog suggested we went onto the Waltzers, his favourite.

The next ten minutes had the quality of a nightmare as I clung to the safety bar in a low-slung contraption which rumbled in tight little epicycles while the wooden deck thundered around and around and up and down, all to the bellowed tune of "Zambezi" and the rattle of mismatched castors. "Roll, pitch, and yaw," I thought grimly. "It might be good training for the space programme, but please God, just let me get out of this alive!" Then a tattooed demon from out of Hell itself appeared and gave our car a couple of hard pushes, just to make sure it was travelling at the very limit of its design capabilities. "I'm going to be *sick,*" I groaned, as my stomach signalled it was about to expel its recent input of sweet-&-sour pork, beer and candyfloss. The fiend from Hell thought this was absolutely hilarious and gave us an extra-hard shove before going on to torment the lost souls in the next car. I *knew* I should have stuck to the dodgems!

We staggered off and I thought Jim and Con looked a bit green, too, but not Rog Peyton, he of the cast-iron stomach, who immediately went onto an even more evil device, a sort of giant centrifuge with long metal arms that gradually lifted so they were vertical. From a safe distance on blessedly unmoving ground we watched in horrified fascination as Rog's little aluminium capsule rocketed straight down at about 6Gs, his head just visible through the mesh cover. Nothing bothers that man!

After that, I hardly ventured out of the hotel all weekend. This was the year of the running battles between Mods and Rockers along Yarmouth seafront, this was the convention—unique in British fan-history—where the management insisted we had half-board terms, so we all sat down together at the same time in the hotel dining room. Rog was disgusted—"the worst food I've ever eaten during a convention," he said, but then he never did care for conventional English cooking. I liked the community atmosphere, which mixed us up and gave me a chance to meet people I might not otherwise have had nerve to approach. Eric Jones, for instance, Grand Master of the Order of St Fantony, who seemed very friendly, and Ken McIntyre, an old boy from London who was an artist, and generously offered to do me a cover for my fanzine.

I enjoyed the convention immensely and felt completely at home, no longer troubled by the insecurities of Peterborough or the tensions of Brumcon. I spent most of my time in the bar, with people like Chris Priest, and Tony Walsh with his pretty (but sharp-tongued) wife Simone. Tony absolutely *lived* for fandom, and he was going to run the following year's convention. In the meantime, he invited us to come along to his BaD group parties in Bristol. John Brunner was there, and I saw him for the first time, icily aloof in red velvet smoking jacket with his terrifying wife Marjorie, who looked and acted like the Duchess of Windsor.

Ethel Lindsay won a prize in the Fancy Dress for her costume "Princess of Zamba," as did Charles Partington as "First BSFA Manned Satellite," after which some of us stayed up for the rest of the night to see dawn breaking over the North Sea. Twenty-four hours later I followed Ted Tubb on another of his

I followed Ted Tubb on another of his late-night "pilgrimages"

late-night pilgrimages, chinking bottles in a conga-line and chanting "Get back to your wives" before being pursued along endless corridors by an irate hotel manager, so heavily-built that we called him "Landburger Gessler" after the evil Austrian overlord in the "William Tell" series then on television. Naturally, throughout the whole weekend not a single person even mentioned the new "mystery" columnist in *Vector!*

However, for Charlie Winstone, it all exploded in his face at the BSFA AGM on Sunday morning. A blizzard was blowing outside but under the mild direction of Roy Kay it had been a sedate, though slightly confused meeting, with no Charles Platt to stir up trouble, no great passions roused. Rog Peyton was given a round of applause for his splendid achievement in putting out *Vector* every two months for two years (during which time Association membership had more than doubled), and the editorship passed to a newcomer, Steve Oakey. Ken Slater came in as the new Vice-Chairman, and then came Charlie's turn, as Treasurer, for the presentation of Accounts.

Now at the time I didn't pretend to understand the mysterious world of bookkeeping and profit-&-loss statements, few of us did. Charlie had never asked our advice, never seemed to be in any difficulty, so we had naturally assumed he knew what he was doing. Unfortunately, it appeared that he didn't, and his errors were exposed in the worst possible way by Ted Tubb, who stood up to interrupt Charlie with a query. "What's this item under 'Expenditure'?" he asked, "Money at a Building Society. Shouldn't that be an 'investment'?" Charlie spluttered and tried to explain, without success. "Don't you know the difference?" demanded an irate Tubb, like a dormant volcano coming noisily into life. It rapidly got worse as Ted went on the warpath with a vengeance. "These figures don't even add up!" he roared, and others started to nod in agreement. Charlie was absolutely crucified, and Roy Kay directed that his accounts should be re-done by the Association Auditor, Chris Priest. Charlie was hardly seen again until it was time to go home.

The atmosphere in the car was strained and difficult. We tried to draw Charlie out of his misery but he wouldn't speak, not even to Darroll, normally the most sympathetic of listeners. On the way back we stopped at Wisbech and took a few photographs outside Ken Slater's little shop-window in Nor-folk Street, but that didn't lift the mood. It was a long, horrible journey back to Birmingham, and I was glad when we finally dropped Charlie at his house. He went in without a word or backwards glance.

That was the end of our meetings in his front room. Charlie's mother was outraged at the way he had been treated, and she forbade us to come to the house again. It wasn't our fault, we had done nothing, but Charlie didn't have the emotional resilience to get past this traumatic shock to his psyche. To him, fandom was now associated with pain and humiliation, and he didn't want anything else to do with it. Remarkably, the BSFA let him remain as Treasurer for a full third term, which was a mistake they would regret. It was the end, too, of the Fanzine Foundation. Perhaps I should have tried to retrieve it from Charlie's house, but I didn't want to face his mother and there was still the problem of where else could it go? I was glad that I had never quite relin-quished that file of *Void,* and wished I had hung onto those issues of *Hyphen,* too.[1]

Within a week or two of the convention, Rog Peyton put out one final *Vector.* It contained my second "Behind the Scenes" column as Malcolm Edwards, in which I explained the birth of fandom as a consequence of the long letter-pages in the early professional magazines, and lamented that when they vanished, the main channels of recruitment into fandom were closed. I suggested that the re-introduction of a fan-feature in *If* magazine, "Our Man

---

[1] Some of these fanzines surfaced unexpectedly at the 1972 Chessmancon, when I was asked to auction off a large pile of material brought along by Manchester fan John Muir. I recognised them immediately, not only by their vintage but also by the address labels, while some even had a sticker attached, "BSFA Fanzine Foundation." I complained to Keith Freeman (then BSFA Chairman), but the auction was allowed to proceed because Muir said they were only "duplicates," and the collection was dispersed. Peter Roberts bought quite a lot and several American fans were only too delighted to snap up other bargains. Charlie must have done some sort of unauthorised deal to clear out his back bedroom, and at the time, I thought it was a thoroughly bad show. I now realise it was probably the best thing that could have happened since at least the important items can be presumed to have gone to good homes—better, cer-tainly, than continuing to moulder away!

Greg Pickersgill added a further note by mentioning that in the September 1968 issue of the BSFA *Bulletin* was an announcement that "The BSFA Fanzine Foundation has a huge surplus of British fanzines to dispose of, some of them as early as 1949" and entreated members to send a 4d stamp to Chas. D. Winstone for a copy of the Foundation's duplicates list. "I was absolutely boggled by the idea that I could get for what seemed like hardly any money at all (maybe a shilling each) fanzines that were legendary even then," said Greg. "I sent off cash and a list by return, and was utterly astonished when I actually got everything I wanted, including about fifteen issues of *Hyphen,* which as has been said, changed my life in various ways."

in Fandom" by Lin Carter, could bring in newcomers once more, and concluded with reviews of *Yandro* and *Riverside Quarterly.*

The twelfth issue of *Zenith Speculation* was finished at about the same time. It had an unusual cover by photographer Jim Groves showing oil droplets suspended in water under strong lighting, but which was likened to the Rorschach inkblots by many readers, who claimed to see all sorts of fantastic creatures lurking among the shadows. The issue led off with Harry Harrison, taking umbrage at Archie and Beryl's review of *Bill the Galactic Hero* in the previous issue. Harry wrote, "When I was writing *Bill* I kept mumbling to myself that old-line, hardcore fandom wouldn't like it. Now it is time to look around and see just how correct these prognosticative mumbles were. I intend to take the look here in the pages of *ZS* because this journal has worked hard to identify itself with stone-age science fiction, and makes vociferous defence of all it holds dear." Harry then went on to castigate Archie and Beryl for having minds that were "too closed," told them to "try harder" to find out what writers were saying, and ended by saying "the only thing that the new wave SF writers have in common is the feeling that SF is an open-ended medium, not closed and restricted to one type of narrative."

Now, if I had been a bit more assertive I could have made a few observations of my own about Harry's letter. For instance it was a bit much for him to blithely class himself as one of the new wave school on the strength of *Bill,* at best a lightweight spoof on *Starship Troopers* and the "Foundation" series. It was also a rather strange position for Harry to *want* to adopt when he was already becoming one of our most-respected writers with novels like *The Ethical Engineer* and *Make Room, Make Room,* both built solidly on orthodox science fictional footings and storytelling techniques. It was hard not to suspect that fashion had something to do with his stance, that and Harry's desire to keep up with the in-crowd and especially with his big pal, Brian Aldiss, who had already embraced the new wave mythology. Lastly, I should have challenged his remark about "stone-age" science fiction, since *Zenith* had never been against change, had only been anxious "not to throw out the baby with the bathwater."

The issue continued with a piece from Michael Moorcock, remarkably restrained for once in his reply to Joe Patrizio's article on J. G. Ballard in the

The image on the left is a magazine cover reading:

ZENITH SPECULATION
review and comment on speculative fiction
APRIL 1966   2/-

HEINLEIN'S NON-FICTION
alexei panshin

1966 - THE HUGO CANDIDATES
* Squares of the City
* Dune
* 3 Stigmata of Palmer Eldritch

& further criticism and discussion by moorcock, harrison, etc.

Vol 1. No. 12.

previous issue. There was a review feature which looked at some of the likely Best Novel candidates for the Hugo in 1966, considering such titles as *Dune* and *Three Stigmata of Palmer Eldritch,* followed by the "Double Booking" column and a healthy "Melting Pot" of letters. However, the big scoop was ei Panshin's "The Non-Fiction of Robert A. Heinlein," a chapter from *Heinlein in Dimension,* the book he had been writing for Advent before he had inadvertently upset the notoriously touchy Heinlein and the contract had been withdrawn.

Interior artwork was by Ivor Latto and Pam Yates. After the London Convention Ivor had gafiated, abandoning his own fanzine and ceasing to write for others, but I think it amused him to keep sending me bits of artwork in his wonderful, crisp style. Pam Yates was very different and counted as a real find. Not a fan herself, she had trained at Art College as an illustrator, and her husband (a research scientist) was a member of the BSFA. Pam had sent a few illustrations to *Vector,* which Rog, in one of his rare slip-ups, had rejected and offered to me. She was just what I was looking for, with an unusual, evocative style that fitted very well with the mood I was trying to create. Even better, she sent me such a wide variety of sketches that I was able to match them effectively to illustrate individual features and articles.

However, fanzines aside, what *were* we going to do about the Brum group? At an emergency Sunday meeting in Darroll Pardoe's Stourbridge home, we discussed the possibilities. We couldn't meet at our various houses since we were all still living with our parents, and a clubroom was financially out of the question. It would have to be a pub, we thought, and Rog suggested "The Old Contemptibles" on the corner of Edmund Street in the city centre, close to the surveyor's office where he worked. We visited it one evening and thought it seemed reasonably comfortable. Perhaps we could get things going and create a minor legend, rather in the way of the London "Globe" meetings? We dreamed that our fame would spread over the years, and foreign fans and visiting Americans would start to drop in to see us. To get things started I decided to put out a single-sheet monthly newsletter, sent to everyone we knew in the area.

We planned the first meeting for May 5th and Rog and I arrived early, agonising in case no one else showed up. Under-age Martin Pitt was found skulking around outside, trying to get up the nerve to venture in, and eventually fifteen or sixteen others showed up, far more than we had been averaging in Charlie's front room. Optimistically, I looked forward to a new era for Birmingham fandom. Two weeks later the second meeting was nearly as busy and to our delight Cliff Teague showed up, as did two girls who claimed to be interested in science fiction. Unfortunately, the night ended on a sour note when one of our newer members got into an argument with the landlord, who threatened to "throw out the lot of you." As I reported, "Alan Roblin lost his head when his beer lost its head." The third meeting went without hitch, and the fourth, though numbers were low, but with the fifth meeting at the beginning of July, the landlord made good his previous threat and ejected us. We didn't drink enough, he complained, and we were annoying his regular customers.

I gave up. As far as I was concerned, that was the end of the Birmingham Science Fiction Group. Afterwards, one or two people may have met unofficially, but in the absence of any claim to the contrary Darroll Pardoe and Martin Pitt announced that they met at the pub on September 25th to toast the anniversary of H. G. Wells' birthday, and then declared the club dead.

Anyway, I was busy! I was immensely cheered when, for the second year running, *Zenith Speculation* was nominated for the fanzine Hugo. Not that I seriously thought it had any real chance of winning, of course, not when the worldcon was in Cleveland, the voters would be almost all Americans and the other four titles were all U.S. fanzines. They were *Yandro,* the previous winner; *Double:Bill,* last year's contender; *Niekas,* another thick genzine; and something I hadn't heard of before called *ERB-dom.* I didn't expect to win, not this year, but the very fact of being nominated again was something to celebrate, and maybe if I kept at it and put out another four or five good issues I might have a better chance in 1967 when the Worldcon would be in New York. It was a powerful motivator.

My July issue certainly looked different, with Ken McIntyre's dramatic cover painting which was titled "Asteroid at Close Approach." It had a curi-

ously dated quality, with jagged pinnacles of rock and sharply defined craters that harkened right back to the early paintings from the British Interplanetary Society, before we understood that thermal erosion and micrometeorite bombardment would inevitably soften any landscape exposed to vacuum for a few billion years. However, Ken's painting had black sky and lots of shadows, which allowed me to try a new trick by letting the picture bleed off on all four edges, with a reversed-out "SPECULATION" in very large capitals right across the top (and a vestigial "Zenith" in script above it).

Inside, there were reviews by luminaries like Chris Priest on *Plague from Space,* Langdon Jones on *A Plague of Pythons* and Brian Aldiss on *The Watch Below,* while "The Melting Pot" was notable for a short missive from Sam Moskowitz in which he took a side-swipe at Alexei Panshin, then added, "Your readers' letters are unusually punchy. Apparently *Zenith* does not invite neutrality." There was a new column in this issue, or rather, a revival of a very old one by "Renfrew Pemberton," which might have been seen as some sort of reward for all my rummaging around among those old fanzines. While the Seattle group's fanzine, *Cry of the Nameless,* hadn't been all that interesting to an outsider, I *had* been impressed with the magazine review column that F. M. "Buz" Busby had contributed for fifty consecutive issues between 1955 and 1959. I liked the sheer *readability* of his column,[2] combining knowledge with good sense, and was really pleased when Buz accepted my invitation to resume "plowing the field" (although somehow, I never had the heart to tell him that in Britain we didn't spell it that way!).

In this issue I had to carry an "apology" to Harry Harrison, because the previous number had made an unauthorised change to his letter about *Bill, the Galactic Hero.* As I explained,

"Harry had made use of a certain four-letter word, but being old-fashioned at *ZS* we chose to omit the word and substitute something similar. Harry wishes to say that this alteration affected his argument." Privately, I thought I had done him a small favour by removing an unnecessary vulgarity but I wasn't going to argue about it!

Also in July I wrote another "Behind the Scenes" column for Steve Oakey, the new editor of *Vector,* and as if that wasn't enough Darroll Pardoe asked me to help him revive *Les Spinge,* defunct since the 100-page mega-issue eighteen months earlier. "Would I write a regular column?" he asked, then added, "Oh, and the deadline is next week." Darroll was getting more and more involved with fandom, and had recently bought Ken Cheslin's duplicator for £50.00.

"I really enjoyed the colour mimeo work," he wrote. "I've always felt mimeo was a lovely medium for colours, being kind of translucent (unlike offset litho inks). I bought the 'Spinge' Gestetner, and vast piles of coloured inks (including white—very useful) came with it, which was fortunate because soon after that Gestetner stopped selling everything except two or three basic colours. Ken also threw in the rights to the *Les Spinge* title (remember, Ken was always the publisher and Dave Hale was appointed by him as editor) so I guess that officially I still own them."

Although I wrote the first instalment of my column in a tearing hurry, it made a conscious effort to use some of the mannerisms I'd admired so much

---

2 No wonder! Buz was a talented writer and it was only a few years before he started selling his own, immensely popular science fiction mega-novels, starting with *Rissa Kerguelen.*

in *Void* and *Quip,* trying to transplant the worldly-wise New York fan-scene to downtown, bucolic Birmingham, writing about people I knew, making up conversations based on the tiniest scraps of truth:

"The other day I was kidding Rog Peyton about that fanzine he's been going to turn out any day now for the past two and a half years. Rog was stung into the retort that a good 'zine needed careful planning, and anyway, he'd prefer to do a fanzine with me. This struck a responsive chord in my egoboo-hungry brain. 'We will co-edit an issue of *Brumble,* Roger Peyton,' I said, 'and we will show Ken Cheslin and Mike Higgs and Charlie Winstone how to turn out a good fanzine.' "

More seriously, in the second part of the column I complained, "Some fans have a peculiar attitude to conventions. They go along with the idea that everything is going to be arranged for their benefit, that a con can be 'good' without their making any effort. They are spectators, who will take part in the festivities only if they deem it worth their while. When a large proportion of attendees are of this persuasion, as was the case at Birmingham last year, they all wait for someone else to do something and of course nothing does happen and the con is a disappointment." Obviously, I was thinking of Ivor Latto, and his indignation that he hadn't been continually "entertained" at the worldcon.

Then I continued with something that came more from the heart, probably because I had been snubbed again at the recent Stourbridge meeting. "Of course, sometimes there are people you simply *can't* communicate with, sometimes fans you've known for years. Even here, in the Centre of the Universe, there are people I've known for ages and yet we have never broken through the barriers between us. One man I've never been able to get through to is Ken Cheslin.

"Ken's a good sort, yet I always get the impression that he doesn't care whether I exist or not, that he will put up with me, but will not open up. My conversations with Ken usually bog down in 'yes' and 'no' responses, and Ken has yet, after two and a half years, to address me personally with a new topic of conversation. Whenever Rog and I go along to see him, it is customary for Ken to address Rog directly and me only by implication.

"I know he doesn't bear me any ill will. We just aren't close. This was always the case with Ken, even at his most fannish. When he met new fans, Ken would steadfastly ignore them, so much so that many of them resented him, but it was purely through a form of shyness that he acted this way. His attitude to me, and perhaps to Charlie Winstone, is purely an extension of this diffidence, never swept away like the cobweb it is. I'm not discouraged, I'm not yelling 'feud,' I'm still persevering. I hope you're reading this, Ken."

I was a little nervous about this portion of the column but it drew just about the reaction it deserved—nothing whatsoever. I might actually have been too kind to Ken because there probably was rather more to his attitude than just diffidence, since he had taken to Mike "The Beard" readily enough. No, rather than writing fanzine articles it would have been much better if I'd asked him, privately, what was his problem.

Darroll knew him much better than I ever did: "I think Ken was rather off-hand with everybody, actually. He was a pretty insecure person (especially after he lost his hand) and this was his way of coping. Nevertheless he and I had enough in common so we were pretty good friends. We started off well when I first met him in 1960 and immediately discovered a mutual love of the *Goon Show*. We just went on from there... But yes, I don't think you were alone in feeling a bit odd with Ken. Others have said the same (including Rosemary)."

Les Spinge 15 duly came out, but *Vector* didn't. It was September before Steve Oakey's first issue appeared, a far cry from Rog Peyton's superb performance. However, all that effort had taken a toll on Rog. He had worked hard for two years on *Vector* and on the Brumcon committee, and now it was Summer and he felt like a break from fandom, wanted to spend more time with his old pals, especially when they went ten-pin bowling. Sometimes I would go along to watch—now I had the car, it was an easy 15-minutes drive over the hill. One night at the bowling alley Rog met a group of lads and girls who didn't seem to have much idea what they were doing. They were impressed with the masterly way he knocked down the skittles, explained they were from the local Young Conservatives club, and had entered a bowling competition. Did he want to help them?

The next time I saw Rog he had joined the Quinton Young Conservatives and I quickly saw the attraction. The club met every Monday night at the local Community Centre, where they had a speaker, a quiz, a visit to another club, or sometimes they just drove out to a country pub. It had about two dozen members, mostly girls, and the club sounded as if it was one long round of parties, dances and social events. Politics?—well, perhaps very occasionally a local councillor might turn up, or we might be asked to deliver a few leaflets, but otherwise it seemed to be almost entirely a social club. Two or three other young men of our age joined at the same time and we soon became good friends. Compared to our experience of science fiction fandom it was an altogether different, more glamorous world!

Actually we kept pretty quiet about science fiction and fandom. It was our little secret, like having a social disease or a mad aunt locked in the attic. The Y.C.s wouldn't have understood. Although by this time Rog had effectively gafiated, dividing his time between the club and his already-huge record collection. My fanzine was an anchor, of course, although it predictably failed to win a Hugo in 1966 and the award instead went to *ERB-dom*. This was my first experience of the voting power of narrowly focussed special-interest groups, which could effectively "buy" an award if it suited them.

Still, in October I was able to celebrate with my third anniversary issue, undergoing a final metamorphosis to emerge as *Speculation,* with a smart new logo and a striking cover. This came from "Riccardo Leveghi," an artist about whom I knew nothing except that my "agent" in Italy had submitted an amazing illustration under his name. The picture arrived as a very large, fuzzy Ozalid print on pale blue paper smelling of ammonia, folded twice over to fit into the envelope. At first I didn't think it would be possible to use it, but fortunately I had infiltrated myself into the BSA Photographic Department, who put it under a plate-camera and reduced it to a size where it looked good. Printed in blue ink on white card, it made a dramatic, almost surreal cover, a million miles away from that sad little "Miktoon" of three years earlier.

It was an exceptional issue in another way because Alex Panshin had now given me a full chapter of his Heinlein book, titled "The Period of Success." I would probably have done better to split it over two issues, because it took up 35 pages and crowded out all the usual features apart from some very brief reviews and one letter—also from Panshin, taking strong issue with Sam Moskowitz's throwaway dismissal last time. We certainly didn't "invite neutrality."

Another dramatic change came about in October, this time because my career prospects suddenly took a turn for the better. From being a floater, I succeeded to a real job, as Publicity Officer for a five-company division of the BSA Group. All the companies operated fairly advanced metal forming techniques, such as powder metallurgy and investment casting, and my position was something of a plum in that I had a lot of freedom and quite a lot of responsibility. Equally important, I now had my own office that had a decent typewriter though not, unfortunately, a duplicator. I still had to use machines in other departments, usually on a Saturday morning.

Meanwhile, *Vector* and the BSFA were both in trouble. The elusive Steve Oakey had vanished without trace, and in December Vice Chairman Ken Slater and Secretary Doreen Parker put out an "emergency" issue. Duplicated once more and with a Spartan layout, it was a very rough issue, as both cheerfully admitted in an editorial titled "Editorrible," but it served its purpose in showing members that the Association was still alive. But only just. Ken Slater had looked at the audited accounts and discovered the BSFA had been living beyond its means and he had a financial crisis on his hands. Not surprising, really, if Charlie Winstone hadn't understood the significance of the figures, and after this final upset he had to resign. Ken Slater's old pal David Barber took over as a caretaker Treasurer, and with both of them living in Wisbech and Doreen relatively close by in Peterborough, they started to get things moving again.

Christmas came and went, enlivened immensely this year by festivities with the Young Conservatives, and in January I brought out the issue of *Speculation* that nearly broke the camel's back. This was the one with Pam Yates' red, jungle cover titled "Garden of Eden," with original "articles" by Fritz Leiber and Bob Silverberg. They'd both been cobbled together from letters, Fritz telling us "All About The Change War" (backed with a good piece I lifted from Dick Eney's *Speculative Review* on my favourite novel, *The Big Time*), and Silverberg writing about his "Blue Fire" series of stories then running in the magazines.

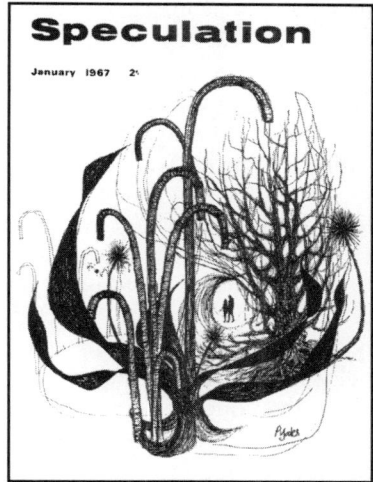

The real punch this time came from Swedish fan John-Henri Holmberg, with a follow-up coming from Buz Busby's "Plow" column. John-Henri took issue with Harry Harrison's previous letter about *Bill, the Galactic Hero* and in a complex argument ended by saying, "Mr Harrison...attacks the basic values he thinks are held by Archie and Beryl Mercer, [but] claims for himself the 'right' to express any views, without fear of criticism or condemnation for those views." Buz Busby took a similar stance about the claims made by the New School, as he called it. "The science fiction reader today is in some danger of being sold a bill of goods as to what he should like, rather than being sold what he *does* like," he said. Buz then went on to discuss the various reviews in the July issue, saying, "What with Aldiss on James White and Lang Jones on Pohl, I get the impression that the New School is a rather intolerant institution, that these boys feel that their way is THE Way."

The January issue had grown to fifty pages and 300 copies, which represented a huge amount of work to type and run off stencils, then collate and staple and finally address and post them out. I managed to get out about half of the print-run before being overtaken by exhaustion and the pressures of the hectic social life in which Rog and I were now engaging, three or four nights per week. The pile of duplicated pages sat in an orange-box and looked at me reproachfully every evening for several months, but fortunately, help was near at hand.

For some time I had been putting little plugs in various magazines, trying to reach other people besides the regular fans. A note in *New Worlds* had brought in a few new subscribers including a Londoner, Graham Charnock, and someone fairly local, David Pringle, who was then a 16-year-old schoolboy living in Sutton Coldfield. Working in publicity, I had access to a huge volume called BRAD—"British Rate & Data," nothing less than a full listing of every newspaper and magazine published in Britain. In fascination, I passed over entries for *Muck Spreader, Ferret Fancier* and similar esoterica, but noted titles that might appeal to SF readers, and sent details and sample copies to *The Writer,* and to the two hippy papers, *International Times (It),* and *Oz.*

Nothing useful came from the writers' magazine, but *Oz* drew a letter from "Robert J. M. Rickard," of Solihull, not a million miles away from where I lived, and I went round to see him. He was short, quietly spoken with thick-lensed glasses and a dense mass of frizzy hair. Bob was studying Industrial Design, but he had a wide range of other interests including Chinese and Oriental culture, philosophy and the works of Charles Fort. He was completely unlike anyone I had ever met before, but we seemed to hit it off well, because he was also a long-time science fiction fan. He was my saviour! Bob helped with the fanzine, proving how very much faster two people can shift paper than one, and we managed to send out the balance of the January issue just before Easter. I couldn't persuade him to come to the con at such short notice, but Bob immediately became a great friend, and we started to see each other regularly. He even wrote me an alarmed letter on *Speculation* 15:

"Not having read a fanzine before, I was surprised at the open attacks on each other made by letter writers and contributors, amazed at the rifts opening between New and Old Schools, and astounded at the state of SF *in toto* (prozines folding, TV-shows in trouble, etc). To me, a newcomer, the whole scene smacks of a general failure. I think this is so serious that I was prompted to write to you, for in all this I can see the seeds of a dismal future…"

I printed his remarks and commented: "This first paragraph was so perfect that I had to use it! These were my feelings at one time—but science fiction and its fandom have been coming apart at the seams now for the last forty years. Crisis succeeds crisis and the only really dismal failure I can see is my inability to get *Spec* published with more frequency."

Meanwhile, the new editors of *Vector* had finally re-discovered the identity of their contributor "Malcolm Edwards" and asked me for a column, which appeared in the March 1967 issue, explaining "fan-speak" with copious quotes from Eney's *Fancyclopedia II*. My column for Darroll Pardoe's *Les Spinge* of the same date presented much more of a challenge. This time I decided to attempt a conscious pastiche of the Irish John Berry, and I wrote a long account of a visit Rog and I had made some months before to Tony Walsh's BaD Group.

John Berry had used a simple, but very effective, technique for many years. He would observe a meeting, or conversation, or minor incident in Belfast fandom and then write it up with massive exaggeration and over-emphasis, throwing in a few witticisms (usually generated quite effortlessly by Messrs. Willis & Shaw). It seemed easy enough, I thought, since I had a fairly good ear for conversation and Archie Mercer could be relied upon for his usual clever wordplay. Accordingly my 8-page piece for *Spinge* contained such snippets as,

"We stayed only a short time at the Walshes', just long enough for me to give Tony a copy of my latest *Nexus* (which Simone remarked was an anagram of Un-Sex, and was that Significant?)."

And my description of the Mercatorial Mansion:

"As Simone had said, and we hadn't believed, it was a large, decaying place, the only house in its road. Mysteriously Victorian, too; we soon heard that the building presented three windows on the exterior of the first floor, and yet from within there were only two….It took quite some time to get used to the labyrinth—I'd ask Archie which door led to the bathroom, and he'd say 'Tenth door,' and I'd shout back, 'Counting from which end?' and losing patience would fling open a door and leap squarely into a broom closet. It really is a fabulous place."

Later, I described the journey back to the Walshes', when Rog and I attempted to follow Archie and Beryl in their Triumph Herald:

"Eventually a car appeared out of the night. It crept ever so slowly up the side-road, then slower still, to stop completely, halfway onto the main thoroughfare. 'There they are,' said Rog. 'Why have they stopped?' 'I do not know, Roger Peyton.' I said. 'Perhaps they are waiting for us.' I tooted my horn gently, to show the Mercers I was waiting. They remained perfectly stationary. I sat and waited, tooted again, flashed my lights, crept backwards until I almost touched their car, and tooted again.

"Slowly, ever so slowly, like a glacier descending to the sea in majestic motion, the Mercatorial motor began moving, swept past in stately grace and dwindled down the road without so much as a flash to show they were even aware of our existence. I guess Archie really concentrates on the road when he drives."

Well, *I* thought it was amusing, anyway. Not so Simone. A month later when we arrived for the Bristol convention she accosted me, eyes flashing, and guns blazing. "Cruel, nasty, wicked, uncaring, ungrateful wretch," were some of the kinder words she used, and "How do you think poor Archie felt when you said such hurtful things about his driving?"

"But it was only a bit of fun," I protested in vain, wondering how I could explain about John Berry's writing techniques to someone who'd never heard of him. I don't *think* Archie himself was the slightest bit concerned, or so I hoped. However, it taught me a valuable lesson, how careful you need to be in fandom, if you don't want to give offence!

"Move Over, Mate!"
Chapter 12

We had a great time at the Briscon. Held in the rambling old Hawthorns Hotel and chaired by the ever-reliable Tony Walsh, the 1967 convention was probably our best yet, although it did give me a nasty surprise at one point.

Starting out early on the Thursday afternoon, Rog and I made the now-familiar drive down the A38 to the Walshes' house in Bristol for a pre-con warm-up party. Darroll Pardoe arrived, as did some of the local fans including Graham Boak, who had recently started the BaD-group fanzine, *BaDinage* (title courtesy of Archie Mercer, of course). We consumed large quantities of Guinness, Simone lambasted me for the great sin of writing my "hurtful" *Spinge* column, and eventually most of us settled down on mattresses in the back room.

This enabled me to get to the hotel next morning ahead of nearly everyone except Ella Parker and Ethel Lindsay, who had arrived on the first train and were already in the lounge, well-settled and ordering repeat trays of tea. Darroll had also been up for hours; he had stayed at the hotel and had been woken at dawn by the sounds of muttering and clattering just outside his window, as a party of geologists loaded themselves and their equipment into a motor coach, a performance they would repeat every morning during the weekend. "They were no trouble to us fans," Darroll said charitably, "as they were away from the hotel from early morning to late at night." It was that sort of hotel, so big and rambling that it could accommodate all sorts of different groups simultaneously.

The Hawthorns was actually the headquarters of the Berni Inn chain and served cheap and enjoyable food, sirloin steaks, duck in orange sauce, schooners of sherry, that sort of thing, in a variety of restaurants replete with oak furniture and orange lampshades. And bars—there were any number of different bars in every corner of the building, as visiting Australian Mervyn Barrett quickly found,

"There were signs indicating the way to the Scotch Bar, the Mexican Bar, and god-knows how many others. For a while I suspected they only had one bar but lots of corridors and lots of signs, the name of the bar depending on one's direction of approach."

At some past time the hotel had been converted from a half-dozen huge mansions, all built to different plans and elevations, and in consequence there were stairs, doors, passages, floors, and rooms leading off at literally all angles. Fans were delighted with one corridor, between the main block and the "Gay Nineties" wing on the third floor, which had no ceiling—it was just a glorified catwalk over the rooftops, open to the stars. All weekend lost souls were wandering in search of their rooms, Ted Tubb being particularly incensed because he was in a sort of private Ivory Tower, far away from the rest of the con, with an untrustworthy lift as his only means of escape.

I wanted to get to the hotel early, so that I could set up a little display stand, constructed from collapsible Dexion tubing and lightweight panels salvaged from an unwanted BSA exhibition stand. My idea was to try to promote *Speculation* a bit more, attract new subscribers and maybe even sign up a few contributors, so I built the display in a corner of the book room, pinned some covers of previous issues to the front panel, and put out my subscription forms. It would be a good place to hang around and talk to people, I thought, even if I didn't sell a single copy. This time I was also thinking of producing a special convention issue, and was on the lookout for material.

Friday night started slowly, with introductions made in "The Brian Aldiss Show," although with no Harry Harrison this year, and with an unusual lack of room parties. I spent most of the evening in the front lounge meeting friends from previous years like Chris Priest, Jim Marshall, Dick Ellingsworth and his wife Diane (she of the lovely, long black hair, looking none the worst for having been "sacrificed" at Repetercon).

I finally met Gerry Webb and his girlfriend Anne Keylock, so nearly encountered on my abortive visit to London, back in 1963. Gerry was tall and slim, with glasses and an infectious grin, and was smartly dressed in blazer and cravat. He talked almost non-stop about his job in the space programme, though I didn't quite understand exactly what he did. It certainly involved frequent visits to Sweden to launch rockets, I gathered enviously, and I also envied Gerry his girlfriend, as did Rog and almost everyone else in the room. Anne was tall and platinum blonde, with a lot of make-up, bright pink lipstick and long black eyelashes, stiletto heels and a tight black skirt. At first, I was a bit frightened of her—she looked way out of my league—but she turned out to be friendly and a good sport.

The programme was stronger this year, with a good number of professionals present, including visiting writers Judith Merril and Tom Disch. Six of them were rounded up on Saturday morning for a panel discussion in which they fielded incriminating questions such as "What Hack Novels Have You Written?" Guest-of-Honour John Brunner led off, blithely ignoring the question completely and talking instead about the way he began writing. "I started telling stories at boarding school after lights out," he said. "By the time I left I had a very good idea of how to tell a story. I had no experience of the outside world but this didn't stop me writing. Science fiction is a good way of writing without showing your lack of experience."

Brian Aldiss endorsed these sentiments, though perhaps slightly ironically. "If you really have done nothing and know nothing, then certainly you should write science fiction. My first novel was actually written fairly directly from life, and was about bookselling. Since then I have presumably done less and know less, and have been writing SF ever since. Like John, I really began *my* career after lights out at boarding school. They did not allow talking, and the master on duty would listen at a grille. If he heard voices he would burst in and ask, 'Who is talking?' and I would put my hand up, to be dragged off and beaten. It was my first form of payment, my introduction to anal erotic literature."

It was an entertaining panel, and cunningly, I had persuaded Diane Ellingsworth to take down the entire proceedings in shorthand and transcribe it afterwards. *One* item in the bag for my convention issue, I thought smugly, and decided to go along to my display stand in the book-room for a while, to see if anyone was interested in *Speculation*.

That's when I had my big shock. In the opposite corner, my old adversary Graham Hall had set up shop on a table and he was completely surrounded with people. I went over and found he was selling a completely new fanzine, something I had never seen before, or even heard about. It was titled *Australian Science Fiction Review,* and I looked at it with incredulity.

Graham noticed my interest and smirked. "Nyah-nyah-di-nyah-nyah," he hooted. "This is better than *your* fanzine, Weston!" I flung him some money and took a copy away to study further. It was a special issue (number 7½) produced by the enterprising Australians for our convention, with a long article on J. G. Ballard and comments by people like John Carnell and Mike Moorcock. With a sick feeling I realised Graham was right, it *was* considerably better than *Speculation*. The editor was someone called John Bangsund in Melbourne, with a whole load of contributors I had never heard of, people like Lee Harding, who appeared to be a professional writer, George Turner, John Baxter, John Foyster, and many others. The magazine was nicely laid out, the criticism was penetrating and well written, and worst of all, while *ASFR* was indisputably a sercon fanzine, an indefinable spark of wit and personality permeated its pages in a way totally alien to a magazine like *Riverside Quarterly*, something I had only rarely achieved myself.

It baffled me! I thought I knew Australian fandom and there wasn't much of it, a few mediocre fanzines like *The Mentor* and *Etherline*, an occasional letter of comment, but now here was something that might as well have come from a parallel universe. A whole new fandom had suddenly popped up from nowhere, fully developed and more articulate than anything in either Britain or America, the most serious competition I had ever faced. And of all people, *ASFR*'s agent had to be the horrible Graham Hall!

I went away to do some serious thinking. My problem had always been to find contributors actually capable of writing good reviews and criticism. There weren't many of them. I still remembered a letter that Dave Hale sent to Charles Platt in early 1964, saying, "The trouble is that there is so little to say or argue about in science fiction that you may be forced to expand your activities to take up social problems and economics." This had seemed to summarise the general attitude in British fandom at the time, but I had never believed it; surely, it *was* possible to write entertainingly about science fiction, I thought, and *ASFR* had proven I was right.

Speculation had to bootstrap its way up from nothing at all, and after three and a half years it was finally starting to attract some good material. But it had been a hard battle! I had started with the Brum group, gone through existing British fan-writers like Archie Mercer, Terry Jeeves, and Alan Dodd, and then found new people like Chris Priest, Joe Patrizio, and Richard Gordon, leavened with comments from professionals like Mike Moorcock and Brian Aldiss. It wasn't enough; that's why I had pushed so hard into North America with people like Al Lewis and Buz Busby. All that trouble, I had just thought I was getting somewhere, and now this...*upstart* had arrived on the scene! I simply couldn't see how it had become so good, so quickly!

Later, Bruce Gillespie explained a few things:

"*ASFR* seemed to come fully-formed for me, too. Certainly, it was already a very sharp, informative and funny magazine with the first issue. But other fanzines laid the groundwork—John Foyster wrote material that was even more acerbic in his multi-named fanzines of the early sixties, but John Bangsund had the divine gift for layout and sympathetic, amused comedy, which Foyster only learned much later. John Baxter was producing much-praised fanzines in Sydney, and Lee Harding's *Canto* 1, from 1964, assembled for the first time the people who later became the *ASFR* team."

That's the ideal way to do it, of course, get some experience on small fanzines, refine your skills, get some other good writers around you and THEN go for it, rather than start off ignorant, with Big Aspirations and none of the where-withal to achieve them, as most of us usually do. So *ASFR* was that rare thing, a planned fanzine, a scientifically designed Construct. No wonder it was so bloody good! They were all a bit older than I was, too, four to six years, which probably helped.

However, something still bothered me. In a letter to Ethel's *Scottishe* John Bangsund wrote, "I read my first science fiction story in 1963." This struck me as being absolutely incredible! How could Bangsund produce something as good as *ASFR* when he had so much less experience of either science fiction or fanzine fandom than I had?

Bruce Gillespie, again:

"The truth is that John Bangsund never had much time for science fiction, and never read a lot of it. What drove him when *ASFR* began in July 1966 was his intense friendship with Lee Harding and John Foyster, both of whom had an encyclopaedic knowledge of SF, and the friendships he formed after *ASFR* became popular. What he had, of course, was enormous skill in layout and writing skills (I have no idea where he got these from) and an instinctive understanding of what fanzines were all about—communication between like-minded people. And a sort of flair for self-publicity, although John would never have seen it that way.

"He was a sales rep at the time, so in his interstate travels he placed copies of *ASFR* in all sorts of isolated newsagents and stalls in the various capital cities, each one of which seems to have been read by somebody who started a new SF club. So we had Alan Sandercock and Paul Anderson in Adelaide, John Brosnan in Perth, Peter Darling, and Gary Mason in Sydney, John Ryan in Brisbane and Michael O'Brian in Hobart—which led to the massive revival of Australian fandom during the *ASFR* days. At the same time, the *ASFR* team knew which authors to send copies to, so the letter column quickly became legendary.

"By contrast, Lee Harding by himself had only published *Canto* 1 in 1964 and was trying to establish himself as a published writer of fiction, while John Foyster had done a huge number of fanzines in the early sixties, but none had the impact of *ASFR*. It was a case of bad cop, good cop. Foyster stirred people into action with his ferocious reviews, and Bangsund made people feel good in his editorials, letter columns, and news sections. Foyster and Harding prob-ably did much of the physical work of duplicating, collating, and posting."

I went back to Graham Hall's table and bought an earlier issue, number seven, dated February 1967, and the more I studied it, the more I realised there was something a bit smelly, here. John Bangsund had been making a determined effort to send copies to Britain, as was obvious by letters from people like Graham Hall, Doreen Parker, Walt Willis, Ron Bennett, even new fans like Phil Muldowney in Plymouth. *ASFR* wasn't really that new at all, had already been published for nine months, and I started to feel I had been taken for a bit of a fool. Surely, Bangsund would have picked up my name and address while he was trawling so widely for support? Maybe he realised *Speculation* was his main competition, was "having no truck with the enemy," as it were, and had deliberately kept me off his mailing list? I felt a bit resentful; this wasn't the fannish way, fanzines usually cross-pollinate each other, always gaining from the exchange. I had automatically sent mine to every other editor and they had all traded with me. Why, Leland Sapiro had even made a point of sending his first *RQ* by express airmail!

The more I looked, the more annoyed I felt. That letter from Walt Willis in No. 7, for instance, was mostly about Brian Aldiss' review of *The Watch Below* in *Speculation,* not in *ASFR*. Walt had mixed up his fanzines, but Bangsund hadn't corrected him, had printed the Willis letter without acknowledging its source. Not very friendly, I thought. Maybe I was taking the whole thing a bit too seriously, but it felt like a sneak attack on my territory, an undeclared outbreak of war.[1]

It was all very discouraging and I went off to the bar to drown my sorrows. Fortunately, I bumped into Gerry and Anne along the way, who tried to lift my spirits. "Anne's just had a new car," Gerry said. "It's a Spitfire. Why don't you two go for a run in it?"

Half-an-hour later I felt a lot more cheerful, bowling along in bright sunshine in a gleaming white open-top sports-car, glamorous blonde by my side, as we shot across the new Severn Bridge and into Wales. The Spitfire wasn't an easy car to drive; very hard suspension and fierce clutch pedal, but it had a lot more "poke" than my wheezy old Ford Popular, and I enjoyed the experience immensely. We drove all the way to Chepstow, nearly fifty miles by the time we got back to the hotel, just in time for the screening of Ed Emshwiller's "experimental" half-hour film, *Relativity*.

Tony Walsh warned us that it was not for the squeamish, that it was "bloody, very bloody," and that those who didn't like that sort of thing had better leave. He was right; some of the early scenes showed the slaughtering and gutting of a pig, its intestines slipping out, and immediately afterwards cut to packets of sausages in a supermarket. Then there was a long sequence, much appreciated by the men in the audience, in which the camera caressed a spectacular, nude

---

[1] I *did* over-react, but *ASFR* was unbelievably good. I eventually established a trade arrangement with John Bangsund, but we never corresponded or became friends, the way I did with Dick Geis and Richard Bergeron. We were both too aware that we were hunting in the same territory!

female body, intimately and at length. Then—shock, horror—a mighty phallus thrust out of the screen, right at us! The film went on like this for another twenty minutes, leaving us in stunned silence.

Well, not quite; in some of the scenes a man wearing what looked like white long johns was seen shifting from one foot to another while humming a few bars of a catchy little tune, repeated over and over. For the rest of the weekend fans would lurch and hum as they walked through the lobby or stood at the bar, entrapped by the best mind-block since *The Demolished Man!*

What to make of it? I was baffled, but was fascinated to hear the film being explained at length by a newcomer, someone I didn't recognise. The name on his badge was Tony Sudbery, and I sidled over and introduced myself. He was a student at York, and yes, he had heard of *Speculation,* would be happy to write a review of the film. We went into the bar and I bought the drinks as Tony carried on with his complicated explanation. That's *two* in the bag, I thought.

We hurried back for John Brunner's Guest of Honour speech. I was curious, because to me he was something of an enigma; this was the second year I had seen him, immaculate in red velvet smoking jacket, moving among, but not actually quite *with* the fans. Somehow, he projected an invisible force field, protecting him from contamination, in a way quite different from other professionals like Brian Aldiss or Jim White. I had read quite a few of John Brunner's stories and had found them interesting enough, but hadn't heard him talk before.

His speech was hard work. Technically, it was faultless, as he read from a prepared text with an air of great panache and sophistication, pronouncing his words with care and precision. He dripped scorn upon the hapless villain of the piece, "Charlie Ignoramus," as Brunner called him, the editor of his current novel, who had made no less than 55 changes to the opening chapter alone. Then John went into all sorts of considerations about the nature of speculative fiction, which were probably accurate enough but I found myself nodding off. I preferred to hear Ted Tubb or Harry Harrison telling stories, as they had done in previous years. It was all too mechanical, I thought, Brunner lacked *spontaneity*.

Still, I thought, there was a written speech up there on the table, and I bet if I creep a bit, he'll let me publish it in *Speculation. Three* items secured!

That evening we had to vacate the main hall, because the hotel had refused to cancel their regular Saturday-evening dinner dance. This meant there was no Fancy Dress parade, and instead Tony Walsh moved everyone to a basement under the main hall for a cider-&-sherry party. With the muffled noise of the band and the shuffling of feet above our heads, it was a disconsolate affair and soon people started to drift away to room parties, although they were particularly difficult to find in the maze of The Hawthorns.

Next morning the BSFA AGM lurched through its usual business, with a Recovery Plan in place under the retained triumvirate of Ken Slater, Dave Barber and Doreen Parker, but who would do *Vector?* Darroll reported, "nobody wanted to be Publications Officer, so being the 'heroic thickhead' that Ken Cheslin later called me, I volunteered to do the job for six months." After that came the bidding session, and with no competition the 1968 Eastercon went to the Manchester Delta group, with a provisional 1969 bid for Cambridge.

In the afternoon Darroll and I were hauled onto the Fanzine Editor's panel, along with Mike Ashley, Graham Charnock, Harry Bell, Mary Reed, and with Beryl Mercer moderating. Seven people on a panel are at least two too many, so we puttered around until someone asked our position on "swear-words," about the most boring subject possible. Beryl would have done better to brush it aside, but instead she made us all explain our position on obscenities, painstakingly plodding from one to another, until it was my turn.

Trying desperately to make it even halfway interesting, I started to tell about the way I had upset Harry Harrison by changing his letter in *Zenith* 12 to remove a four-letter word I thought was unnecessary. It was a difficult choice, I said, because I wanted to respect Harry's wording but I didn't swear myself in my fanzine and didn't see why I should have to print something I was unhappy about, especially since it didn't add anything to the argument. Suddenly I was interrupted.

"SHIT! SHIT! SHIT!" bellowed Graham Hall from the back of the room. "What's the matter with you, Weston? The word is SHIT! SHIT! SHIT!"

We were aghast. People looked around in amazement. Tony Walsh strode down the centre aisle, face grim, and told Graham to leave. He shouted some more choice Anglo-Saxon words over his shoulder as he was escorted from the room. That rather put paid to the fanzine panel, which fizzled out soon afterwards.

The next item was much more interesting, as Mike Moorcock came on to deliver a speech titled "The New Fiction." Like John Brunner, he had typed it neatly in advance, but there the resemblance stopped. Halfway through he threw up his hands with the despairing cry, "I've missed out a page," but by then no one would have noticed the omission, because by then no one knew what he was talking about. As Darroll commented, "Mike appeared to be roaring drunk, and indeed took numerous drinks from the bottle at his side, but I suspect he was acting the part to a considerable extent."

After the first few minutes of delivering what was essentially a serious and critical paper, Mike began to emulate that scene from Amis' *Lucky Jim* in which the protagonist gets drunker and drunker. The audience was probably far better entertained by this hamming than by a formal and reasoned talk about science fiction. Perhaps Mike was as far gone as he seemed—or perhaps he preferred to have a bit of fun! Certainly, he became remarkably lucid for the questions about the future of *New World* that followed. And I had my eye on that typed speech, my fourth bag of the weekend, although unfortunately Diane wasn't around to record the subsequent discussions.

That was almost it, and Sunday evening went in a blur with a St Fantony ceremony, followed by the traditional room-party with traditional Shorrock home-brewed punch ladled from a plastic bucket. My last memory of Bristol is staggering back with Gerry Webb to his room at 5.30 on Monday morning for a final drink, long after Anne had retired. We crashed in and woke her up, and while Gerry looked for the bottle, I used a convenient ashtray by the bed to dispose of the remains of a small cigar that had long since expired. "Hey, Gerry," I mumbled, "this ashtray has little black caterpillars in it."

"Thank you very much," snapped Anne, reaching out to snatch the ashtray away, "those are my eyelashes."

Happily took turns to hurl the books
over the dark rooftops

Then we saw a pile of cruddy British paperbacks that Gerry had bought by mistake at the auction, rubbish all of them. We managed to get his third-floor window open, and happily took turns to hurl the books over the dark rooftops, one by one. "*I hate science fiction,*" I remember saying with the deepest conviction at the time, but I didn't mean it, honest I didn't!

It had been an excellent convention, Rog and I thought, as we drove back to Birmingham. We now both felt completely at home in fandom, and were all the more surprised to find afterwards that Ethel Lindsay didn't see it the same way. "I have to admit that at this year's convention I was conscious of not being fully integrated with the whole," she said in *Scottishe* 44. "We have got bigger, of course, but there is no use sighing after the good old days of Kettering when the numbers were just right. Anyway, I don't think the increase in numbers alone accounted for the feeling I sometimes had of being among strangers. In the past I have always been able to talk to fans from sixteen to sixty. That, I felt, no longer held good."

Ethel's remarks were sparked off by finding a quote card that read, "NO! ETHEL MIGHT OBJECT!" which worried her because she didn't know who produced it, whether it was meant seriously or as a joke, if it had a kind or unkind meaning. "Up until this year I *would* have known," she said. "I wonder—did British fandom change, or did I?"

This prompted renewed talk in *Scottishe* about the state of British fandom. Chris Priest said, "I mentioned this 1963–64 thing because I feel quite genuinely that at this time a rift developed in fandom…whether I am aware of this rift because I was one of the newcomers, or whether there is another reason, I don't know. In 1965, I was talking about a 'new' New Wave, then last year there was a 'new,' new, New Wave, and so it goes on. Tell me, did it all start in 1964? Or does the tide constantly come in?" While Darroll Pardoe said quite simply, "the trouble with British fandom today is that the New Wave ever existed. Too many people came in all at once and they identified with themselves as a group, rather than with fandom generally."

Buck Coulson contributed a thoughtful letter in which he probably answered Ethel's lament as well as anyone could. He said, "An individual's position in fandom changes. Stick around long enough and you're considered a BNF, whether you've ever really done anything outstanding or not. Then I look around for people who *I* consider BNFs and suddenly realise they're out of fandom or have retired to FAPA. You're a British BNF, now, Ethel, and the younger fans approach you with awe—or don't approach you at all in case you might not speak to them if they did."

This was my first introduction to the "Revolving Door" theory of fandom, the idea that people go out as fast as others are entering, along with the implication that a fannish generation is about five years. However, I was much more preoccupied with the new competition from *ASFR,* which Ethel praised highly, giving it her vote for the 1967 Hugo: "the subject of science fiction is treated with real seriousness; there is no doubt that the main interest is SF. Yet it is always a *fannish* 'zine—the twinkle of good humour is never lacking. Science fiction is treated as a subject worth study, but is not given an over-rated value."

All this meant I would have to try even harder, make a big effort with *Speculation.* Thank goodness I had signed up all that material so that I could get out my special convention issue without delay. Only, it didn't work out like that.

Life had suddenly become very hectic. At BSA, I was producing a quarterly house-journal (printed by letterpress!), arranging conferences up and down the country, from London to Glasgow, as well as organising a stand at the London Motor Show. In the Young Conservatives, Rog and I had both succeeded to committee posts, and I was putting out their monthly magazine. Six of us had a weekend in a caravan at Weymouth, and then we took a holiday flat in Cornwall for a week during the gorgeous weather of late July. There just wasn't any time to publish a fanzine!

Rog started a romance with Arline, one of the girls from the YCs, and disappeared completely from sight. I struggled to keep up with fandom, did two more "Malcolm Edwards" columns in April and July for *Vector,* and another column for Darroll's *Spinge* in June. The latter was an experimental, stream-of-consciousness affair in which I described the "slices of my life, stratified and insulated, facets of interests and experience and personality, each with their minor triumphs and tragedies."

There was no organised fandom in Birmingham now, but I saw a lot of Bob Rickard, usually on Sunday mornings when I drove over to his house and we read the *Sunday Times* together. We talked about science fiction and I gave him my unwanted fanzines. He did a cover for the YC magazine, started to work on a cover for my Briscon issue of *Speculation,* and even typed the stencils of John Brunner's speech. I was more and more impressed with Bob, writing in my editorial, "He is the man who will one day revive the Birmingham Science Fiction Group."

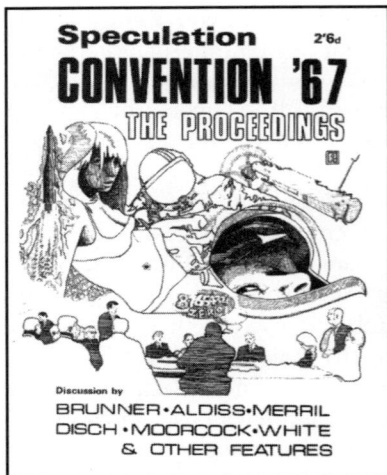

Speculation 2'6d

CONVENTION '67
THE PROCEEDINGS

Discussion by
BRUNNER·ALDISS·MERRIL
DISCH·MOORCOCK·WHITE
& OTHER FEATURES

In August, I bought a little red sports car, an MG Midget, and soon afterwards started to see Eileen, who actually worked in the same office as Rog Peyton, and who had come along to the Young Conservatives at his suggestion. Suddenly life became even busier, and it is a minor miracle that *Speculation* 16 ever appeared at all. But it finally did, in October, as I attacked it in a "sudden, savage desire to get the thing off my back" and produced 40 pages devoted almost entirely to the convention, shorn of other features but with superb, professional-standard cover artwork by Bob Rickard.

"As is usual with the successes of my life," recalled Bob, "I had no idea what I was doing and was searching for some kind of graphic style. I had experimented with merging disparate drawings and images by overlapping their shadows. I would cut out likely photographs of machinery, figures or portraits and copy them using the new-fangled photocopiers, and re-copy a number of times until the mid-tones were eliminated, leaving stark black and white shapes. Some of these I traced and re-drew, then made collages of them. Many of the Punk Generation fanzines used similar cut-&-paste techniques to more radical effect, but I like to think I beat them to it."

The cover layout was strongly influenced by my involvement with engineering trade journals, with a splash heading, "CONVENTION '67—The Proceedings." Inside, there were four major items plus my own 5-page report, titled "The Speculator at the convention," in which I tried to emulate the light touch of John Bangsund, with only indifferent success. By this time, of course, *ASFR* rather than *Speculation* had been nominated for a Hugo at the New York Worldcon (though it didn't win, the honour going instead to *Niekas,* a large, diffuse genzine).

"Never has so much time gone into an editorial," I wrote. "Originally, those three pages didn't take very long to write, back in early May, although it was a lot of trouble to bring them up to date in July. And the August re-stencilling took even more time, only to be scrapped in September. Three editorials written without seeing print! And what was intended as a hot-from-the-press Special Report on the Easter convention has become instead a peculiarly dated post mortem."

By then Bob Rickard had commenced the second year of his course at the Birmingham School of Art & Design, which had moved to new premises on the campus of Aston University, sharing their facilities, including the Students' Union. When I next called him I was amazed to hear that he had already started a science fiction group at the university, which had held several well-attended meetings. The next one would be a special event with a Big Name guest, and Bob invited me along. Who was the speaker? None other than John Brunner.

New Blood
Chapter 13

John Brunner didn't even lift his eyes as I slipped in, a little late, because traffic had been heavy and the meeting in the Union building had started at six o'clock. I took a seat at the side, waved to Bob and looked around at the fifteen or twenty students in the room, mostly male with a few girls here and there. So this was the new Aston group; I wondered what they were making of John Brunner?

His talk sounded familiar, not so much because of what he was saying but because of his manner, so very formal and correct, pre-supposing a degree of knowledge of science fiction in his audience which few of them would be likely to have. He should have kept it simple for a little group like this, I thought; he would have done better to just sit on the edge of the table and talk about his ideas, the way he wrote his books, that sort of thing. Then John finished his talk and started to answer questions, and I jotted down a few notes on a pad, thinking I might be able to do something with his remarks in a future issue.

Eventually the meeting ended, John Brunner departed, and a man wearing a blue blazer shepherded us out of the room. He was broad-shouldered, square-jawed, with blond hair and a stern expression, a tough-looking character who looked as if he wouldn't stand any nonsense from students. His name seemed to be "Bernard" and I gathered he was something to do with the university.

Bob led the way to the bar, which looked a bit grubby, with grey-painted walls, bits of paper everywhere and scruffy-looking students sitting around with their feet on the furniture. I bought the drinks and met some of the group members. One of the girls had long hair and glasses and wore a brown, corduroy overcoat; she was Pauline E. Dungate, who eventually confessed she had thought I was John Brunner's secretary. I talked to several of the men— Robert Hepworth, Alan Denham, Alan Donnelly, Tim Stannard (who was studying law), and Ray Bradbury—that's a fine, science fictional name, I told him—who was a trainee silversmith.

"Bernard" looked at me suspiciously, but in the end joined us and I discovered his name was actually Vernon Brown, he was a technician at the university, and he was an SF enthusiast. After we had been talking for a little while, he mentioned that he had once been in contact with a science fiction group in Birmingham. "When was that?" I asked. Vernon thought for a moment and said that he had found a little slip in a paperback, around 1964, and he had received a letter from "a chappie in Quinton, can't remember his name." "Was it Rog Peyton?" I suggested helpfully. Vernon agreed that it was indeed, but that Rog had said the group met in someone's front room and played games all night, and he hadn't liked the sound of that, so had never replied. I shook my head sadly. "I think you made the wrong decision, there, Vernon," I said.

Eventually, the others went and Bob Rickard and I found a quiet corner. I congratulated him on getting the group together, and asked him how he had persuaded John Brunner to appear. Bob explained that the Union encouraged student groups to invite speakers, made the room available free of charge, and even covered speakers' expenses. "Someone came up with Brunner's address," he said, "who was then living in the exotically-named London district of Frognal. We were hugely surprised when he wrote back, agreeing to come along. A few of us met him at New Street station, absolutely awed to be in the living presence of a famous person who made a living writing SF, so conversation was sparse and awkward on the way to the Aston campus."

Bob said he was a bit disappointed that the group was not working out in quite the way he had intended. With his strong interest in the works of Charles Fort, he had wanted to form more of a speculative society, but everyone just wanted to talk about science fiction! I sympathised, insincerely, and started to discuss *Speculation,* because I wanted to get another issue out quickly. I had been holding some items for nearly six months already, including Buz Busby's "Plough" column on *The Moon Is a Harsh Mistress.* Would Bob do a cover to illustrate it? He agreed, and then I had a sudden brainwave; since he was at Aston University, surely he could get electro-stencils cut for me at the special students' rate? Great! Just like old times, I thought, because for the last three years I had been paying an extortionate amount, with all the risk and inconvenience of having to send my artwork away in the post.

I went home feeling enthusiastic about this new group in the city and determined to make up for lost time; *ASFR*, watch out! Unfortunately, once again real life had other ideas. I was seeing Eileen most nights of the week, which cut down on my time severely, and my job was busier than ever. Not that I was the only one to be forced away from fanac; Darroll Pardoe produced just one issue of *Vector* before having to quit, to be replaced as editor by my friend Tony Sudbery. Darroll also had to abandon his revived *Les Spinge,* with a final blast at the "introverted, involuted state of British fandom," before he disappeared to Ohio on a two-year research grant.

On the "Revolving Door" principle, however, another fanzine immediately appeared from the United States, with the resurrection of Dick Geis' *Psychotic.* Its strong editorial presence and unique "alter-ego" dialogue had made it one of the most charismatic of the 'zines from the early sixties, and this new incarnation contained some surprisingly perceptive comments about the SF field. The lights of fandom continued to come on again, and competition was hotting up!

Fortunately, although *Speculation* 17 (February 1968) was late, the issue was a good one, and this time I had some help in putting it together. Bob Rickard had invited the Aston Group to a collating-party and most of them came along, out of curiosity if nothing else. So, with my printed pages packed into three large suitcases, I borrowed the wheezy BSA Cortina again, and drove straight from work to Aston University, where Vernon opened up the biology laboratory. Its long, wide benches were absolutely ideal for collating, and in no time they were covered in pages in a veritable fanzine production line.

Although it needed some careful management. Each person had five or six stacks of pages, which they put together into sub-sets, and then brought to the end bench for final assembly and stapling. The problem was that they all worked at different speeds, one moving like lightning and getting too far ahead, others hopelessly slow and fumbling, falling far behind. We kept hitting bottlenecks, which necessitated swapping people around in order to catch up. Even so, the issue was finished in less than two hours, fully collated and stapled, a job that would have taken me weeks, unaided. I gave each of them a copy and announced we were going to the pub across the road, where the drinks would definitely be on me.

Vernon had to check the gas taps

I packed my case, Bob Rickard donned his "Rupert Bear" chequered scarf, but the super-conscientious Vernon decided he couldn't leave without making a quick safety check. "Fair enough," we thought, and waited while he inspected the gas- and water-taps, of which there were many, to make sure that none of the "students" (he said the word darkly, making it an insult) had interfered with them. Then, as everyone piled into the corridor, Vernon paused again, torn between the demands of duty and pleasure, and went back inside his beloved laboratory to check the taps just one more time. "We'll see you down there," we shouted.

Bob's cover artwork was superb, with one of his dramatic collage-type illustrations for Buz Busby's "Plough" column, and under his supervision the cover graphics took their final format, with boxed illustration and logo run at full width across the page. Solid reviews had come in from Joe Patrizio, Graham Charnock, and Brian Stableford, the latter two appearing for the first time. At last, I was starting to find those new writers I needed, who had seemed so plentiful in Australian fandom. Bob, too, proved no slouch at criticism, contributing "All Kindsa Vomity Stuff" in which

Speculation - 17

VOL.2 NO.5   FEBRUARY 1968

THE PLOUGH IS A HARSH MISTRESS / F.M. 'BUZ' BUSBY

he took a hard look at Harlan Ellison's new collection, *I Have No Mouth and I Must Scream*. The issue was finished off by "The Speculator" being hopeful about "The SF Scene—1968," a good "Melting Pot" of letters, and a new feature titled simply "Opinion." This presented snappy, one-paragraph opinions on authors and stories, culled from letters and from other fanzines as a shameless device to plant comment-hooks and encourage reader-participation.

Greg Pickersgill, then living remote from any fans, remembers the issue. He had joined the BSFA in early 1967, and subscribed to *Speculation* a little later. He said, "I recall issue seventeen with Busby's piece on Heinlein, 'The Plough Is a Harsh Mistress' splashed on the cover, and wondered why it was called that. Bloody hell, it all seemed to sixteen-year-old me to be so grown-up and Serious and Important. And, amazingly, it was!"

An encouraging late letter came in from Sam Moskowitz. "I have just finished issue fifteen," he said, "which in many respects is a complete change-of-pace. It is much lighter, less critical, and almost fannish in tone. This is not a criticism, merely an observation, for I found the issue eminently readable and well-balanced." Good, I thought, maybe I'm on the right track after all. And maybe I could push it along a bit further at the 1968 Eastercon, which this year was going to be organised by the Manchester group and held in Blackpool.

Except that Thirdmancon didn't happen quite as advertised because only a few months before Easter the Delta group lost their hotel, and at short notice relocated everything to the little spa town of Buxton, out on the Derbyshire moors. Their new hotel, the St Ann's, was a crumbling Georgian relic, and it promptly slid into bankruptcy a week or two before the convention.[1]

Eileen hadn't really met any science fiction fans and was a bit wary, but I persuaded her to come along, explaining how she would enjoy meeting all the interesting and amusing people who would be there. I was probably dwelling over-much on fond memories of Bristol, which had been a very civilised affair, because as it turned out Thirdmancon was not exactly the best introduction to convention-going. We were conscious of strange people everywhere, including one man dressed in black who spent the entire weekend lurking behind the floor-length draperies in the con-hall. Perhaps because of the mixed interests of the Manchester group the convention attracted a record attendance, but a good proportion of them must have been horror, supernatural, and film fans who went around in costume most of the time.

Fortunately we had booked late, hadn't been able to get into the St Ann's, and stayed instead at a modest but clean hotel a few hundred yards away, venturing across to the convention for major programme events such as Ken Bulmer's GoH talk on the Saturday afternoon. This took place in the main hall, a long narrow room that had a huge astronomical painting by Eddie Jones at one end, a magnificent backdrop featuring a red giant star against the blackness of interstellar space.

Ken Bulmer appeared early, a wiry little man with hair down to his shoulders at the back and a great drooping moustache. He radiated nervous energy and began his speech at a furious pace, clutching a huge pile of papers, and pausing only to *ad-lib* at Ted Tubb's expense. "I've divided my talk into a number of sections," he told us, "each with a centre, some soft and some hard." In one of his "hard centres," he said, "The hatred of science is the single dominant thread in modern speculative fiction." Another nugget was, "a writer has to learn to write before he can forget about writing." It was Ken's fightback against the excesses of modernism. However, in one throwaway line to me afterwards he gave his most accurate prediction of times to come. "Fan-

---

[1] The convention's clever name was probably the best thing about it. Something about Manchester seems always to guarantee disaster, generation after fannish generation, from Supermancon in 1954, through Buxton in 1968 to the 1972 attempt, which also lost its hotel. The curse continued to its 1976 culmination in the howling wilderness of Owens Park (run by a completely different set of people). This dread record ensured that no group dared to organise a convention there for over twenty years, and gave rise to the legend of the Manchester Dead Zone.

tasy," he confided, "that's the coming thing. They'll all want fantasy, not science fiction."

He went on for over an hour and our attention may have wandered slightly, but fortunately, we were sitting behind a veritable apparition, a young man in pink lounging pyjamas with what looked like a tasselled Turkish fez perched on top of his long, flowing blonde hair. Eileen studied him with fascinated interest, never having seen anything like it before. It was the first appearance of Bristol fan Peter Roberts, soon to become a fannish icon for his bizarre fashion-sense.

"I travelled up in Archie Mercer's car with the other BaD people," said Peter. "For some in my age-group this was the time of bells, beads and caftans; my vaguely hippy outfit was a Yugoslav pillbox-&-tassel hat (a gift from a holiday), and a sort of red, Chinese-dragon-print cotton top which was indeed a pyjama top (the accompanying bottoms, which I didn't wear, were black, giving a vaguely Mandarin look). I don't recall what trousers I wore, but probably flairs and maybe even 'loons.' To be fair, I was a teenager and it was 1968…"

Actually, it must have taken a lot of courage to appear in this get-up in the middle of the afternoon. Most of us just wore our normal working clothes at a convention—that is, sports-jackets, suits, or blazers, complete with collar and tie—what else? Although some youngsters had turned up dressed a bit more casually, some even wearing jeans. I didn't know them and they tended to keep to themselves, but fellow novice Bob Rickard ran round furiously with the new fans and we hardly saw him all weekend until we finally had to *drag* him out of the hotel, late on Monday morning. He'd had a wonderful time, met all sorts of interesting people, he assured us, as we drove back in the worn-out company Cortina I had borrowed for the occasion, my MG sports car being in dock for emergency repairs. One of them was Greg Pickersgill attending his first convention. We met briefly at Buxton, but neither of us took much notice of the other.

Greg said, "I distinctly remember talking to you for a while in a corridor. I also remember being passed on the stairs by Harry Bell. It was that kind of first-con experience. All I can think of is how much OLDER everyone seemed than me, and how essentially unapproachable they were, even the people whose names I knew from fanzines. (We're talking about people maybe five years older than me, but that's a long time when you're sixteen, and a particularly naïve, socially, sixteen as I was.) I was genuinely in awe of people like, for God's sake, Chas Legg, because he was a STUDENT—we're at the time of the student uprisings and high politicisation here, remember, when people like me looked on students as some sort of advance elite front-fighters for the new age. Remember what I said earlier about 'naïve'?"

I told Bob about my old nemesis and sparring-partner Charles Platt, who had made a fleeting visit to the con, along with Michael Moorcock and Tom

Disch. I had first noticed him in the book-room, peddling back issues of *New Worlds* in a shaggy overcoat too big for him, with a great growth of gingery whiskers and bare feet. Curious, I asked why he wasn't wearing shoes, on what was after all a pretty cold Easter weekend, but he just looked at me blankly. I think he was making some sort of Statement.

Later that evening Eileen and I went for dinner in the nearby Chinese restaurant, and I exclaimed in amusement at a strange item on the menu. "Fishmaw soup," I said. "I wonder what that is!" Suddenly I became aware of a high-pitched sniggering noise. "Heh, heh, heh, Weston doesn't know what fishmaw soup is," tittered a familiar voice. I looked around and saw it was Charles Platt, still bare-foot, at the next table with Tom Disch, who had the good grace to look slightly embarrassed. I should have smiled sweetly and asked Charles to explain, which would almost certainly have put him on the spot. Instead, I gave him a dirty look. "Who is that rude person?" asked Eileen. "No one to bother about," I told her, "just someone I used to know."

On Sunday we stayed for the business meeting before taking a drive into the surrounding moors, to have lunch at a strange little pub, high up on the crest of a bare hill, miles from anywhere, but nonetheless absolutely full of people. Before we left we saw my friend Tony Sudbery step down from the editorship of *Vector*, to be replaced by Michael Kenward, who soon afterwards went on to become editor of *New Scientist*, a somewhat larger editorial role. The putative Cambridge bid for 1969 had disappeared without trace, and Ted Tubb had formed an emergency scratch committee with various other London worthies such as John Brunner, Gerry Webb, Anne Keylock, and Daphne Sewell. They didn't have a hotel yet, but promised more news as things progressed.

After Buxton, Bob was super-keen and so was I, and with the help of the Aston Group we managed to finish *Speculation* 18 in record time, so that it appeared in May, only one month after the convention. It was an excellent issue, with another surreal cover from the mysterious Italian artist Riccardo Leveghi, once again sent to me as a folded Ozalid print requiring photographic reduction (by BSA). The BSA Press printed it as a wrap-around cover, with stencils typed on the BSA machine, and duplicated on a BSA Gestetner on Saturday mornings. How fortunate I worked for such a useful company!

The issue featured an abridged version of Ken Bulmer's speech (just the "hard centres"), set off by a splendid illustration from Ivor Latto, along with the usual departments and another innovation, "The Critical Front," a heading devised to pull together the book reviews into what I called "the battleground, the front line of *Speculation.*" Newcomers this time were David Redd, a young Welshman who was already selling stories to *F&SF,* and Michael Harrison, a London writer who had just made his first sale to *New Writings in SF.*

They appeared alongside Chris Priest, Brian Stableford, Bob Parkinson (an early 'sixties fan, making a welcome reappearance), and Peter White, returning to fandom after a 3-year absence during

THIRDMANCON 1968
Guest of Honour Speech
by KENNETH BULMER

which time he had become a fully-qualified airline pilot, flying Boeing 707s from Shannon Airport.. His letters invariably came on Irish-green "Shannon Inn" notepaper, and I commented, "Talk about 'sense of wonder'; to me, SF can hardly compare with the miracle of heaving that huge chunk of metal into the stratosphere." (At the time, I had yet to make my first flight.) Finally, and amazingly, I had managed to achieve a sort of accommodation with Graham Hall, who contributed a long review to the issue. He certainly could write well, even though we still couldn't stand the sight of each other!

The "Melting Pot" was full to overflowing, with letters from professionals like Larry Niven, Brian Aldiss and John Brunner, but the most interesting came from two of my American fan-correspondents. First, Rick Norwood, of Riverside, California, commented on my special convention number:

"The outstanding issue at Bristol seems to have been that of the New vs. Old, with a choosing-up of sides that goes something like this. For New Wave we have experimental writing, human problems, soft science, and subjective viewpoint, as opposed to technical problems, hard science, and objective viewpoint for the Old School. The convention seems to have been a rally for the New Wave, with very little said for the opposing point of view. The one point in the *Speculation* picture of the con where it looked as if there would be a real confrontation, the process was bogged down in definition. This was where James White brought up the subject of hard science versus soft, and Judith Merril waved-away the issue, 'it is very easy to research science.' Apparently, she has never felt the need to go beyond Freshman Physics in her research. In fact it is very hard indeed even for a technically-trained writer to keep up with modern discoveries—Judith Merril's casual dismissal of the problem simply shows her lack of interest in the subject."

Willem Van Den Broek, of Ann Arbor, addressed himself to a subject dear to my heart, by commenting upon the overall quality of the magazine and the direction in which it should go. "The biggest problem, as I see it, is that most of your reviewers still fail to make themselves entertaining. Although I don't doubt they are recording their reactions accurately, it takes a *lively* reaction to be interesting. People like Algis Budrys or Damon Knight will always have a stimulating reaction to any book, no matter how awful, because they're interesting writers. Since *Riverside Quarterly* seems to have taken up most of the 'serious criticism' category, it looks as if the area you are trying to carve out is that of 'interesting comment by interesting reviewers,' the sort of thing you get here in a magazine like *Newsweek*. Things are improving with *Speculation* and I usually find myself more motivated towards science fiction after an issue than when I first pick it up."

His remarks paralleled my own thinking about *Speculation*. I was trying to act as a commentator on the current SF scene, exploring divisions caused by the "new wave" controversy, looking at new books and new authors, and generally providing an on-going discussion forum. The difference between this and earlier attempts like *Inside* and its successor, *RQ,* (and even the prestigious *SF Horizons*) was that they were essentially sterile set-pieces, taking frozen snap-shots of the field rather than considering it in all its fast-changing complexity. That's why I had been so upset at first sight of *ASFR:* it had gone for exactly the same niche, and now it wasn't the only one, either! Because the lights of fandom were now blazing brightly, with competition coming not only from *Psychotic* and Bill Donaho's *Habakkuk,* but also from the mighty *Warhoon,* which had awoken from its slumber. Editor Richard Bergeron sent me his new number 23, and it was so impressive it made my teeth ache!

The summer fled past, while I struggled with another issue. The very success of the May number had caused letters to pour in, while my projected lead article was growing steadily longer. This was Richard Gordon's study of Brian Aldiss, which was going through draft after draft as Richard corresponded with Brian and kept adding further thoughts. Meanwhile, Bob Rickard left the College in July and started to look for a position in Industrial Design, while Eileen and I decided to get engaged and started saving hard to get married the following spring. This was *serious,* and I started to raise some money by selling various items. I sold my brass telescope to Mike "Beard," and my cherished American *Galaxy* magazines to Greg Pickersgill, who bought a large part of the set, from 1950–56, for £15.00. He complained bitterly afterwards that I had overcharged him, while I regretted it almost immediately and offered to give him his money back!

The 1968 Worldcon took place in Oakland, and once again, *ASFR* rather than *Speculation* was nominated for the Hugo. The prize went to another special-interest group, however, and was taken by *Amra,* the magazine for fans of heroic fantasy. "One day we'll get there," I thought, and rang Vernon to arrange a collating session. I was finally ready to go with number nineteen.

The Aston Group had become sufficiently established to survive without the guiding hand of Bob Rickard, but he came along to the first meeting of the new academic year, at which we put together the September issue. It was a massive 64 pages, and newcomers must have been totally bewildered by the entire experience! Bob was now shown as "assistant editor," and had produced the cover, another of his collages, printed in red and illustrating Richard Gordon's article on Brian Aldiss. This dominated the issue, along with a "Plough" column and scads of reviews. The "Melting Pot" was awash with luminaries like Philip Jose Farmer, Piers Anthony, and David Masson, and the first appearance of my local subscriber, David Pringle. There was also an incredible WAHF column that listed Terry Carr, Brian Aldiss, Sam Moskowitz, Ken Bulmer, L. Sprague de Camp, John Foyster and Robert Bloch, among a grand total of forty-seven other letters received. We seemed to have struck a vein of pure gold, the trouble was that we just couldn't mine it fast enough!

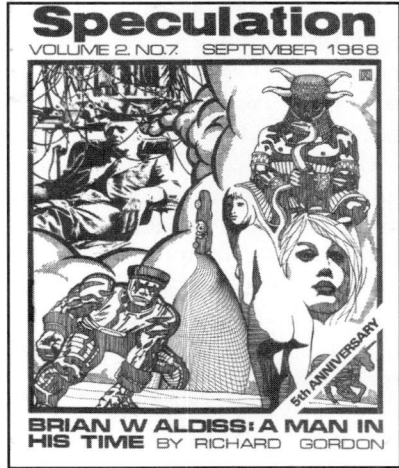

Interestingly, the issue contained reports on two of the first academic conferences about science fiction. American fan Tim Hildebrandt described The Secondary Universe, organised by the University of Wisconsin, while I commented upon a similar event held by the Brighton Festival of the Arts, which appeared to have been totally dominated by the New Wave. This was where Tom Disch made his famous remark about "the old-timers are like corpses wired for sound," and Michael Moorcock said that writers and editors of the old school were "pig-idiot illiterates." The only "Old Guard" writers present were Ted Tubb and Ken Bulmer, who went down for the day at their own expense, not having been invited as delegates.

This was also my "Fifth Anniversary Issue." "Much to my surprise," I said, "we made it, five years after the very first issue of *Zenith,* the little magazine which became the slightly-pretentious *Speculation* you hold in your hands today." Reviewing our progress, I continued, "We were the first to mention the New Wave vs. Old Guard argument, the first, I think, to begin talking seriously about the changing nature of SF." I ended by saying that "Michael Moorcock has figured pretty prominently in our first five years, and to begin our second half-decade we asked Mike if he would contribute a column. In this issue we are pleased to publish his first instalment, the inside—and re-markable—story behind *New Worlds.*"

"Remarkable" was an understatement. I must have caught Mike at just the right time, for when I asked him, he sent a 3000-word manuscript by return, received after almost everything else was already printed. It was a fascinating account of Mike's journey from 17-year-old editor of *Tarzan Adventures* to publisher of *New Worlds,* and of the way he was keeping the magazine going while being "faced with writs and bills that now appear to be delivered in bundles at regular intervals during the day." It was simply too good to hold over, so I hastily bolted on his column to the back of the issue, pushing the page-count even higher, and it saw print just six days after receipt.

David Pringle's LoC prompted me to get in touch and suggest a meeting. He lived on the other side of the city from Bob and myself (or rather, we each lived at the apexes of an equilateral triangle, all remote from each other), so I suggested we should rendezvous in a city-centre pub, and in November the three of us met in the basement of the Temple Bar. We seemed to get on well; David was seven years younger than me, with a slightly gloomy air that concealed a genuine enthusiasm for science fiction. I thought he was remarkably well read and perceptive, and suggested he might like to try his hand at reviewing for *Speculation.* It was great fun to be able to talk SF face-to-face, and I vaguely wondered if we could ever get a local group going again.

The anniversary issue brought another deluge of letters. The only thing now holding back *Speculation* was my inability to publish more often, and I had a bright idea to solve this problem. Bob and I would edit alternate issues, keeping them down to only 30 pages, in this way greatly increasing their frequency. That decided, I gave Bob my files for the November issue and started work on the January number. This was the point at which everything went horribly wrong, so much so that *Speculation* 20 became legendary as the "Special Disaster Issue." In a retrospective, I wrote,

"While this sort of thing is more-or-less the Fanzine-Editor's Burden, I'd like to purge my soul by telling you about some of the difficulties which may have resulted in the odd unreadable line or two in the last issue. Bob Rickard and I decided to embark upon a Great Experiment by sharing the editorship. The trouble was that while looking for a proper job in Industrial Design, Bob was working night-shifts at a sweated-labour factory making plastic gnomes or something of the sort, with the result that he had just about enough energy to stagger home and sleep all day, never mind cutting stencils. So things were bound to happen slowly, and just when a big effort was called for on the stencilling front, Bob came down with an attack of some deadly disease. Offering my condolences and taking back the load I had so joyfully shared out only a month or so before, I glumly surveyed our office typewriter, which was broken, and promptly contracted 'flu myself on the day it was repaired.

"The story could go on for a long time, but some further highlights concern the stencils Bob had already done, which wouldn't print properly since his portable typewriter hadn't cut them deep enough. I struggled to re-cut these at work by staying late in the evenings, and managed to print half the issue without incident on the next weekend, only to find on the following Saturday that the Gestetner wasn't working (it turned out that a junior girl had 'pushed the thing over' because it got ink on her!). We survived the University's bungling with our electro-stencils, and I arranged another printing session the following week. However, I had bought cheap and very nasty Swallow-brand ink, and on getting home I found this had soaked completely through every page, ruining eight sets of 350 copies.[2]

"Since by then Christmas was upon us, we pushed the whole mess into a dark corner and forgot any idealistic deadlines. After that it was pure anticlimax and largely Bob's show, with an epic afternoon in the college print room using purloined paper and ink, followed by a bitter little collating session in the Chemistry Lab. during which Bob stapled his thumb and shed copious amounts of blood over the pages. And Michael Moorcock thinks *he* has troubles!"

Bob recalls, "The Union had all this equipment just lying there, unused for most of the time, and so we moved in furtively; no staff knew, and we lived in dread of being discovered at any moment by the caretaker. All I can remember of the collating session is that I stapled my thumb to one cover. Briefly, before the pain kicked in, I stared at it stupidly, as it dangled from my extremity, wondering why I couldn't put it down like the previous copies. Somewhere out there its lucky owner has a sample of my DNA, and in one unlikely future I could be cloned from it."

Speculation
VOLUME 2. NO.8.   JANUARY 1969

STRANGE WAYS OF EVOLUTION BY FRANZ ROTTENSTEINER

---

[2] The evil Swallow brand was run by sadists with some perverted grudge against duplicating machines and all who used them. Their ink had special non-drying properties, their blue correcting fluid dissolved stencil wax, and the stencils themselves were so flimsy that when you peeled them from the carbon, the centres of all the enclosed letters like o, p, d, g, and so on, were left behind, creating nasty little black blodges. One experience was enough; no one would ever knowingly buy a Swallow product for the second time.

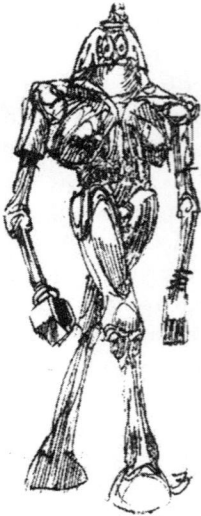

Bob's January issue was slender but packed, and he did a cover illustrating David Pringle's long analysis of *Bug Jack Barron,* to which was appended a very complimentary 2-page letter from Norman Spinrad himself. The Austrian critic Franz Rottensteiner did a demolition job on Gordon R. Dickson (a bit of a sledgehammer to crack a very small nut, I thought privately), there was a lively "Opinion" feature, and a "Melting Pot" brimming over with letters from professionals. One of the triumphs this time was a series of working sketches from Jack Gaughan, done for an anthology called *Invasion of the Robots.* He sent drawings of big robots and small robots, flying robots and marching robots, a robot in Gestapo hat and one well-endowed robot captioned "advertisement for a mechanical Maidenform." I think Jack might have been a bit fed up with robots by the time he finished, because on the last of the pictures, in large and ornate red lettering around the margins and in every square inch of space there is the legend, "ClaNk! cLAnk! CLAnk! ClanK!"

My February issue came quickly afterwards, with more of Jack Gaughan's robots on the cover, and a feature interview between the Danish critic Jannick Storm and J. G. Ballard, in which the Great Man made several inflammatory remarks such as, "I think [fans] are a great handicap to science fiction and always have been." This was followed by Buz Busby's "Plough" column, Bob Parkinson's acclamation of Philip K. Dick, and wall-to-wall professionals jostling for position in both "Critical Front" and "Melting Pot" columns. Fritz Leiber, Tom Disch, Harlan Ellison, Piers Anthony, Bob Shaw, Alex Panshin, Terry Carr, they were all there, with a wonderful two-page letter

Speculation
VOLUME 2. NO.9.   FEBRUARY 1969

AN INTERVIEW WITH J. G. BALLARD BY JANNICK STORM

from Samuel "Chip" Delany describing his experiences at the academic Secondary Universe conference the previous Spring.

Speculation had finally attained those "bright, sunlit uplands," that plateau above the clouds where all problems melt away in a golden glow of contentment. All I had to do was keep on pubbing and anything was possible—why, one day I might even win a Hugo! First, I was getting married, and then a few weeks later would be the Oxford convention.

Bitten by the
Organising Bug
Chapter 14

Saturday March 8th 1969 was an important day in my life, because at twelve o'clock I was getting married. However, nothing stops for science fiction, and that very same morning the postman delivered a large, unexpected parcel. Curious, I opened it to find a bundle of review copies from *Books & Bookmen,* the trade magazine I had been trying to cultivate for months. There was the MacDonald edition of *Stand on Zanzibar,* all 500 pages of it, along with five other titles, and the editor wanted "1000 words, within the next seven days, please." I was overcome with competing emotions of delight and horror; great to break in, and to actually be *paid* for writing reviews, but what awful timing! Somehow, though, I managed to get the review done, only a few days late, though I had to cheat a bit on the Brunner book.

After our honeymoon, Eileen and I moved into a little ground floor flat while the builders finished our new house. I was looking forward to the day when I would finally have a den, where I could put up shelves for my books, install a desk, and who knows, maybe even get a duplicator. However, at first things were more difficult than ever, with my possessions split between two locations and my post still going to my parents' address. We were also very hard up, with so many new bills to pay, and I didn't think we could afford the 1969 Eastercon, just a few weeks later. With the rather bizarre title of Galactic

Fair, the convention was being held in Oxford's swish Randolph, an expensive hotel with very high room rates.

Rog Peyton was in a similar situation, having married about six months earlier and finding finances tight, but looking for a chance to return to fandom after his dalliance with the Young Conservatives. Neither of us wanted to miss the con, so a week before Easter I suggested we went down to Oxford on the Saturday morning and stayed for just one night at a bed-&-breakfast place, which would keep our costs down but enable us to attend most of the convention. It would also give Rog the opportunity to introduce his new wife, Arline, to science fiction fandom. She had never met fans before and was understandably a little nervous at the prospect.

We drove down together to the Cotswold Lodge, an ivy-covered Victorian pile on the main road about a mile out of town. The front garden was overgrown, and the heavy front door groaned in protest as we entered a silent, deserted hall, festooned with wrought iron and stained glass. Rog spotted a brass hand-bell and gave it a ring, and with a creak another door opened and Boris Karloff entered, dressed from head to toe in moth-eaten black. "The lady of the house died yesterday," he told us, "and she is resting in the parlour. Do you want to see her?" Hastily, we declined his kind offer and an elderly retainer took us to our rooms along a gloomy corridor, asking us to carry our own cases since "his back wasn't what it used to be." He opened our doors with a ten-inch, cast-iron key.

WHEN DID YOU LAST CHANGE THE SHEETS?

We got out of "Castle Drac"

"We were expecting something horrible," said Rog, "and it *was*. Floral wallpaper—with a different pattern on each wall! There was a screen in a corner, hiding a table upon which rested a magnificent crockery punch bowl and two gallon-sized drinking mugs. At least that was what I thought they were, until I noticed there was no en-suite bathroom, then the full horror of the situation hit me." Dumping our cases, we got out of "Castle Drac" as quickly as we could possibly manage!

The Randolph was easy to find, right opposite the Bodleian Library. We went straight to the bar, where Eileen and I were immediately overwhelmed, by old friends and complete strangers in equal measure. Straightaway I met Tom Clareson, editor of the American scholarly journal *Extrapolation,* who was making a brief visit to England. We had been actively corresponding because I was intrigued by the way we seemed to be approaching the same subject matter from diametrically opposite directions, and by the whole new phenomenon of academic interest in science fiction. Then we were joined by the author Dan Morgan and his attractive wife Georgie, and good old Ken Bulmer with his wife Pamela. The Germans were there in force and I said "hello" to Waldemar Kumming, and then to the Scandinavians, Lars-Olov Strandberg, Kjell Borgstrom, and several others. James White came over and made Eileen his friend for life, when in his soft brogue he invited her to join his Society for People of Normal Height. We saw Bob Shaw, Gerry Webb, Ted Tubb, all the usual suspects; I waved across at Bob Rickard, greeted Vernon Brown and some of the other Aston Group people, and Eileen started to tease Graham Boak.

Suddenly, however, Daphne Sewell appeared to bring me abruptly down to Earth by telling me I was "on" in half an hour, as moderator for the panel "Looking Back on SF." "But that's tomorrow, Daphne," I protested, but she was implacable, saying briskly that "it had all been changed," and that was that. I was annoyed, because I had been enjoying myself immensely and just wanted to carry on drifting through the whirl of socialising. Reluctantly, I found panellists Donald Wollheim and Michael Rosenblum, and we tried to find a few things to talk about in the few minutes before the programme began.

We went into the main hall, and I found we would be sitting on a low platform beneath a huge backdrop of the space-station from *2001*. This was actually a full-size cinema advertising poster for the film (which, after the con was over, Gerry Webb took home and carefully pasted over an entire wall of his dining room). The panel wasn't a great success, despite my best efforts, because the two of them started to reminisce about early British fandom, which wasn't the point, really. Trying to get back to the topic, I asked Don Wollheim what he thought of the recent *New Worlds* and was a bit embarrassed at the resulting outburst, especially since Michael Moorcock was sitting among the audience.

Later, Mike wrote to *Speculation:* "Wollheim and I are not strangers. Last year he visited me and took me out to lunch. This year he told his audience what my opinions and delusions were, and it was the first time I had heard his opinion. I have heard harsher and better-argued opinions from the lips of my friends and I have been less amused by them than by Wollheim's, but I have never felt contempt for those people as I feel for Wollheim and the sad sods he represents.

"Thank God for John Brunner, Ken Bulmer, and the few people who still seem prepared to bring a note of reason to the proceedings. I have a feeling I'm not made of such stern stuff. To hear people I have liked braying like donkeys, betraying great areas of illiteracy and lack of understanding as they babble their incoherent insults at an audience that by and large seems to appreciate these performances, makes me genuinely sad and deeply depressed. Next time a convention comes round it will be that much easier to make the decision not to attend.

"I wonder if SF fans have ever considered that there are beings of superior intelligence, with certain alien thought-processes difficult for the fans to understand, living and working amongst them? Rest assured, science fiction fandom, we mean you no harm."

My panel over, I wandered around feeling a little unsettled. Once lost, a good mood isn't so easy to recapture, and I didn't get back into the swing of things until later that evening when the "Cosmic Carnival" began. The hall had been cleared for this event and chairs lashed together to make a square inside which the contestants paraded in fancy dress. Some of the costumes were ingenious, but the most outrageous was Keith Bridges in his role as the "Arcturian Dustman," naked to the waist and looking like a giant grape with his head and ample upper body dyed bright purple through generous application of Gentian Violet. He won a prize, but the next few weeks must have been difficult for him in the tax office where he worked, while the top layer of his skin wore off!

Somehow, the carnival turned into a St Fantony ceremony, and the mock-pageantry led into a tournament of medieval-style jousting, with the "Knights" entering the square and kneeling to their "Ladies" before fighting for their favours. They wore helmets and full armour, with wooden swords and shields (apart from Derek "Bram" Stokes, who leapt around with long blonde hair and very white body, in loincloth and medallion and very little else). The "Black Knight" was particularly lethal, cutting down his opponents with a mighty clatter of sword on shield, and the majestic figure of Brian Burgess was equally impressive in "Ned Kelly" helmet and olive-green armour studded with rivets. Looming over the contest, he wielded his sword with such abandon that he knocked out his opponent, who had to be taken to hospital with concussion.

Earlier, our Guest of Honour, Judith Merril, dressed in flowing robes, was carried into the hall on the shoulders of an honour guard. "Unfortunately, they brought her in on a large butcher's tray," commented Rob Hansen in *Then,* "and someone in the audience gave voice to the image that had occurred to more than a few others when he yelled, 'Where's the apple in her mouth?' "

On Sunday morning, E. J. "Ted" Carnell chaired a panel on the New Wave movement, with panellists John Brunner, Dan Morgan, Charles Platt, the poet Edward Lucie-Smith, and someone I didn't know, called George Hay. This was a slightly odd mixture, especially since Ted Tubb was in the audience along with Michael Moorcock and Judith Merril, all of whom might have had something to say. Brian Aldiss was also present, although for some reason he was making only fleeting appearances at the convention. Bob Rickard captured the entire discussion for *Speculation* on his trusty tape-recorder.

John Brunner led off, saying reasonably that, "for me, the 'new wave' is largely an optical illusion." Giving the outsider's viewpoint, Lucie-Smith followed by saying, flatteringly, that "the great quarrel in the SF field has been partly about the growing pains of literary responsibility. SF suddenly finds itself not a minor genre but a very, very important part of new literature." Then Charles Platt (representing *New Worlds*) chose to define the new wave by "saying what it *isn't,* because for many writers it started with them being disenchanted with things as they were." He couldn't resist the usual insulting sideswipe, adding, "A lot of science fiction could have been written by hermits living deep underground with no contact with the outside world."

Dan Morgan was having none of this. Unlike the others he gave specifics rather than sweeping generalisations, choosing to look at three novels claimed by the new wave—*Camp Concentration, Bug Jack Barron,* and *Stand on Zanzibar*—and quickly illustrating how in every way they were conventional—but very good—SF novels. If Carnell had gone straight back to Platt we might have had an all-out confrontation, but unfortunately he let the initiative pass to George Hay, who spoke at length but said very little, citing Marshall McLuhan, the "fall-out from current technology," "sociological implications," and other buzz-words. Rather than the anticipated fireworks, the discussion veered onto the far less interesting subject of the obscenities in *Bug Jack Barron.*

Determinedly, Dan Morgan brought the panel back on-topic. "I would just like to say a few words about a failed writer for literary magazines who came to science fiction and tried to make it something that it isn't, nor ever was. This man is capable of writing competent, even brilliant SF short stories. But he has the effrontery to insult our intelligence—you and me, the average science fiction reader, for whom he has publicly voiced his contempt in the *Speculation* interview, with such drivel as 'Generations of America,' and 'Dr Christopher Evans Lands on the Moon.' The dreadful irony about this is the way in which this cynical view has been slavishly followed by one pseudo-Ballard after another, in the so-called stories published in *New Worlds.*" He concluded, to considerable applause, and the panel went on for another half-hour, with interjections from an increasingly irritated Ted Tubb in the audience. Eventually someone asked Mike Moorcock a direct question and he leaped to his feet, shouted, "I've got a train to catch," and rushed off, not to be seen again that Easter.

That was the high point of the programme. Judith Merril's Guest of Honour speech at the Sunday night Banquet (an innovation for a British convention) was appallingly bad, rambling, and incoherent, and though Bob Rickard dutifully recorded it, we decided not to use it in *Speculation.* Merril was not a very good GoH, and no one was impressed when Graham Hall attached himself as her "toy boy" for the weekend and moved into her suite. He was subsequently seen looking exceptionally flushed and greasy, boasting loudly about ordering expensive meals, bottles of champagne and brandy and so forth, all "on the room bill," to be paid by the convention committee.

Chris Priest commented, "John Brunner paid the bill, something he remained bitter about for many years afterwards. He didn't have to stand those expenses personally, but he felt very keenly that Merril and her acolytes had thoughtlessly taken advantage of the convention, which didn't have a lot of money."

Meanwhile, unnoticed, unseen, newcomers on the scene were burrowing among the undergrowth of the convention, rather as did those small, rat-like mammals during an earlier age of dinosaurs. Bob Rickard remembers Oxford vividly because "that was where Leroy Kettle was sick on John Brunner's dog." It was Roy's first convention (he had booked for Buxton but developed appendicitis), and at the time he was training to be an engineer at Warwick University and was finding it hard going and extremely boring.

He wrote in *Wrinkled Shrew,* "I was spending a great deal of time reading SF and went to the convention as a catharsis. The hotel had a sort of Gormenghast magnificence, with vast winding corridors and buttresses and things, and I knew only one or two of the fans there, Peter Roberts and Greg Pickersgill. These were strange people—certainly not engineers. Peter was quietly bizarre, a little aloof, and to my mind at the time, extremely knowledgeable and intellectual (that is, artistic). People with very long hair who had a habit of wearing outré clothing (pyjamas during the day) were uncommon, particularly among the shorthaired, shiny-suited, white-collared fascist fans of yesteryear. I can't recall saying much to Peter that con, except struggling vainly to impress him with half-remembered facts of little relevance and less consequence.

"Greg was a different kind of different. He was more like I wanted to be; unsavoury, uncaring, degenerate, appropriately rude, well-read, rebellious, well-stocked with SF esoterica, perpetually teetering on the brink of total alcoholic abandon, fannish within his own carefully defined limits, extremely faithful to his friends, a budding writer. I spent more time with Greg at that con than now seems reasonable, but we were the only two people to go to *every* programme item. Funny how things change."

Roy, Peter, Greg, and others at Oxford like John Hall and Graham Charnock would later become "Rat fandom" and would transform the British scene more thoroughly and completely than the earlier New Wave ever had. However, for now, the most prominent new face at Oxford was that of George Hay.

George was a strange, otherworldly character who had stalked the margins of SF fandom for many years. He had written four long-forgotten SF novels in the 1950s and had then gone quiet, suddenly re-emerging at this convention. Tall and thin, bald on top with grey hair down to his shoulders, and invariably wearing an oversize sports-coat with the elbows out, he was involved with every fringe-group going. An incredible "ideas man," he would pick up the telephone at a moment's notice and call anybody, anywhere, and talk at them non-stop until they either gave him what he wanted or fell down in a coma. He generated new projects and organisations on a daily basis, most of which never had the remotest chance of leaving the ground.[1]

Dave Langford described George: "Peering through thick glasses invariably mended with sticky tape, he would loom at people and weave strange spells of nagging energy and erudition. He wheedled the Science Fiction Foundation into existence at the North-East London Polytechnic in 1971, an SF think-tank intended to push his own personal agenda. Perhaps it would have become a lobby group, urging Parliament to pay attention to antigravity, relativistic paradoxes and ion drives. Instead, there was a coup led by Peter Nicholls, which seized control and changed its direction. George had aimed for the stars but the critics preferred academic respectability."

A little after the Oxford convention George started calling me regularly, and, being curious as to what he actually *did,* how he earned a living, I visited him at something he called "The Environmental Consortium." This turned out to be a table in an architect's office, and after two hours of listening to him talk over lunch in the Family Planning Clinic across the road, I left, none the wiser. George struck me as well meaning but hopelessly impractical; however, when he made a bid for the 1970 con, no one else stood up and he was awarded the job.

Eileen enjoyed the Oxford convention immensely. I came away enthused, and sharing the work between our little flat and my BSA office, I made short work of another *Speculation*. The May issue came out within three weeks, a good, solid number with several innovations and another printed, wrap-around cover by Eddie Jones.

My editorial took the form of a diary, recording day-to-day events as they happened, for instance: "2nd February— heard from Harry Harrison, with an article for the special Heinlein 30th anniversary issue. I see I'm the third person to suggest Harry as the next editor of

---

[1] Brian Aldiss remembers, "George always wanted SF to be a sort of teaching tool. I argued that SF had to exist as literature or it was nothing. His approach, I thought, was mistaken. His most brilliant plan was that a Martian fighting machine should be built as a memorial to H. G. Wells; he saw it striding over Primrose Hill, and I have always regretted that this inspiration was never translated into reality. Of course, George also founded the Science Fiction Foundation."

Analog." There was the first instalment of a new column, "Vision of Suburbia" by Chris Priest, and a long review by Ken & Pamela Bulmer of *Dangerous Visions,* along with other reviews by Messrs Pringle, Hall, Stableford and Sudbery.

Once again, the "Melting Pot" bubbled and seethed with contrary opinions. For instance, the academic Ivor Rogers added a good-natured perspective on Tim Hildebrandt's earlier report from his elevated position as director of The Secondary Universe conference. He said, "I missed the shook fists, raised eyebrows, and one particularly intense exchange between Judith Merril and William Tenn that blew a fuse on the recorder, although at supper that night we had a dramatic reenactment." He made some wise observations on Chip Delany's "wipe-out of the Professors at the Modern Language Association," and concluded that "the professional litterateur can kill a good thing pretty fast"—the first indication I had seen that the new-found academic interest in science fiction might not be altogether a good thing!

However, it was the Ballard interview in the previous issue that attracted the most attention. Dan Morgan said, "I should think quite a few people will be up in arms about Ballard's comments on fandom—they bloody well ought to be!...Most of our writers came from fandom in the first place and aren't ashamed of the fact—most of the writers, that is, except for culture-snobs who dropped in via the literary magazines." Bob Parkinson added, "Someone once said that Ballard characters typically stand around giving themselves away. The interview, for those who would read, is a give-away about Ballard himself. However, I doubt whether many will see just what it does say...Ballard, like Heinlein, is losing contact with reality."

To my surprise, Charles Platt also wrote, and commented on the interview, though possibly with ulterior motives. "The Ballard interview was excellent," he said, "so refreshing with its individuality and conviction. Such awareness of environment and image is rarely seen in fanzine articles. How sadly ironic that Ballard's condemnation of 'almost illiterate' SF fans is followed immediately by F. M. Busby's asinine reviews of mediocre category fiction. This article is typical of the fan's self-indulgent, chummy, chatty, verbose, uninformative, and totally unperceptive commentary on that which is interesting to him and his friends. So very dull. I am glad this kind of article doesn't generally appear in your fanzine."

Charles then went on to insult Dan Morgan, and to praise some remarks made by Phil Harbottle about John Russell Fearn, the man who single-handedly brought science fiction into such disrepute in Britain with his dreadful stories under various pseudonyms like Vargo Statten and Volsted Gridban. Platt's letter presented me with the usual dilemma; would his contribution cause more trouble than it was worth? Print it or ignore it? Unwisely, I chose the first option, thinking that something so obviously 'over-the-top' would provide a little light relief. I even added an ironic comment, "I'm pleased you came back from retirement at my special request to begin a couple of feuds, Charles, and I'm sure this will liven-up things no end. Of course, I don't believe a word you say here, because anyone who can agree with J. G. Ballard's opinions of science fiction and simultaneously admire Vargo Statten is simply pulling a few legs!"

Well, so much for light relief! The July issue (number 23) picked up strongly on this little aside. In his "Suburbia" column, Chris Priest said, "J. G. Ballard and John Russell Fearn must make two of the strangest bedfellows, yet there they are, linked with not so much as a blink of an eyelid in Charles Platt's incredible letter." Chris went on to say what he thought of Fearn, an opinion given relevance by the announcement just before the Oxford con that Phil Harbottle had been entrusted with the job of editing a new British SF magazine, to be called *Vision of Tomorrow*. Phil, as we all knew to our cost, was absolutely nuts about Fearn, having devoted years of his life to tracking down stories in obscure places, and finding *thirty-four* complete novels in the *Toronto Star Weekly* alone. He had compiled a massive biography, *The Multi-Man*, which had attracted the attention of Ron Graham, a rich Australian businessman who shared Phil's obsession, and we were worried what would result from this odd combination.

Chris continued, "What I am concerned with is the continuing public opinion of science fiction and how it may fare if Fearn's novels are reprinted in any quantity. Charles Platt's remarks that Fearn wrote 'professional fantasies' that were 'full of imagination and drama' is as wild and irresponsible as he claims Fearn's techniques, ideas and plots to be."

Phil Harbottle piled in, taking me to task over my "silly and sarcastic footnote" and demanding to know "the truth," whether I had invited Platt to write a hypocritical letter to stir up controversy deliberately, or if he had written in "all sincerity" and I had implied "he is something between a hypocrite, a liar, or a joker." This struck me as a bit of a no-win question, to which I could only retort that: "I added my footnote—call it flippant if you like—because I found Charles' attitude to be incredible."

Platt was also represented in this new issue, with a long review and a letter to the "Melting Pot," in which he said, "*Stand on Zanzibar* was impressively thorough but also impressively dull. I always find it hard to enjoy a book whose author shows no sensitivity toward human beings and human character, and in *Zanzibar*, I felt Brunner had compiled a social document, which covered everything except the real emotions and thoughts of the people who would have to live in the world he represented. Incidentally, I thought *Make Room! Make Room!* failed in exactly the same way; written within the conventions and style of stereotyped formula fiction, however *authentic* the background."

He reviewed Philip Jose Farmer's two Essex House books, *Image of the Beast* and *A Feast Unknown,* which were causing a minor sensation in some quarters with their scenes of bizarre sexual acts, violence and mutilation. Typically, Charles took a dissenting view, claiming the first book was "an unusually successful gothic-fantasy novel…amazingly vivid and subtle," and the second title was "perfectly paced, well-plotted, and creates from pulp myth a story which is real and vital and relevant to the present day." It was a well-written review, although I worried whether Charles really *meant* any of it, and I really should have edited out his gratuitous insults aimed at Ted White.

Speculation
VOL 2. NO. 11.   JULY 1969

STAND ON ZANZIBAR
-review inside

DISCUSSION PANEL :- THERE AIN'T NO SUCH THING AS 'NEW WAVE'!

Otherwise, the issue was notable for the somewhat bizarre cover illustration by Pam Yates, and Pam Bulmer's long review of *Stand on Zanzibar.* There was a strange "Jerry Cornelius" fragment from Michael Moorcock, and Bob Rickard's transcript of Ted Carnell's panel from the Galactic Fair which I titled, "There Ain't No Such Thing as the New Wave." For the first time I ran a double photo-page, something proposed by my German friend Waldemar Kumming for his own fanzine, *Munich Round-Up.* The idea was that he should paste up his convention pictures into a composite montage, have them professionally printed, and we would split the costs. These pages show some of the highlights from Oxford; the tournament, the banquet, the *2001* backdrop. It would have been wonderful if we could have produced similar pages for previous cons, of which so few records survive.

Finally, I added a back-page editorial supplement in which I commented, "The last three months have probably been the most exciting period of my life." I described how we had just been privileged to witness the Apollo 11 moon landing, and shortly afterwards the early probes to Mars. During the same period, Eileen and I had moved into our newly built house at Kings Norton in a pleasant little development, which backed onto the heavily wooded cutting of the Birmingham-Worcester canal, giving a view from my study window of the frequent waterway traffic. For the first time I had produced an issue of *Speculation* at my own desk, in comfort, rather than being perched on the edge of my bed with a heavy typewriter on my knees. Happy, happy days!

The following weekend I was abducted. On the Sunday morning I was digging rather futilely at the heavy clay in my little front garden when a small brown car drew up outside. The driver leapt out and came running towards me, waving his arms wildly in excitement. He had wild grey hair, he wore sandals and his shirt was hanging out, and he looked like nothing so much as the archetypal science-fictional Mad Scientist. It was my first meeting with Jack Cohen, a man whose enthusiasms can sometimes be overwhelming!

Before I quite realised what was happening I had been bundled into his car, protesting weakly "my wife will wonder where I've gone," and was being driven across Birmingham to meet someone called "Judy," while Jack told me his life story. He was actually "Doctor" Jack Cohen and he worked in the Zoology Department of the University of Birmingham, specialising in what might be called "weird beasties." He told me with some pride that he had once worked professionally with Isaac Asimov, which had been a special thrill because Jack was a long-time science fiction fan. Quite by chance that summer he had employed David Pringle as a lab assistant, who showed him my fanzine, and Jack had realised this "fandom" thing was just what he needed.

The following week I visited him one lunchtime at the University and was fascinated by his workroom, where battered copies of *Neutron Star* and *Childhood's End* shared shelf-space with academic textbooks and jars of crottled greeps. Jack took me down into the basement bestiary, where he reached into a large glass tank and with the cry of "...and look at these *beautiful* cockroaches" held out a handful of the nastiest, most repulsively squirming horrors I'd ever seen, and then regarded me reproachfully when I conspicuously failed to share his enthusiasm. Jack was a real character and I was delighted to have someone else to talk to, now that I wasn't seeing Bob Rickard quite so often and David Pringle had gone off to Leeds. However, little did I know that I was in danger from something a great deal more threatening than anything Jack had to offer. I was about to be bitten by the Organising Bug!

It all started innocently enough. One evening in the early autumn I was sitting in my parked car outside Cannon Hill Park, waiting to meet Eileen on her way home from work, when I was amazed to see a poster displayed by the Midlands Arts Centre for something titled "An Afternoon in Middle-earth." I thought this was quite remarkable. *The Lord of the Rings* was an obscure work of fantasy, almost unknown outside a small circle of enthusiasts, and yet a respectable organisation was sponsoring a conference to discuss the trilogy! Of course, there was a local connection; the MAC was only a few miles from Sarehole Mill and the lost fields of Hall Green, where Tolkien had spent his childhood days. Even so, I thought, maybe they might want to run a conference about science fiction?

My inspiration came from many sources. From my chat at Oxford with Tom Clareson about the growing academic interest in SF, from the *Speculation* report on the American Secondary Universe event, and because by now I had organised a half-dozen or more big industrial conferences for the BSA company. However, in the end I was just *lucky,* because next morning when I telephoned the MAC publicity officer I found he, too, used to work for BSA. We knew the same people, had a pleasant little chat, and he was happy to set up a meeting with their Director of Courses, who agreed surprisingly readily to sponsor a conference the following June, under the snappy title of "Speculative Literature—science fiction today." He asked whether I could get any professional writers to take part, and I said I probably could; while he had never heard of Bob Shaw or Ken Bulmer, he was impressed when I mentioned Brian Aldiss. "How about Colin Wilson?" he asked brightly. "And maybe Dennis Wheatley?"

From the comfort of my new study, I fired off letters to most of the British professionals of my acquaintance, and to James Blish, who was in the process of moving to England, inviting them to the conference. They all accepted, of course—after all, they were actually going to be *paid* for their presence, with hotel and travelling expenses also refunded, a much better deal than offered by conventions. Then, I needed to get on with *Speculation* because the next issue was going to be something special. It was my "Heinlein" issue, commemorating the thirtieth anniversary of the appearance of "Lifeline," his first published story, in August 1939, and I was already running late.

I saw Jack Cohen quite often during the next few months, visited him at the University and at home when he moved to a little house at the top of the Lickey Hills. One Sunday morning Eileen and I turned up to find the place in a state of uproar because Jack's python had made an escape bid, and had disappeared under the floorboards. Since the house was part of a terrace and the crawl spaces were interconnected, the neighbours were understandably alarmed at the thought of a four-foot snake at large! Snakes, bats, dolphins, Jack loved any weird creatures, but he hadn't yet met other fans, and it was only at the infamous "Sci-con" that he had his first large-scale taste of science fiction fandom. Afterwards, Jack claimed to have had "the best weekend in my life," which just goes to prove once again that a convention is what you make of it, because almost everyone else thought it was a complete disaster.

George Hay had confounded traditional wisdom by taking the 1970 Eastercon to London for the first time in nearly twenty years, with truly awful results. Because a few people had complained about the cost of the Oxford Randolph, George had gone for the cheapest hotel he could find. Unfortunately, where London hotels are concerned the words "good" and "cheap" simply do not go together. He ended up with the Royal, in Southampton Row (scene of the 1951 & 1952 cons, and by the look of things, not decorated since).

Imagine, if you will, a vast, shabby, 400+ room establishment with corridors "long enough to land a B-29," as Graham Boak commented, and with just two tiny lifts which could only take two or three people and never rose above the third floor. (Eileen and I were in a closet on the sixth.)

Attendees were bullied into paying in advance, the staff were hostile, and the management was so totally oblivious that they claimed not to be aware that a convention was taking place—or simply didn't care, since the place was due to be demolished a few weeks after Easter. Dinner was served for a period of about half-an-hour only, but *not* to couples with children (which hit the Shorrocks, among others). John Brunner ordered wine with his meal and was told, "Get it yourself." A porter gave a V-sign to Ethel and Ella when they asked for help with their luggage, and in the morning, the queues for the cold, greasy breakfast stretched from the restaurant across the lobby, while indifferent waiters left guests to clear their own tables as best they could.

In the evenings, we sat in a gloomy lounge, with a huge brickwork arch which looked like the entrance to a railway tunnel and through which we imagined a train would come racing at any moment. The bar closed at 10.00 p.m., and afterwards you had to queue at a serving hatch where a night porter would grudgingly sell warm brown ale by the bottle, no glasses available. It was a nightmare hotel, one normally used only by back-packers and economy-class tourists.

Into this unpromising location, George had decanted a strange mixture of computer scientists, environmentalists, psychologists, poets, a Member of Parliament, educational research specialists, and of course, the obligatory scientologist, but he forgot to provide very much about science fiction. On Friday night there was a talk from Professor Willis McNelly, visiting from California, on Saturday we had James Blish's GoH speech, and that was about it. Arthur C. Clarke turned up but wasn't introduced, let alone asked to speak. George simply wasn't *there* most of the time, too busy being a Media Star, racing around London being interviewed by radio and TV, newspapers and journalists, peddling his own peculiar brand of fantasy and half-baked idealism.

The programme created an aching void, a sense of waiting interminably for something that was never going to happen. On the Saturday afternoon I had been asked to run a "*Speculation* panel," but in the hours before it was due to begin I became uneasily aware of throngs of people hanging around waiting, asking, "When's your panel going to be on?" Something conceived as a relatively minor item had become, in the absence of anything else, the key event of the afternoon. The panellists were Chris Priest, Pam Bulmer, David Redd, Michael Kenward and Bob Parkinson, and we spent over an hour working on our arguments about the "State of SF." Inevitably, though, the poetry reading over-ran, and so instead we all went across the road to a pleasant little Indian restaurant (who said they would go out of business when the Royal closed down, since everyone who stayed at the hotel came over to eat with them).

This was the weekend during which we experienced the spectacle of Michael Moorcock and his friends, who wandered around carrying asses's heads and waving a whisky bottle. Mike had roundly condemned fans and the low level of discussion at the Oxford convention: "one begins to suspect that one has fallen into a nest of paranoid schizophrenics or, as it were, is trapped in a loony bin." At Sci-con, Mike and his pals shouted and made animal sounds during the speech by Raymond Fletcher, M.P., and sat in the middle of the hall during John Brunner's poetry-reading session, disrupting the event by talking, laughing, and passing the bottle. When John complained, Mike Dempsey (editor at Hutchinson) threw a glass at him, which shattered noisily on the floor in front of the speakers' table, the fragments cutting open Brunner's right shin and drawing copious quantities of blood, leaving John "with a scar I shall carry for the rest of my life."

Just a few good moments came out of the shambles of Sci-con, almost like ghosts of the convention that might have been. Tony Walsh went over the top with his fancy-dress costume as usual, this time coming as a perambulating rubbish heap with junk tied on all over him, labelled "The Real 1984." Tony's message was, "this is the future, and it stinks!" and he had drenched himself in butyric acid to make his point. *Not* a good idea!

A *real* "Malcolm Edwards" appeared at Sci-con, as my pseudonym of four years earlier took on a life of its own! It was an incredible coincidence, but an excellent boost for Malcolm, since people kept coming up and saying how nice it was to meet him for the first time after reading his columns in *Vector*. He was a member of the Cambridge University SF Society, and I thought he had the right attitude when he said, "science fiction is pretty good and there ought to be more of it." Our first conversation, however, was not promising: "My *father* wears trousers like that!" said Malcolm in disgust, staring at my sturdy suit trousers, while I looked at his pink satin bellbottoms and thought privately, "my *wife* wears trousers like that—in bed!" Yet another generation gap had opened up in British fandom!

And not everyone was unhappy; for some, attending a con for the first time, (in Rob Hansen's words) "the meeting with kindred spirits and the sheer wonder of being with so many people who read science fiction gave Sci-con all the magic of any other first convention. One first-timer so enchanted was Ian Williams, who, fired by enthusiasm, returned to his native Sunderland and formed a new SF group in the North-East."

Some of us were concerned at one stage about Brian Aldiss, who fell into such a deep slumber during a particularly tedious explanation of "A Scientific Theory of Mysticism" that his sleeping head swayed perilously away from his chair and towards the hard, unforgiving floor. Later that night, Brian found Rog and I waiting for the film show to start, staring glumly at the torn piece of white paper taped to the wall, which was the best George had been able to provide for a screen.

Brian recalls, "In that horrid hotel there were marble steps leading down to the hall where films were to be shown. Ted Tubb had held a party there, featuring his homemade plonk. More than one young fan became deeply icky and threw up over those steps—just before it was film-time. No time to mop it up! And more than one person slipped up in the spew and slithered down the steps into a deep pool of it."

It was all very squalid, and Brian said that he was pretty fed up with the whole affair and was going home in the morning. We said we felt very much the same way ourselves. Brian then confided that this was the second time he had been asked to be Guest of Honour but had then been required to step down. We were suitably shocked, as he went on to explain how he had been invited as GoH for 1969 in Oxford, but when a new committee had taken over, headed by John Brunner, they had wanted to have Judith Merril instead. George Hay had heard about this, thought it was a bit poor, and so he had asked Brian to be GoH in 1970, which he had accepted. Then George heard that James Blish was moving to England and he did exactly the same thing, pushing out Brian once again in favour of a supposed bigger "name."[2]

Rog and I were suitably disgusted, and promptly offered to make amends. We would bid for the 1971 Eastercon and would do it properly. We promised to find a decent hotel and make Brian our Guest of Honour, but he wasn't enthusiastic, seeming deeply cynical about fandom. He wished us well and went off to bed, leaving us plotting and scheming into the small hours. Next day we duly stood up at the bidding session and faced opposition from—of all people—Brian Burgess, who said he wanted to run a convention in the seaside town of Swanage. Few of us had heard of the place, but it hardly mattered, because the idea of Brian running anything was so ludicrous that it was hardly worth putting the matter to a vote, and Rog and I won our bid by a minor landslide.

I had been bitten by the Organising Bug again—for the second time in six months!

---

[2] Chris Priest comments, "As I recall, Brian was going to be GoH but the committee couldn't get its act together. John Brunner and some others swept in to the rescue, and as part of the package, they said they wanted their own choice of GoH. Brian took this as a personal snub by Brunner...which it might have been, or might not. I suspect not. John was clumsy, vain, pretentious, self-absorbed, and many other things, but he was never malicious."

Vigilantes and Voters
Chapter 15

Birds were singing, the sun was shining, and at last, it was the June weekend of the Speculation conference. I was excited and more than a little apprehensive; this was my baby and goodness knows how it was going to work out! After the disappointments of Sci-con I was ready for some serious talking about science fiction, and so it seemed was everyone else, because more than half the registrations were from fans. This hadn't really been our intention—I had vaguely expected to draw in locals who were curious about SF, perhaps some of the "arty" crowd who usually patronised the Midlands Arts Centre. After all, this was going to be a "respectable," semi-academic conference, *not* a convention.

Unfortunately the MAC had completely lost interest, however, and did none of the publicity they promised. They left it all to me, and so I promoted the event through the usual fannish channels—and attracted keen fans from all over the country. The Centre hadn't cared about the programme, either, so I organised it myself and invited five speakers—Brian Aldiss of course, and Ken Bulmer to represent the earlier British writers, with Chris Priest for the modernists. James Blish came as the only American author (and as a major critic in his own right), and Bob Shaw, largely because we didn't very often get a chance to see him. Then Brian suggested his friend Philip Strick (from the

British Film Institute), and at short notice Professor Willis McNelly came along as our token academic. In the end, about the only thing the Centre did was to produce an attractive programme book, from text I provided.

Chris Priest and his wife drove up from London on Saturday afternoon with Ken and Pamela Bulmer, and stopped at our little house in Kings Norton, where Eileen served an early dinner, before we all set off for a pre-conference get-together. The MAC people had booked accommodation at the Cobden Hotel on the Hagley Road, but when we arrived, we discovered to our horror that it was a strict temperance hotel, with no bar! Nothing for it but to adjourn to the nearest pub, and so a two-dozen-strong procession of science fiction writers, wives, and faithful fans straggled off along the main road towards the dubious comforts of the saloon bar in the Ivy Bush.[1] I could hardly believe that I was walking along in humdrum old Birmingham, actually talking to the great *James Blish,* one of the foremost names in science fiction, author of books I had read in awe, like *A Case of Conscience* and *They Shall Have Stars*. Truly, a cosmic moment!

We were thrown out at half-past ten, of course, to the great disgust of Judy Blish, a highly assertive lady who persuaded a reluctant landlord to sell us several bottles of whisky so that we could continue our party back at the hotel. Hiding the bottles under our coats and taking care not to make any suspicious clinking sounds, we smuggled them past the receptionist and up to the Blishes's room, where Ken

"Send up some glasses," she demanded

Bulmer and I volunteered to sortie out and steal toothbrush-glasses and coffee-cups in the time-honoured British way. Just as we were leaving, however, and before we could stop her, Judy Blish picked up the telephone and called room service. "Send up two dozen glasses, we're having a party in here. And

---

[1] Later to become a beacon of fannishness, when Ray Bradbury took over as landlord and hosted the BSFG in his upstairs room for several years.

some ice," she demanded imperiously, with the authority of one used to hotels that did as they were told, with none of this temperance nonsense.

It was a great little party. Ken Bulmer told stories about Bert Campbell, and Chris Priest regaled us with a hilarious account of the afternoon he spent in a tent with Brunner and Ballard, surrounded by thousands of hippies, at the recent "Phun City" freak-out near Worthing. Some time after midnight, Brian Aldiss grew pensive and sat on the bed, drawing out a splendid fountain pen and envelope, and started to jot down some notes for tomorrow's talk. Unfortunately, just at that moment I was demonstrating to Bob Shaw how aircraft could fly in a parabolic path to create weightlessness conditions, and my arm intercepted Jim Blish's whisky glass with disastrous results. The contents went all over Brian's envelope, instantly turning his notes into a soggy, unreadable mess and creating interesting blue patterns on Jim's pillow. Eileen and I went home soon afterwards, although I understand the party went on to 5.00 a.m.

Next morning I had a headache, but still managed to enjoy the conference enormously. The Arts Centre was situated in an attractive spot in woodlands next to the River Rea, and we were in a large, hexagonal auditorium, panelled in wood, with the speakers in the centre and spectators occupying benches all around. I recognised most of the faces, fans from all over the country like John Steward from London, Vic Hallett from Cambridge and Gerald Bishop from Exeter. Local supporters turned up in force, people like Tim Stannard, Jack Cohen, and Vernon Brown with some of the Aston group members.

Bob Rickard set up his tape-recorder and the morning session went quickly, with presentations from Philip Strick, Chris Priest, and Bob Shaw. We had a jolly lunch and resumed with James Blish, whose assigned title was "The Good, the Bad, and the Indifferent." This was a "clever" title of mine, intended as an opportunity for him to discuss specific stories, but instead he chose to talk about literary criticism, reading his paper quickly and incisively while the audience listened in respectful silence. Blish ended, "No critic has the lifespan to wait time out—and his only recourse is to make himself the master of his subject as best he can, and defend his perceptions of the good, the bad, and the indifferent against juries, shifts in taste, ignorance, popularity contests and all other forms of mob action—including other critics who are trying to create or mount bandwagons."

Ken Bulmer had a very different approach. "My technique for giving a talk," he said, "is to write it out completely, and then carry out a running commentary on what I've written." He started with a quip about my programme titles: "When Peter sent me the programme I was intrigued by James Blish's title. Then, when I saw the order of the speakers I understood immediately what he meant by 'the good, the bad, and the indifferent.' Later on, we will doubtless hear Brian Aldiss' reaction to being given the 'indifferent' slot, but as for myself, I'm delighted to be numbered among the bad boys. Villains have always had more vitality and have been more interesting than heroes!"

Ken couldn't resist playing the audience for laughs, but he actually delivered a very serious and important speech, concluding, "Although SF is widely acclaimed today by all manner of unlikely people…it is this very acceptance and proliferation that is at the root of its own current weakness. Science fiction is *not* a respectable literature. It is a literature of revolt. But there is so much of it now, most of it unreadable, that its sting has been drawn."

A somewhat subdued Brian Aldiss now took the floor for "Civil War in Science Fiction." The title had been meant to refer to the New Wave business, but unfortunately I had omitted to brief Brian as to exactly what I had in mind, and so with some ingenuity he interpreted it as an excuse to talk about H. G. Wells and *War of the Worlds*. This was currently his favourite subject, he said, since he had very recently recorded a programme about Wells for a BBC Radio series. Brian also explained the reason for his reticence:

"I've come here in rather low water because I'm now about 8½ months gone. I have about a fortnight to finish a novel I've been working on for a very long time (*A Soldier Erect*). So, to change the metaphor, I'm suffering withdrawal symptoms from the world, and if I seem inarticulate it's because I'm battling away in the recesses of my mind with the Burmese jungle. So perhaps what I'm really talking about today is the SF novel I can write when I can break free from Burma."

He concluded his talk by saying:

"What one would like to see, I think, is a grasp of this whole complexity, dealt with in a sort of modern equivalent of the simplicity H. G. Wells used. I don't mean copying him, but if one could find a present-day equivalent of his simplicity then I think you might have a new wave that is something like a tidal wave."

Willis McNelly gave the final presentation of the day, and briefly discussed some contemporary novels which used SF themes, saying in conclusion, "For Heaven's sake, let's not make science fiction an enclave that only the initiated can join." Afterwards, the audience joined in, with a spirited and enthusiastic discussion that went on for a remarkable ninety minutes until 6.30 p.m., when I had reluctantly to bring the conference to a close.

A great day, I thought, and I was looking forward to hearing Bob Rickard's recordings, which we were going to transcribe for *Speculation*. The people at the MAC were also pleased and a little surprised at the support we had received, inviting me to come back the following summer. It didn't even occur to me until many years later that while they paid a £100 fee to each speaker, plus travelling and hotel costs, I had done the whole thing for nothing. I had simply never asked, and they had never offered. I bet George Hay wouldn't have missed a chance like that!

Organising the conference had been a good trial run for the 1971 Easter convention, which was going to be a far bigger thing. By now, Rog and I had brought Bob Rickard and Vernon Brown on board our committee, and we had spent several weekends trying to find a suitable hotel—absolutely the key factor in deciding success or failure. The trouble was that Ken Cheslin had been right, all those years ago; Birmingham *was* a bad city for hotels. A return to the Midland was out of the question, and my first hope had been the Imperial, scene of the 1959 convention. Unfortunately, while the manager was helpful and I liked the layout, we thought it was too small and a bit tatty, and we had promised Brian we would do things properly, with a decent hotel on a par with the Randolph. But where to find it?

We thought the problem was solved when we visited the St Johns at Solihull, a modern building with a huge ballroom and an attractive bar, just a few hundred yards away from a busy shopping centre. Unfortunately, it was a fairly snooty establishment and I could tell the manager regarded us with great suspicion. "A *science fiction* convention?" he enquired in distaste, while I hastened to assure him that we weren't all Monster Raving Loonies. He was unconvinced, and next day sent a polite letter declining to accept our booking. It was the same story with the Leofric in the centre of Coventry, which would have made a wonderful convention hotel but they had plenty of business anyway and didn't want to risk it, and at the Queens in Leicester, another good hotel that suddenly had cold feet. This was ridiculous, I thought. There was no risk involved. After all, we had been holding SF conventions for—how many years now?

Amazingly, we didn't know! I queried people like Tony Walsh and Ron Bennett, but no one could tell me when the annual convention series had started. Eventually I asked Ken Bulmer, who had been a fan back in the 1940s, and persuaded him to try to list all of the previous conventions. He did, and to my slight disgust, we turned out to be number 22; what a pity, I thought, just one year earlier and we could have made a big fuss about "Coming of Age." Now at least we could give the convention a name. Normally it would be some sort of play on the town or city, but since we didn't know *where* we would eventually end up, I thought we should simply call it "Eastercon 22" and take it from there. Only a month or so later, Ken Bulmer wrote apologetically to say that he had forgotten the four pre-war and wartime conventions, but by then it was too late and we had committed to our chronology.[2]

A decent letterhead goes a long way, I thought, and that "22nd annual convention" gave us a reassuring pedigree. Even so, I had to tell a few little fibs

---

[2] Upon which all subsequent British conventions have been based, though with a little tinkering by Rob Hansen and Pat McMurray to compensate for one or two other errors in Ken's original listing.

when we visited the Giffard Hotel at Worcester, not absolutely ideal, but almost our last chance at finding anywhere in the Midlands. It was very modern, all concrete and straight lines, crassly planted among the historic buildings of the old town, but it was big enough, and had a superb lounge with plate-glass windows overlooking the beautiful medieval Cathedral. The manager was cautious, but was taken in by my story that it "was a sort of literary event," and in early June we made a firm booking. He gave us room rates of £2.00 per person per night (shared) and £3.00 (singles), which I thought were pretty good.

The months went by and registrations came in steadily, so that by the beginning of 1971 we could report 298 registered members, one-third greater than ever before, and over seventy hotel bookings were received by return-post after we sent out the booking form. We seemed to be on a roll, and for one heady week it looked as if Damon Knight, Kate Wilhelm and Frederik Pohl would all be coming to Worcester. Suddenly, however, we hit double trouble. Brian Aldiss resigned as Guest of Honour, and this was immediately followed by the start of a postal strike.

Brian's letter was a bombshell! The only reason Rog and I had taken on the convention was to do justice to him, and now he was dropping out for no very good reason, saying vaguely that he "might be living in Hong Kong for a while." No Eastercon had ever lost their GoH before, and the postal strike made it impossible to find anyone else, and we couldn't receive hotel bookings or advertising copy for our programme book. We were in a deep hole.

Somehow, it all worked out. Anne McCaffrey had just moved to Eire from the United States and graciously stepped in as last-minute GoH. We invited Ethel Lindsay to be Fan Guest (an innovation at British cons) and Phil Rogers as Toastmaster (another innovation, stolen shamelessly from Worldcons). The American artist Vincent Di Fate sent us some wonderful illustrations, which showed Worcester Cathedral transposed to an alien landscape. We used these for the cover of our programme book, badges, and a special first-day postal cover, all printed in dramatic black and purple.

My good friend Andy Porter in New York collected our advertising copy from fans and publishers and managed to get the material flown into Britain in a Diplomatic Bag, thanks to the help of

Jim Young, an SF fan in the U.S. Foreign Service. Somehow, people managed to register despite the postal strike, and were assigned rooms in the Giffard or in one of the nearby overflow hotels, the Diglis, Star, and Talbot. We hit a record of 404 members, of whom 284 actually attended, far more than at any previous Eastercon, with vast numbers of newer fans. It was the first appearance of Rob Holdstock, John Piggott, and John Brosnan, and Worcester witnessed the emergence of the Gannet group with Harry Bell, Ian Williams, Ritchie Smith and Tom Penman. The convention saw the full coalescence of the Ratfans with Greg Pickersgill, Roy Kettle, Graham Charnock, and John Hall, while Malcolm Edwards, Peter Roberts and Graham Boak were already prominent fan-editors and took part on the fanzine panel. All this newly focussed energy would now bring about the rapid and complete transformation of British fandom during the mid-'70s.

Peter Roberts wore fetching, canary-yellow overalls, and Darroll Pardoe, back from his American posting, had married his Rosemary and metamorphosed from clean-cut bushy-tailed student to spectacularly-bearded wild man. Mark Adlard, a new contributor to *Speculation,* appeared in cravat and sportsjacket, looking every inch the English country gentleman. We had a full quota of Europeans, with critics Jon Bing from Norway and Jannick Storm from Denmark, Michel Feron from France and Gian Paolo Cossato from Italy. Don Wollheim and David Gerrold, and John Berry represented the United States, and the German contingent included Tom Schlück, Waldemar Kumming and others, who presented me with boxes and boxes of my favourite "Henry Winterman" cigars which they had bought duty-free on the ferry.

Brian Aldiss came after all, his Hong Kong adventure having proved something of a mirage, and he checked in at the neighbouring Talbot and seemed to enjoy himself. However, he later said, "At the time I was suffering from an undiagnosed illness which turned out to be hepatitis A, B, and probably C as well. A couple of sips of a good red wine and my body seemed to turn into a slagheap. I remember two burly fans carrying me out to the Volvo and Margaret driving me home to die. On that fateful drive, I coined a perfectly splendid few Famous Last Words and was pretty pissed off later to find myself recovering. I have long since forgotten what those Last Words were, but I know John Brunner's name came into it."

When planning the programme I had a sudden flash of insight; instead of the usual sweeping generalisations, I thought, let's actually talk about specific works of *science fiction,* let's put on the verbal equivalent of a book review column, as it were. This vision didn't quite translate into reality in the way I had envisaged, but I did manage to get James Blish to talk about an individual author with his keynote item, "All in a Knight's Work." The title was conceived when we thought Damon Knight would be present at Worcester, but as Jim Blish said, "It still seemed like a good idea, but with some shift in emphasis. Since I don't have Damon out there to embarrass by talking about him for a solid hour, I'm going to talk instead about the consequences of some of the things he has done." Another session on the same lines was the debate between Philip Strick and my pal Tony Sudbery, on "The Case For and Against Philip K. Dick."

However, the high spot of the weekend was undoubtedly the Fancy Dress Show on Saturday night. As Rob Hansen comments in *Then:* "This was probably the first totally successful Fancy Dress held at a British convention. Previously, it had been no more than an excuse for established fans to have a bit of fun, but now the quality of many of the entries and the obvious seriousness with which some people were beginning to approach the Fancy Dress marked a sea-change in attitudes towards costuming in British fandom."

Nearly fifty entrants took part, an incredible number, but the odd thing was that the upsurge in support was entirely spontaneous. We hadn't made any special effort to push the Fancy Dress, and people must just naturally have felt motivated this year. Fred Hemmings took first prize as a "Space Viking," Ramblin' Jake Grigg was a "Pirate of Ersatz," Doreen Parker came as C'Mell the cat-woman (she had worn something similar before, but it gave her an excuse to show off her legs!), and Brian Hampton was "The Tooth Fairy." Ken Cheslin came back from gafia as "Ethelred the Unready," and Dave Kyle donned bushy eyebrows, false nose and glasses to take a prize as "Ted Carnell—Spirit of First Fandom."

The Aston Group put on a particularly fine show, with Alan Denham as "Overlord" from *Childhood's End;* Alan Donnelly as a "Yellow Martian" from Barsoom; Richard Doron as "The Fly", and Pauline Dungate as "Kali," from *Lord of Light.* Vernon Brown appeared in full Viking gear, with helmet but *no* horns, while Ray Bradbury was splendid in dress uniform as "An Officer of the Imperium." (Later, the group toured the neighbouring pubs in their costumes, and "Prof." Doron as "The Fly" vastly impressed the locals by sucking up beer through his proboscis.)

Eileen and I were determined to enter into the spirit of things, but I was stuck with the job of Master of Ceremonies and had to announce the various entries. In the end we went as "Gully Foyle and Olivia" from *Tiger, Tiger,* my costume being a dinner suit and full Maori devil-mask, liberally applied with black grease paint. It looked terrible! Eileen simply bought a large square of red silky material and cut a hole in the centre to create a gown, with a high collar made from silver cooking foil and a white wig from the joke shop. It was surprisingly effective, and she won a prize as "Best Lady's Costume."

For comic relief, Brian Burgess entered as a waiter, carrying a tray with a pork pie and a bottle of Worcester Sauce, and Phil Rogers paraded in blonde wig and fishnet tights as some sort of dancing girl. (One of the girls on the hotel staff thought he had "pretty good" legs, and Doreen told me that he received at least one offer from someone suffering from gender-confusion!) Gerry Webb appeared, bizarrely, as "Dr Death" in skull face-mask, top-hat and full morning suit; he had hired the suit for a friend's wedding the following morning—in London, after which he rushed back to Worcester for the Sunday night revels. Not to be outdone, Jack Cohen brought various alien friends to the party, including a fox-cub, a talking bird and his pet "Mesklinite," a giant black tropical centipede which scuttled around the stage furiously under the lower gravity before finally disappearing up James White's sleeve.

Next morning, the Business Meeting proved unexpectedly stressful. First, the 1972 convention was swiftly awarded to the Manchester Delta group, and the new Novacon was announced to general acclaim. Then the discussion moved on to the possibility of Britain being able to host a world convention before the end of the decade. Although having first floated the idea in *Speculation* only six months earlier, I was understandably taken aback when from the front row dear old Dave Kyle attempted to pin it very firmly to my coattails, proposing that I should be chairman of a British bid. I might have gone along with it, I really might, if I hadn't just come from a difficult meeting with the Giffard's manager, who was not at all happy.

He had been very helpful, had not given us any trouble, but he didn't like the way some fans were behaving. He had noticed—couldn't *fail* to notice—that some of them were coming into the hotel heavily laden with backpacks and bedrolls. One idiot actually set up a primus stove in the main lounge! We had some very conspicuous freeloaders and people who tried to bunk down in the lounge and in the dealer's room, while the fragrance of "certain substances" was wafting gently through the upstairs corridors. The manager expected me to Do Something about it.

I was under pressure. I told the business meeting that we were letting ourselves down, spoiling a good relationship with the hotel management. I said that it didn't particularly matter *what* people did in their rooms, whether they freeloaded, brought in drink, or smoked pot, as long as they were discreet about it, didn't make it obvious. Dave Kyle nodded wisely at the sense of this request, and stood up to address the floor. "We must all watch out for this sort of thing," he said solemnly. "I suggest we should appoint some 'vigilantes' to patrol the hotel."[3] Immediately, there was pandemonium! Ken Eadie, a Wolverhampton fan, jumped up and earnestly volunteered to be a vigilante (Ken wasn't very bright, but he desperately wanted to be *involved*).

Others violently denounced the whole idea. Dave Kyle tried to explain why he thought it was a good thing, while I stood on the stage despairingly, saying, "No, no, there's no need for anything like that." It was all very discour-

---

[3] Due to an inaccurate fanzine report by Peter Roberts, the vigilantes suggestion was forever afterwards attributed to me rather than to Dave Kyle, which I always thought was a bit unfair!

aging, and afterwards I went for a walk with Eileen along the banks of the River Severn, muttering dark thoughts and consigning all thoughts of World-cons to the deepest part of the river.

St Fantony took the floor at lunchtime. Now, I had always enjoyed seeing the "Knights" parade in their colourful outfits, although many fans were not so enthusiastic. Chris Priest, for instance, commented on the first time he saw them that "St Fantony very nearly put me off fandom completely," and Jim Linwood was even more critical, saying, "The whole business was sickening exclusiveness, not part of any fandom I wanted to belong to."

I thought they were both wrong, that St Fantony was a clever bit of fun, a splash of colour and novelty, something uniquely British in its evocation of past times, done with fannish flair and good humour. As Eric Jones had ex-plained it to me at Yarmouth, it all began as a bit of leg-pulling, back when he moved from the Liverpool group to Cheltenham in the late '50s, and the Order was revived in 1965 for the London Worldcon in order to entertain the large numbers of overseas visitors. However, by the time of the Worcester convention their objectives seemed to have subtly changed. Keith Freeman wrote in our Programme Book, "Throughout fandom, people were working hard and receiving no recognition for their efforts...the ceremonies bestowed honour upon their recipients. Those elevated to the Order are chosen for two reasons—one being the amount of work they have done for fandom, and secondly, their conviviality and sociability."

Both Rog and I felt we might be so "elevated" at Worcester. We had been in fandom for the best part of eight years and had both kept busy—Rog with *Vector* and the BSFA, me with *Zenith,* and here, at our convention, was the perfect opportunity for St Fantony to bring us aboard. After all, we were friendly with almost everyone in the Order—Phil, Doreen, Archie, Beryl, the Shorrocks, Ken Slater, and with the "Chief Executioner," Eddie Jones.

But as Beryl moved through the audience, selecting candidates for the initiation, I realised it wasn't going to happen. They inducted Bob Shaw and James White, which was fair enough since they were both long-time fans as well as professional writers. But it started to appear that the Order had reso-lutely set its face against admitting anyone from later than about 1963. (The Manchester group being perhaps the only exception, largely because of their close relationship with the film-making Liverpool Group, I suspect.)[4]

---

[4] This was the high-water mark of St Fantony. There were other ceremonies during the early '70s at which the Order continued to "elevate" their friends, their wives, and profession-als, but never anyone from the "new" fandom, which was increasingly coming to dominate fannish affairs. As a result the Knights became steadily less popular, until their final appearance (probably in 1975), when to their evident shock they were greeted with boos from a large section of the audience. Why weren't we "elevated"? After Worcester a female member of the

Peter Roberts wrote a piece in *Egg* in which he said, "I think many fans dislike [St Fantony] because of their fairly blatant attempts at creating an elite of fans and their wretchedly childish ceremonies." In *Then,* Rob Hansen summed up, "Younger fans already felt antipathy towards St Fantony for the reasons Roberts cites, and because of what he and others perceived as the closed and exclusionary nature of its parties at conventions."

On Sunday afternoon we showed our main film, *Charly* (from "Flowers for Algernon"), which everyone agreed was beautifully done and very moving. There was a Banquet in the evening at which Toastmaster Phil Rogers was surprised to be presented with the Doc Weir cup, being momentarily struck speechless until he recovered with the retort, "This is no good to me, it's empty!" On Monday morning we did something unprecedented, treating the entire convention to a two-hour boat-ride along the Severn on *S.S. Belle* (Bob Rickard observed, "If this boat sinks then the whole of British fandom will be wiped out!"). And that was the end of Eastercon 22.

We made some new converts. One was a young American girl, Mary Goodaw, who was sent along by the local newspaper. She appeared on the Friday and I was then amused to see that she stuck with the convention in a state of dazed fascination, right up to the riverboat trip on Monday. After-wards, she sent me a copy of her long, serious report from the paper. "They wanted me to write about you people as if you were Martians or insects," she said. "I'm afraid the article is a bit dry and dull compared to the good humour and fun evident throughout the convention—and the pleasure I had myself."

Bob Rickard commented, "The Worcester convention proved to be one of the pivotal points of my life. Not only did I find the Ace paperback editions of Charles Fort's four books in the dealers' room, but I had the privilege of meet-ing James Blish, and learned he was possibly the youngest member of the long-defunct Fortean Society."

It was a good con, a successful con, but I felt *drained* when it was all over, had tried to do too much myself and had learned some valuable lessons. For instance,

---

Order told me that I had been blackballed by the then-Grand Master, apparently because I "rubbed him up the wrong way." Rog Peyton heard another story, that Eddie Jones had put it about that neither of us wanted to join the Order, and so they never approached us. The latter sounds mildly unlikely, and could easily have been checked if anyone had bothered to ask. It was never true; at one time, I would have *loved* to be a Knight of St Fantony, and so would Rog.

It was a tragedy, really, that something with so much potential for fannish spectacle should be destroyed by its own narrow-mindedness. If only the St Fantony people had realised it needed above all else to engage with and involve newcomers, the group might still have been active today. This was particularly relevant at Worcester, where new groups like the Gannets and the Rats were emerging, and new fanzines like *Fouler, Egg,* and *Cynic* were becoming influ-ential. If he had lived, I don't think Eric Jones would have made that mistake!

I'd had the mistaken belief that you simply set a time for programme events and people turned up and got on with it. *Wrong!* In reality I ran all over the hotel, looking for speakers, chasing-up panellists, reminding them they were on in ten minutes. We didn't have any mechanism to make it happen (they now call it the Green Room). I discovered that the various events needed to be introduced, and wound up when they over-ran, or a substitute had to be found at short notice. Someone had to be responsible (that's what the "ops" room now does). Why did I have to erect the screen for the films, take it down again, and run around switching off lights and checking speakers? (It's now done by the "tech" team.) As for the film programme, poor old super-conscientious Gerald Bishop sat up all night, running and re-running each spool to make sure there was no hitch!

It was just as bad for the other committee members. Vernon worked very hard, and afterwards complained, "After setting up the tables and notices for registration, Rog Peyton and I ended up running the desk most of the day on Friday. Then we found we couldn't lock the door to the Art Room from the outside, had to leave it by the fire-exit and go out through the cellars. Back to the desk again, except for a few minutes of fiddling with the projector for Jack Cohen's slide show. Which leads me to think that while an organising committee should be small, three or four members at most, there should be a larger sub-committee or group of people responsible for all these details, leaving the main committee free to deal with major worries." (Vernon was groping towards the concept of "gophers.")

As John D. Berry commented, "The very first person I saw at the con hotel was Pete Weston, who looked precisely like a harried con chairman. It wasn't until some time on Sunday night that I saw him relax, have a drink, and join the party." By then I was feeling disenchanted with the whole business. I seemed to have spent the entire weekend making sure things happened, rushing around without meeting anyone, setting up events without listening to them, and worrying about other people's problems. After an exacting four days, I wanted to enjoy the convention myself—and suddenly discovered that it was over, that there wouldn't be another for six months.

Although that *was* progress; six months was better than twelve! Thanks to the Aston Group, we could now look forward to Novacon, a new autumn convention. It was an idea that came out of a collating party for *Speculation* 26, in May 1970, in the Biology Lab at Aston University. Mentioning that the group was particularly strong this year, Vernon said they would rather like to take on some sort of project, to bring themselves into better contact with mainstream fandom. "Why not run a small convention?" I suggested, my mind already full of plans for next Easter. "You could use the Imperial Hotel—it's a bit small for an Eastercon, but there's a good bar and the manager reads SF. If you organised something at the end of October or in early November, I'm sure you'd get enough support."

While the original concept was mine, Vernon chose the name, and with the Aston Group he did the work to make Novacon a reality. Before then, however, the Organising Bug would bite me one more time. All these projects were coming together, feeding off each other. The Aston Group swelled the audience for the Speculation conference, which then helped to boost Eastercon 22, and that in turn provided a platform for the second Speculation conference in the summer of 1971. Meanwhile Rog Peyton was moving Andromeda, his speciality SF book business, to the city centre. We had started a bandwagon rolling, we were finding more and more people interested in science fiction, and it only needed a small push to pull all the loose ends together into a revived, resurrected, new-style Birmingham Science Fiction Group.

Rog and I went back to the Imperial Hotel and hired their George Room, which had the great advantage of being adjacent to the upstairs bar. We scoured the membership lists from my conferences and from the Worcester con for local addresses, checked BSFA members, old fanzines, Rog's customer records, even dug up names from the previous Brum group, and sent out a letter announcing an inaugural meeting on Friday 25th June, just two weeks after the second Speculation conference. That night the two of us met in the foyer with some trepidation. Would anyone turn up? Imagine our delight when we peeked into the George Room and saw row after row of people, fifty at least! I recognised some of the faces, Geoff Winterman from the old group (the "Ancient Brummies" as Darroll called us), and Pauline Dungate and Ray Bradbury from the Aston group, but mostly they were complete strangers. Rog and I marched down the centre aisle and took our seats at the front table, and I thought this was going to be the most satisfying project yet.

Rog and I had enjoyed a brief, pleasurable sojourn with the Young Conservatives, and we borrowed heavily from their organisation. Fan groups tend to be small and ephemeral, a few people meeting in a pub or someone's home for a time until enthusiasm dies and the group falls apart. We were more ambitious, were going to start a training programme for local fandom, luring newcomers with the tempting bait of science fiction. So, we outlined our plans for regular meetings, guest speakers, a monthly newsletter, a committee and an annual AGM with election of officers and presentation of accounts.

They loved it! Enthusiasm was heavy in the air, and people volunteered for committee positions. Tim Stannard agreed to write a Constitution, borrowing equally from the Y.C.s and his car club. He had been a founder member of the Aston group, now ran a solicitor's office and was a useful man to know. Vernon became Treasurer and Rog took on Publicity. The meeting adjourned to the bar, where we met some of the newcomers, among them Hazel Faulkner, who had attended the first Speculation conference, and Stan Eling, who had found us through the second. He was thin and wiry, with a mass of frizzy black hair and a slightly squeaky voice, and came with his attractive wife, Helen. Stan said he had been reading science fiction all his life, and the new club was just what he had been hoping for. Rog and I congratulated ourselves, and we started to look forward to the prospect of a mini-convention every month.[5]

1971 had been an exciting year, but I hoped the biggest thrill might be still to come. Greg Benford had suggested I should stand for TAFF again, with the promise of going to Noreascon, the Boston Worldcon, at the beginning of September. I had mistakenly stood once before, prematurely, in 1966 (through bad advice at the time), but five years had made a big difference in my support, particularly in the United States.

I thought I had a reasonably good chance of succeeding this time, despite running against long-time fan Terry Jeeves, and I did so much want to attend a Worldcon, especially *this* one. Everyone expected Boston to be a great con, and I had been in touch with Tony Lewis and some of the other NESFA people for years. I wanted to meet them, and my friends Arnie Katz and Andy Porter in New York, and Charlie Brown, Ted White, and all the other fans I had heard so much about during the past six or seven years. Eileen would come with me; this would be our great transatlantic adventure, and we began saving money to pay for her fare.

There were a couple of other candidates, of course. Per Insulander was a big-name Swedish fan but was hardly known outside Scandinavia, while Mario Bosnyak, the German entrant, was an absolute outsider. He admitted he had never even *heard* of fandom until 1967, had never worked on a con, published a fanzine or written many letters, and I didn't consider him to be a serious contender. Anyway, he had already been to the St Louis Worldcon in 1969, so I didn't really see why he should want to run now. My friend and nominator, Waldemar Kumming, would have been a much stronger candidate from Germany, although apart from the Heidelberg Worldcon in 1970 the Germans were quite insular and had comparatively little involvement with international fandom.

Imagine how dismayed I was when the results were announced. Mario Bosnyak had won by 138 votes to my 84, with Terry Jeeves coming third with 66. The breakdown explained everything; Mario had received 106 votes from Europe (against my 33), with 46 votes coming from Italy alone (when they had taken no part in the contest in previous years). I felt sick with disappointment. And something smelled. What had happened soon became very clear, as was explained in a long letter Waldemar Kumming wrote to rich brown, whose fanzine *Beardmutterings* was the only one to show much interest in the situation. Waldemar said,

---

[5] It worked. The BSFG was still going strong in 2004, with Vernon as Chairman and Rog as Newsletter Editor. At the first (successful) Novacon a hasty meeting was convened to bolt on the convention to the group's Constitution as an annual fixture in the Birmingham area.

"The rumour of soliciting votes...seems to boil down to various fannish trips [he made] within Germany and Italy, and a somewhat aggressive manner in telling all and sundry, and especially fans with some influence, about being a TAFF candidate. These trips quite likely cost about as much as the TAFF trip. It has to be said at this point that the money for these trips, as for the visit to St Louis, did not come from Mario's funds but was paid by another fan (Molly Auler), who was at the time employing Mario as a personal secretary.

"Pete Weston would have had a splendid opportunity at the 1971 British Easter convention at Worcester to milk some TAFF dividends from his excellent organising of the con. He preferred to lean over backwards to avoid even the semblance of doing so. On the other hand, Mario may have approached the line of the 'just barely permissible' too closely for comfort."

TAFF had always relied upon a certain amount of integrity, among both candidates and voters, a willingness to play by the (implied) rules. There is even a clause on the voting form, that states, "If you think your name may not be known to the Administrator, then in order to qualify please give the name of an active fan who is known to them and to whom you are known." If invoked, this clause would probably have disqualified a large proportion of Mario's votes, but who wanted that sort of grief?

Waldemar Kumming was right. It cost only five shillings to vote, and I *could* quite easily have run round the Aston group and signed up twenty or more supporters, none of whom would known anything about fandom, TAFF, or the other candidates. I could have done the same thing at Worcester, but didn't, because I was very conscious of the need to be "squeaky-clean," didn't want to be called a hustler. I had chosen to rely upon the natural constituency of informed voters, people who *cared* about TAFF and knew what it was all about. Mario Bosnyak was playing by different rules, and as a result the Americans received a delegate that they didn't know, hadn't voted for, and who disappeared without trace immediately afterwards.

Afterwards, the rules were tightened up so that a winning candidate had to receive at least 20% of the first-place votes on both sides of the Atlantic. That would have disqualified Mario Bosnyak. But it was too late to do me any good. I was saddened and disappointed. Eileen and I didn't have our big adventure, and now we had discovered she was expecting our first baby in the Spring, I never *would* get the chance to go to an American Worldcon.

The End of *Speculation*
Chapter 16

At the beginning of 1969 I wrote to as many writers as I could, inviting their comments on the thirtieth anniversary that coming July of Robert Heinlein's first story, "Lifeline." An amazing number replied and I produced the result in *Speculation* 24 as a special feature, "After 30 Years—A Symposium." It wasn't intended as a tribute, although some contributors treated it as such, but rather, I sensed that we were on the cusp of a change in critical mood, and I wanted to explore contemporary *attitudes* towards Heinlein.

Spurred perhaps by Michael Moorcock's earlier dismissive remarks, "a trivial writer, with the same faults as Fleming, and just as unreadable," I brought together a collection of sentiments that ranged from the once-universal adulation to what Harlan Ellison termed "a vague disrepute." My own

Speculation
VOLUME 2. NO.12.   SEPTEMBER 1969

AFTER 30 YEARS: SYMPOSIUM ON THE WORK OF ROBERT A. HEINLEIN introduction said, "I have been fascinated to see once again how many different meanings can be read by different people into the same story. As a result I think some of the material in the following pages will reveal slightly more about its writers than about Robert Heinlein."

The issue was full of star names, all with their own viewpoint. Harry Harrison said "[he] is a natural born writer...he has the spark to communicate, in great quantities," and Daniel Galouye recounted some anecdotes from his personal meetings with Mr Heinlein. More penetratingly, Algis Budrys commented, "You cannot show me the other SF writer who can afford to ignore Heinlein. We can all see several who think they can, but that mistake becomes less common the closer you get to the championship circles."

The list continued, with words of praise from Fritz Leiber, Robert A.W. Lowndes, Ken Bulmer, Poul Anderson, Jack Williamson, and Harlan Ellison. Others were more critical, such as Brian Aldiss, who called Heinlein "a very foreign writer," and Norman Spinrad, who blamed him for "the generally stagnant and juvenile nature of the SF field in the '60s." The most balanced verdict came from John Brunner with an exceptionally thoughtful and well-considered piece, and the most unbalanced from M. John Harrison, who said, "Heinlein is a purveyor of shoddy goods," and that "his crypto-Fascist militarism...leads to Chicago" (the riots at the U.S. Democratic convention had just taken place, with Mayor Daley's brutal crackdown).

Both my regular columnists participated. In the "Plough," Buz Busby discussed *Starship Troopers* and *Stranger in a Strange Land,* with some insights into the author's attitudes, based on his own first-hand conversations at the 1961 Seattle Worldcon. In "View of Suburbia" Chris Priest expressed a personal reaction: "My attitude to life is poles apart from Heinlein's. I do not like or agree with most of his heroes. I do not like or agree with his philosophies. Sometimes, I cannot stand his writing style. But there is something about a Heinlein book which reacts chemically with my brain, and which sucks me into his private world against all my better judgments. Only once in my life have I ever read a book that has so interested me that I have become oblivious to the real world. That occasion was on a train journey several years ago, when I missed my destination by four stops and suffered great inconvenience as a result. The book was *The Puppet Masters,* and it is the compulsive quality in this novel and in so many others of Heinlein's, that is for me what distinguishes his work."

I was pleased with the issue, and in due course received a very pleasant letter from the Great Man himself, the start of an occasional correspondence. I suppose authors like to feel appreciated, just like anyone else!

As I had hoped, the symposium provoked further reactions. In Issue 25 (January 1970), Brian Aldiss wrote, "I was surprised you got so much enthusiasm, even from such bright chaps as Fred Pohl. Enthusiasm for Heinlein in

1945 was one thing; in the greatly different world of 1969, entirely another.... Some of your contributors say things that just stun me.... I prefer to think that you occasioned a sort of jolly SF party where everyone got together and enthused about the super plot-twists and fab alien-bashing in *Starship Troopers,* and now the partygoers are sober again and back in the real world, a little bashful about what they said in their cups the night before."

But I was startled by a letter from Swedish fan Mats Linder, in which he said, "I must quote a paragraph from *The Puppet Masters,* Signet edition Page 53: 'I felt warm and relaxed, as if I had just killed a man or had a woman—'

"Some hero, huh?" said Mats. "I'd say he's sick...I'm aware that Heinlein wasn't thinking of this guy as a sick person; very likely, he himself thought this a natural reaction. And it might even be an occasional slip, but it does fit the general picture of Heinlein, the author, as seen by me, the reader."

I was rocked back on my heels, couldn't believe it, had to go and check the reference in my copy of *The Puppet Masters.* It's there, right enough. How could I fail to have seen it before? It stopped me in my tracks; did I agree with this sort of mind-set? No, of course I didn't! So, this one observation from Mats Linder was more instrumental in changing my own attitudes towards Heinlein than were the entire contents of the previous issue.

What would BSFA members make of all this, I wondered, coming in "after the party," so to speak? Because this issue went to the entire membership as a substitute for the non-appearance of the official journal, *Vector,* which was once again in difficulties. The Association paid for me to print an extra 250 copies, and perhaps I thought it was a good way to promote *Speculation.* If so, I was disappointed; my experience, nearly seven years earlier, had proved that the BSFA was *not* fandom, and its members, by and large, did not write letters to fanzines.

The main reason I agreed to their request was because I had finally bought a duplicator, a Gestetner model 260 which I had seen advertised in *Exchange & Mart* at only £30.00 (to put that in context, our mortgage payments on the new house were £28.00 per month). The address was in Southall, and by arranging a convenient "business trip" the following week I was able to collect the machine from a family of Indians, staggering down a narrow flight of stairs from a room above a corner shop. It was an obsolete model but in good condition, with automatic feed and responsive inking. So now, comfortably ensconced in my little study, I could do *anything!* (I even had a typewriter—the old office Imperial had been thrown out because the service man said it needed expensive repairs, although I used it without trouble for the next fifteen years.)

However, in the following weeks I came to regret my agreement with the BSFA, since with 50 pages and 600 copies, that was 15,000 sheets—30 reams of paper—far too much to be handled comfortably. Night after night I laboured over the duplicator, and it was a major trial to collate that many copies, even with the dutiful help of the Aston Group.

Speculation
VOLUME 3 NO.1   JANUARY 1970

FREDERIK POHL • MICHAEL MOORCOCK
CHRISTOPHER PRIEST • JAMES BLISH

Still, the new issue was full of Big Names that even BSFA members would recognise. The cover showed one of Dick Bergeron's "killer robots," with a splash line announcing "Pohl—Moorcock—Priest—Blish." Inside, in the "Critical Review," James Blish provided a long essay on Brian Aldiss's novel *Barefoot in the Head,* Pamela Bulmer did a landmark review of Samuel Delany's *Nova,* and Brian Stableford reviewed *The Left Hand of Darkness.* There were fourteen pages of outspoken letters and three columns; first, Frederik Pohl, with some fascinating remarks about Cyril Kornbluth's "Shark Ship" and Poul Anderson's *Satan's World.*

Fred was followed by Chris Priest, who dismembered some of the awful stories in Phil Harbottle's new *Vision of Tomorrow* magazine, and used this as a platform to muse upon the whole business of being a writer. Chris asked, "What is there in writing that makes it an activity which is attempted unsuccessfully by many, admired (in general) by most, and practiced successfully by only a comparative few?" He went on to say, "I hope that when I read science fiction by other writers, that they have had the sense to wipe their boots and have left their hack formulas behind." Chris expressed a certain amount of idealism, coupled with a realistic perspective on having to earn a living from writing—he had now been a full-time freelance author for eighteen months.

Finally, controversial as ever, there was another instalment of Michael Moorcock's column, cobbled together with Mike's permission from two long letters of comment. He took another swipe at Heinlein, "he's a mediocre writer whose work doesn't bear discussion in literary terms. As for the sociological and psychological terms in which his work would have to be discussed, I doubt if you'd print my private view of poor old Heinlein's problems."

Mike also made several extreme statements about the Oxford convention, roundly condemning Don Wollheim and Dan Morgan, and other (unspecified) people there as "a nest of paranoid schizophrenics," which provoked a heartfelt editorial comment. "We markedly part company on Mike's attitude towards fandom. I feel that fandom has achieved amazingly much for a small, scattered group of people with no commercial backing. People who complain about fandom ought to stop and look for any other amateur group that has done more, for its size. I'm rather proud to be involved with fandom."

In number 26 (May 1970), Don Wollheim hit back, saying, "It has never been my habit to dodge questions and issues when confronting the public. I felt free to say what Mike described as the 'cold truth' because Moorcock was in the audience, and no one could say I was talking behind his back, and he could be free to comment, refute, or run away. He chose the latter."

Greg Benford joined in, saying, "Michael Moorcock surely likes to have both sides of the argument..." and there were lengthy contributions from John Foyster and John J. Pierce (then fronting something called "The Second Foundation," which opposed the New Wave polemics). All this was given fresh topicality by some last-minute editorial remarks, in which I reported on the recent Sci-con and the bad behaviour of Mike and his friends, culminating in the nasty episode in which a glass had been thrown at John Brunner.

By now, *Speculation* was feeding on itself, becoming largely self-sustaining, and this certainly made the job of editor much easier. Round and round we would go, one contributor setting off another, with more letters than I could print. All I had to do was occasionally throw another book on the critical bonfire to keep the flames burning brightly!

This time, for instance, Fred Pohl's column was devoted to Jim Blish's previous review of Brian Aldiss' *Barefoot in the Head,* while in a letter, Jim Blish added to Fred's earlier remarks about Kornbluth's "Shark Ship." Chris Priest devoted a large part of *his* column to discussing what Fred Pohl had said about Poul Anderson, and in a long letter, Samuel Delany commented on Pam Bulmer's previous review of *Nova.* As if this wasn't incestuous enough, the writer David I. Masson made a rare appearance with an interesting article on the use of language by SF writers, quoting examples from the work of—who else?—James Blish, Brian Aldiss and Samuel Delany, while to conclude, Brian Aldiss contributed a long, merry eulogy to Michael Moorcock and three of his recent novels, including *Behold the Man.*

Speculation was ready to take off, but unfortunately, I had other demands on my time. After securing the 1971 Eastercon, Rog, Vernon, and I were spending weekend after weekend in visiting various Midlands towns in search of a suitable hotel, and after that came my Speculation conference in June. My job was keeping me busy—for the first time we had a stand at the Hanover Fair—and I was also trying to carve out a garden from the desolation at the back of our little house in Kings Norton. Still, I kept pegging away at those

stencils, and in the summer was vastly encouraged to hear that at last, *Speculation* was back on the Hugo ballot. About the same time, David Redd sent me a photograph of a pub in Pembrokeshire, called the Speculation Inn, which I thought might make a good cover picture. I promised David I would visit it as soon as I could.[1] In the meantime, I decided to call on some of the London publishers.

Victor Gollancz was the most important, with an extensive SF line in their distinctive yellow dust jackets, and managing director John Bush had always been kind and supportive, sending me review copies almost from the beginning. However, their offices in Henrietta Street, just along from the Covent Garden vegetable market, were a surprise, to say the least. I had imagined a major publishing concern, slick offices and sleek black vans racing through the night, that sort of thing. Instead, I found a narrow, Georgian building with a sort of shop-window and a solid door, on which I hammered until an old lady admitted me to a dark hallway. My impressions were of dust, bare floorboards and an equally bare flight of stairs, and I found John Bush in a small upstairs office, behind an old table piled high with papers and books. In reality, I realised, Gollancz was a pretty threadbare sort of operation.

Several years later Malcolm Edwards joined them, and commented, "Gollancz's building had been their home since 1928, and showed few signs of having been redecorated since. At the front was a display window, in which was arranged a desultory selection of recent titles. You went in, through an internal lobby, and turned right into the reception/telephonist's area, where the formidable Margot fulfilled both jobs. She was already in her 70s when I went there in 1976 and had been there for a couple of decades, becoming increasingly deaf, not the best qualification for either of her jobs. The switchboard still had those cords that you pulled out and plugged in to connect people. John Bush's office was on the first floor facing on to Henrietta Street. His secretary sat in the bit next to him, separated by an old painted plywood partition. The walls were brown up to dado level, and dingy cream above. The stairs were worn and very slippery, from decades if not centuries of use. People regularly fell down a flight because they were so treacherous (and ill lit). Once I fell down from the second floor to the first. Livia Gollancz's office door was at the foot, and I tumbled through it with a great clatter. She looked at me spread-eagled on the floor and said, 'There's no need to knock.' "

Dobson Books were even worse. They had a peculiar list, with very good names like Eric Frank Russell, Fritz Leiber, and Jack Vance, mixed with some decidedly second-rate authors like John Rankine and Arthur Sellings. Their

---

[1] So much for good intentions! It was nearly thirty years—just before Christmas, 2003—before I finally managed to visit David, and see the Speculation Inn, along with Geoff Winterman and Greg & Catherine Pickersgill.

books were amateurishly produced—I still remembered their gaffe with *I, Robot,* by "Issac Asimov"—with type apparently reproduced directly from the (small) Ace paperbacks, printed with 2-inch margins all around. I had often wondered why they did such a poor job with their books, but all became clear when I visited their premises at 80, Kensington Church Street.

This was just along from Hyde Park, not far from glitzy Knightsbridge, but the area had seen better days and the address proved to be a large, run-down house with an overgrown front garden. The door was opened by Dennis Dobson himself, an amiable old buffer who looked like Lord Longford, bald, with long grey hair around his ears, wearing a faded grey three-piece suit, half-moon glasses and a slightly vague expression. "Come in, come in," he said, welcoming me into a dusty front room piled high with papers, books, boxes, a scene of clutter and disorder, mixed with household items and dirty crockery. Dobson appeared to be more of a hobby than a business, and the only mystery was how they ever managed to publish anything from such a shambles![2]

It was September before Issue 27 appeared, instantly notable for Bob Rickard's brilliantly executed cover illustration of the first Speculation conference. From photographs, he had created a clever montage of line drawings that was actually much more effective than the unadorned photographs themselves would have been. The issue was dominated by transcripts from the conference, but there was substantial other meat as well, notably in "The Critical Front," where Tony Sudbery reviewed John Brunner's *Quicksand* at length, and Pam Bulmer wrote about *The Left Hand of Darkness.* However, the issue continued the process of giving Michael Moorcock sufficient rope to hang himself, which

---

[2] Rog Peyton had a similar experience. "A few years later I walked the length of the road, unable to find the number I was looking for. All I could see was a row of decrepit old buildings, set back from the road, long disused and obviously about to be demolished. I was about to give up when I suddenly noticed a bare light bulb, just visible behind very grimy, cracked and patched windows. The front door hadn't seen a coat of paint since the war, and it was opened by Dennis himself, who invited me into a very dusty corridor, about 20 feet long, lined both sides with five-feet-high piles of paper. He told me that these were unsolicited manuscripts that one day they would get round to reading! Then he introduced me to his wife Margaret, and their new 'trainee' editor, Phil Otterill, and we spent an interesting afternoon talking about SF. I recommended various books including *The Prisoner* novels, and Dobson eventually published two of the three.

"After Dennis's death, Dobson stopped publishing but continued selling stock. Their last title was Colin Kapp's *The Timewinders,* which made it into uncorrected proof stage (very few were printed—I own one of those) but no finished copies ever appeared. When the premises were finally demolished, Margaret Dobson, with son Oliver, bought a castle in Durham where they now store their remaining stock of books and organise tours around the castle. Margaret runs the local post office—or she did five years ago, when I last contacted her."

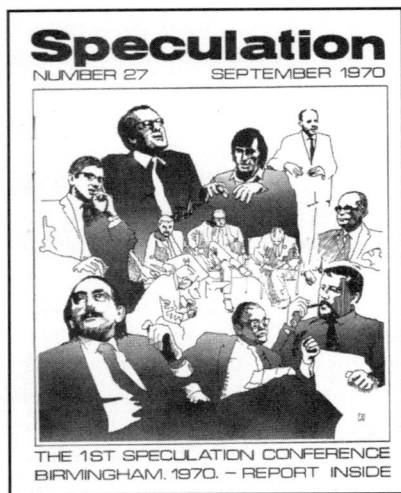

Speculation

NUMBER 27   SEPTEMBER 1970

THE 1ST SPECULATION CONFERENCE
BIRMINGHAM. 1970. – REPORT INSIDE

he did in spectacular fashion with the latest instalment of his column.

Mike began, "Have just returned from a horribly active holiday on Exmoor and ache in every muscle from riding, hiking, climbing, and swimming. The only ache I lacked was a headache. On my return, *Speculation* supplied the lack. I had the impression, in the main, that it was a local magazine published and circulated on the Island of Dr Moreau. Fanzines are where one publishes one's unconsidered remarks—the sort of remarks one would modify or discard if writing something professionally. It is like having a conversation at three o'clock in the morning on the third day of a convention—everyone says a lot of silly things."

He then went on to make some extremely unconsidered remarks of his own, and made the disastrous mistake of trying to excuse the infamous glass-throwing incident at Sci-con. "As for a 'new waver' hurling the glass, you know very well that the person who threw the glass has nothing to do with science fiction and was merely a poetry-lover who was offended by Brunner's remarks about me, after I had left the hall." Mike added, "I also made three separate attempts to make the peace with John Brunner, but his paranoia has gone too far, it seems."

I disagreed, in a footnote commenting that "far from having nothing to do with science fiction," the phantom thrower, Mike Dempsey, was SF editor for Hutchinson, who had published Lang Jones' *The New SF*, with Michael Moorcock's introduction. This whole business was now turning nasty, as James Blish entered the fray to write about Sci-con (where he had been GoH) in the same issue's "Melting Pot" column. "The chain of incidents at the poetry reading and thereafter can only be described as ugly—this is the first convention I have ever attended in which there was actual blood shed—but was at least partially redeemed by John Brunner's magnificent conduct under fire. I'm a little puzzled, though, at your telling us who *didn't* throw the glass but not who *did*. Surely it's no secret; in fact, the man was present all the rest of the evening, receiving congratulations for his offences from various previously-respected figures."

In the following issue Jim Blish would tackle Moorcock head-on: "As your footnotes show, Mike is a very poor reporter, regardless of what other merits he may have..." And John Brunner himself was provoked to write a two-page letter in which he described exactly what happened at Sci-con and afterwards, and ended by saying, "There are a handful of people around the SF field nowadays who seem determined to destroy the atmosphere of goodwill which I have enjoyed so much over so many years. They appear to have fallen into the ancient trap of believing that you can't get to the top without treading on other people *en route*."

The whole thing had got out of hand, and to my secret relief Mike Moorcock wrote no further columns for *Speculation*. Vivid and entertaining they had been, but they had stirred up as much trouble as Charles Platt ever did, and I rather resented Mike's insults. "Island of Dr Moreau" indeed! I wondered, too, how we had come to this. Why had Moorcock become the Scourge of Fandom, when he used to be the life and soul of the party at conventions? Had the experience of editing *New Worlds* changed him in some profound way, his avowal of the so-called new wave alienated him from his previous values?

I was far happier with a jolly little note from Mark Adlard upon my conference issue: "I think Bob Rickard should be congratulated on his cover. This is further proof (if any were needed) that the camera cannot compete with the artist when it comes to presenting character. Just look at the North Oxford tilt of Aldiss' head as he scents his audience at Cannon Hill."

Mark was the latest of my discoveries, whom I had found through another note in *The Writer,* a well-educated man in his thirties who had written a little fiction—he had sold short stories to *She* magazine—and had suddenly encountered science fiction. "I suppose I am an example of someone who discovered what SF might do without ever having seen an SF magazine," he wrote. "But having discovered the field I then felt as if I wanted to swallow the whole thing, Knights of St Fantony and all."

Originally from the North-East, Mark was living in Cardiff, where he was Sales Manager for GKN's steel stockholding operation. This attracted my professional interest since I was trying desperately hard to advance my own career in industrial marketing (and had just commenced a 3-year night-school course). Mark was working on a novel, writing in the early hours of each morning, five o'clock to seven, this being "the only time I get any peace." His perspective was that of the non-pulp English tradition of science fiction (Wells, Stapledon, Huxley), which came across in the reviews he subsequently did for *Speculation,* and his "novel" was eventually published as the much-admired three book "T-City" series.

Issue 28 appeared in January 1971, delayed a little because of the looming imminence of Eastercon 22, but with an excellent line-up. The cover splash line proclaimed, "Special High-Power Review Issue" under another Ivor Latto illustration, which I titled, "Reviews—set 'em up and knock 'em down."

It led off with Alexei Panshin's review of *I Will Fear No Evil,* in which Panshin said, "Heinlein has been better served by those publishers who had the courage to reject this book than by the two who have accepted it." He was

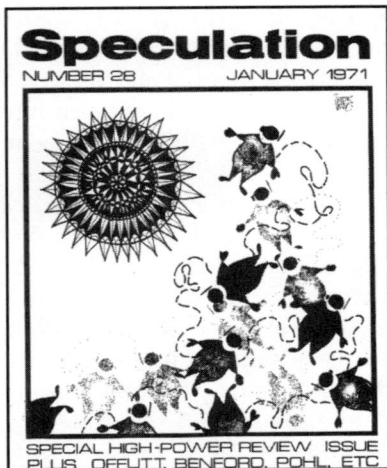

Speculation

NUMBER 28   JANUARY 1971

SPECIAL HIGH-POWER REVIEW ISSUE
PLUS OFFUTT, BENFORD, POHL, ETC

followed by Fred Pohl, Greg Benford, and Andrew Offutt, then Chris Priest discussed *Tiger, Tiger* and suggested Anthony Quinn for the leading role in a film adaptation. There were long reviews by Messrs. Redd, Stableford, Sudbery, Adland, and from the Australian Bruce Gillespie, and in "The Melting Pot," Mike Moorcock's column attracted considerable comment. Ian Williams probably said it all, "I can't make up my mind whether [Mike] is a sincere, sensitive person with genuine doubts about his own talent, or just somebody who wallows in maudlin self-pity and virtually stands up and begs to be crucified. Perhaps there's more of him in Karl Glogauer than most people might have thought."

Eight months would pass before the appearance of Issue 29 (October 1971), a period of both success and failure. During the intervening months I had run the Easter convention and the second Speculation conference, and with Rog had launched the new Birmingham SF Group. In that same interval I had lost the TAFF contest, and while *Speculation* had been nominated a fourth time for the Hugo, it had once again failed to get the Award. However, Noreascon had announced voting totals, and as I announced on the cover, under an illustration by Vincent Di Fate, "49 first-place Hugo votes is pretty good!"

Speculation

October 1971 No. 29

49 first-place
Hugo votes
is pretty good!

This was a thick issue, with transcripts of Jim Blish's and Tony Sudbery's talks from the Eastercon 22 programme, and four pages of photo-montages from the convention, that I had greatly enjoyed putting together. There were some substantial reviews, but two new entrants rated special mention. First, the critic Robert Conquest contributed a long and thoughtful review of the original collection *Three for Tomorrow,* and then in "My World and Welcome to It," Larry Niven discussed the evolution of "Known Space" and the problems resulting from its complexity.

But it was becoming more and more difficult to produce *Speculation* on any sort of regular schedule. I was unhappy with my job, and for a brief period left

BSA before returning, which was probably a mistake. By this time Eileen was expecting our first child and had given up her own job, causing finances to be tight once again, there was the burden of my night-school course, and of course, once baby Alison arrived in April, all hell broke loose! Under these circumstances it was probably a minor miracle that Issue 30 finally appeared in June 1972, a mammoth 72 pages, complete with a spectacular Bob Rickard wrap-around cover illustrating his feature article, "After Such Knowledge," on the work of James Blish.

SPRING 1972 NO. 30

Rickard on Blish's After Such Knowledge

The issue was notable for a number of reasons. It saw the first appearance of Tom Shippey, a local man who had found one of the little cards we had put around to advertise the Birmingham SF Group. Tom was a University lecturer in Medieval English at the time, and as I wrote, "he is awesomely well-read and speaks at least seven languages, including Old Icelandic." It was a minor tragedy we hadn't met before, because it turned out that until recently he had lived on the other side of the canal at Kings Norton, only a few hundred yards away. We could have had so much fun talking about science fiction in the local pub, just over the bridge! As it was, Tom had missed both the first Speculation conference and the Worcester convention, and the most active years of my fanzine, although he immediately began to contribute long, thoughtful reviews. In this issue, he tackled Brian Aldiss' new collection, *The Moment of Eclipse,* and Donald Wollheim's *The Universe Makers,* a semi-autobiographical volume. On the latter, Tom concluded, "Too often, large bundles of facts and insights are tied up with very slender threads of assertion. If you just don't believe the assertions, the book becomes useless."

There were four photo-pages from Chessmancon, and fifteen pages of letters, the first coming from American fan Jerry Lapidus, who perceptively noted, "For the past few years *Spec* has been unquestionably the leading magazine in the English-speaking world for SF criticism and discussion of the field. Then issue 29 came—and there's a difference. This reads more like an issue of *SFR;* a bunch of people, mainly professionals, talking *about* the field, about science fiction, but with precious little real criticism."

To which I answered, "Right! But I didn't think you'd pick up so fast on my—ah—equivocal philosophies towards fan-publishing. My attitudes are still subject to change, even after nine years of toil on this one fanzine. Last summer I was enraptured by the idea of face-lifting *Speculation* into a much more 'chatty' magazine about personalities first. I voiced these thoughts at the second Speculation Conference, and met with great disapproval from Philip Strick and Mark Adlard in particular, and in the end the last issue was a compromise." I also noted, "Incidentally, this heresy is by no means a recent phenomenon; I see from my file of ancient back-issues that I was jumped on as long ago as 1965 by Charles Platt for publishing what he called 'Zenith True Confessions' instead of criticism (I had dared to print a bit of gossip about John W. Campbell...")

My "equivocal" attitudes came through strongly in a nine-page editorial, which, among other things, reported on Chessmancon, commenting, "It was a very good con, despite the forebodings held by almost everyone due to the ever-shifting hotel and almost total lack of communication from the Committee... The Blossoms was an excellent hotel and the staff must go on record as being about the friendliest I have ever seen. The little barman, who cheerfully served single-handedly until five in the morning, only to reappear next morning at half-past nine. The porters, who—far from hounding fans—actually helped them put insulting messages on the hotel notice board, and gleefully took part in the Mammoth Paper Aeroplane Contest down the stairwell."

However, I was a little unkind to Brian Aldiss, first reporting that "for once in his life he completely miscalculated the extent of his popularity," by advertising in the Programme Book, and by placing lots of little postcards on every flat surface, urging fans to nominate him for the newly-instituted Europa Award, to be presented in Trieste in July. Rarely can any campaign have been so counterproductive, and in spontaneous reaction a lot of people voted instead to nominate James White's *All Judgment Fled* as the novel entrant for the Europa.

Then I quoted the *Sunday Times* report on the convention. "A growing rift in the ranks of writers is apparent," it proclaimed. "They seem a convivial lot, but in private disparagement is rife. 'You can't take him seriously,' shrugs one, 'he's still in the world of space-opera.'"

I ventured to suggest that the 'one who shouldn't be taken seriously' was Guest-of-Honour Larry Niven, and I wondered who might have said *that* to the reporter. The paper's very next paragraph continued with an attributed quote from Brian Aldiss, "Basically you can divide SF writers into highbrow and lowbrow," he said, making it clear that he himself preferred the imaginary worlds of writers like Plato and Swift. "And later," I reported, "after Fred Pohl's talk had generated a real argument among the professional writers present, Brian let the mask slip completely. It was clear who he regarded as 'lowbrow'—at Chester, it was Niven and Pohl."

Another author might have taken umbrage, but Brian was more sneaky. Instead, he sent me a wonderful item that he called *a jeu d'esprit,* written while he was in a holiday mood, just before departing for Lower Bavaria. The title took me all evening to pick out painfully in Letraset, "I'm only a yellowing skull, without any yellowing ears, and yet I can hear every word you say as clearly as if it were yesterday." The cover splash on Issue 31 (December 1972) titled it more succinctly, "Aldiss—Hounded to the Grave?" and it was a little gem, impossible to summarise, one of the wittiest pieces Brian has ever written. It made a series of subtle (and not-so-subtle) retorts to my comments, as when the widowed Margaret is interviewed about the departed Brian, and says, "He felt that Weston was far too glib in his diagnoses, and wielded far too much power in his rotten little magazine... Weston had the infernal cheek to pretend"—her voice rose to a shriek—"that he and my husband were mad about Heinlein's work!"

The cover showed a giant statue of King Kong that had recently been erected in the Bull Ring, to the astonishment of Dave Kyle and Forry Ackerman when they passed through for the third Speculation conference at the University, and announced, "Novacon-2*[sic]* in Birmingham—Where else can you see an 18-foot gorilla?"

Inside, we ran "The Most Controversial Speech at Chessmancon," the Fred Pohl talk that had caused so much argument, a carefully-worded piece in which Fred stirred up the other professionals with his vigorous defence of the traditional values of science fiction. Fred quoted a remark he had made to Algis Budrys, "A. J., I don't mind your having people settle all the great problems of humanity in your stories, but can't they do it while they're dodging fire-lizards on Venus?" Uproar broke out, and Harry Harrison commented, "God, up there in a dirty moustache!"

Other noteworthy features of the issue were "The Critical Front," which contained four major book reviews by Tom Shippey, along with David Pringle's review of Ballard's new *Vermillion Sands* collection and the Canadian Doug Barbour's evaluation of *Again, Dangerous Visions*. There was also a report on the recent Eurocon at Trieste, with a set of photo-pages from Waldemar Kumming and the announcement that *Speculation* had won the first Europa Award for Best Fanzine.

Well, this was an unexpected honour, but my satisfaction was tempered slightly by sight of the actual Award itself, which my pal Vernon Brown kindly brought all the way back from Trieste, carrying it carefully on his lap since it

was very fragile. It was a ceramic trophy about eighteen inches high, replete with knobs and curlicues, finished in tasteful dark-brown varnish and looking like nothing so much as a Victorian table-leg. Rather wistfully, I contemplated the elegant bronze plaques that the runners-up had received!

Surprisingly, Issue 32 appeared relatively quickly, in March 1973, a 68-page issue that was instantly memorable for the cover picture of my nine-month-old daughter Alison, looking somewhat reproachfully at the camera and chewing on *Have Spacesuit, Will Travel* above the title, "Digesting Her First Heinlein novel."

It was a good, solid issue, with the major feature being Larry Niven's GoH speech from Chessmancon, titled "Alternatives to Worlds." We pulled out all the stops for this one. Printed on special gold paper, the speech had no less than eleven original illustrations by "Ames"—Andrew Stephenson. I had met Andrew at Worcester and he had subsequently been writing stories for Rob Holdstock's "fiction fanzine," *Macrocosm,* but he had also been doing some fine artwork for Malcolm Edwards in *Vector.* I thought Andrew was the right person to bring Larry Niven's concepts to life, and was proven spectacularly correct; his drawings were superb, with a draughtsman's attention to detail and a keen sense of humour, as shown by the spaceship in the title spread that was a disguised slide-rule!

Larry Niven was equally impressed, and wrote a fan letter saying, "Mr Stephenson, you are a genius!" He sold the article to *Analog* and suggested Ben Bova should use Andrew's artwork, which he re-drew to exploit the finer reproduction available, and later, Larry re-sold the whole package to paperback. Andrew comments, "Larry had taken a liking to my work and put my name forward to Jim Baen at *Galaxy.* Later, he remarked that I drew what he imagined, or words to that effect. His work was tricky at times, with all those odd entities and situations. I enjoyed inferring absent details, filling gaps as consis-

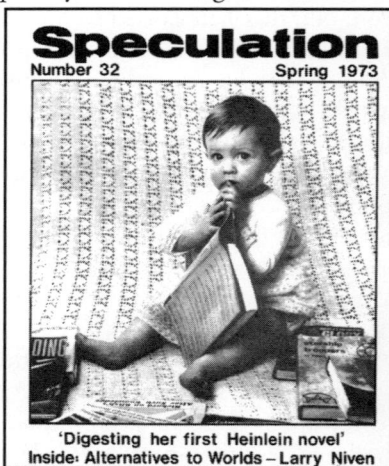

tently as possible." Eventually, Andrew contributed a considerable amount of work for *Galaxy,* his biggest job being the interior art for *Inferno.*

Larry Niven himself appeared in the "Melting Pot" column of Issue 32, writing, "The piece by Brian Aldiss about Brian Aldiss had me in hysterics. Where was this marvellous, witty writer when *Report on Probability A* was being written? I'm a monomaniac regarding that book, with good reason; after Heicon I was trapped on the Amsterdam–New York charter flight for something like ten hours with no way to even leave my seat, and with only that one book in my possession. I actually got about forty pages into it before I went back to staring at the ceiling. If Brian Aldiss had met me coming off that plane I'd have hit him with something heavy."

The most remarkable item in the entire issue, however, came in a three-page letter from Jim Blish, who left an unanswered question that must be right up there with Fermat's Last Theorem. Jim started by wondering what was so special about his famous story "Surface Tension": "to many fans it was the only story my name brought to mind, and there were even more who remembered it, but could not remember or had never heard of the author. *And I couldn't see why.*" Then, he said, in 1972 he had Darko Suvin as a house-guest for a few days, and miraculously, he had the answer.

Jim said, "It explained the popularity of 'Surface Tension,' it explained the popularity of some other works of mine, the reason why the larger number of my conventional pieces had quite failed to be memorable, and a good many other things too... I'll never forget that evening's discussion, which was to me indeed like the Descent of the Dove, but for every good reason I'm keeping it close to my chest until I think I've digested all of it." So there we have it, "James Blish discovers the Secret of writing memorable fiction"—and he didn't tell anyone!

In my editorial I ruminated about "whither *Speculation?*" What tack do we take for the future, I wondered, and considered the flavour of the magazine, the way it had developed through the interrelationship of the various people who wrote for the magazine. I even looked forward to celebrating "the ten-year stretch" in October, and said that my tenth annish would be number 35, unless "some major catastrophe intervenes."

It did, and it was my own fault. I made two disastrous decisions, which together killed off *Speculation*. First, I had been tremendously impressed with John J. Pierce's mammoth essay on Cordwainer Smith, in his own *Renaissance,* and foolishly offered this a home, not considering that I already had a backlog of material and didn't need a reprint from someone else's fanzine. Even worse, having had difficulties with duplicating the previous issue, I accepted an offer from one of my subscribers, Jim Diviney, to print the next one by litho. Jim told me that he had bought a printing press, pending his discharge from H.M. Armed Forces, and he would be able to do the work very cheaply.

This sounded good, so I painstakingly typed out another issue, pasting it up on oversize paper masters for reduction to quarto. Of the 36 pages, 25 were devoted to the Cordwainer Smith article, accompanied by a superb cover and five wonderful interior illustrations from Andrew Stephenson, true works of art, in every sense. I sent off the originals to Jim and waited...and waited. It was nearly nine months before he finally advised the issue was finished, by which time it had been completely overtaken by other events. We had moved house, I was looking desperately for another job, and another baby was on the way. I drove down to his army camp in Gloucestershire with little enthusiasm, and collected Issue 33—not collated and stapled, as I had hoped, but as loose sheets, patchily-printed on flimsy paper. It seemed that starting a printing business was not quite as easy as Jim had imagined.

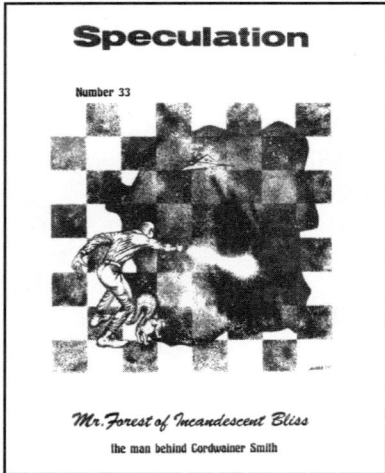

Speculation

Number 33

Mr. Forest of Incandescent Bliss
the man behind Cordwainer Smith

I no longer had my comfortable study but was in an older house, needing decorating, for which we'd had to pay far more than we had expected. I was overwhelmed, hard-up, didn't have the heart—or the time—to do anything with the issue except to put it into my attic, where it sat for another two and a half years before I finally put copies together and distributed them as a supplement with *Maya* in 1976. It was an ignominious end to *Speculation,* a whimper rather than a bang. If only I had carried on, exactly as before, with the usual mix of letters and features, produced on my trusty duplicator... Even then, I suspect, it could not have gone on for very much longer. Times had changed; when I started, back in 1963, there was almost no serious discussion of science fiction. By 1973 there were a multitude of sources, fanzines, books, and *Foundation,* the journal of the SF Foundation, that bizarre hobby-horse of George Hay's which had taken on a real life of its own, largely thanks to its first Administrator, Peter Nicholls.

Living a life at least partly in the mundane world, trying to earn a living and bring up a family, I simply didn't have the time, the resources, or the ability to compete. *Speculation* had come a long way, had reached heights I could never have imagined when I first produced that little purple *Zenith.* I had published the fanzine for nearly ten years and its passing left a void; I would have to find some other big project to keep me actively involved with fandom.

The Canadian critic Susan Wood once suggested in *Maya* that she was awed by *Speculation*. In reply, I noted that, "with one issue, I counted up and found that every single contributor had a degree (for what that is worth) save me. What a state, to be given an inferiority complex by one's own fanzine!"

Weston Discovers America!
Chapter 17

Yippee! I had won TAFF—on the third attempt! They gave me the good news just after Tynecon and I was delighted. It isn't usual to stand more than twice but because the last contest had been a bit exceptional, to say the least, my nominators had persuaded me to try again, up against my friend Peter Roberts, and winning this time by a convincing majority, 154/65. So I was going to a Worldcon after all, to the 1974 Discon in Washington, D.C. What an adventure!

Sadly, Eileen would have to stay at home with our daughter Alison, who was only two years old. A great pity, because the American fans would have loved Eileen. Still, I started to make my plans but after only a couple of weeks, we hit a problem. Yes, that's right; we were going to have another baby! And the estimated date of delivery was the end of August, right at the same time as my TAFF trip. How did *that* happen! What was I going to do? It struck me that we couldn't have hit such a precise two-week slot like that if we had tried! Fortunately for me, Eileen was incredibly generous. "You go;" she said, "you'll never get another chance to visit America." That was the way it seemed then; almost no-one we knew had crossed the Atlantic except for a few Travelling Jiants like Dave Kyle and Bill Burns. It was a big thing, expensive, not something you did without good reason.

I received the TAFF money from this side of the pond—there wasn't much of it—and started to look around for the cheapest flights. The best deal seemed to be with Court Lines, one of Britain's biggest travel companies. How to organise the trip? I wasn't going to have a lot of time—two weeks was about all the holiday I could take from my job. And I was a bit handicapped because I didn't know many people in the Washington area except Dick Eney and the Gillilands (not realising that Ted White had moved back to Falls Church several years earlier). That was the trouble, I was a little out of touch, had been far better connected back in 1971 when I *should* have made my trip. Still, Eddie Jones advised me not to be too concerned because "you'll meet plenty of people over there."

In May, however, I suddenly had other things to worry about. My employer, BSA, finally crashed and I was made redundant, in the middle of a recession, which was a bad time to be out of work. A few worrying weeks followed before I found a job in market research with the Delta Group, although they weren't very happy that almost immediately I would be taking two weeks off.

The trip was getting very close and I had to make some decisions. It would have been nice to get some help from the American administrators, Len & June Moffatt, but I didn't know them, had met them only briefly the year before, and they were West Coast fans anyway. In the end I arranged to fly into New York at the beginning of Worldcon week, and from there I thought I could easily get up to Boston and see Tony Lewis and the other NESFA people, and perhaps travel down to the convention with them. Not an ideal plan, but it seemed reasonable at the time.

Then I wondered; what to wear? I needed something casual but practical, and they said it was going to be *hot* in Washington. Eventually I chose a brown suede jacket (with lots of pockets) to travel in, a really natty pair of bold-checked flairs, a coral shirt, and a cream-coloured lightweight suit for dressing up. I also bought a portable tape-recorder, the smallest I could find, in order to dictate notes every night for my TAFF Report. Now I was all set to go.

Except that one week before I was due to leave England the whole of the mighty Court Lines Group collapsed into bankruptcy. My ticket was paid for, but suddenly all bets were off. In panic, I tried to telephone their head office. So did ten thousand other people. The lines were jammed, the local travel agent couldn't tell me anything, newspaper headlines screamed it was the biggest-ever travel crash, airlines were turning passengers away, thousands of families had lost their holidays. Chewing my fingernails, I worried, why *do* these things always happen to me?

Fortunately, the travel industry got itself together at top speed. After some nudging by the government the heads of all the major operators held an emergency meeting and announced that Court Lines tickets *would* be honoured.

(This was actually the beginning of the present ABTA guarantee scheme.) So on Saturday 24th August I said goodbye to Eileen, who was by this time very advanced in her pregnancy, and travelled down to London to meet Peter Roberts, who was kind enough to come out to Heathrow and see me off. The plane was delayed, but I boarded in the late afternoon and slumped thankfully into my seat; after all the upsets, I was finally on my way!

I had only flown before on a few short trips to Europe and I was still nervous about the whole idea, so the prospect of an eight-hour flight was a bit daunting. With hundreds of people on board, the 747 seemed enormous, more like a ship than a plane, and it was so *noisy,* a continual droning roar, impossible to ignore. I peered out of the window but couldn't see anything except clouds. They served a meal, then started to show a film, but I couldn't see the screen very well so I tried to read my book, but couldn't concentrate because of that terrible roaring. Sneakily, I opened one of my plastic half-bottles of duty-free whisky and took a good mouthful. After a few more tots I started to feel happier, the engine noise receded to a dull thundering and I fell asleep, thinking about my mission.

In late 1973, my alter ego Malcolm Edwards had revived the idea of running a world convention in Britain before the end of the decade. Inadvertently echoing Eileen he had said, "I want to go to a Worldcon, am never likely to get to the USA for one, and therefore have to resort to bringing the mountain to Mahomet." We got together, and with Peter Roberts formed a provisional committee and made our move at Tynecon, the three of us going up onto the platform at the end of the Sunday-morning business meeting to outline our plans.

We had no very clear idea where to hold it and we didn't know when. I stumbled through an analysis of current and likely bids, explained the infamous 3-year rotation system and why we should aim to take on the supposedly weaker Midwestern zone, and urged the need for a massive, pre-emptive strike before any serious American opposition could get off the ground.

I was cut short in mid-flow. An attractive (American) lady with red hair stood up in the front row. It was Ruth Kyle.

"Peter, Britain's *fine* in '79," she said, to thunderous applause.

And it was. In one brilliant stroke of inspiration, Ruth gave us our year, our slogan, and our momentum. That morning almost the whole membership of Tynecon (one of the most successful of British Eastercons) signed up as supporters, and Peter and I agreed that whichever one of us won TAFF, we would put our case at Discon and stake an early claim to 1979. So now in my luggage I was carrying a thousand fliers and campaign badges and I was going to have to talk up our British bid at every opportunity. I dreamed of standing on a platform to make a speech in front of massed fans, but they couldn't hear me because of the terrible noise...

…and woke up with a pounding headache and the feeling that I was trapped in a long, grey metal tunnel with someone hammering loudly and continuously on the outside, a roaring, ringing, echoing noise that was never going to stop. The lights had been dimmed in the cabin and it was actually not very warm. Most people were asleep. I looked at my watch and found it was only nine o'clock. Only halfway! I tried the headphones for some music, but couldn't concentrate with my headache and that continual, penetrating background rumble. The journey seemed as if it would go on forever and I couldn't keep drinking whisky, not for four more hours.

Before landing, the flight attendant brought round some green and white forms. The white one was a straightforward Customs Declaration, and after pondering over it, I decided I wouldn't need to declare my Worldcon campaign badges. The green form was for Immigration, and it was absolutely ridiculous! Give your age and date of birth, it said, in *three* separate places. Then there was a whole series of silly questions, like "Are you seeking entry to engage in criminal or immoral activities? Have you ever been involved in espionage or sabotage or involved in any way with persecutions associated with Nazi Germany?" and "Have you ever been arrested or convicted for an offence involving Moral Turpitude?" The answers were pretty self-evident, and I wondered whether in the whole history of the world anyone had ever answered "yes."

Eventually we landed and disembarked into the sticky night of August in New York. The first thing that struck me was the *heat,* the hot, clammy air. And that dreadful *smell!* It reeked of dead fish and sewers, and some of the other passengers held handkerchiefs to their noses as we walked across the tarmac into the terminal building, down a staircase and into a long, grey cellar. There we were herded between rows of metal bars into an arrangement of stalls, rather like a giant cowshed, under a large notice saying "Aliens." A burly policeman watched us, chewing gum, his belly hanging over a belt liberally festooned with guns, ammunition, riot-sticks, and maybe hand grenades for all I knew. Then they brought on the sniffer dogs. Welcome to America!

It took well over an hour to be "processed," to have my passport inspected, my forms stamped, and to collect my luggage, and it was after 2.00 a.m. by my body clock when I went through the final doors. And there, bless them, were the fans, Steve Stiles in the lead with a half-dozen others I didn't know. A tall, white, slightly chubby young man took my hand. "Hi," he said, "I'm Andy Porter. What did you think of the latest *Algol?*" I grinned bravely, and asked the question that was foremost in my mind, "What's that horrible *smell?*" They looked taken-aback and I realised they couldn't smell anything, didn't know what I was talking about. Steve suggested that maybe it was the mud flats; JFK Airport is on reclaimed land, right next to Long Island Sound, and the shoreline is tidal. Perhaps that was it? None of them was bothered by the heat or the stench, and I suppose you get used to anything, if you live with it long enough.

Andy and Steve took me back to Steve's apartment for a party, and I tried to be a real fun person although for me it was by now after 3.00 a.m., and it had been a long day. Finally, they all went home and Steve showed me to the room they had kindly provided. It had its very own air-conditioning unit built into the window and the air was cooler, though I wondered how I would ever sleep with all that buzzing and wheezing only a couple of feet from my head...

Next day I was introduced to bagels and lox and rude taxi-drivers, then flew up to Boston, where Tony Lewis met me at the airport and gave me a quick tour of the city. He pointed out landmarks like the Copper Kettle and the hideous, green-painted girders of the elevated expressway that some lunatic city-planner had caused to be driven through the historic waterfront district. He showed me City Hall, which turned out to be an inverted pyramid, obviously designed by the same demented architect who created Birmingham's Central Library (the building that Prince Charles said "looked like a place to *burn* books, not store them"). Then we went to a NESFA meeting in someone's house and I met a whole lot of friendly people like Bonnie Dalzell and Spike MacPhee, talked about *Ringworld,* and then went to a fish restaurant where I had my first clam chowder.

Tony took me to MIT, where he showed me the MITSFS library with its wall-to-ceiling shelves of leather-bound volumes of *Amazing* and *Astounding.* We went out to see his wife Susan at work, and she sat me in front of their big computer to try a game in which you were supposed to land a rocket on the Moon by balancing speed, height, and fuel supply. I managed to make a crater fifty-feet deep, which she said was about par for the course. So much for daredevil space-jockeys flying by the seat of their pants!

I was anxious to get to Washington early, so took the overnight Amtrak from Boston, which seemed another never-ending journey. It meant that I arrived on Wednesday morning, before the convention had started, suffering from mild jet lag, and feeling vaguely disoriented. The Sheraton Hotel was immense, a sprawling conglomerate reported to possess over four miles of internal corridors, a labyrinth of wings, extensions, halls, and function rooms radiating off in all directions. Even more confusingly, it was on a slope, so that from one direction my room was in the basement, while simultaneously being on the ninth floor at the other end of the building. I was immediately lost. And it was so *cold* in my room. Outside, the sun was shining brightly but the hotel was air-conditioned, almost to the point of being uncomfortable. I dragged an extra blanket out of the cupboard and took a nap for a few hours before venturing downstairs to the lobby, where I hung around hopefully, looking for a familiar face.

Suddenly I was a neo all over again, watching fans arriving, talking, and greeting each other, while I recognised no one in this strange new fandom. They were all much more casually dressed than I was used to, some of the men wearing shorts and T-shirts, the women even less; halter-tops and bare midriffs were common. Then a tall, grey-haired man arrived wearing a familiar red blazer. It was good old Dave Kyle. I was so pleased to see him! Dave introduced me to the co-chairs, Jay Haldeman and Ron Bounds, and to Ron's girlfriend, Bobbi Armbruster. They were very kind and showed me around, so that by the evening I suddenly experienced an odd switch of perception; looking at so many familiar faces (familiar, on two hours' acquaintance), I felt suddenly at home, as if I had known American fandom for years.

That was the night I went out with DUFF-winner Leigh Edmonds and his girlfriend Valma Brown from Australia, with a crowd of their friends to a restaurant a few blocks away. We seemed to get on well together, and I made a start on the important business of telling people about the British Worldcon bid. As luck would have it, a number of the other diners were from the Chicago area and they said they had been thinking of mounting their own bid for 1979. "Nah, you don't want to do that," I assured them, quickly signing them up as pre-supporters and giving them our little blue badges. It was a good beginning. Then, back at the hotel I rang home and had some wonderful news; now I had another daughter, and mother and baby were both well!

I was struck by the sheer size of it all. The largest U.K. Eastercon had seen about 400 people, but Discon II had ten times that many. Anyone who thinks this is a good thing has to experience the football-match crowding, the sheer frustration of trying to find friends in a mob, particularly since the hard core, the keen, active types who publish fanzines, organise conventions and comprise fandom-as-I-know-it, are still counted in hundreds. Ridiculously, at the Worldcon the original founding body had become an outnumbered, statistically insignificant special interest group among much larger proportions of casual readers, *Star Trek* and media fans, and so on. And from my privileged position, I was able to see a little way behind the scenes and gradually came to realise that the mighty Worldcon, the very highest pinnacle of fannish excellence, was actually running on a wing and a prayer. The original organising committee had crashed and burned, and the convention had only been saved by heroic, last-minute efforts by Ron and a brave few others. This was an absolute revelation![1]

On Thursday morning Joe and Gay Haldeman (whom I had met at Chester in 1972) invited me for lunch at a nearby coffee shop with some other fans.

---

[1] Much later I realised this was quite a common state of affairs, that in fact very many American Worldcons are doomed to catastrophic failure. Except for Boston, of course. Never Boston!

Going through the revolving door meant instantly swapping the icy air-conditioning of the Sheraton for the full furnace blast of noonday Washington in August. The heat was a solid wall! It was like stepping fully-dressed into a very hot sauna, and I ran the last hundred yards, soaked to the skin with perspiration. Gay was very kind and sympathetic and gave me a cold drink, and now I understood why everyone was dressed so lightly. "How on Earth did they ever *settle* this country?" I gasped.

The convention started that afternoon in a most peculiar way. In a huge, crowded hall, Harlan Ellison stood on a table, and traded insults with Isaac Asimov at the other end of the room.

"You Dirty Old Man Asimov!" shouted Ellison.

"Stand Up, Harlan!" retorted Asimov.

This went on for a half-hour or so to the delight of the fans, though somehow, I wasn't entirely happy at the exchange. It was obvious that this was a familiar double-act, that these two larger-than-life personalities were putting on a show, but I thought it was an unedifying spectacle, not exactly *dignified*. And after the "dialogue" was over, I noticed that Harlan went stomping around the hall, cursing and insulting the fans quite rudely, acting his part as "Mr Tough Guy," although he was perfectly correct with me. No, I decided, too false, I didn't like it at all.

Asimov and Ellison were almost the only professionals in evidence that afternoon, and I wondered where all the others were hiding. It was nothing like our British cons, where Brian Aldiss, Ted Tubb, and Ken Bulmer were so visible and such integral parts of the scene. At Discon, the authors appeared briefly for programme events and then vanished mysteriously to some presumed Valhalla in the attic. They kept out of reach of their anxious admirers apart from a few carefully planned encounters, like the one staged that night by the committee.

They gave me a box and a boater

It was a Meet the Celebrities party, but done in the American way, the authors given straw boaters and large name badges and asked to stand on low boxes. As the TAFF-man, I was similarly equipped with box and boater and dutifully stood there while the fans streamed past with their autograph books, pausing occasionally to squint at my badge, decide they'd never heard of me, and hastily look away before going off to find someone more famous. It was quite humiliating and after a half-hour, I decided I'd had enough of that, jumped down and went off to find someone I could talk to. I liked the straw hat, though, and wore it most of the weekend. Leigh Edmonds said I looked exactly like a *Void* boy, and I thought there could be no higher praise!

There was another, first-time Brit at Discon, and this was John Jarrold, a 21-year-old who had decided to come to Washington after attending just a couple of British conventions. By all normal rules of engagement he should have been swallowed up, lost among the masses, but John Jarrold travels under a kindly star. He said:

"I just remember having a WONDERFUL time. Les Flood was there, and he introduced me to just about every author under the Sun, Larry Niven, Keith Laumer, Leigh Brackett, Ben Bova, Jack Williamson, Roger Zelazny himself (the GoH) and MANY others. It was an amazing time. At the Meet the Celebrities party I ran into John Brunner, who said, 'Oh, Hi, you made it.' Then I remember running into R. A. Lafferty in the bar. Les Flood bought me drinks there at least twice and introduced me to Ray Lafferty. I was incredibly lucky."

That was the main thing I missed, *the bar*. The American fans didn't seem to drink—or rather, the hotel bar played a far less important role than it does at our Eastercons. Just a few months earlier, we had literally drunk the Tynecon hotel dry—did someone say 3,000 gallons?—and to us the bar was the focal point, the axis around which the convention revolves, a friendly, inexpensive place where you could sit and meet everyone, sooner or later. But Discon had no counterpart, and I thought this resulted in an odd vacuum at the heart of the convention, meaning you had to wander around aimlessly and hope you bumped into someone. Very hard on the feet!

There *was* a hotel bar, of course, a small, brightly-lit area just off the foyer, with stools and a thuggish-looking barman who continually polished glasses and supervised an enormous array of strange-looking bottles, serving things like Screwdrivers and Manhattans to Gordon Dickson and Jerry Pournelle and a few others affluent enough to afford them. On the second day, I went in with Leigh and Valma and ordered three beers, receiving a dirty look and three small, very expensive tins of very cold, very fizzy Budweiser, no draught beer being available. I didn't do that again! Later, we went out to a supermarket and bought a few six-packs of Michelob, which I smuggled up to my (freezing cold) room to accompany the duty-free whisky at room parties. However, I had to drink most of it myself, the American fans preferring to guzzle Coca-Cola, Dr Pepper and root beer.

I spent a lot of time that weekend with the Australians because we seemed to have a lot in common, culturally, and very much the same sense of humour. We joked together about the Great American Cutlery Shortage; we had discovered that no matter how many courses you had, they only gave you one knife and fork, and you were in trouble if you should accidentally leave them on the first plate. "I think the correct etiquette is to wipe them carefully on the tablecloth after the first course," I suggested helpfully, and they agreed with me that the Americans were probably too busy making space rockets to be able to provide a full set of cutlery.

Leigh had the look of a bedraggled student, with owlish glasses, wispy beard and ponytail, and a stocking cap he kept firmly on his head at all times. Valma was small and slight with chestnut hair and freckles and a big smile. They were a lovely, fun couple, and I was highly flattered when he wrote in his trip report, "It was an enlightening experience chatting to that horribly sercon person who had produced *Speculation* and finding that he was one of the finest fannish people I'd met in many years."

I met Bob Tucker at the Aussiecon Party, somewhere high in the towers of the Sheraton, where Leigh and Valma presented him with a bottle of Jim Beam they had bought at Sydney Airport, and asked for a demonstration of how it should be properly drunk. Tucker obliged with his "Smooooooth" routine (although privately, I thought the stuff was a bit rough compared to a good Scotch whisky), and then we sat around on the floor, talking about nothing in particular. People were smoking, so I lit one of my little Henry Winterman duty-free cigars, which attracted Tucker's attention. "What's in that thing you're smoking?" he asked. "Why, tobacco," I said in surprise. "Just tobacco? Let me have that," he said, taking a deep mouthful. I have no idea of the possible significance of this exchange.

John Jarrold, of course, had no trouble finding room parties:

"Gardner Dozois and Jack Dann had the room next to mine. We rode up in the elevator together, not knowing each other, and ending up tailing right to the end of the corridor. My room had two double beds and a closet which was bigger than any hotel room I'd had at a U.K. convention. Gardner and Jack had booked a twin room but were given a suite, so I heard cries of joy as they explored all the unexpected space. They had parties every night, to which I was invited. Good job I was young!"

There was simply too much to see and do. Simultaneous programme events, a huge Art Show, a continuous film programme, and a half-dozen syndicate discussion rooms that I didn't even find until the last day. These were occupied by groups like the N3F, SFRA, and so on. There was a Georgette Heyer Tea (in Regency costume, please), and a Burroughs Dum-Dum (in leopard skins, maybe?). The basement book room was enormous, crowded with tables and over a hundred dealers selling old magazines, comics, filmstrips, artwork, posters, and models—you name it, it was there. I managed to pick up some old *Astounding*s at very moderate prices and U.S. SFBC titles at just a dollar each, these apparently being a drug on the market. Bill Rotsler gave me a personalised name badge, and Larry Niven offered a campaign button for Trantorcon in 23,309.

On Saturday night I was fascinated by the Masquerade (we call it the Fancy Dress), where the participants mostly enacted some little tableau or scene, rather than just stumbling on and off in the British way with a cardboard box on their heads. We saw over one hundred costumes, some of them very beautiful, including excellent renderings from Philip José Farmer novels *Flesh* (the antlered Stagg and virginal attendant) and *The Maker of Universes* (the "Harpy"), and plenty of slave girls in chains because of the influence of the John Norman Gor books. The top entries were the Resnicks, incredible as "Ice King and Queen," and Drew and Kathy Sanders as "The Golden Apples of the Sun." Someone told me these were really serious costuming fans, who spent most of the year making their outfits. I could easily believe it.

The business meeting took place on the following morning, at which Kansas City was awarded the 1976 Worldcon and preliminary bids were heard for 1977. This was my chance, and I took the platform to deliver an earnest five minutes about Britain's intention to host the Worldcon in 1979. It seemed to be well received and I sold more pre-supporting memberships, so successfully in fact that later, Mike Resnick, prospective chairman of "Chicago in 79," discovered that all his potential committee members had signed for Britain. With good grace he came on board, too, and by the end of Discon I had collected over two hundred pre-supporters and our pre-emptive strike had been well and truly delivered.

I was greatly honoured when Ron invited me onto the top table for the Banquet and Awards ceremony on Sunday evening. They expected me to say a few words, so I made a bit of an effort and put on my cream suit and a ruffled shirt with a big maroon bow tie. It turned out that I needn't have bothered, since Ron wore his usual open shirt and jeans, but I always think it's better to be too smart than too scruffy. We sat high on a dais with Roger Zelazny and the other guests, overlooking some eleven hundred other diners whose tables stretched away under the bright lights into the middle distance. I looked over my shoulder at the row of gleaming Awards, and quipped to Ron, "You realise this is the closest I'm ever going to get to a Hugo!"

Finally, the meal was cleared away and our Toastmaster, Andrew Offutt, got to his feet. Now, all he had to do was to introduce the Guest of Honour and supervise the batting order for the presentations. But this was the night Andy Offutt went mad. He talked, and he talked, and he talked. Everyone fidgeted, but still he talked. The audience was growing restless, muttering, and complaining, and still he talked. Suddenly Harlan Ellison marched determinedly down the aisle from the back of the room, mounted the steps to the dais, and hissed so loudly that it was picked up by the microphones, "Andy, shut up!" There was a universal gasp of relief but it was premature. Andy Offutt just smiled serenely and carried on. He spoke for a total of one hour and fifteen minutes, and sat down to total silence.

Late, much too late, Roger Zelazny stood up and in just one minute thanked the committee, before sitting down to a standing ovation. And then the Hugo Awards were presented, handsome silvery rockets given to various winners, to Ben Bova, Harlan Ellison, and finally, for Best Novel, to *Rendezvous with Rama* (accepted by publisher Betty Ballantine, on behalf of Arthur C. Clarke). Somewhere in there I made my few remarks about TAFF, but like everyone else in that room, by then I just wanted to get out. We had been sitting for nearly five hours, far too long, and afterwards everyone had only one question, "What was the matter with Andy Offutt?"

That was it, really. I was checking out on Monday, and while I finished packing Gay Haldeman came by to pick up a book or something. "Oh, it's so *cold* in here, Peter," she said, walking over to the window and flipping up the concealed lid on the plain metal box that had been making such a racket for the last five days. Expertly she adjusted the controls, switching the fan from "Full Boost" to "Off." Immediately the noise-level dropped, and so did my face; it had never even occurred to me that the temperature of individual rooms could be adjusted!

I spent the rest of the day in Washington with Leigh and Valma and with Alexis Gilliland, who had kindly volunteered to give us a quick tour of the major sights. At first we were worried about Alex because he had a leathery, expressionless sort of face with a peculiarly slow, laconic way of talking, and we thought he might be hard work. But very quickly we realised that he had a wonderful, dry sense of humour that was an absolute delight. He took us to the Washington Monument, where we rode the lift to the observation deck at the top, and then to the Smithsonian, where we gawked in unabashed wonder at the Mercury, Gemini and Apollo capsules. Our final destination was the Lincoln Memorial, which we all thought was tremendously moving. Alex lined the three of us up on the steps, overlooking the Reflecting Pool, and insisted on taking photographs with each of our cameras. Then, all too soon, I had to head for the National Airport, where I said goodbye to Leigh and Valma and caught my flight to Melbourne, in Florida, where I was going to spend a few days with Sam Long.

Sam was a busy little Rupert-Bear character whom I had met years earlier at an Eastercon when he was stationed in Britain with the U.S. Air Force. He now worked as a weather-forecaster at Patrick Air Force Base, and he had suggested I should come down to Florida, where we could have a really good time, see Cape Canaveral and let off one of his weather rockets. Well, I didn't need very much persuading to see the fabled Cape, and after discovering the cost of a flight from Washington to Florida was really amazingly cheap, I thought I would definitely give it a try.

The flight took just over an hour and I arrived at Melbourne, a small, almost deserted airport with a fresh, cool wind blowing from the sea. Sam was waiting for me in his red MGB sports car, of which he was very proud, and as we drove to his beachfront apartment, I thought this was just too good to be true. What a wonderful life, working for the space programme, living by the sea in beautiful Florida. I was looking forward to seeing the sights and meeting the local fans, but when I mentioned this to Sam he just looked at me blankly. "Oh, there aren't any fans in Florida," he said.

I was disappointed, I was sure Sam had mentioned some local fans. Perhaps I had misheard. But then we arrived at his apartment, and I was disappointed again. The complex *did* face the ocean, but there was a 4-lane highway between us and the beach, and it wasn't exactly a beach but a rather nasty-looking strip of gravel with dense beds of seaweed just off-shore. "Oh, you can't bathe there," said Sam. "Rocks and dangerous currents." We parked and went inside the apartment and had something to eat. "What shall we do tomorrow?" I asked eagerly. "Oh, I have to go to work," said Sam. "But you can come along." Slowly, the realisation was dawning that it might have been a bit of a mistake to come to Florida.

The following day we went into Patrick Air Force Base ("Oh, it's nothing to do with the Space Programme," he said), and I spent the morning watching Sam consulting his instruments and writing reports about the weather. In the afternoon things brightened up, and we went along to the firing range, where I watched the technicians make ready a met. rocket. This was a solid-fuel job about six feet long and four inches diameter, which launched from a short ramp and went up ten miles or so before the instrument package separated and parachuted down. It was indeed quite a thrill to go into the blockhouse and press the button to send the rocket on its way!

Then Sam drove us along the coast road towards Cape Canaveral itself. I was thrilled, as the silhouette of the Vertical Assembly Building appeared on the horizon and in the far distance several of the launch gantries. Sam stopped the car in a lay-by, we walked over to a chain-link fence, and he pointed proudly inside. Wow! They had a whole array of rockets in there, many of which I recognised. There was a V2, an obsolete Ajax-Hercules, a Redstone, a Thor, many smaller types, and towering over all of them was the mighty Atlas, all gleaming silvery-white in the Florida sun. I asked Sam if we could get any closer. "Oh, that's a restricted area," he said, so I stared at the rockets for ten minutes or more, before reluctantly

---

[2] What Sam Long didn't tell me, and what I didn't discover until I returned in 1987, was that just a short way down the road there was a gate in the fence, and a sign, which said, "Welcome to the Visitor Centre." I could have walked around the rocket garden at leisure, seen the fantastic exhibits inside the Museum, watched the film-presentations, bought souvenirs. But we didn't do

climbing back into the MGB and turning back, away from the Cape.[2]

On the way home, I noticed signs for something called "Walt Disney World," and asked Sam about it. "Oh, that's a rip-off," he said dismissively. But I had read about the new Disney project that had opened a year or so before, and thought I might give it a try. It would be better than more weather forecasting, anyway. But how to get there? It was in central Florida, probably a hundred miles away. "There's a bus," my friend conceded, and we stopped by the bus station in Melbourne, where I put my name down for next morning's excursion. Then we went back to his apartment, where I dictated into my tape recorder for an hour or two, catching up on my final impressions of Discon.

Next morning, bright and early, Sam dropped me off at the bus station and I climbed aboard a large, single-deck coach, a bit battered, but air-conditioned. We sat there for a while, waiting for other passengers, but none appeared. With a deep sigh the driver engaged gear and off we went. It was a strange feeling, being the only passenger on a bus that could hold fifty or sixty. Sam later explained that the bus company had a franchise, which meant they had to operate the service if any passenger wanted to use it. So because of me, the poor driver had to make a two-hundre- mile round-trip and hang around all day at Disney World. No wonder he was so uncommunicative!

Disney World was incredible. I rode the monorail to the "Magic Kingdom," walked down Main Street, went on all the rides. I saw "20,000 Leagues Under the Sea," "Pirates of the Caribbean," "The Haunted Mansion," and went back twice for the incredible, breath-taking "World in the Round," a huge, circular theatre that presented a film programme with 360-degree views of the great sights of the world. It was a wonderful day, although I only wished that Eileen had been there; no matter how marvellous the sight, there's something lacking if you can't share it with another person. Finally, I left Disney and caught my bus, resolving that I would return to New York the following morning. Two days in Florida had been more than enough!

That was almost the end of my trip. Back in New York I met Leigh and Valma again at an uptown party hosted by Dave Emerson and Asenath Hammond. I stayed with Andy Porter and watched him type file cards for *Algol,* then we walked the Brooklyn Bridge and visited Sam Moskowitz at his frozen-food company. I met Moshe Feder and Jim Young, spent a pleasant evening with Arnie & Joyce Katz at 55 Pineapple Street, and Andy took me to the top of the Empire State Building and across the harbour to climb up inside the head of the Statue of Liberty. I did all the usual tourist things, but I enjoyed them, sampled New York food, met the fans. All too soon, I was boarding my plane, and slept solidly through the entire flight home. Now all I had to do was to write my TAFF Report.

---

any of that. I had come 5000 miles and fallen short at the last two hundred yards because Sam Long "wasn't interested" in that stuff, had "seen it before." I find it hard to forgive him for that.

Professional Stuff
Chapter 18

I was in trouble as soon as I got back from America. My new boss at Delta telephoned just after I arrived home on the Monday morning, heavily jet-lagged, and was unsympathetic, demanding I came into the office immediately. Eileen was still recovering from having Lucy, we now had two young children to look after, and a lot of decorating and other work needed to be done in the house, and central heating installed before winter. Hard up again, I offered to teach two night-school classes at the local college for their Diploma of Marketing course, Tuesday and Thursday evenings. They paid £5.00 per session, which was very useful, but it took me another evening each week to prepare my notes and mark the homework papers. Life was suddenly very hectic.

Just then I didn't have time to think very much about my TAFF Report, but I did start to do a little writing for *Science Fiction Monthly*. This new magazine had first appeared in February and it was a mess, a great floppy thing full of the worst, most garish covers from the New English Library paperback line. However, it had already run some new material, stories by Brian Aldiss and Chris Priest, and a film-review column by Australian fan John Brosnan, and I scented an opportunity. For years I had been writing the occasional review for *Books & Bookmen,* and sometimes readers' reports for John

Bush at Gollancz. I thought this might be a more regular market, and I needed the money.

Contriving a business trip to London, I visited the gloomy, church-hall offices of NEL at High Holborn, just across the road from the site of the old Globe meetings, and introduced myself to Julie Davis, the editor of *SFM*. She looked nineteen though she might have been a few years older, and she knew nothing about science fiction and very little about editing. I offered to help, give her any advice she might want, but not surprisingly, found I wasn't the first through her door. Julie had already been visited by John Brosnan, Rob Holdstock, old-time fan Walter Gillings, and Malcolm Edwards. She was confused, didn't understand this "fandom" business, didn't know who to believe. Gillings, a retired newspaper man, had already sold her a series on "Modern Masters of Science Fiction," but she was receptive to my idea for some articles on well-known SF themes like space travel and parallel worlds. Their rate was £10.00 per thousand words, which would pay a few more bills.

While *SFM* lasted I sold a number of these theme articles to Julie, and I was pleased when Charlie Ryan subsequently picked them up for his new *Galileo*. But I was irritated to see such a wonderful opportunity being squandered. Here was a major publisher with a good budget, colour printing and proper distribution, but the magazine was being spoilt by fundamentally incoherent strategy and hopelessly incompetent editing. Julie tried hard, but she really didn't have a clue, as was proven when she innocently accepted a "popular science" article from some idiot who solemnly trotted out the ludicrous theory that insect life could evolve quite spontaneously out of pond mud, something disproved over a century earlier by Pasteur and others.

By the time it finally ceased publication in May 1976, *Science Fiction Monthly* had seen twenty-eight issues. Initially, circulation had exceeded 100,000—huge numbers for Britain—but all along it had suffered from a fatal confusion of purpose; it could never decide whether it was a proper magazine or just a vehicle for reprinting cruddy NEL cover paintings. Even so, it had a tremendous effect upon British fandom, attracting floods of newcomers to the London Globe meetings and submerging the already-moribund BSFA beneath more than 1200 enquiries. At its deathbed a few secrets were spilled; for instance, it was revealed that Malcolm Edwards had negotiated a special rate of £15.00 per thousand for his material, because he was "more important" than other fan-contributors. I shook my head in rueful acknowledgement of a truly great hustler, but John Brosnan was less forgiving and went ballistic with rage!

Well before then I was expounding my thoughts on science fiction publishing to Anthony Cheetham, ex-editor at Sphere, who had recently secured a top job as managing director of Futura Publications, a new paperback house backed by the considerable muscle of the British Publishing Corporation.

Rog Peyton had known Anthony for some time, and because he seemed friendly and approachable we had invited him along to address the February 1975 Brum Group meeting at the Imperial Hotel. He gave an excellent talk about the problems and rewards of SF publishing, and the evening was a great success.

Afterwards—well, you know how it goes. Some of us were hanging round the bar, rabbitting on about the merits of various authors, and discussing the stories we were going to write, one day, when we got around to it, when Anthony came over and joined in. I had never met him before, not even corresponded, but I found we had similar tastes, both liking Fritz Leiber (but not other fantasy), Larry Niven, some Heinlein, Jack Vance, and so on. I told him about my frustrations with *SFM,* and the way I thought it *should* be edited, but didn't make any particular effort to be ingratiating since I figured that with all the other eager busybodies in fandom he was long since spoken for. Anyway, at the time I was feeling fed up with the incompetence of publishers generally, and with the uselessness of *Science Fiction Monthly* in particular.

Eventually Anthony retired to bed, and that was that, until the following Wednesday morning, when I received an intriguing white envelope through the post. His letter began, "I'd like to persuade you to edit a new anthology series."

Yippee!

Except that…in some ways this would prove to be a poisoned chalice. Oh, it was certainly a wonderful surprise and I was overjoyed at the invitation, but I had no idea how much work it would involve, the time it would take. It sounds great to be an editor but I found out with *Speculation* that editing can often be a thankless task, and as Richard Bergeron said in another context, "You can be an editor or a writer. Not both." In the previous year, spurred by redundancy and three weeks' unemployment, I had been trying to develop a sideline as a free-lance writer, and had managed to sell a fair volume of professional work, mostly journalism for the technical press, with those *SFM* articles for light relief. I had even started to collaborate with Tom Shippey on a projected series of science fiction stories (which eventually came to nothing). The advent of the anthology swiftly put paid to all that!

Anthony wanted to call the anthology "Andromeda," after Rog's bookshop, and he envisaged it as an annual fixture on his new list, stressing also his desire to encourage new writers. The only trouble, I thought, was that this was Rog's title, not mine, and I wasn't entirely sure of the propriety of using it; how about the Speculation anthology instead? But no, Anthony had made up his mind, and *Andromeda* it was going to be. "I've written and explained it to Rog," he said vaguely. Our rates would be £10.00 per thousand, and he would pay me a straight £100.00 for editing the book. Now I had six months to assemble the first number, which would appear the following spring.

My first move was to write to all the professionals I knew, then to put an announcement in *Locus* and the *SFWA Bulletin,* with a letter to all my old *Speculation* contributors saying, in effect, "this is your chance." Not because I necessarily wanted to play favourites, but because these were the people most likely to succeed at writing fiction, if they ever turned their hands to it. Half of them had already broken through anyway, people like Chris Priest, Mark Adlard, Brian Stableford, David Redd, and so on. Then I made a big mistake. I advised *SF Monthly* and *The Writer,* both places where, I reasoned, I might expect to find aspiring Young Hopefuls. This is known as "leading with your chin."

Good old Brian Aldiss was the first one to respond, bless him, with "Appearance of Life," a story specially written for *Andromeda* that was so absolutely, perfectly *right* that I couldn't find words to thank him enough. It was such a good story that he could have sold it anywhere, to better-paying markets where it would have gained a great deal more exposure, but Brian was being kind, helping me to get started, and I was very grateful.[1]

A deceptive calm then followed for two months, during which time I bought excellent stories from George R. R. Martin and Michael Coney. I also saw most of the material which circulates endlessly around the market, stories often written by established writers on their occasional off-days, sometimes years old, sent out time and again, pieces not entirely bad but which don't excite, don't inspire anyone to publish them, except in desperation. In fact, I suspect that's how a lot of SF *does* eventually get into print. However, with only one book per year I didn't have to be desperate, so I was determined not to compromise, not to accept any story I wasn't completely sure about, no matter who was the author.

One day while slogging through the pile I accidentally dropped a peanut-butter sandwich onto a particularly dismal manuscript, and started to wonder about the feasibility of introducing an Editors' Tip-off System, to trace where a story had been on its previous travels. Suppose Harry Harrison put a coffee-stain on the back page, Ken Bulmer filled in a few "o"s on page one, Julie Davis bit off the corners? Fortunately, those brown peanut-butter stains quickly came off, or they might have been misinterpreted further down the line!

I learned a few things that ten years of fan-editing had failed to teach me. One is that good stories do not grow on trees; an editor has to work hard to get decent material before competitors snap it up. It helped, of course, that word-rates for *Andromeda* were fairly high by British standards, but even so, this was an unknown new venture and professional writers already have commitments.

---

[1] Despite this limited exposure, "Appearance of Life" was tipped as a *Locus* recommendation for the 1976 Hugo Award in the Best Short Story category. If it had appeared in a U.S. collection, it might well have done a great deal better than that.

Agents were completely hopeless. One of them, representing an established writer, wrote a letter that went something like this: "When I first took on **** he sent me a huge pile of stories, so many that I thought I'd never get through them, but I've worked away and managed to place all but four, and now I'm pleased to send these to you." Well, thanks very much, I thought, looking without enthusiasm at the yellowed, dog-eared manuscripts he had enclosed. What a sales pitch!

Then there was the agent who sent me three long stories by someone I had never heard of, the sheets unnumbered and unbound, so they all fell into a pile when I opened the envelope. Of course, he hadn't enclosed return envelope or postage, and I had to resist a strong urge to throw the whole lot away. Later, his client wrote to me direct, asking if I had seen her stories, since she had been trying to get them back from the agent for six months at least.

My worst experience involved Keith Roberts and his agent, Giles Gordon. I had very much admired Keith's "Pavane" series, and sent him my letter about *Andromeda,* inviting him to contribute. I heard nothing for months and then, on the weekend of my deadline, he sent me a long piece titled "The Big Fans." It started well, with a future England in which giant windmills had been built to supply power, but swiftly added complications which involved ley-lines, the Little People, and so on. It wasn't for me, but tactfully, I sent it back with an apologetic note explaining, quite truthfully, that I had already selected the stories for the first book, which was now closed.

Keith Roberts went berserk. He sent a wild letter in which he accused me of breaking our "contract." I had *commissioned* a story and then rejected it! He was furious, and accused me of lying about my deadline. I would hear from his agent, he said. Giles Gordon sent an even wilder letter. He was going to sue! He was complaining to Futura! He would get me blacklisted by the SFWA! I would never do anything else in the science fiction field!

I was very upset. I hadn't commissioned *anything,* only sent Keith Roberts the same letter as I had sent to everyone else. Surely I was able to reject a story I didn't like, that came in late, without prior warning? I made a special trip to see Anthony Cheetham, who was more amused than concerned, and advised me to forget it. "Giles is known to be a bit erratic," he said, which wasn't much comfort. Years later, however, I discovered with some relief that Keith Roberts had managed to fall out with almost everybody else in the SF field, so at least it wasn't just me!

But none of this prepared me for the coming storm. My notices appeared in the magazines, and hundreds of would-be writers must have thought, "Aha... Here's my chance."

The stories started to arrive daily, in bundles. Six, eight, ten, twelve per day! All the rejects from the *SFM* Story Competition, all the rejects from the *Sunday Times*/Gollancz writing competition, I saw every one. Each morning

Editing *Andromeda*

the postman brought another armful of manuscripts, and I grew to dread his approach. My little girl Alison started to say, "More rubbish, Daddy."

I filled a crate in my study and started on a second, and fell far behind on reading. Most people submitting seemed to be absolute amateurs, without the most basic idea about writing. One envelope was tastefully decorated with blue spiders, painstakingly drawn in ballpoint ink. Another was so unbelievably bad in every possible way that I wondered if Charles Platt had come back from the grave to hoax me again. Then there was a woman who wrote asking if I would consider her story, but who didn't actually send it, or an SAE. I didn't see why I should waste my time with that, so ignored her, and she wrote again, and again, every week, asking with increasing desperation if I would consider her story. Maybe I missed something good, but I figured that if she didn't know enough to let me actually *see* it, then it probably wouldn't be very exciting.

Purple ink in exercise books, illiterate scrawl, no return envelope or postage with a good half of them. Did people really place so little value on their work? Did they expect me to subsidise them? Ten pence per envelope would be a fair average, and I received over 300 stories all told. I was trying hard to do the decent thing, acknowledge submissions, read them quickly, make helpful comments. But they weren't helping themselves. When I asked the advice of an older, wiser editor, he said bluntly: "No return postage—then throw them away." This seemed a bit hard, so I started to send stories back without a stamp; let the authors pay a few postage dues and they might catch on!

One man wrote to me, saying he had a story to submit but he wondered if I would require a stamped, addressed return envelope. He enclosed a stamped, addressed return envelope for my reply.

I just couldn't face it, and told him I was full up. That's what happens, after a while; cynical, you might call it, but you learn to tell whether a story is going to be any good just by looking at the accompanying letter. Little things, like if the author can't spell the word "story" then he probably isn't going to make it. All right, I know Samuel R. Delany, for instance, can't spell for peanuts, but "story" isn't really a very hard word, is it?

I showed one letter to my pal Adrian Mellor, the sociology post-grad, after we fixed the leaking hot water pipe in my bathroom. It said, "I am enclosing a story of 5,261 words length."

"You gave it away, baby," he said sorrowfully.

I lost my temper with one clown who sent a manuscript, just one among a dozen that morning. It joined the pile. One week later he sent a terse little letter, demanding to know why he hadn't yet heard from me. A week later he sent me a registered letter, in which he took me strictly to task for not answering, hinted that he might take his story elsewhere, and ended with a thinly veiled threat to sue if I dared to use it without his permission. I was so annoyed that I wasted ten minutes finding the wretched manuscript (it was halfway down the pile, waiting its turn), read it quickly (well, the first two pages. That was enough, it was variant 6-B on the Atlantis theme) and wrote back telling him what he could do with his story. Naturally, he hadn't bothered to enclose return postage.

The whole thing was a complete waste of time, because out of all those manuscripts I didn't find a single piece I could take for *Andromeda,* although I did find four or five possibles, stories that were flawed but seemed to have something about them in one way or another. Late one night I came across a surprisingly good story, written by a 17-year-old schoolboy and very nearly acceptable for publication somewhere, if a little reminiscent of Anderson's Trader Team. I wrote him a long letter back, trying to be as helpful as I could, saying what I thought could be improved and inviting him to resubmit, and was really quite surprised when I didn't ever hear from him again.

And the really good stories, the ten which eventually appeared in the first book, where did *they* come from? From just the places you might expect. From friends, existing professionals like Christopher Priest, who sent me "An Infinite Summer," possibly his finest short story. And dear old Bob Shaw, with "Waltz of the Bodysnatchers," who told me that he had been writing a novel, "but stopped and did this story instead, because you were saying at Coventry how disappointed you were with the material you were getting."

Harlan Ellison, whom I had only met briefly at Discon, surprised me by sending "Seeing," a really brilliant story, and the others came from fans who were starting to carve out names for themselves in the SF field. I published Andrew Stephenson's second story, the excellent "The Giant Killers," commenting, "Is there anyone else who can complain that he doesn't get enough time to concentrate upon writing because he is too busy painting *Galaxy* covers?" I was fortunate to receive stories from Rob Holdstock, Ian Watson, Terry Greenhough, and a surprise submission from Naomi Mitchison. And for the second volume I introduced first-timers Mike Scott Rohan, Bob Rickard, William Wu, and Tom Shippey, with Dave Langford's third story and an unusual piece from *SFR* editor Dick Geis, so my original hope paid off; fans *could* write science fiction if they tried!

The trouble was, I had put in six months' work to earn that £100.00, less my costs. It wasn't much, and the second two volumes took a lot longer. Although I'm still proud of those three collections, they weren't a commercial success. Anthony Cheetham had lost interest long before I submitted the first manuscripts, and the books crept out from Futura, unloved and unwanted.[2]

Editing *Andromeda* was satisfying, if not particularly lucrative. Editing a science fiction magazine called *Vortex* might have been fun, if things had worked out differently.

My first encounter with *Vortex* was at Novacon 6, when I noticed that Rog Peyton's book stall had acquired a preproduction "dummy" of a proposed new British prozine. I was vaguely interested, since after the demise of *SF Monthly* I wondered whether this might be a possible replacement market. One look told me to forget it. *Vortex* had a well printed colour cover but was clearly oriented much more towards fantasy and the macabre than suited my taste, while the interior illustrations and layout were really crude. I dismissed it as just another in the long line of bungles and missed chances which have dogged publishing in the U.K. whenever anyone tries to produce any sort of SF magazine.

The first two issues confirmed my opinion. They made *SF Monthly* look good! But then in April 1977, Rog Peyton told me that the publisher of *Vortex* had visited his bookshop and had said that he, too, was disappointed with the magazine and was looking for a new editor.

"I mentioned your name," said good old Rog.

Sure enough, the man telephoned me a week or two later. His name was Edward Shacklady and he said he needed help. Would I get in touch with the editor, Keith Seddon, straight away? Now, I had never previously heard of Seddon. Certainly he wasn't a fan, and it was clear from his two issues so far that he couldn't know much about science fiction, or about editing, and after recent experiences I'd had enough of trying to give advice to people who didn't really want it. I said as much.

---

[2] There were only three *Andromeda* collections. The third had an incredible line-up, with original stories from Fritz Leiber, Larry Niven, Chris Priest, David Redd, Ian Watson, David Langford, Tom Shippey, William Wu, and Darrell Schweitzer. It made no difference, the book sold only small numbers and was generally ignored. But I was very proud of it, and of the previous two volumes.

"I'd heard you were looking for a new editor, Mr. Shacklady," I said. "That's how I'd prefer to be involved."

"All right," he said. "Work out your budget and call me back on Friday."

Now immediately, I was a bit nonplussed. I mean, budgets are important and all that, but at such an early stage I would have thought there were a few important things to discuss first. From his point of view, what were my qualifications to run a magazine? From mine, who was he, and what was it all about, anyway? But still, it was his money, and that gave him some privileges, so I tried to estimate how much time would be needed to edit a monthly magazine on a freelance basis, costed it out, and dutifully rang him up and gave him a figure.

"That wouldn't pay for a cover painting," he said scornfully. "I don't think you know what you are talking about, Mr. Weston."

Fighting back a strong feeling that maybe *he* was the one who didn't know what he was talking about, I asked for clarification.

"What exactly did you want me to include?" I asked. "This is my fee for doing all the editorial work."

"Oh no," he replied. "I want a complete price for *everything;* stories, artwork, layout, the lot. All I want to do is print it."

I asked a few other questions, like what sort of rates was he paying authors and artists at the moment, but he wouldn't say. "You tell *me,* Mr. Weston," he said slyly.

I started to have second thoughts about the whole business; it was getting smelly. But I discovered I had developed an itch to get my fingers on *Vortex.* I knew I couldn't possibly do worse than the present incumbent, and after all, didn't I once produce a big fanzine every couple of months? With actual money available, surely I could easily find a few willing artists; and Bob Rickard was pretty good on layouts. Realistically, I knew it wouldn't last for very long; but what the heck, press onward!

So I thought about it a bit, shopped around, and from *SFM* days established rates for wordage and artwork, which didn't look too unreasonable. I called him back with a new figure.

"All right," he said. "Now where can we meet?"

Feeling quite excited, I made my way to our rendezvous. We had arranged to meet in the bar at the Charing Cross Hotel, on the night I was coming down to London for a One Tun meeting. This could be it, I thought, the start of something big, and so with some care I packed my "references" in my bag— a few issues of *Speculation* with big names inside, *Andromeda* 1, and some copies of *Science Fiction Monthly* that contained my articles.

Meeting Edward Shacklady was a let-down, all by itself. He was a small, drowned-rat sort of figure with a cold gleam in his eyes. "Nasty Man," I decided instinctively, but pressed on, secure in the knowledge that he obviously

Vortex story—meeting Edward Shacklady

had money to spend, and if he owned a publishing company then he must have at least some idea of what he was doing.

"Now then, Mr. Weston, when can you start?" he asked, ignoring social preliminaries and not even glancing at my credentials. Once more, the overwhelming impression of *wrongness* swept over me, the feeling that we were approaching this thing from the wrong direction. I tried to explain my conception of how a magazine should be run—more-or-less straight science fiction, with articles and interviews and news features—in fact I had prepared tentative contents pages for a couple of issues.

He wasn't interested in that sort of thing.

"Look at these," he said proudly, withdrawing colour proofs of the third and fourth issues from his briefcase. I looked.

"Er... I've never really been very keen on running illustrations in single process-colours," I said, as tactfully as I could. "I mean, the cyan isn't too bad but the magenta's a bit vile, and you can hardly see the yellow."

"I think it looks good," he snapped in annoyance.

Anyway, we talked a bit more and I said I wanted three things. If he expected me to take full responsibility for assembling the package, I would want a schedule, a mutually binding contract for a minimum number of issues, and money in advance for the first number.

We agreed that he would give Keith Seddon his marching orders, and I would take over with the seventh issue, in July. Triumphant, I decided to take a taxi rather than the Tube to the One Tun.

Only—it didn't happen. After a few weeks, I rang to enquire about progress.

"Having a few problems," he said. "Can't talk now. Just get on with it."

"But what about the contract?"

"You don't need to worry about that. You can trust me."

"Oh yes," I thought to myself. I smelt a great big rat, and I wouldn't trust Mr Edward Shacklady with a lump of cheese.

Another few weeks went by, and I told my proprietor that if he wanted a July issue, time was running out fast.

"We're having a big meeting up here next week," he said, revealing for the first time that he didn't actually own the company. "Keith Seddon's father doesn't want me to change editors."

Aha! I thought. That's where Seddon—and *Vortex*—came from. His father was a director of the printing company.

Finally, it became obvious that the whole thing was a dead loss, and I withdrew from the mess with a certain feeling of relief, mixed with disappointment, of course, and regret that people like Jim Barker, Alan Hunter, and yes, Larry Niven, had taken some trouble, all of which had been in vain.

There is an epilogue to this story.

Some months later, I had a mystery telephone call at my office.

"Keith Seddon here," he said.

Embarrassed, I didn't know what to say. After all, though I wished him no ill will personally, I had tried to take his job.

"What do you know about *Vortex?*" he queried. He was the editor, and he was asking me!

Apparently the poor chap hadn't tied things up contractually, had trusted Shacklady, and now the magazine had gone defunct with its fifth issue and he was out of pocket. I couldn't help him and said so. What a shambles! And what a terrible waste—for *Vortex,* in its brief life, had excellent mechanical reproduction and first-class distribution. What I could have done with that opportunity!

Tales from the BSFG
Chapter 19

Coal Bunker

It was May 1975 and I was at the top of the garden when Rob Jackson telephoned, and I had just that very minute dropped a concrete coal bunker on my foot. We didn't burn solid fuel any more, and I wanted to use the bunker as a composter for garden rubbish, but it was heavy and had slipped out of my fingers. So there I was, howling and screaming, hopping around among the dying weeds and decaying grass cuttings, as Eileen put her head out of the kitchen window and shouted that Rob was on the 'phone. It was a big garden, and it took me a half-minute to hobble back to the house.

"Hello, Rob," I said tersely. "I've just dropped a concrete coal bunker on my foot."

"Er, hello," said Rob, ignoring all the obvious questions and coming straight to the point in his usual incisive way. "Er, Peter Nicholls can't come up to Newcastle to talk to the SF Group and we're in a bit of trouble and I can't think of anyone else, so I wondered if you'd like to take his place? First week in July?"

Well, I thought, pausing for reflection, Rob certainly knows how to flatter you into accepting an invitation! But I was tempted, anyway. I rather liked the idea of talking SF for an evening with the Gannets, even if it did mean a two-hundred-mile train journey.

"No, he can't come," said Eileen firmly. "He spends too much time on science fiction as it is."

There then ensued an argument broken by frequent asides, "Hang on, Rob, we're discussing it," until my wife played her trump card (which she'd only just remembered). "Anyway, we're going on holiday that week."

So I had to decline. But then he started to talk about his plans for his fanzine, and this set me thinking. I had first met Rob at Novacon 3 with Dave Langford, Kev Smith, Chris Morgan, and other members of the Oxford University SF group. He had gone back to Newcastle, joined the Gannets, and in 1974 was Treasurer of the hugely successful Tynecon. Now Rob had taken over *Maya* from Ian Maule, and under his inspired editorship it was rapidly becoming a significant focal point.

I was missing the soapbox that writing editorials for *Speculation* used to provide, and the British fanzine scene was starting to take off, with titles like Pat Charnock's *Wrinkled Shrew,* Peter Roberts' *Egg,* and so on. I wanted to be involved, if only marginally. Besides, my pal Vernon Brown kept saying that I had gafiated, had become mercenary and only wrote for *SF Monthly.* So, I asked Rob, would he like me to do a column for *Maya?*

He said he would, and I set to work that same night. "Keep it simple," I thought to myself, "just write about things which have been happening, in fandom and real life." So appropriately, I titled the column "Slice of Life."

For instance, just the previous weekend Adrian Mellor had asked if he could pop round for a chat. Adrian was a postgraduate student at the University who had been attending meetings of the Birmingham Group for six months or so. He was the sort of person I had always wanted to attract, intelligent, well-read, with interests of his own and anecdotes to tell; he was able to contribute something, rather than just being one of those who came along to listen to the programme and then went home. Adrian was working for a doctorate in sociology, and for his thesis he was examining the nature of the attraction that SF seems to have for its enthusiasts.

This sounded familiar and I was a bit wary at first, remembering the wordy Stephen Pickering and several other amateur sociologists in the fanzines. However, there was nothing trendy or pretentious about Adrian, he read a lot of science fiction himself and was genuinely fascinated with fandom. Having interviewed other local fans, he said it was now my turn. But, as the long-suffering Vernon could have told him, for me Saturday afternoon was a busy time. "If it's fine, you'd better bring your boots because I'll be digging the garden," I told Adrian. "If it's dull, I'll be working on the bathroom."

The bathroom won that weekend. Eileen was out, and we carried on a fine, fannish conversation while I hammered away, replacing floorboards. Our house was nearly forty years old and needed a lot of things doing to it; recently we had demolished a wall between toilet and bathroom proper to make a larger area, which now needed to be re-tiled, painted, and so on. But didn't we have a merry chat! Adrian looked through some of the items from my collection, and asked to borrow *The Enchanted Duplicator, Fancyclopedia II*, and assorted current fanzines including *True Rat* and *Zimri*. Then I brought him my file of *Speculation,* beginning with that tiny purple copy of *Zenith* 1 from 1963.

Each one stirred fond memories, like the time the Aston Group collated an issue in Bob Rickard's crummy, unheated flat on the Hagley Road (one of a long series of Bob's crummy flats) during a bitterly cold week near Christmas, with poor old Bob coughing and wheezing with 'flu before having to stagger off to work night-shift at the sorting office. We had another Adrian in those days, a quiet chap who never said a word but who could collate at twice the speed of anyone else. We used to give him a huge pile of pages and leave him to it. "Are there any more at home like you?" Bob once asked him, when we were doing a particularly thick issue.

Happy days! Those Saturday mornings when Bob and I would bluff our illegal way into the print room at Aston University and duplicate away, on tenterhooks in case a patrolling caretaker caught us. The bloodstained copies of number 18, when the stapling machine ran amok and attacked Bob, the Swallow ink that wouldn't dry, the duplicator we had to fix with paper clips, all those other minor disasters! Producing *Speculation* was always a team effort, though the actual composition of those teams fluctuated wildly over the years.

So there we were, Adrian sitting on the lid of the W.C. reading *Zenith,* me nailing down floorboards, talking science fiction.

"I'd better be careful or I'll hit a pipe," I said, just as I hit a pipe.

A fine jet of water under incredible pressure hit me in the face. I pulled up the floorboard again and found I had put a nail into a half-inch copper pipe.

Swearing, laughing, crying, I asked Adrian to put his finger over the hole while I found the stopcock. I ran down to the garage and turned off the main. Upstairs, water continued to flood out and started to come through the kitchen ceiling.

"It's getting warm," called Adrian.

Damn! I had holed the central heating system! Panicking now, I switched off everything that could be switched off in the boiler-house.

"It's getting very H*O*T," wailed Adrian in anguish.

I ran back upstairs to find him sitting in a puddle, trying to hold a sponge over a geyser of hot water that was erupting merrily from under the floor. Wasn't there a valve on the hot-water cylinder somewhere? There was indeed, and it slowly cut off the flow.

"My wife will kill me," I said. "Must get a plumber."

The first three I called were out, or watching football matches. The fourth tried to be a bit more helpful. "Knock the nail all the way in," he said. "That will hold it, and I'll come and fix it properly on Monday." He lived in the next road.

Finally, I found a man who came along and soldered up the damage, giving me a look, that seemed to say, "I've met idiots like you before." Vainly, I mumbled something about having done a bit of plumbing myself (true, two washing machines installed and a new sink unit), but he wasn't impressed. At least, while we were waiting, it gave Adrian and me a good chance to talk about the mysterious lure of science fiction, a subject fresh in our minds after Bob Shaw's talk to the BSFG the previous night.

Bob and Sadie had only recently moved across to England from Belfast, and we had wasted no time in inviting them along to the Brum group. Bob's title was "Getting and Developing Ideas for SF Stories," and he gave us a mixed talk, part-serious, part-comic, along with some excellent advice for aspiring writers. He told us about his life, how he had started to sell professionally, back in the 1950s, about the way in which he and other young hopefuls had practiced with writing exercises, taking very simple opening lines and developing them into stories. Bob gave us an example of the sort of thing he meant:

"He sat on a rock and looked at the floor."

So far, so good. But then we began to get confused, because Bob seemed to be talking a bit out of context.

"Ask yourself some questions," he said. "How big, what colour, what did it smell like?"

"What? The rock?" some people asked.

"Floor?" others wondered. Heads turned in puzzlement, all around the room, seeking enlightenment.

"Flaw?"

"What flaw?"

"What's he on about?"

I turned, very casually, towards the delectable Sadie, who was sitting on my left.

"Do you think he means *flower,* do you think?" I asked.

"Why of course he does," she replied in surprise, as if to say, "What else?" The word spread around the room. "He means *flower.*"

"Oh. Why didn't he say!" Satisfied, attention went back to the talk.

Later, in the bar, we mentioned this little point of confusion to Bob.

"Yes, but that's how we say it in Northern Ireland," he said. "We don't sound the middles of the words."

"But you're living in England now, Bob," I pointed out, "and we can't understand what you're saying."

"You're right," he said in a very Northern Irish way. "Floor. Flooore. Flahwr."

"Don't you get talking like that Peter Weston!" said Sadie, clearly alarmed at such a terrible prospect.

For me, the best part of Bob's talk that night was when he described his childhood and his awakening interest in space and the stars. This really set my mental bells ringing, with so many parallels between his life and my own. Listening to Bob, as he told us about the way he tried to make a rudimentary telescope out of a cardboard tube and a couple of lenses, I remembered trying to do the very same thing myself. Although I was more fortunate than him because eventually I was able to buy a complete brass telescope from Army Surplus, whereas Bob could only find an eyepiece that he carried around hopefully for months, searching without success for the other bits!

It was a good meeting. But they were *always* good meetings, back in the glory days of the Birmingham SF Group at the dear old Imperial Hotel in Temple Street. The month after Bob Shaw we had Tom Shippey, talking about Tolkien, and the following month Dave Kyle visited us with his new book on the History of Science Fiction.

There was the time we saw James Blish bark across the room at his wife, towards the end of his talk on "Science in Science Fiction." The immediate mental picture that conveys of a fierce, domineering Jim Blish is completely false, however; he really did *bark!* It stopped conversation completely for a moment, but had the desired effect of setting Judy Blish rummaging in her handbag for her husband's cigarettes. "You never really know what these authors are like until you meet them, do you?" said Vernon.

Afterwards, sitting in the comfortable upstairs bar at the Imperial Hotel, pinching spring onions from Jim's ham salad, I was feeling pretty pleased with our progress. His talk had attracted an audience of fifty-five, and we had nearly eighty paid-up members on our books. It was a long way from the hard times of 1966, when the "old" BSFG was disintegrating and we were struggling to get the club onto a better footing. We failed then, and I remember thinking the trouble was that we were penniless innocents, with no experience, no resources, and no strengths to draw upon. We needed to have some older, wiser heads around, who would crawl occasionally out of the woodwork and regale us with stories of times past, as they did in cities like Los Angeles, New York and London, all places with long histories of fannish activity.

Now Rog and I were able to dodder around at group meetings, annoying the youngsters with stories of how much better things were in the Grand Old Days of 1963 when Cliff Teague still walked the Earth and we ate melted ice cream every Sunday afternoon. Now we *were* the veterans, and we had succeeded in creating a local fandom in our own image.

It went on from there. In the first ten years the Brum group hosted almost every big name author in science fiction, including Larry Niven, Theodore Sturgeon, Joe Haldeman, Fred Pohl, and Jerry Pournelle. We managed to get Isaac Asimov, during his one and only trip to Europe, with a special meeting at the Holiday Inn that attracted over 200 people. We invited Samuel R. Delany, who lectured an uncomprehending audience about Wittgenstein at such length that Rog (the chairman) fell asleep by his side, and I dropped into a deep slumber and fell off my chair with a resounding crash. But sometimes we made our own entertainment, like the quiz-night one summer evening in 1975....

"In what novel was the principal character named Wade Harper?" asked the fan at the back of the room.

There was a moment of stunned silence, as the audience considered the sheer impossibility of the question. The faces of the team being challenged took on expressions of despair, brows furrowed, and teeth clenched with the intensity of their concentration. The seconds ticked by, and I was sure they didn't have the slightest idea of the answer. Vernon frowned and looked at his watch....

"*Three to Conquer,*" said Laurence Miller. "By Eric Frank Russell."

Then it was the turn of Pauline's team. Rather than the usual, boring method of splitting everyone into teams and asking them questions devised by the Committee, Vernon had introduced an ingenious new system in which teams made up questions to ask each other. Of course, to make it fair, both parties had to be shuffled around each time, and by nine o'clock things were getting a bit complicated.

"Who won the Doc Weir Award this year?" asked Pauline, sneaking in an unfair fannish reference.

"The What?" chorused her opponents.

Rog Peyton grinned. He, Vernon and Pauline were probably the only three to have even heard of the Award, out of the thirty or so present in the room; other than, of course, the actual 1975 winner himself.

That was the end of a round, and now Vernon started to work out the score. First, he drew a series of lines on a large piece of graph paper, then took out his slide rule. Those in the front row heard an arcane rumble, "Two points if they get it right," he muttered, "but only one point to the following team, if they answered the question the others missed, and deduct one point from the first team if they couldn't, adding that to the score of the team who asked the question in the first place...."

He scribbled away while the hum of conversation grew and grew. Ray Bradbury (now a member of the Magic Circle) began to do conjuring tricks. Rog started to sell books. Others went to get refills, fan-wives talked about whatever it is fan-wives discuss when they get together, and Adrian Mellor took rapid notes for his sociology thesis. Waiting for the quiz scores, I looked around at the familiar flocked wallpaper of the George Room, at the keen fans—Vernon, Pauline, and Hazel Reynolds, each of whom had chaired Novacon, and group Treasurer and archivist Stan Eling with his wife Helen, who was chairing the next one. I nodded to David Hardy, our astronomical artist and cover illustrator for *Analog* and *F&SF*, at Rog Peyton, owner of the U.K.'s largest SF bookshop, David Sutton, one-time editor of *Shadow* and now doing professional horror anthologies, Adrian Cole, who had just sold a 180,000-word novel to a U.S. publisher, and Chris Morgan, who had been a steel buyer with British Leyland in Oxford but had recently moved to Birmingham and become a freelance writer.

slice of life
— peter weston

Brum Group faces

Dimly, I sensed the ghosts of others not at that particular meeting. Jack Cohen, fandom's amiable Mad Scientist and chairman of Novacon 4; Bob Rickard, whose magazine *The News* had so impressed the Fortean Society that they had recently flown him out to Chicago and were commissioning him to write a book on Fort's mysteries. Other good friends like Tim Stannard of the old Aston Group, now a wealthy socialite and solicitor, driving an Alfa Romeo with a big house in Edgbaston. Geoff Winterman, one of the few other survivors from our front-room era and now headmaster at a large West Midlands school, and Tom Shippey, Oxford's youngest Fellow, the man who reviewed SF for the *Times Literary Supplement* and set the science fiction questions for BBC TV's "Mastermind" programme.

We seemed to have brought in so many new people, in just a few brief years; Hazel and Stan (both coming in via the Speculation conferences), Laurence Miller, Dave Cox, Dave Holmes, Kevin Easthope, and of course Gillon Field, though tragically she died in 1974, just as she was getting really involved with the group.

One of our new recruits was Steve Green, who fondly remembers those good times: "The post-*Star Wars*, post-*X-Files*, post-internet generation will probably find it impossible to grasp how much of an oasis the Brum Group represented for SF fans in the mid-1970s. Alongside the Andromeda Bookshop (with which it formed a perfect symbiosis, each feeding the other), they were beacons for those of us who considered Ellison and Aldiss far more interesting topics for conversation than the relative merits of Aston Villa's back two.

"I still recall the first meeting I attended, back in February 1977, when the aforementioned Brian Aldiss followed his general comments on contemporary SF with a bizarre tale involving KGB minders and a palace basement crammed with busts of Josef Stalin. I was hooked, and each third Friday that year proved just as electric; the next few months included appearances by Chris Priest, Bob Shaw and Anne McCaffrey. Not forgetting a certain Peter Weston, hotfoot from Suncon, whose Miami slideshow fired my 17-year-old imagination like one of Richard Burton's audience hearing of Mecca for the first time; by the end of the evening, mesmerised by Pete's victory speech, I'd already determined Seacon '79 would be my first Worldcon. Just as soon as I got this other event called Novacon 7 out of the way, that is.

"More than a quarter-century on, I cannot conceive how my life would have diverged had I not wandered into the foyer of the late, lamented Imperial Hotel that February evening: too many friendships unforged (Pete among them), too many pints undrunk, too many issues of *Critical Wave* unpublished (actually, on second thoughts....)"

We were visited by Flying Sorcerers, when a representative from the Aetherius Society came to talk to us, a little man who explained with great dignity that Jesus Christ was alive and well on Venus, where he was directing Earth's resistance to the Cosmic Overlords. He gave us a smudgy newsletter which was full of exciting accounts of interplanetary battles. "Just last weekend," he said, "members of the Society went up a mountain in Wales and through the massed power of their prayers (and their little black boxes), they successfully repelled an invasion from Saturn." Tom Shippey decided that he had heard enough of this nonsense. "Next time, don't stop them," he said, "then we'll believe you."

Steve Green said, "As I recall, there were two of them. After five or ten minutes of high-octane bollocks, the main chap told us, 'You may laugh.' I think he meant it as a nod to our scepticism, rather than the way we took it— as an instruction."

Rog Peyton recalls, "It was a wonderfully light-hearted meeting where several of our members had fun arguing with their speaker, particularly our own vicar, Bob Vernon. I don't think their speaker enjoyed it anywhere near as much."

Shortly afterwards we moved away from the Imperial Hotel, because we were getting tired of the continual changes in management and their attitude, which ranged from indifferent to actively hostile. Fortunately, we had a refuge, because Ray and Carole Bradbury had become landlords at the Ivy Bush pub, just a mile or so out of the city-centre, and they welcomed us to their excellent upstairs room with its private bar. By this time we had brought even more new members on board, Paul Oldroyd, who was supposedly studying medicine at the university, Mike & Bernie Evans, Tony Berry, who had been active with the Leeds group, and Martin Tudor, who went on to become our most successful fannish fan. Poor Martin was so diffident that he lounged silently against the bar for at least six months before anyone spoke to him.

We hosted Dave Langford at the Ivy Bush, on the publication of his first novel, *The Space Eater,* and Brian Aldiss when he told us about his new book, *Helliconia Spring.* We entertained Eddie Jones, who discussed SF Art, Frederik Pohl, who talked about *Gateway,* then John Sladek, Brian Stableford and Barry Bayley.

However, not all meetings were entirely successful. Take the visit of Colin Kapp, who started by flourishing a 15,000-word manuscript that he proposed to read to us, *before* he started his main talk! Having explained that this might take a little longer than he anticipated, we managed to side-track him into a preamble, but he was only halfway through this when the landlady threw us out at ten past eleven (Ray had by this time moved on to another pub). I asked Colin if his story "Lambda One" had been influenced by a similar story in *Astounding,* but he just looked baffled—apparently he didn't read much other science fiction. All I gathered from the evening was that Colin worked in some sort of plastics factory down in Gloucestershire, and he wrote his stories on night-shift when there was nothing much else to do. This led to Steve Green's suggestion for the creation of the "Kappometer," an absolute scale against which the boredom quotient of all future speakers could be measured.

In those days we were full of enthusiasm, and our most ambitious project was to build a Carnival Float for the Lord Mayor's charity procession, which each summer made its way through the streets of central Birmingham. Vernon was chairman that year, and our publicity officer was Alan Cash, who was very enthusiastic about the idea. Alan was a keen photographer who had previously been the driving-force behind the abortive "Brum Group film." He had already made a whole series of 8mm films of his own, somewhat reminiscent of the old Delta group productions at Repetercon, so we had "Alan Cash and the Birdman" and "Alan Cash meets Flash Gordon," that sort of thing.

Vernon formed a working party with his new wife Pat, Alan, Chris Suslowicz, Anne Gaye and one or two others, and they found a suitable working-space in a shed at the bottom of Anne's garden in Yardley. The theme for the procession that year was maritime, and so our little band decided they would create a sea-monster. It was cramped in that shed, but over a month or more they managed to build a rather splendid monster out of timber, cardboard and papier-mâché. It wasn't a complete job, but more like a Loch Ness affair, with just a long neck and head standing seven or eight feet high, complete with gaping jaws and rows of ferocious teeth, the whole thing painted in bright sea-green. The idea was to mount it on the back of a truck, and drive it through the streets while group members gave out leaflets and collected money in buckets.

I was the driver, since I was the only one with any experience of handling commercial vehicles and I had a friend who operated a delivery business. So, the night before the procession I borrowed his flat-bed truck and drove over to Anne Gay's house. Once there we discovered several technical problems, the most serious being that they had built the monster *inside* the shed, and it was in consequence too big to come out through the door! Much struggling then ensued, until the beast finally emerged from the ruins of the shed and we discovered it was too heavy for us to lift onto the back of the truck. Eventually, with the help of local residents we managed to get the thing on board, and we had a jolly time trying to fix it securely, so that it wouldn't fall over. Finally, at about nine o' clock in the evening, I set out for home, a distance of about ten miles.

I drove slowly along the main roads, anxious not to lose my load. Cars hooted and youths shouted derision, and I was very aware of the amused glances my monster was attracting. I left the truck on the drive outside the house, and early next morning my three little girls were delighted, coming out in their nightdresses and dressing gowns to pose for pictures with the monster. Then I had to make the journey into the city centre (more derision), to rendezvous with Alan and group members in a back street where the other floats were being assembled. Our effort was very creditable, but unfortunately we realised we had forgotten something important—no notice about the BSFG, nothing to explain what it was all about! Chris and Pauline Morgan appeared wearing flotation jackets, with a rubber dinghy and paddles, and climbed aboard the truck to pose as innocent boaters being attacked by this terrible creature. Other members stood ready to walk alongside with their collecting buckets, then the policeman signalled, and off we went!

We ground around the city streets at two miles per hour, the crowd cheered, the money flew through the air, and in half an hour we were back in our back street, the parade over. "Now what, Vernon?" I asked. "What do we do with it now?" He gave me a stricken look. It was a detail that hadn't even been considered. There we were with an eight-foot green monster on the back of a hired truck. What to do with it? We couldn't just scrap it, not after all that work. Maybe a play-school might want it? Several other ideas were suggested, none very practical, and in the end I telephoned Bob Vernon, our man in the dog collar.

Bob was a Church of England vicar who had joined the group a year or two earlier. He was a pleasant, urbane individual with whom I used to enjoy long discussions about religion, trying to "pin him down," as he put it. While I respected Bob's beliefs, they did seem a trifle amorphous, and I was always intrigued how he could read science fiction and agree with me about almost every subject, and yet there was this central, hazy area where my atheism and his faith collided. The attraction now was that he had a modern church in the nearby suburb of Bordesley Green, with an adjacent church hall that I thought might make a suitable repository for "Nessie."

Bob reluctantly consented, and we delivered our load, dragging it into the hall and through two double-doors that opened onto a large, raised platform in an alcove at the rear of the room. As we left, I turned and looked back at the giant, grinning green head standing proudly aloft between the sliding wooden doors, looking like nothing so much as a pagan idol in a temple, awaiting its worshippers for the next sacrifice. "You're might have a bit of trouble squaring this with the Bishop, Bob," I said. "I mean, I know the Church of England is pretty flexible but they might draw the line at this!"

Monster, "I think he likes you"

The Brum group achieved a lot in those first ten years. We celebrated with Tencon, a mini-convention in June 1981, with a splendid Tenth Anniversary commemorative book, assembled by Rog Peyton, in which Archivist Stan Eling documented every meeting. By this time group members were already veteran convention organisers, having run Novacon since 1971 when it was first bolted onto the Constitution in a smoke-filled room. Initially, we decided that Novacon wouldn't be just a smaller Eastercon but would instead aim to be more fannish, and to that end, the early guests of Honour were fans, rather than professional writers—Doreen Rogers, then Ken Slater and Dave Kyle.

These worthy intentions didn't last long, however, and within a few years GoHs were to include John Brunner, Dan Morgan, and Anne McCaffrey, and the convention started to get bigger. And bigger. The first Novacon attracted 144 attendees, but by the fourth the total was over 200, and we were rapidly outgrowing the old Imperial Hotel. This was the year at which Jack Cohen was chairman, and where the Banquet meal (chicken) resulted in three-quarters of the membership contracting food-poisoning. Rog became chairman for 1975 and decided he had to move to the more modern, more up-market Royal Angus, and caused himself some problems when he did a radio interview that morning and mentioned there would be a Fancy Dress. Little did he expect that people would register as "walk-ins" *and* enter the Fancy Dress, without appearing to realise that the whole thing had a science fiction theme. So Rog found himself in the embarrassing situation of having to introduce entrants like "Ena Sharples" and other popular TV characters. Rog says he still shudders at the memory of that evening!

Tom Shippey recalls, "The main thing I remember about being an SF fan in 1970, and simultaneously a young academic not yet in a secure position, is that it was a bit like being gay. It was something you had to keep secret, for fear of severe professional disapproval—they would just assume you weren't serious, or that you had some disqualifying defect of character. At the same time, fans had ways of recognising each other, and formed an automatic support group, bound together more tightly by social rejection. So going to a fan convention—and speaking at a fan convention, out there in the open, in public, without having to watch what you said, and to people you knew what you were talking about—well, this gave a sense of extreme liberation.

"I don't think I ever delivered better 'presentations,' as the Americans call them, (they weren't really lectures, because of the audience participation, not to say interruption) than I did at a succession of Novacons. I remember speaking about history in science fiction, about magic in science fiction (both of these got published in *Foundation,* and still appear in revised form in repeated editions of the Clute and Nicholls *Encyclopaedia*), and also—but this was to the Brum group—on language in fantasy and sf: and this wasn't just about Tolkien, I remember Philip José Farmer got a sound airing too. At the end of the latter one Roger Peyton commented dolefully, 'Well, does anyone feel qualified to say anything about any of that?' but in fact they did."

The Angus was the new home of Novacon as it continued to grow, and grow, up to 1981 when Rog was Chairman again, Brian Aldiss was GoH, and attendance threatened to exceed 500. This caused the hotel to panic when they discovered their insurance cover was limited to that number, and the committee had to introduce a cut-off and actually turn people away.

Novacon permanently allied itself with fannish affairs by innovating the "Nova" Award for fanzine excellence. As Dave Langford describes, "Before plans for the automatic canonisation of each award-winner could be finalised, the Nova settled down as merely a hearty pat on the back for the editor of the fanzine chosen as Britain's Best in a given year. From 1973 to 1976 the winner was decided by a select panel of judges, chosen for their vast knowledge of fandom and ability to shout at one another late into the night. Thus at Novacon 3 in 1973, when I attended my first convention, the first Nova was posthumously presented to Peter Weston for his famous fanzine *Speculation*—not that Peter was particularly posthumous, but his fanzine was.

"Not all was well; too many judges were turning up in cement socks at the bottom of the Angus lift-shafts after announcing their decisions. Drunkenly, I suggested to Stan Eling that the Nova could be awarded by popular vote if some idiot sprained his brain drawing up rules, and drunkenly, he told me to go and do it. The result was, in Kevin Smith's words, the three-volume presentation set of Nova Award rules, with the seven appendices. The embarrassing moment came the following year at Novacon 7, where under my foolproof new rules and frighteningly impartial guidance, the Award went to *Twll-Ddu*, edited by, well, um. Oops!"

The Nova was first conceived by Gillon Field, a relatively new member who showed tremendous promise before her untimely death in 1974. Gillon actually constructed that first Award, which went to *Speculation;* unfortunately, she had to make it in a great hurry, and it consisted of just three rectangular pieces of blue perspex, cemented to a square piece of blue perspex. It took pride of place on my windowsill for a few months, next to my Victorian ceramic table-leg from Trieste, until inevitably the cement dried out and the Nova fell apart, about the same time that I knocked over the Europa table-leg, which shattered into a million pieces.

Afterwards, the Nova became rather more elaborate, as Dave Langford said: "Every year Ray Bradbury—the Benvenuto Cellini of Birmingham—toils in his secret laboratory to construct a Nova trophy, which is sometimes unique and sometimes considerably more than unique; one year it might have hypersonic streamlining and a megadeath strike capability, next year a built-in cigar lighter."

More recently, Ray standardised production on a cast pewter rocketship, modelled on the cover illustration from the very first Novacon Programme Book, a fine, Gernsbackian craft, with tailfins and portholes, rivets and rocket tubes, blasting off on a fiery column of exhaust gases. It is a most worthy presentation piece, and recognising my plight as the only winner without an actual Award, Ray kindly presented me with my very own Nova rocketship at the end of 2003. Who needs a Hugo, anyway!

Novacon NOVA Award for Best Fanzine—1973: *Speculation*
edited by Peter Weston

Worldcon!
Chapter 20

After Discon our 1979 Worldcon bid was well and truly launched, and Malcolm, Peter and I settled down for the long slog, promoting, manning tables at conventions, taking memberships, and producing progress reports. Very quickly, we decided there was only one possible site in the whole country and this was the Metropole Hotel in Brighton, the only location with the right combination of conference facilities and on-site bedroom accommodation. Besides, Brighton was a wonderful location, with its seaside setting, its Regency connotations, and its convenience to London, the airports, and the Channel ports.

By early 1976, we had over 600 pre-supporters, but we were starting to struggle under the workload, and we decided to enlarge the committee with three other, carefully chosen members. Their names were announced in the second PR, with tongue-in-cheek introductory blurbs by Malcolm:

"Rob Jackson is one of the fastest-rising stars of British fandom. He first came into prominence as a member of the highly successful Tynecon committee. Since then he has taken over editorship of the fanzine *Maya,* and so transformed it that in little over a year it won both the Nova Award and the *Checkpoint* Poll. Rob is a qualified doctor, although so far he is only allowed to practise on children.

"*Leroy Kettle* is the earnest and taciturn young man who has assumed the awesome duties of Membership Secretary. A committee member for Seacon, the 1975 Eastercon, he is best known as a fan writer of huge repute; he and his fanzine *True Rat* have won the *Checkpoint* Poll in so many categories in the last couple of years that it takes Roy several hours to list them (not that it stops him). His first published story appeared in the latest *New Writings in SF,* several earlier tales having resulted in the immediate demise of the three magazines concerned.

"*John Steward* is perhaps the least-known to fandom at large, although he has enthusiastically attended conventions for a number of years. He has been persuaded to take on the job of Treasurer, for which he is professionally qualified, as well as having a big mattress to stuff the money in."

After eighteen months of referring to ourselves as "the British Worldcon," we thought it was about time we had a name, and the same PR announced that we were now Seacon '79, a title chosen after a certain amount of anguish and smiting of foreheads. The problem was that we simply couldn't make a catchy name out of any combinations of Brighton, Britain and con. In desperation we circled round and round the obvious title of Seacon, but were put off by two reasons; first, that it had been used for the 1975 Easter convention, even though that actually took place in Coventry! (Originally the bid had been for a seaside hotel; the committee simply couldn't find one.) Second, and more serious, Seacon had been previously used by a Seattle Worldcon, and in some ways it was their intellectual property, should they ever wish to bid again at some future date. We debated the matter endlessly, and in the end decided it was the only possible name, completely missing the obvious alternative of Channelcon, which didn't occur to anyone until the Eastercon returned to the Metropole in 1982.

By the time of our third Progress Report in April 1977, we had also adopted our official symbol, Harry Bell's fannish lion, had 800 pre-supporters (with over 350 coming from the United States), and had added another recruit to our little team. Again, Malcolm did the introduction:

"We felt the need of a man of mature years and a receding hairline to cope with advertising and publicity, and soon hit upon the ideal victim in *Graham Charnock*, a man of vast experience in the advertising world and in fandom. Those with long memories still nostalgically recall his fanzine *Phile*. Lovers of incomprehensible New Wave writing still affectionately remember his stories in *New Worlds* (of which he became Associate Editor), where he appeared in the famous New Writers' Issue alongside the vast, festering foot of Robert P. Holdstock—an experience which haunts him to this day. Later he became (in no particular order) a bookseller and rock-and-roll star (playing in a punk-rock group, 'The Burlingtons,' and featured on Mike Moorcock's still-to-be-deleted album 'New Worlds Fair'), was on the committee of Seacon '75, and assisted (as he does to this day) the lovely and talented Pat Charnock (no relation) with her fanzine, *Wrinkled Shrew.*"

A little later, Pat herself came onto the Steering Committee, along with Eve Harvey and North-East fan Kevin Williams, making a total of ten people in the inner core of decision-making, all of them among the most active and influential British fans of the decade. I had also been keen to involve Greg Pickersgill, but through an unfortunate misunderstanding at a One Tun meeting, this never happened.

We were roaring towards the Millennium (our target of 1000 pre-supporters), but we still needed to present our formal bid at the business meeting of the 1977 Worldcon, which this year was "Suncon," held in fabulous, fannish Miami Beach. Several of our committee planned to get across for the convention, taking 2000 sticks of Brighton Rock, our badges with the "fannish lion," and our bidding song:

> *"And it's time, fen, time,*
> *Time to raise your voice,*
> *And let your friends know*
> *That you have made your choice,*
> *And we all agree, that it would be mighty fine*
> *To hold the con in England in 1979."*
> —Vera Johnson, 1976

"I'm glad I haven't just bought them a doll," I said to Lee Hoffman, as we came out of the toy shop in the town of Coral Springs, Florida, my arms full of presents for my family back home. "I always think people who buy dolls for little girls are taking the easy way out because they can't be bothered to find something more original. My girls don't want any more rotten dolls."

I concluded my diatribe, and with a perfectly straight face Lee handed me a beautiful Apache Indian doll.

Oof! I started to back-pedal frantically. What I meant, of course, (I told Lee) were those cheap, nasty identikit plastic dolls of which we already had a cupboardful at home, mostly in pieces. Whereas the beautiful doll Lee had kindly bought for my three little girls was an "ethnic" representation of an authentic American Indian costume, more of a collector's display item than something to be dismembered by young children. That was my story, and I don't think she took offence, anyway!

It was the mid-point of a fairly strange day, my last before returning to England. Earlier, I had emptied a huge sack of money onto Tom Perry's kitchen table in their house in Boca Raton, the takings from our successful Worldcon bid. And I do mean huge, with hundred-dollar notes mixed in with the mound of fifties, twenties, and smaller denominations.

"Look, this one's ripped," announced Tom's son, Mark.

"Throw it away," said Tom dismissively, "it's only a ten."

"There's nearly as much here as you earn in a week, Tom," I said, playing up to his reputation in British fandom as a Rich American.

"Yeah," he replied, with an expression on his face which seemed to say, "I should be so lucky."

"We could go a long way on this money," Lee remarked thoughtfully.

Eventually we finished counting, finding 24 uncashable cheques made out to the administrators, "Mercury Services," by people who clearly hadn't read the instructions on the Suncon site ballots, and a Scottish pound note which, by the look of it, had been in somebody's wallet for the last thousand years. (When I finally arrived back in Birmingham that note was to save my life, being the only item of British currency remaining in my pocket and just sufficient to pay a reluctant taxi-driver, with a handful of nickels and dimes for a tip!)

The pile totalled over $10,000, and I started to wonder how to get the money safely back to the United Kingdom. I mean, it would be asking for trouble to turn up at Immigration Control with great wads of notes stuffed into my socks like some sort of Drug Baron, and I would never be able to explain the intricacies of the Worldcon bidding process to the Customs Officers, especially since I didn't entirely understand them myself.

We decided to take the loot in to the nearest bank, but the cashier at the Bank of Coral Springs was bewildered by the foreigner with the funny voice and the sack of money, and his suspicious request to transfer it to an offshore account. I realised for the first time that the American banking system is very different to ours in Europe. Instead of the "Big Four" clearing banks with their myriad branches in every High Street, each little U.S. town seems to have its very own bank. It's all because of their Constitution or something, but it means they don't have a lot of corporate experience to draw upon. This place was way out of its depth and they didn't know how to handle us at all.

I finally gave up trying to explain about Hugo Gernsback, and asked, "Can you tell me where I could find the nearest branch of Barclays International?"

"I think there's one in Boston," the woman offered helpfully.

In the end Tom came to the rescue, had the money put into his account, and got the bank to write a Certified Cheque which I put into my pocket very carefully, to take home to our Treasurer, John Steward. And then it suddenly hit me; we had actually won ourselves a Worldcon! Now life was going to get *really* interesting!

We had come to Suncon, to the Hotel Fontainebleau on Miami Beach, in order to publicise our bid, to present it formally at the business session and of course to hold some parties. "We" being committee members Rob Jackson and I, together with Peter Roberts, who very conveniently had won the TAFF trip that year. We felt reasonably confident against the relatively little-known New Orleans bid, but you never can tell. As Rob said, "We had heard an odd, unattributable, and worrying rumour that the New Orleans bid was running us very close on postal votes." From our side of the Atlantic it was difficult to judge, and for all we knew, masses of local people might vote, having calculated that it was a lot easier to get to Louisiana than Brighton. Just in case, I thought, we had better show that the Brits were fun people by having a big party. No sticks of Brighton Rock, unfortunately; after six months of correspondence with the U.S. FDA people, we had been refused an import licence on the grounds it was a dangerous foreign substance which might contaminate clean-living American citizens.

My idea was to have a short, sharp blast on the Saturday night, starting at midnight and lasting for just an hour, rather than one of these long drawn-out affairs where people wander in and out and nothing ever happens. "We'll need to put on a bit of a show," I said. "We can use those slides of Brighton. What else can we do? How about our bidding song? Has anyone seen Vera?"

The Suncon committee let us have a suite, and we packed them in. Vera Johnson duly appeared with her guitar, fandom's very own Country & Western artiste, and she led us through a few rousing choruses of the bid song, then we put on a grand knurdling tournament and ended with a Hum-and-Sway, events which, so we assured the Americans, were traditional at *all* British conventions. The only trouble was that to my recollection, no one had knurdled since 1966, and I had only ever *seen* one Hum-and-Sway, back at my very first con in 1964. So a bit of improvisation was in order—but it seemed to work well enough!

Rob Jackson thought so, too, and said, "I remember the manic excitement of the Britain in '79 party where Pete worked himself up into a frenzy of euphoria and infested the audience with enthusiasm and delight; and the almost anticlimactic feeling, a sort of mental exhaustion, when the bid result was announced."

Linda Krawecke was there, a young American fan from the New Orleans area, who none-the-less liked the look of these crazy Brits:

"What I remember most was just having a really good time. The drink seemed to flow and someone mentioned something about 'beercans stacked to the moon,' and there was something like—the Astral pole? Yes—I didn't know what it was at the time but looking back at it now—it must have been the Astral pole thing. And I remember Peter Roberts in his wonderful, orange-striped jacket. It seemed really cool, and somehow very, very, British. The friends I was with at the time agreed that the Brits seemed to know how to party, and that having an SF con to attend in the U.K. would be a good way to combine travel to a country we'd always wanted to visit with the kind of fun and hospitality the Room Party indicated. We all made a pact to get to Seacon. Only two of us made it in the end, and since half of our little group ended up staying in the U.K., you may just be grateful that there were only two—or you may have ended up with a larger invasion than you had!"

Our Victory Party on Sunday night was better prepared. This time we had a much larger room, which was just as well since word had gone round and people were queuing outside from 11.30 p.m. onwards. The day before, Rob and I had knocked ourselves out with the effort of fetching the drinks, when we borrowed Joyce Scrivner's car and four large suitcases with which we drove downtown to a liquor store. We bought three hundred dollars worth of beer and soft drinks (the owner was impressed, gave us his card, and offered to stay open especially for us, if we wanted any more) and nonchalantly staggered through the hotel foyer with the heavy cases with brave smiles and only an occasional clink and rattle to betray the contraband within. (The object was to avoid the exorbitant corkage fees levied on outside drink.) We made a return visit for the second performance, but with their usual efficiency and directness my pal Tom and his wife Alyx made things much easier by simply bribing a porter to bring up the crates to our room by the back-stairs.

I was surprised to see how many Americans seemed to know our National Anthem,s but I suppose old habits die hard. Vera belted out the bidding song, then one about English food, with a chorus of "And chips," which I thought particularly appropriate. Tom Perry did a zany, Bill Bryson-like sketch on cultural differences between the two countries, and Kathy Sanders performed a splendid belly-dance. This came about through a piece of pure luck; earlier in the evening we had exchanged a few words prior to the Banquet, and Kathy had asked hesitantly if we would like her to appear. She and husband Drew were among the small number of Masquerade Masters at the time, and their costume had been really incredible. So, too was Kathy's dance routine, which went on for ten or fifteen minutes before the admiring fans.

More knurdling, then we ended the party with another Hum-and-Sway, much more ambitious this time. Imagine hundreds of people sitting cross-legged in concentric circles on the floor, taking a drink, then linking arms, and humming loudly in the total darkness, while swaying rapidly from side to side. The leader intoned the ceremonial words to call up the Spirit of Trufandom, and gave the blessing, "May you all produce the Perfect Fanzine." Yes, for a few brief moments there, once I got them to shut up, I think we did succeed in evoking the Cosmic Guiding Principle of fandom. It would be churlish for anyone to suggest that it was only Rob Jackson with a sheet over his head!

Much later that night Ron Bounds and Bobbi Armbruster helped me get into the exclusive Hugo Losers' Party in the penthouse suite, where Joe Haldeman grinned at me and said, "Hey, Peter, you just missed Robert Heinlein by five minutes. He was asking after you!" Joe certainly knows how to wound!

It was a warm Florida night and we went out onto the balcony overlooking the Atlantic Ocean. Far out on the horizon you could see the twinkling lights of the gambling ships, and low in the sky there was a spectacular full Moon, huge and glowing brilliantly white.

"It's so bright," said Bobbi, "it reminds me of that Larry Niven story..."

" 'Inconstant Moon,' " said Ron.

"...Where the hero thinks the sun has gone nova on the other side of the Earth, so he and his girlfriend go for their last hot-fudge sundae."

"I've never had a hot-fudge sundae," I said wistfully.

"WHAT!" Amazed, well-fed American faces turned to me in shock, clearly not believing this terrible tale of want and deprivation.

"We'll get one now," said Ron.

"But Ron, it's five in the morning," I protested weakly.

"So?" Bobbi enquired, genuinely puzzled.

We took the elevator down to the basement and when the doors opened, I was amazed to see the restaurant was full of people. (I now realise that Americans never sleep. All night long they eat, do their shopping, buy cars and go to chiropractors.) And there in the faded glitz of the Hotel Fontainebleau I had my first, and best, hot-fudge sundae, with delicious creamy American ice cream drenched in hot, sticky chocolate-fudge sauce with a whipped-cream topping. Bliss! But, I thought, let's see them try this stunt in Brighton; at 5.00 a.m. they'll be lucky to get a cheese sandwich!

One of those insomniac Americans was Linda Krawecke, who had been carousing with some of the new friends she met at our party. "We wanted to stay up and watch the sun rise over the Atlantic," she said, "but everyone was getting very tired. We checked with the front desk to see when sunrise would be—and it wasn't for a few hours yet. We didn't think we would make it. Then we saw Ray Lafferty wandering around the lobby (as he did late at night at cons—he never slept as far as I knew). We greeted him and explained our dilemma. 'Sun'll be up in 40 minutes,' he said. We told him, No, every source said it wouldn't be up for awhile. 'Forty minutes,' he said, and wandered off.

On faith, we went out to the beach anyway—just to see the ocean again before dozing off—when we see a line of grey then pink, and don't you know it, in 40 minutes the sun came up. After that, we believed R. A. Lafferty unquestionably had special powers. He made the sun rise for us."

The following day I had two more hot-fudge sundaes, and a 3-scoop banana split which defeated even me. Funny I hadn't noticed that page in the menu before! And in that very same elevator, I stood behind Robert Heinlein, all the way up to the top floor. Now, I'd corresponded with him, off-and-on, for seven or eight years, but it's different when you

I discovered ice cream sundaes

meet someone face-to-face (or in my case, face-to-back-of-head). I noticed his grey hair was close-cropped, which made him look very strict. And what could I say, anyway? This wasn't the right time or place, I didn't want to act like one of the autograph brigade, and he was promoting a drive to donate blood, which didn't much appeal to me—I hate needles! So diffidence won and I missed my chance to meet one of the greatest names in science fiction.

However, I *did* get to see one of the greatest films in science fiction—*Star Wars*. It was on the Thursday afternoon, before the con had really started, but Peter Roberts and I were already feeling a bit left out from the various witticisms being made by the fans. What exactly was a Wookiee and why should we let him win? Why all the heavy, asthmatic breathing? And I didn't get the "Chinese Restaurant" joke, with the punch line (told in a solemn voice), "Use the Forks, Luke. Use the Forks."

We decided we had enough time before the opening ceremony to go along to a local cinema and see *Star Wars,* although we were warned there'd be long queues and we would never get in without advance booking. Strangely, the cinema was almost totally deserted and we couldn't understand why. We sat through the epic, emerging slightly stunned to find that outside it was raining. *That* was why everyone with any sense had stayed at home. Because "rain" doesn't adequately describe the sort of tropical deluge that faced us, with road and pavement already under inches of water, traffic stopped, and no other pedestrians in sight. There we were, standing under the dripping canopy and contemplating our dwindling chances of getting back to the hotel in time for the opening (it didn't matter for me, but it was rather more important for Peter to show his face as the official TAFF delegate from the U.K.).

We waited for ten minutes or more until a taxi came by and stopped at our frantic waving, although the driver made no attempt to come across to our side of the street. "Sadist!" I thought, as we ran through the swirling torrent, getting thoroughly soaked in the process. Although at least it was warm rain.

Peter later described the experience in his TAFF Report, "It was more like riding in a boat than a cab; the road was awash and invisible, rain thundered on the roof, the driver peered through the downpour, gripping the wheel like some old sea dog. We two sat in the back, keeping an eye open for sharks. 'This is OK,' growled the cabman. 'I've seen worse.' "

Rob, Peter and I manned the Seacon '79 desk all weekend and kept on signing-up more pre-supporters, with some help from the other Brits at the convention, people like Mike & Pat Meara, Vernon & Pat Brown, and Graham Poole. We kept an eye on the activity at the rival New Orleans table and started to feel more and more confident, particularly when one of their people came over and asked Rob, "What is this 'fandom' thing anyway?" We realised that they were pretty much unknown, that they didn't have much behind their bid apart from vague slogans like "Crescent City in 79."

I delivered our formal presentation at the Sunday business meeting and the adjudicators retired to count the votes, emerging surprisingly quickly to announce that Britain had won the 1979 Worldcon. (No figures were given, but I was told our majority was about four to one.) And then to our total surprise, chairman Don Lundry handed us a big sack of money, the accumulated funds voters had paid to take part in the site-selection ballot. We hadn't understood the rules, hadn't expected it, and were totally taken aback! And an hour or two later I was counting the proceeds with Tom and Alyx. Yes, we had won our Worldcon, there was no going back now!

By the time the great day finally dawned we had over 5000 members and 3500 of them turned up, making Seacon '79 the third-biggest world convention ever held until then. Now, today this may not sound so impressive but at the time it was absolutely unprecedented; British fandom had never done anything like this before. We were in completely uncharted territory. The London Worldcon had been a long time ago, none of its organisers were still around, and the difference in scale was simply enormous; a factor of ten, at least!

In retrospect, it could all have been a disaster. We, the committee, didn't begin to realise the enormous potential there was for things to go wrong. Yet we sailed through with apparent ease, and to this day, no one has ever had anything bad to say about Seacon '79.

How did we succeed? Because, I think, it was that rare thing, the product of a completely *united* fandom. For once British fandom came completely together, fanzine fans and con-runners, the fannish fans and the sercon devils, along with all the various local clubs and factions, so that the convention was not run by any one regional group or sectional interest; just about everyone was involved, in one way or another. As Rob Hansen noted, "The committee was almost a roster of Britain's most active fans of the previous ten years, with Peter Weston as chairman and *thirty-nine* others listed in the programme book in various roles."

In *Drilkjis,* Kevin Smith wrote about his feelings of anticipation: "I was excited about it. So was most of British fandom. It was going to be BIG, for one thing, and so it turned out. It was seven times as big as the biggest Eastercon. At Seacon '79, we Brits were outnumbered by foreigners— about three to one. And the feel of it was going to be different. This was a *Worldcon,* damn it, not just any old British con!"

We went to Brighton because in 1979 that was the only possible site, to the rambling corridors of the Metropole Hotel with its seafront position and its oil sheikhs, its huge complex of exhibition halls and its obliging manager, Fred Hutchins. I always got on well with Fred. He never really understood what it was all about, probably thought in private that we were a bunch of lunatics, but as far as he was concerned he was going to have a full hotel at a normally quiet time of year. He could see we weren't going to smash up the place, and it was none of his business if we wanted to walk around all day wearing pointy ears.

The complex was so enormous that most people needed a few hours to find their way around. There were eight huge halls in the exhibition centre, plus further function rooms in the hotel itself, and in the end we used them all. Hall 1 was a two-storey affair with a wide balcony at first-floor level, and naturally we used that for the main programme and big events. We put the dealers into Hall 3, also a double-decker, with a bar in Hall 2 and an alternative programme stream in Hall 4. The Art Show went into Hall 7, and we used Hall 5 for a massive fan-room, almost a convention within a convention, with its own bar, programme items, and row of slot-machines.

All that space beckoned so temptingly that we kept adding more attractions, but every extra hall cost us more hire-charges. So, to Treasurer John Steward's disgust, as fast as money came in, we spent it! Malcolm Edwards was particularly guilty in this respect, bringing an art exhibition from Dragon's Dream/Paper Tiger into Hall 6, and a special *Star Wars* exhibit into Hall 8. Late one evening Eileen and I were given a private viewing of this last item by Craig Miller, the genial Californian fan in charge, and we were suitably impressed by the terrific range of hardware from the film that they had somehow managed to get into the building.

John Steward was an FCA, a highly qualified Accountant, and he took his responsibilities seriously. He worried quietly all weekend about cash flow and trial balances, and on Friday evening he came to me with a sheet of figures that suggested we had run out of money. I shrugged my shoulders; at that stage, what more could we do, except hope for plenty of walk-ins? Fortunately, next day they came in droves. We were always short of money with Seacon '79, had made an early mistake in selling memberships much too cheaply, at only £11.00 per head for full attending status. It meant we had to be mean with ourselves—all the committee members paid for their own rooms, for instance. In my case I had to pay for two rooms—one for Eileen and myself, the other for our three young daughters and their granny, who we brought along to help look after them. On several occasions we boiled eggs in our electric kettle and toasted bread for a cheap lunch, and I never once went into the top-floor Starlight Restaurant. Ridiculous, really, but we were so worried about losing money! In the end, while Seacon '79 had total revenues of over £50,000, we cut things much too close for comfort and our final margin of income over expenditure was somewhat less than £1000.

After being harried so unmercifully at Worcester, however, I had learned the need to *delegate,* and we worked on the principle of section heads taking total responsibility for their areas. So Malcolm arranged the main programme, Roy Kettle ran the book-room, auctions and films, Rob Jackson handled the Banquet, and helped by Coral, also looked after the Fancy Dress. John and Eve Harvey ran the fan-room, merchandising operations, and newsletter, Pat Charnock managed membership, Graham produced our publications, Peter Roberts ran the fan-programme, and my old pal Tim Stannard from the Brum Group (a solicitor by vocation) was responsible for legal matters. Martin Hoare took on our internal security operations, and we gave the job of administering the Awards presentations to Dave Langford, thus beginning his long and fruitful association with the Hugos.

Dave comments, "I remember sitting at my desk at AWRE Aldermaston in 1979, furtively going through Hugo nomination ballots and recording the counts on Government-issue squared paper. (There was plenty of computer power to hand, but no spreadsheet software, and I didn't fancy all that data entry via punched cards.) One interesting discovery was the shamelessness of certain authors, like the one who entered her latest book in all five nomination slots for Best Novel. My lips are sealed; not even wild flying dragons would persuade me to name names.

"Then it turned out that the Hugo rules stated that the final ballot should be determined from the nominations, **but without saying how**. It would have been entirely legal to base the ballot on the works with fewest nominations, or the first five alphabetically, or various naughty Anglocentric possibilities which occurred to me. Instead, I virtuously took the common-sense route and even drafted an amendment to get this incorporated into the rules.

"A disembodied voice intoned, 'For you, Langford, the war is over,' when the figures began to disclose what had previously seemed unthinkable—that I myself was a contender in the fan-writer category, and likewise my *Twll-Ddu* as fanzine. This had never happened before. So I turned over the vote-counting to David Pringle, and contented myself with organizing the physical trophies. My college friend Adrian Smith, a dab hand at woodwork, produced the solid English Oak bases for the traditional rockets—which, in those pre-Weston days, were rather nasty and pitted. The Hugo assembly kit, a box of assorted threaded rods and nuts, came in handy for repairs during a *Twll-Ddu* production crisis that summer, and for years I was able to brag that mine was the only duplicator in fandom to incorporate parts of a Hugo."

In the very first *Ansible,* Dave also reported on the drama surrounding the arrival of the awards from the engraver, complete with creative spelling: "the Dramatic Presentation Hugo is a 'SCIENCE FICTION AGHIEVEMENT' trophy, and the Campbell Award was marked 'Seacon 1978'."

John Harvey commented, "Eve appeared to have the fan-room mostly under control by Friday; the TV games machines were glowing red hot and bulging with 10p pieces. The man with the Big Sack had arrived to empty them, when Eve remarked, "Didn't we have eight machines?' 'Of course,' I replied. 'Well, there's only seven now.' 'WHAT!'

"I rushed madly around the room, counting. Only seven present. I spent the next hour with Martin Easterbrook, going frantic looking for the missing machine. Nobody could have pinched it—could they? Hotel staff said they'd seen people struggling with one—through the doors to the *street!* Which master criminal, in broad daylight, under our very noses...? Visions of Seacon having to pay £2000+ came to mind. In the end we tracked the machine to a suite in the hotel and were less than polite to the miscreant who, it turned out, had ordered a machine, had found them delivered to the Fan Room, and liberated one for his own use without telling anyone!"

As for Pat Charnock, she may have been in a state of shock all weekend, and only remembers fleeting impressions: "Good con. Big con. Met loads of good people. Drank a bit. Good hotel—really like the Metropole. Spent most of my time in the office, as I was in charge of membership, and shy. It was a good place to be as I could squeak with delight at the very first sight of famous Americans."

We appointed session-chairmen for the main programme, people with presence and loud voices, such as Peter Nicholls and Rob Holdstock. Over and above that, I had asked Kevin Williams to be Operations Manager, in overall charge of the smooth running of the whole event. It was a job he performed superbly, with the result that I found myself totally superfluous to requirements, reduced to hanging round the Ops Room and asking hopefully, "Anything gone wrong?" only to be repeatedly disappointed, and told to go away.

I was only called upon once, late on the first night (early morning, really). After a busy and stressful day, I had just fallen into bed and was slipping gratefully down into a swirling pit of drunkenness and exhaustion when there came a furious hammering on our bedroom door. Dragged awake, I blinked sleepily at the circle of panicked committee faces round the bed, gradually registering their cries of anguish and distress, which were terrible to behold. "The hotel is closing down all the parties! You've got to *do* something!"

The hotel security people were on the rampage and had just evicted the SFWA from their top-floor party suite, something for which they had paid over £100 per night (big money in 1979). People were not happy. Somebody had to complain to the management, and it looked as if that somebody was going to have to be me!

Dressing reluctantly, I was propelled downstairs by anxious committee members to the lobby, where I went over to the desk and stood there politely, being ignored by an indifferent night clerk. Suddenly, feeling very tired and emotional, I felt something snap inside my head and all that niceness and civility stuff went out of the window. I began to "do a Khrushchev," hammering and banging on the counter, and complaining loudly that I wanted to see the manager. Soon, their chief security man appeared, a squat, Edward G. Robinson-like thug with a scar and a nasty disposition. He didn't like me on sight, and I didn't like him. Accusations began to fly wildly, "I've brought you a half-million pounds' worth of business," which he countered with, "Bunch of crazies all over the place!" Consumed by red rage I shouted at him, and he shouted at me, we stabbed fingers and gestured, and I threatened to get Fred Hutchins out of his bed and he threatened to have me thrown out of the hotel, and I said we would sue, and after ten minutes of this, he started to back down. The watching crowd of fans broke into applause as, shaking like a leaf, I crept up to the last surviving party enclave in the Ladies' Powder Room on the Sixth Floor, where I sat on the carpeted floor with Mike Dickinson and Peter Roberts, who sympathetically plied me with his herbal cigarettes.

Next day we went to see Fred Hutchins with a carefully chosen team of heavyweights including Jerry Pournelle (SFWA President), Tim Stannard and R. Lee Smith, the captain of the uniformed security company we'd hired (a team of retired local policemen). Fred gave us a cup of tea, apologised profusely, and told us that he would call off his security people for the rest of the weekend. There would be no more trouble. And there wasn't.

Kevin Williams described my antagonists, "...a bunch of characters led by a guy called 'Kurtz,' whose ominous name well described the nature of his security operation. He turned up in the Ops Room one afternoon and announced dramatically, 'We're going to call the bomb squad. Somebody has padlocked a metal box to the leg of the piano in the Sussex Lounge.'

" 'Oh…that's just Filthy Pierre's nose-flute,' we said. 'We'll get him to move it.' Kurtz remained unconvinced of the existence of any such person until Filthy Pierre came, unlocked his box, and went away with it. In fact, there were very few security problems at Seacon. Both Kurtz and R. Lee were surprised about this, in a convention of such a size. 'We get more trouble with the Conservative Conference,' our man said, towards the end of the weekend."

After that first incident I think the only other time I saw Fred Hutchins was at breakfast on the Tuesday morning, when he came up to our table with a slightly puzzled expression on his face. "Excuse me, Mr Weston," he said, "but do you know anything about a twelve-foot tower of beer-cans that seems to have been piled against the wall in the Norfolk Room?"

"Not a thing," I assured him blandly, shaking my head. "The *stunts* some of these science fiction fans get up to!"

In reality, of course, I knew quite a bit about the tower, which we had constructed the previous night at the Gopher Party. The concept of gophers was something Rob and I had brought back from Suncon, and at Seacon '79 it took on a life of its own. We ended-up with a whole army of volunteers, fans who would willingly run all over the place with messages, helping with set-ups and doing all those other chores, and the Party on Monday evening was our way of thanking them.

Once again, Rob and I went out to buy drink, with a big wad of money in my pocket and empty suitcases in the back of the car. As we hurtled through the back streets of Brighton I had a moment of *déjà vu;* "I think we've done this before, Rob," I said. Unfortunately, this was Brighton, not Florida, it was lunchtime on Bank Holiday Monday, and all the shops were shut. Fi-

THE BEER HUNTERS

Looking for beer

nally, we spotted a street corner off-licence and hastily parked. We went into the shop and I put £300.00 on the counter.

"We want to buy beer," I said, "A *lot* of beer."

The shop-girl looked at all that money, which was probably going to represent the biggest sale she had ever made, and responded in classic British manner. "But we're closing in ten minutes," she said, in desperate hope that we would go away and trouble someone else.

Arriving back at the hotel's loading bay, we were met by Martin Hoare with his walkie-talkie, who briskly called our uniformed security men. They moved like clockwork, opening up the goods entrance and whisking our booze away to a safe hiding-place until the evening. Then, just before midnight, we took it all down to the basement room we were using for the party. "We'll build a Tower of Beer-cans to the Moon," I said, "it's an old fannish tradition." The fans started to stack the tins into a giant pyramid and I seized a Magic Marker and wrote out instructions on a piece of cardboard:

"Tower of Beer-cans to the Moon—A concept originated by Terry Carr and the Berkeley boys in the early 1960s, and recently revived by Arthur C. Clarke and Charles Sheffield. Object of the exercise is to take full beer-can from top of tower, dispose of contents in some way, and neatly stack can to form a cosmic funicular tower on the other side of the room."

The gophers set to their task with great enthusiasm. We knurdled, we had the Astral pole, and Kathy Sanders gave us her full belly-dancing routine. Many of the Big Names came down to join in; Brian and Margaret Aldiss, resplendent in evening dress, Fritz Leiber, Bob Shaw, Theodore Sturgeon, and most of the committee. Halfway through we were raided by 'hotel security' in the form of a squad of 'Imperial Stormtroopers,' in full *Star Wars* kit, courtesy of Craig Miller. It was a great party and eventually I left them to it, the Tower by this time half deconstructed. From the evidence next morning, some sturdy souls stayed awake until the job had been finished!

The Gopher Party and that little altercation with security were about the only times I actually had anything to *do* that weekend. Apart from the Opening Ceremony, that is. That had been my baby from the beginning, something I had fought hard for at committee meetings against the doubts of the others, something I was determined to do properly. I firmly believed that conventions often fail because they never get properly *started*. They just sort of creep into life while no one is looking, never develop a good head of steam, a sense of presence, the feeling of involvement which is so necessary if attendees are going to knit together to make the whole greater than the sum of its parts.

The rest of the committee were unenthusiastic, they could see problems. And what exactly did I have in mind? Music, I suggested. At Discon I had been very impressed by the colour and spectacle of the Alexandria Pipe Band, which Dick Eney had marched through the convention one evening (though I never found out exactly why). And a bit of comedy would be good. What if I brought along a fake machine-gun and pretended to mow down the rest of the committee? They looked unimpressed. All right, I said, so what if *they* were to mow *me* down? They brightened visibly at this idea, but still said "no."

In the end, Kev Williams came to the rescue. Kevin was a manager at Procter & Gamble and was well used to organising things. He and his wife Sue had already agreed to paint our backdrop for the main hall, a huge thing that would stretch across the width of the back wall and would necessarily drop through two floor levels. It must have measured something like 30 x 20 foot, in white, with Harry Bell's fannish lion symbol, and our slogan, "Britain's fine in '79,"

"So," said Kev, "how about if, for the opening, we have the backdrop rolled up on the floor, and we project the symbols of previous Worldcons onto a screen. We'll play some music while this is going on, gradually getting louder, until at the right moment we give 'em a full blast as our backdrop goes up. A sort of audio-visual build-up, and then Peter can come on and say his bit, and he can have his marching band, too, if he wants it."

Well, Kevin certainly sold me and the rest of the committee too, although his proposals caused considerable technical difficulties and I never did find out how he managed to transport that huge, heavy backdrop and get it rigged up the way he wanted. His choice of music was superb, and his slide show worked wonderfully during rehearsals, as the conventions marched through the years to a stentorian voice-over: "1975–Melbourne; 1976–Kansas City;" and so on, culminating in the awe-inspiring moment when the voice said "1979–Brighton" and our backdrop slowly came up, to the dramatic theme from *Rocky*. It brought tears to my eyes, it really did!

What about the band? Well, since we were in Brighton I thought it would be nice to have the Royal Marines. Of course, we couldn't afford the entire regiment. In fact, it turned out that we couldn't afford any of them! Apparently this sort of thing is a nice little earner for well-known regiments, so the best we could get were a half-dozen members of the Caledonian Pipe Band. Still, I thought, the bagpipes and the uniforms would make a bit of a splash as they marched into the hall, and the Americans would appreciate it, so we went ahead with the hire.

The big day came, Thursday 23rd August. We had decided to start a whole day earlier than usual, to give five days of programme events. "Don't be late," we had said in our publicity. "Don't miss the opening ceremony," and the main hall was filling with people as the magic time of 2.15 p.m. approached. We were ready to begin the show, to switch on the warm-up music, which would come from speakers, strategically placed around the hall by our tech crew, at low volume to begin with, but gradually getting louder until the moment came for the slide show. Our guests were waiting in the wings, Brian Aldiss in a splendid loud-checked Swedish jacket, Fritz Leiber more sober in grey suit. But *where* was our band? They should have arrived an hour or more ago! Just then I took a telephone call from their leader. "Stuck in heavy traffic on the way down from London," he said. "Won't be more than another half-an-hour."

I gritted my teeth. We, the amateurs, had done everything right, yet we were going to be late because of the so-called professionals! I had a hurried discussion with Kevin; should we go ahead anyway? Someone pointed out that we didn't actually need the band at the beginning of the show, maybe we could spin it out a bit. We compromised, left things for ten minutes, and then switched on the music. There was a ripple of excitement from the audience.

By now there must have been well over 1500 people in there. Just then the phone went again. It was the leader of the band. "Still stuck," he said cheerfully; "won't be more than another half-hour."

Kevin and I debated what to do next. In his words, "The sound technician had all the music set up, the gophers stood at their posts, by light switches, ready to haul on ropes to raise the banner at the prime moment. Sue was ready with the spots, Andy Firth had the bathing belles in the bar alongside the main hall, buying them drinks and keeping them warm. I stood on the balcony ready to cue the slides and give all the signals for the sound, banner, spots, bathing belles, and band. But no band. The tension on the balcony was palpable. 2.30 p.m. came and went."

"Let's run the warm-up music through again," Kevin suggested. "That'll buy us some more time." The trouble was, it did start to get pretty loud towards the end of the first stanza, and people began to get restless when the music went round for the second time. Suddenly it stopped. Dead silence. "Break in the circuit," said one of the techies, as they scurried off to find the problem. I began to chew my nails because it was all going wrong. After an anxious few minutes, Martin Hoare came back on his walkie-talkie; "found it," he said. "Some idiot American pulled all the plugs out of the speakers down here on the floor." Problem fixed!

"Right," I said. "We're not waiting any longer. Let's get it rolling, Kev," and this time we went right through the sequence. First came the opening anthem, then the lights went down, the slides ran through, and as our backdrop was solemnly raised to the sound of *Rocky*, a spotlight picked out our fannish lion and the audience went wild. Toastmaster Bob Shaw introduced our Guests, and they came on, one by one, Fritz Leiber, Brian Aldiss, and Harry Bell, followed by Coral Jackson's bevy of Brighton Bathing Belles in bright turn-of-century costumes, who trooped onto the stage and made a fuss of the Guests of Honour and the Chairman. Yes, the band *did* arrive, marching on with about thirty seconds to spare. Seacon '79 was well and truly launched, and everyone who had been involved in the ceremony was left trembling and covered in a fine film of sweat.

One last comment from Kevin Smith:

"But oddly, the feel of Seacon'79 was *not* different; it was familiar. I felt at home. The feel was fannish and familiar, but there were lots of new people who fitted in and contributed to it. Legendary American fans and unknown British neos—I was meeting both for the first time—added enough vitality to break up the established rounds of British fandom without ruining its fannish ambience. It was great, I tell you! It was great."

After breakfast on Tuesday the committee meeting came together for one final meeting to wrap up any loose ends, congratulate ourselves, and decide who would get the solitary left-over Hugo Award. Then I had to leave Brighton, leave fandom behind, and start on the long journey home to Birmingham, back next morning to a difficult, demanding job and a hard-driving, unsympathetic manager.

Brian Aldiss waved goodbye. "Poor old Pete," he said. "From now onwards, life is going to be downhill all the way."

Epilogue

Brian Aldiss was nearly right. Things certainly went downhill after the Worldcon, as almost immediately I was swept up in a fresh wave of job problems that took most of my attention, until I finally surfaced in the spring of 1980 with a new position as General Manager of a troubled subsidiary of the Wilmot Breeden engineering group. I hung onto fandom by my fingernails for three busy years, before beginning to surface again in early 1983.

It started with a renewed involvement with the good old Brum Group, and in turn, the person responsible for that was, as ever, Rog Peyton. The coming year had looked like being something of a crisis point for the group, since no one particularly wanted to stand as Chairman and some problems had accumulated. In desperation, they had asked me, several times from October onwards, but I wasn't interested. However, at Eileen's New Year party Rog saw his chance, and while I was slightly under the influence he signed me up, irrevocably, in front of witnesses, to take on the job.

Until committed, I genuinely didn't want to do it, but then I began to get more and more interested in the idea. I had been Chairman several times before, and it's usually not a good idea to repeat yourself, but still, that was 1973, and a lot had changed since then. Maybe local fanac would help me get started again, a return to my roots, a chance to recapture a sense of purpose by concentrating on smaller-scale objectives? In fact, I was intrigued by the possibilities inherent in the Brum Group, became interested again in the original, forgotten idea of building a local *fandom*.

It seemed to me that quite a number of new and talented people had joined the Group while I had been away, people like Paul Vincent, Steve Green, Martin Tudor, Tony Berry, Chris Baker (the artist "Fangorn"), and others, fans-in-the-making, just looking for the right door. Maybe we had been in training camp for too long, and it was time to head out and aim for the Tower of Trufandom? This would be my mission; to pass on the spark, like the Fairy in *The Enchanted Duplicator*.

Eileen was a bit concerned at the possible workload involved, but I reassured her that it would "only take up one night per month" for committee meetings and so on. That was never realistic and within weeks I was in the thick of it, from a long-winded and unsatisfactory AGM in January to an equally long-winded but action-packed EGM in March, where we defended Novacon against the usurpers who wanted to wrench it bloodily from the grasp of the Brum group. A lot of accumulated tension was around, for which the second meeting seemed to act as a sort of catharsis, and I realised the group had become very insular, out of touch with mainstream fandom, and not terribly popular. It needed to be woken up!

So there I was, busily publishing manifestos, conceiving projects, lobbying for support, and generally bleeding and dying for my beliefs. And one of those projects was APA-B. The idea came from dim recollections of APA-L, the weekly APA run by the Los Angeles group, and partly from my own half-forgotten memories of the joys of pubbing. This was just what the group needed, I thought, something to focus creative effort and energy, something to build involvement between BSFG members and help bring them closer to fandom proper. And it was just what I needed, too, because in no time I was typing stencils and cranking out pages once again, as if my life depended upon

it. There's nothing like a target, a deadline, an obligation to deliver, and I had promised to put a fanzine into the first mailing of the new APA-B in June 1983.

I called it *Prolapse,* to Eileen's considerable disapproval. "Look it up in the dictionary," I wrote, "it means 'falling down' (that's fannish), and 'to slip out of place' (which is exactly what's happened to me, as the microcosm has moved on during my absence). I'm perfectly aware there is another meaning, of course; after all, in my previous incarnation I aspired to a sort of third-rate 'pro' status, and now I've 'lapsed' back into fandom."

The first issue had a Steve Green cover which featured my appearance in the Fancy Dress Parade at the 1983 Eastercon—Albacon—in Glasgow:

"Not much of a Costume, is it?" they said.

"Why don't you have a sword with that shield?"

"Maybe if he had a dragon on his shoulder?"

I felt a bit of an idiot, standing in a curtained-off alcove with the other contestants, wearing their glittering costumes, false heads, and so on, while I stood there with my trousers tucked into my socks, a rucksack on my back, fanzines sticking out of the pockets of my faithful, battered old suede jacket, and my Shield of Umor on my arm.

One of the committee tried to move me on: "Only contestants allowed in here."

Somebody else was photographing the costumes, looked at me rather doubtfully, and decided not to bother.

Then the compere, Anne Page, asked me what I was supposed to be, frowned at my card and spelled it out slowly, "J-O-P-H-A-N in Search of the Perfect Fanzine." She looked at my shield and frowned again. I could almost hear her thinking, "Wonder what fantasy trilogy that's from?"

Actually, I was rather proud of that shield, and it had taken a considerable expenditure of energy and effort to get it to Glasgow. It was made it in one frantic Saturday afternoon of creativity in my workshop, the week before the convention, after I had decided to make a special effort to be really fannish, and to go to the Fancy Dress as Jophan.

It began life in 1968 as the facing for a display board, when I was still with the BSA company, a piece of aluminium sheet used for an exhibition in France. I took it with me when I left, along with various other bits of wood and metal, on the general basis that it might come in useful. So, fifteen years later when inspiration struck, I had to remove the lettering with an abrasive pad, then I cut the sheet into a rough triangle and drew a large, grinning face in felt-tip pen.

Next step was to put the thing onto a thick bed of latex foam, to act as a cushion, and then I started tapping away with a small hammer and punch. Aluminium is malleable stuff but each tap only produced a dent about 1/2-inch long and 1/8-inch deep, and it takes a long time to get anywhere, since you don't want to tear the sheet. Finally, I sprayed the face with some aluminium car-paint to brighten it up a little, outlined the features in black gloss paint, and bent the top into a chord and secured it with a piece of broomstick, which held the shape and gave me something to grip. As a finishing touch, I added a strip of polished brass across the top; that was originally due to be used as a rain-deflector on my back door!

"It has a sensitive fannish face," said Eileen, inspecting my masterpiece, a huge curved shield about 40 inches by 30 inches.

It looked very fine, but when I boarded the train to Glasgow I found I had a problem. The Shield was too big to put on the overhead luggage rack, too long to go behind the seat, so I had to sit and hold this great parcel, wrapped in brown paper, for five hours, with Steve Green, Martin Tudor, Chris Suslowicz, and Tony Berry chuckling all the way. We were going to Albacon to restore the good name of the BSFG; I had two hundred pounds in my pocket, money prised from the clutches of a reluctant Treasurer, so we could hold a Brum group party.

Was it worth all the effort?

I shambled around the Fancy Dress area in front of a disinterested crowd, and only one person applauded. That was old-time 'fifties fan Mal Ashworth, who had chosen that year to return from the glades of gafia. He was almost the only one to recognise the Shield; such was the state of British fandom in 1983!

APA-B was a success—the first mailing contained nine titles, the second, thanks to the efforts of intrepid OE Cath Easthope, seventeen. It did the trick and launched several Brum group members into mainstream fandom, and under a different name, the APA survived for a number of years. The Brum group was revitalised and returned to the Imperial Hotel for a second long stretch, and the whole period became known as the "Birmingham Renaissance." Very soon, though, I found myself once more forced away from fandom by mundane pressures...

As for the Shield, I enjoyed making it, and in 1987 donated it to the Fan Auction at Conspiracy, the British Worldcon, where it was bought by Greg Pickersgill. I was delighted that it went to a good owner, and trust he will keep it well-polished. After all, Greg, you know what might happen if you don't!

Epilogue on Epilogue

My 1983 re-entry to publishing was abortive, sadly, overtaken by real-world events before it had really got started. There were only two issues of *Prolapse* (though it drew a fantastic letter-column, with comments from Terry Carr, Lee Hoffman, Ted White among many others), because in October, just after my fortieth birthday, my job blew up in my face, again. This was a familiar story and I was so fed up that this time I did a "Victor Kiam," borrowed a lot of money and bought the company. After that, with our house on the line, I had little time for fannish activity, though I continued to attend British conventions and a number of Worldcons during the late '80s and '90s.

An unplanned consequence of all this was that one afternoon I found myself in Los Angeles, listening to Craig Miller complain about the high price and general non-availability of the Hugo Award rocketships. I had just told Craig about the chromed Jaguar mascots that my company made, and he asked the obvious question which had never previously occurred to me: "Why doesn't your company try and make the Hugos?"

I came home, examined the spare Hugo trophy I had wrested—wrestled—out of Malcolm Edwards' sticky grasp back in 1979, and decided that yes, we could do it. Using the existing Hugo as a master pattern, we made a cast-iron mould into which we poured a zinc-based alloy, using gravity die-casting techniques, rather than the cruder sand-cast rockets that Charlie Brown had previously supplied. The result was a slight re-design, a major improvement in quality of finish (no more "meteor impacts"), and a reduced price. I supplied the Hugos for Los Angeles in 1984 and every year afterwards (apart from Chicago in 1991, who cleverly produced their own, plastic, self-destructing trophies). They are normally chromium-plated but were gold-plated for Magicon in 1992, to mark the 50th Worldcon, and again in 2003 for Torcon, for the 50th anniversary of first presentation.

It sometimes strikes me as ironic that I should have wanted a Hugo so badly and never won one, and I have now produced over five hundred of them!

Otherwise, I still hang around conventions and try to participate in the programme. A whole new crop of actifans have appeared, too recently to appear in this book, who regard me as a historic curiosity, a fossil, to whom Mark Plummer can comment, "The earliest events in this (present) story took place a year before I was born," and Claire Brialey can ask in fascinated horror, "What was it *really* like to publish a fanzine back in 1964?"

Yes, the Revolving Door keeps on going round, and my role is to be a sort of permanent doorman to British fandom, watching them come in, and after five or ten years go out again. Long may it continue!

"Where Are They Now?"
Appendix 1

Aldiss, Brian

Brian writes, "My wife Margaret died of cancer in November 1997. Directly after the funeral, when silence fell over me and swallowed me, I wrote a book about her illness and life, and our love and our family. It is entitled *When the Feast Is Finished*. Strangely, though, the feast was not finished. When I was at my lowest ebb, a young French woman called on me and on her second visit declared she was in love with me. I cannot explain the passion this aroused, and from then on I entered into a richly creative period of my life, full of women and new friends and happiness.

"The following books have been published since that day: *The Twinkling of an Eye* (autobiography); *White Mars* (a utopia); *The Squire Quartet* (4 volumes); *A.I.* (stories); *The Cretan Teat* (comic novel); *Super-State* (dark SF novel); *Affairs at Hampden Ferrers* (local Voltarian novel). To be published shortly: *Jocasta* and *Sanity and the Lady*. Also around, an opera and some pamphlets and poems. Life is a miracle!"

Barber, Dave

Dave lost touch with fandom in the early '70s, and says, "I spent most of my time at work (I worked away from home and late into the evenings for several years) and what spare time I had was taken up with home life. I continued to read SF, but it seemed to change for me, and though I still read it, I am only really happy with the 'old style' of writers. (Asimov, Heinlein and of course Eric Frank Russell!) Now I have more free time, I am looking to see what SF has on offer. I am thinking about dropping in at a convention some time in the future if they will have me."

Barker, Jim

Jim Barker started up his own graphic design/illustration business in 1982, dropped out of fandom in the late 1980's and, apart from the occasional convention appearance and fanzine cover, hasn't been seen much in fandom since. Jim's professional work includes illos for *SFX* magazine and BBC television and various Scottish book publishers. He has a website at *www.cartoonise.com*.

Bell, Harry

Harry went to Noreascon 3 in 1980 with Jim Barker, but has not attended another U.S. convention since. "In the '80s I continued with the Silicons and Novacons and published fanzines," said Harry, "and I also continued drawing cartoons for fanzines round the world, but found it less and less fulfilling, especially when more and more they failed to see publication. I took up painting and became increasingly successful. And I got married. The Gannets had shrunk to a tiny and uncomfortable Rump, so without making a conscious decision, I found my life had become something which no longer had much room for fandom. Today I'm a professional artist, having quit the Civil Service in 1979 and graduated in Fine Art from Newcastle University in 2001. I still keep in contact with a few fans (more since my connection to the Internet), but I don't see much of the old spark being fanned into flames again."

Bennett, Ron

Ron still attends conventions and is still writing for fanzines and recently has had published a small number of SF and mystery novels.

Blish, James

James Blish died in 1975 and was buried in Oxford. During his last six years in England he was a major figure at British conventions, with a high point at the 1974 Tynecon, where he took the lead role as "The Mighty Oz" in his wife Judy's production of *The Wizard of Oz*.

Brown, Vernon

After Eastercon 22 and Novacon, Vernon became more interested in continental fandom and went to several European conventions, including Trieste in 1972, from where he kindly brought back the first Europa Award for *Speculation*. At the inception of the new Brum Group he went onto the committee and with only a few brief respites, he has stayed there ever since, now being almost chairman-in-perpetuity. While Vernon first met his wife Pat at the group in 1973, they got together in 1976 at a fan-party, attended Suncon in Florida, and married soon afterwards. He retired from Aston University in 1996.

Brunner, John

John died in August 1995 on the first night of Intersection. Chris Priest wrote, "John Brunner's sudden death at the Glasgow Worldcon came as a profound shock, but not, sadly, to those who had been in contact with him recently, a surprise. Every conversation I had with John in the last two or three years was spiked with his unhappiness, frustration, and disappointment. His health had become intermittently poor, his finances generally shaky and his career seemed at a low ebb. But in earlier years he was buoyant. John was the first major SF writer I came to know personally, and although I often found his company uncomfortable, because away from home he put on a defensive veneer, I never ceased to admire him, like him and more often than not love him." (*Ansible* 98)

PW adds, "While John's professional work is well documented, it is probably less well known that he was a great supporter of British fandom. He almost always attended conventions, he took a major role in organising both 1969 and 1984 Eastercons, and he provided much of the impetus for the rescue of the BSFA in mid-1975 when it was very close to being wound up."

Bulmer, Ken

Ken was GoH at Novacon 3 in 1973, but seems to have quietly slipped away from fandom in the early '80s, and Beccon in 1983 was probably his last Eastercon. Paradoxically, Ken's greatest professional success came late in his career with his series of science fantasy novels under the pseudonym of Alan Burt Akers, commencing in 1980, with at least fifteen titles published. He also wrote under a dozen or more other pen-names, at least eight used solely for non-SF, such as his Hornblower-style sea adventures by Adam Hardy.

Ken has suffered poor health in recent years with at least one major operation, but still keeps in touch through the kindness of Dave Langford and the indispensable *Ansible*. In 1998, Dave produced Ken's TAFF Report from 1955 (including one chapter even the author had forgotten!), which is now on-line at the TAFF web-site.

Burgess, Brian

Brian died of heart failure in January 1997, aged 65. He had seemed very much older since his stroke some years ago, and intensely regretted missing his first Novacon in 1995 (having been at every one since the beginning); his fan involvement dated back to 1952. Greg Pickersgill adds: "Brian was a real fan, a genuine enthusiast for science fiction, fantasy, fandom and conventions; he brought the same cheerful optimism to his other interests—he was widely travelled and made friends all over the world, and was something of an authority on G. A. Henty—and was a kindly and good-hearted fellow, with maybe rather more than the usual quota of eccentricities, but in every sense one of us." (*Ansible* 115)

Burns, Bill

Bill attended London Circle meetings in 1970, where he met U.S. fan Mary Ensley, who had come over on Don Lundry's Heidelberg Worldcon charter flight. At Heidelberg, Bill tracked her down, and he moved to New York in 1971, where they married and have lived ever since, with frequent trips to the U. K. for fannish and family events. Noreascon 4 will mark their 33rd anniversary.

Bill owns a computer consulting business and in his spare time is webmaster for a number of web sites on the history of science and technology. One of his favourite projects is the eFanzines.com site, an "electronic news-stand" where fanzine editors are provided with free web space for their fanzines (and production help as needed), together with a compilation of Trip Reports and other memorabilia, including a section showing Peter Weston's recent photographic record of British fandom. Bill won the "Doc Weir" Award in 2003 and the FAAn Award at the 2004 Corflu for his superb web-site (*www.efanzines.com*).

Charnock, Graham

"Where have we been since doodley squat?" muses Graham. "Well, we're obviously not in Kansas any more, Toto. Just going through the usual traumas of marriage, counselling, buying leather sofas from warehouses on the North Circular, bringing up children, children becoming adults, parents becoming children, etc. Pat occasionally dusts off her folders of *Wrinkled Shrew* with a bemused smile. She is a dedicated mother to our two grown-up sons, visiting them regularly whenever the prison authorities allow, whilst I have special dispensation to take care of the cats and occasionally change their nappies. They hate it; I've got so many claw tracks on my forearms my doctor is convinced I'm a junkie. That's what I tell the police too.

"I am engaged in writing the ultimate hermetically-sealed science fiction novel, called *Levelland,* presently 200,000 words long and no end, agent or publisher in sight. To keep body and soul together I have a day-job with a left-wing book distributor in Hackney Wick, where I have been elevated to the dizzy heights of deputy trade sales manager. If you want to know where to go for a copy of the *CPAG Guide to Housing Benefits and Council Tax Legislation* 16th Edition, look no further. And as you know I have recently re-invented myself as an SF fan, and contribute regularly to *Chunga,* the best fanzine in the world since that one by the late Terry Hughes, and even since Charles Platt's *Garbistan,* which is why I am longing to read your memoirs."

Graham made a surprise appearance at the 2003 Eastercon with "The Astral League Revival Tour" and distributed a new issue of his personalzine, *Vibrator.* Some still claim that he is the world's very best fan-writer.

Charnock, Pat

"I lead a quiet life in Harringay, working for the local council and paying off the mortgage. I have two grown sons—one's into science fiction and dungeons and dragons, and the other spends long weekends at computer gaming conventions. The noisiest things in the house are Graham and the cats.

"Many women take a career break to raise their kids. Me, I went on working but took a fandom break. I'm thinking I could still wangle my way back in, and win the Nova yet. I spent a long time not writing anything apart from procedure manuals and memos, but in the last year I've started editing our newsletter at work, and now I write a lot of it too. In the autumn, I'm going to sign up for the 'remind yourself how to edit a fanzine' evening class. Meanwhile, I read a lot, investigate my family history, prune shrubs, and cook huge pots of chili con carne for the cats."

Cheslin, Ken

Ken died suddenly and unexpectedly on 4 August, 2000; he was 63 or 64. In recent years he had battled heroically against low income and a cranky photocopier to reprint classic fan material in the millennial "Atom 2000" and many volumes of John Berry's articles. (*Ansible* 158)

Cohen, Dr Jack

After more than thirty years at Birmingham University, Jack finally decided to move on, and has now carved out a multi-faceted career, both as a reproductive biologist and as a successful author, of textbooks and of popular science. He now works with mathematician Ian Stewart and they have published a number of titles, including *The Science of Discworld* with Terry Pratchett, and *Wheelers*, an SF novel. Jack still appears at conventions and was a guest at Boskone in 2001.

Edwards, Malcolm

Malcolm writes, "After the 1979 worldcon I remained fairly active in fandom for the next two or three years, publishing fanzines. Then, at the beginning of 1983, John Bush retired as Managing Director of Gollancz, and I took charge of their SF list, which pretty much put paid to that (fanzines, I mean). I chaired the 1987 British Worldcon bid, but stepped down from the committee the December before the convention after my marriage broke up (I remained titular chairman, but Paul Oldroyd, as is generally recognised, actually chaired the convention).

"Since 1987 I've been inactive in fandom, but connected because of my career in publishing. I ran the Gollancz SF list until 1989, and then moved to Grafton/HarperCollins. While having moved out of being a specialist SF publisher in 1991, I have always had a list under my general charge; first HarperCollins/Voyager, then, when I moved to Orion in 1998, Millennium/Gollancz. I still manage to attend at least one convention a year, on average, somewhere (Eastercon in 2002, World Fantasy in 2003), and still regularly see many friends from the 70s—Brosnan, Holdstock, Kettle, and so on."

Hall, Graham

Graham Hall died of cirrhosis of the liver in 1980, aged 33. He had recently married and settled in Culver City with his Californian wife Susan. (*Ansible* 12)

Harrison, Harry

Harry writes, "Twenty-five years. They've gone by rather quickly. A big move—from San Diego back to Europe. Been in Ireland ever since and greatly enjoying it. Good and very bad. My dear wife Joan died a short while ago. We were together fifty years; I could have used fifty more. She is sorely missed.

"The kids have done well. Moira re-married very happily indeed. Gave up farming and went back to school. She is now Dr. Harrison and teaches graduate students molecular biology. Todd married and is still working in medical R&D in California.

"And the writing has gone well. My *West of Eden* trilogy broke out of category and sold very well in mainstream. A million and a half copies of the paperback; can't complain! Another series, alternate history, *Stars and Stripes Forever* doing well. And Russia! All my books now in print there and I am top of the SF sales there. My publisher invited me over and I was guest of a con— and let me tell you—they practice *real* fanac! If you get a chance to go—go!

"Life is a bit quieter now. I get to more cons, see old friends before they snuff it. Too many good mates have gone to the big publishing house in the sky. After some time dawdling about I have started a new career/gone back to an old career—in graphic novels.

"The cinema. As I write this my *Stainless Steel Rat* books are in pre-production in Hollywood with Twentieth-Century Fox. Golconda Films in London now has my *Technicolour Time Machine* at the script stage. One can but hope…

"Life goes on."

Hay, George

George died in 1997 following an operation. Chris Priest said, "He had a great sense of humour, and was a man of exceeding good nature. When he was in hospital last year, I cracked a bad-taste joke about the medical staff thinking for three days he was delirious, until they worked out he was telling them about the SF Foundation. The next time I saw George I made the same joke, and he laughed and laughed." (*Ansible* 124)

Higgs, Mike

Mike did not attend another convention after 1965, and became much more involved with graphics and comics fandom. He became a full-time artist and edited a series of large-size "Nostalgia" books, including the complete adventures of "Dan Dare," reprinted from the beloved *Eagle*. He married Cynthia and they still live in North Birmingham.

Howett, Dick(y)

During the early 1980s Dicky Howett finally abandoned all fannish activity, consolidating his cartoon career by drawing for Marvel Comics and broadcasting his own "humorous" short stories on local radio. These days—apart from writing media articles (a book is due at the end of 2004), Dicky collects and restores items of "historic" TV and film hardware (cameras, lights, microphones), some of which he rescued literally off the scrap heap. His collection of television studio equipment is acknowledged as significant. Also, he assists the national Museum of Photography Film & Television in the hunt for rare items. However, Dicky's hoard of electronic dinosaurs doesn't languish. Parts can be seen regularly, hired as authentic props in feature films, TV series, and popular music videos. Recently, reconstructing a 1950s US TV studio, Dicky filmed (and appeared in) sequences with Hollywood star Kevin Spacey.

Jackson, Rob

Rob is now the consultant psychiatrist in West Sussex, managing substance-misuse services for the county's specialist NHS trust. He helped run Mexicon 2 in 1986 and was on the committee for Conspiracy, the '87 Worldcon, but found that experience exhausted his fannish enthusiasm for quite some time. In the '90s he devoted more time to training junior doctors and helping Coral care for infirm family members. Rob says, "Coral, who helped to run Seacon '79's Fancy Dress, is now a full-time homemaker but is also very involved in helping promote the crafts of weaving, spinning, & dyeing locally. Offspring: Dulcie (now 23) graduated in French & Italian, and is now working in radio advertising in Bristol; Hugo (18) studying acting, but also into Japanese anime & historically accurate mediaeval re-enactment, & Veneti, (12)." Rob is now back in some contact with fandom electronically via the "Memory Hole" Mailing List and other e-communication with old Gannets & other pals.

James, Edward

Edward ceased all fan activity after 1965 (going to university) until the early 1980s, when he organised a public series of lectures on science fiction at the University of York, where he was a Senior Lecturer in the History Department. At this time he started reviewing and writing on SF and going to cons again, surprising his old pal Peter Weston by turning up for the Leeds Yorcon in 1985. The following year he became editor of *Foundation,* with which Edward continued until 2001, and he has since published a number of books on science fiction and related subjects. He became Professor of Medieval History at Reading University in 1995 and launched an MA in Science Fiction; he is currently Secretary of the Science Fiction Foundation.

Jarrold, John

After a few years away from fandom John re-entered in 1982 with fanzine *Prevert* (one previous issue in 1975), which moved from personalzine to genzine and won the 1985 Nova for Best Fanzine. Through the mid-'80s he was reading for various publishers, including Macmillan and Gollancz, so when Toby Roxburgh left Orbit/Macdonald in late 1987 he started as editor of Orbit in January 1988. (John still thinks about that with a true sense-of-wonder.) He ran the Orbit, Legend, and Earthlight publishing imprints from 1988 to 2002, before becoming a freelance editor and publishing adviser. John has lived by the sea in Sussex since 1990, and swears he would never live in London again. He now provides advice to aspiring writers as "The Script Doctor" with a web-site, *www.sff.net/people/john-jarrold/*.

Jones, Eddie

Eddie died in October 1999 at age 64, after weeks in hospital following a stroke. Rog Peyton comments: "Eddie was, in my opinion, one of the very best SF artists in the 1970s. At his most prolific he was painting eight commissions a month. For the last 10–15 years he had moved out of the SF field and spent his time painting military figures for a model shop in Liverpool. He made an unexpected appearance at the 1999 Eastercon, where he was surprised that anyone in science fiction fandom remembered his artwork or his name." (*Ansible* 148)

Jones, Langdon

Jim Linwood writes, "Lang is very much an 'old Labour' councillor in Bracknell, but still has an interest in Peake and classical music. His eyebrows no longer meet in the middle."

Kettle, Roy

Roy is alive and well in London and is now Something Important in the Civil Service. While he is reported to still see a few old friends, he has not been to conventions for many years and is out of touch with fandom generally. Claire Brialey adds, "I was quite surprised to encounter, in a professional context, one Roy Kettle, who was indeed a senior civil servant, albeit by that stage a denizen of the Department of Work and Pensions. This was a contact that proved to be very useful when a few weeks later we needed to contact fans from before our time whose work we wanted to include in the fanthology for the 2003 Eastercon."

Kyle, Dave

Dave and Ruth continue to reside in Potsdam, New York, and Dave has been seen occasionally at American conventions. In the 1980s he wrote three "Lensman" novels.

Langford, Dave

Abandoning nuclear weapons research in 1980 to take his TAFF trip and scrape a living as a freelance writer, Dave says, "This was a career move which continues to be unprofitable, dozens of books later." He publishes the SF/fan newsletter *Ansible*, launched in 1979 and going strong after 25 years. As of early 2004 Dave has won an incredible 23 Hugos—17 as fan writer, 5 for *Ansible* as fanzine, and one for best short story—plus two BSFA Awards, two Nova Awards, the Skylark Award, and the European SF Award (shared). He has been a guest at many SF conventions in Britain and the U.S.A., and once each in Australia and Finland. His first book of 2004 was his SF story collection *Different Kinds of Darkness*.

PW adds, "*Ansible* is indispensable and the on-line back-issues provide a tremendous resource for research into the recent past of British fandom." (*www.dcs.gla.ac.uk/Ansible/*)

Lewis, Albert J.

Al Lewis turned up unexpectedly at the 1972 Chessmancon, with his wife, Linda, whom he married in 1969, and with a baby boy. He appears to have attended occasional meetings in the Los Angeles area for several more years but then withdrew entirely from fandom.

Lindsay, Ethel

Ethel Lindsay died early in June 1996 all too soon after the cancer diagnosis that left her determined to enjoy her expected 6–12 remaining months. (*Ansible* 108)

Linwood, Jim

In late 1965 Jim and Marion moved to Nottingham to start a family and his fannish contacts were restricted to close friends. Jim says, "I drifted away from fandom in the late '70's, having decided to spend more time getting an education to further my career. I got a Master's degree in Earth Science from Kingston University, became a fellow of the Geological Society and a Chartered Water & Environmental Manager. As a Planning Engineer looking after London's rivers I progressed (because of legislative changes) through Greater London Council, Thames Water, National Rivers Authority and the Environment Agency. I'm now pretty much retired but do voluntary work for Kew Bridge Steam Museum. We have lived in Isleworth for 30 years and have no plans to move."

Commenting on the events in Chapter 2 (originally in *Maya*), Jim says, "I thought, '*parallel childhoods!*' because I, too, made a refractor from army-surplus lenses and a cardboard tube and my observatory was an outside toilet in the 'mean yards' of our terraced block. The gap between the door and the frame was just big enough to hold the telescope firm enough to permit steady viewing. Unfortunately, the neighbours using their loos thought the heavenly bodies I was viewing were more earthbound and women wagged their fingers at me in the street shouting, '*I saw what you were up to last night!*' Still it was worth it, to be the only kid on the block to see the Luna craters, Jupiter's moons and the phases of Venus. Eventually I got paid to look through real telescopes."

Mellor, Adrian

Adrian died of cancer in 1999. PW writes, "In 1978 he was offered a Sociology post at the University of Liverpool and moved away. We exchanged Christmas cards for a few years but never met again. A former colleague comments that 'he put a lot of energy into his teaching, and setting up an M.A. before his retirement, which meant that he did not publish as much as he should. I was very fortunate to work with him on a project about Liverpool writers and fiction, as well as the setting-up of the Shrewsbury Quest, based on the Cadfael novels.' A web-search indicates that he published a number of papers in the general area of sociology & science fiction, and Liverpool

University's School of Media & Cultural Studies now awards an Adrian Mellor prize, for excellence in undergraduate dissertations."

Mercer, Archie

Archie died in March 1998, after years of poor health; in 1971 he moved with Beryl to the tip of Cornwall and, amazingly, appears to have dropped out of fandom completely, keeping in contact with only a few close friends. He became involved instead with various local activities, and at his death was vice-chairman of the Cornwall Humanist Association. (*Ansible* 129)

Mercer, Beryl

Beryl died in October 2003. PW notes, "She was the perfect complement to Archie; once they were together, they didn't seem to need anyone else, and after a few years in Bristol fandom they quietly moved away, never to be seen again at fannish events. I resumed contact with Beryl only just before she died, and she told me she missed Archie dreadfully, and was in very poor health. However, Beryl had remained close to her two sons, David and John, and was proud to have been a great-grandmother. She had written a fantasy novel, *Merlin's Quest*, although it had not been accepted by any publisher at the time of her death."

Moorcock, Michael

Michael Moorcock is alive and well and still writing, in Texas—"M. J. 'Tex' Moorcock, The Old Circle Squared, Nr Austin, TX," as he signed a recent e-mail. There is slightly less of him than there used to be, thanks to the 2002 amputation of two gangrenous toes, which he advertised for sale as AUTHENTIC RELICS in the May 2002 *Ansible*.

Invited as Guest of Honour to the 1975 Seacon at Coventry, Mike cried off a month or two before, and never again attended a British Easter convention.

Nadler, Harry

Harry Nadler died from a heart attack in March 2002. Although he had not attended many conventions since the early '80s, he had run the Manchester Festival of Fantastic Films for the previous thirteen years. Ron Bennett writes, "Great enthusiast for cinema and life. Great dry wit. Always an absolute joy to be with." (*Ansible* 176)

Pardoe, Darroll

After returning from the United States Darroll married Rosemary, and to some extent dropped out of active fandom while he concentrated upon earning a living. In 1977, tired of commuting into London, he took a job in the chemical industry in exotic Widnes. He and Rosemary moved to Liverpool and from there to Chester, where they still live. Darroll says, "In the early eighties Peter-Fred Thompson got me thinking about Buddhism, and in 1986 I met the Zen teacher whose student I have been ever since, Hogen Daido. In the late '80's Thorsons published a book that Rosemary and I had written on the legend of the female Pope. In 1990, I joined the Chester branch of a well-known charity, and since then it has taken up quite a lot of my spare time. So here I am in 2004, retired but very busy and still never regretting for a moment having married Rosemary on a snowy day in 1970."

PW adds, "Peter-Fred was a young lad of fourteen who lived across the road when we were at the Beeches Drive address, and came over to help me with duplicating the last few issues of *Speculation*. This brought him to fandom and ultimately, Darroll to Buddhism! Funny old World, isn't it!"

Parker, Doreen—see Rogers

Parker, Ella

Ella Parker had not been involved in fandom for many years, and the 1971 Worcester convention was her last. She entered a hospice and died in February 1994. (*Ansible* 79)

Perry, Tom

Tom's involvement with fandom was always episodic; he took fandom by storm in the mid-sixties with just four issues of *Quark*, then disappeared until his surprise reappearance at the 1976 Mancon, after which he produced two more issues. Moving to Florida in time for Suncon, he promptly vanished again until a further brief resurgence in the early eighties, at which time he was already a fan of desktop computing. Sadly, he died in July 1997.

Gary Farber wrote, "Tom's zines were like his writing: always thoughtful, carefully done, fannish, yet substantive and of import. He combined the fannish touch of a Hoffwoman or a Tucker, with the care and weight of a Boggs. He was a fan always to be taken seriously, yet who rarely, if ever, fell into taking himself too seriously or indulging in pomposity. He was, simply, one of the greats." (*Ansible* 121)

Peyton, Rog

Rog writes, "Having got married in 1968, my SF activity was at its lowest and my wife 'requested' that I dispose of these hundreds of 'old books and magazines.' So I sorted out a few boxes of unwanted items and sent out a catalogue of books to sell. Before very long I found myself dealing in SF in my spare time, opening Andromeda Bookshop in 1971 and giving up my job in the building trade to go full-time in 1973. Not exactly what my wife had planned!

"My involvement with the Birmingham SF Group hasn't stopped. I'm currently producing the monthly newsletter. Over the past 33 years I've held virtually every committee post—chairman, publicity officer, newsletter editor (my current job) and been on the committee of Novacon—our annual convention—several times, even chairing a number of them—and once I was Special Guest. Somehow, I've also found time to be on the committee of a couple of Eastercons, and attend about 140 assorted conventions, and be auctioneer at a large number of them. I also produced a couple of issues of a fanzine, *Land of Laughs,* in the late '80s.

"Meanwhile, back on the professional front, I was running Andromeda, acting as agent for artwork rights for the late Eddie Jones in the '80s, and in 1989 I started publishing SF under the Drunken Dragon Press imprint.

"Andromeda grew over 30 years to become one of the largest, if not THE largest, specialist bookshops in the world. And then September 11th happened and everything fell apart, resulting in Andromeda going into voluntary liquidation in January 2002. But selling SF was in my blood, and in November 2002 I sorted out a few boxes of unwanted items (oh, you heard that phrase before!) and started up again, using the very apt name Replay Books, selling second-hand items on eBay."

Pickersgill, Greg

PW writes, "Greg Pickersgill did not make much of an impact at Buxton, nor the following year at Oxford, but we most definitely took heed of *Fouler* (joint effort with Roy Kettle), when it appeared in 1970, designed to shock and wake-up the cosy fannish Establishment. Rob Hansen credits *Fouler* as 'having begun the revolution in British fanzines' that would lead to the 'Golden Age' of the mid-'70s, but Greg only went on from there, refining his message and his own penetrating writing style, never letting up with his demands for greater effort and higher standards, an idealist who is his own strictest critic.

"In later years Greg has become an icon, the 'Grand Old Man' of British fandom, who more than anyone has succeeded in reconciling supreme fannishness (the love of good fan-writing as exemplified by Willis, or Tom Perry) and the sercon orientation of something like *Warhoon* (or perhaps *Speculation*), and shown there really is no conflict between the two. Harsh and intolerant of muddle-headedness, but generous with his time for projects that he feels worthwhile, Greg has also been surprisingly kind to some lost souls who most fans have generally shunned.

"His most notable contribution in recent years has been 'Memory Hole,' an incredible collection of fanzines, painstakingly stored, indexed and noted on his web-site, without which research for this book would have been impossible. In his accompanying e-mail news-group, Greg's own acerbic contributions provide the driving energy that keeps the exchanges fresh and entertaining. (*www.gostak.demon.co.uk*)

"Greg married Catherine McAulay in March 2003, and they remain half (or two-thirds) of the Haverfordwest SF, Helmet and Marching Society. Greg won the 'Doc Weir' Award in 1978, was a Guest of Honour at Follycon, the 1988 Eastercon, and will be GoH at Interaction, the 2005 British Worldcon in Glasgow."

Pitt, Martin

After the demise of the Ancient Brummies, Martin continued to provide artwork to fanzine under the Santos by-line and attended several conventions. Since then, he says, "I have hunted the Loch Ness monster (successfully—it tasted delicious), got married in Prague (still married to the same female, Eva), consequently acquired two children, managed a small chemical plant, and published a couple of (technical) books. I ended up with a PhD, and for the past 15 years have been teaching chemical engineering in Yorkshire. I live in Leeds, but work in Sheffield. With family life and professional obligations, my SF activity has been confined to reading (and a lot less than I would like)."

Platt, Charles

Charles Platt emigrated to the USA in 1970. He became a highly success-ful journalist and essayist, and now lives in Arizona. His two books *The Dream Makers* contain an excellent series of interviews with most major SF writers.

Pratchett, Terry

No real need to comment on what Terry has done since that first appear-ance at Peterborough in 1964. He is now an international mega-star and, of course, is a Guest of Honour at Noreascon 4.

Priest, Chris

Chris writes, "In 1968 I gave up my last job, and began writing for a living. I was lucky: within four months, I had obtained a contract from Faber for my first novel, £50 down, the rest on publication! Starvation wages, even back then. I've managed to keep going ever since, with many ups and downs. For much of the time I was living in Harrow, in north-west London. After a pe-riod of relative mobility, living in different places, I settled in 1991 in Hastings, where I still am. I'm married to Leigh Kennedy, a writer born in Colorado, now a British Citizen. We have 14-year-old twins, Simon and Lizzy. We shall all be at Concourse in Blackpool, Easter 2004, where I am guest of honour. In 2005, I'm to be guest of honour at the Worldcon, in Glasgow. In between we will be trekking to Germany for Palatine Con, where I am...this is becoming repetitive. My most recent novel is *The Separation;* I'm working on a new one at the moment."

Pringle, David

After graduating in 1972 David spent the next ten years in Leeds, married his wife Ann and had a son, James. He started writing articles and reviews for the early *Foundation,* and in 1977 became its Reviews Editor. He says, "When Peter Nicholls left the SF Foundation, at the end of 1977, Malcolm Edwards and I found ourselves competing for his job. In the event, Malcolm became the new Administrator and I became a so-called Research Fellow (my brief was to research the usefulness of science fiction in education—although in fact I was just a kind of glorified librarian for their book collection). I com-muted weekly from Leeds, staying mid-week in digs in Barking, Essex. That was just a two-year appointment, alas, and it didn't look as though I would have a future there, so I began applying again for 'real' jobs and in the autumn of 1979 began work as Information Officer at Leeds Polytechnic. That was the year of the British Worldcon, which, as I recall, was run by Peter Weston and Malcolm Edwards... I was the Hugo ballot-counter for that event—I always seem to have wound up playing second fiddle to these guys!

"In 1976, I had co-edited a small-press book with James Goddard, entitled *J. G. Ballard: The First 20 Years* (Bran's Head Books), and in 1979 I had another small book published—*Earth Is the Alien Planet: J. G. Ballard's Four-Dimensional Nightmare* (Borgo Press). I also contributed quite a few entries to Peter Nicholls's *Encyclopaedia of SF* in that same year. I became overall editor of the journal *Foundation* when Malcolm Edwards resigned from that post in 1980—but from a distance: I was still living in Leeds.

"We began *Interzone* in 1982 (Malcolm, myself, and six others), and I moved with my family to Brighton in that same year. Have lived here ever since, initially working as Personal Assistant to the Director of Brighton Polytechnic. I moved back into librarianship in 1985, but left that in 1988 to work as Series Editor for Games Workshop Publishing (a job that lasted three years, until 1991). I have been a freelance editor and full-time *Interzone* editor/publisher since 1991, living somewhat parlously from a financial point of view... I have written or edited various books over the years, including *Science Fiction: The 100 Best Novels* (Xanadu, 1985), *Imaginary People: A Who's Who of Modern Fictional Characters* (Grafton, 1987), *Modern Fantasy: The 100 Best Novels* (Grafton, 1988), etc."

Redd, David

David writes, "After a brief burst of sfnal activity in the late '60's/early '70s, I returned to being a respectable person, a civil engineer, a husband, and a father (in that order). Infrequent SF stories continued to appear in *Asimov's, Scheherazade* etc, most recently in *Fantasy Annual* 5, a print-on demand book from Cosmos—demand it now! Similarly, infrequent fannish pieces surfaced to general incomprehension in Ken Cheslin's *The Olaf Alternative* and elsewhere. More interestingly, I appeared on "Who Wants to Be a Millionaire?" and wrote up the experience for Sandra Bond's wonderful *Quasiquote* 5. (Since you ask, £16,000, but I had children at college)."

PW adds, "Recently I took up David's 30-year-old invitation and, along with Greg Pickersgill, finally visited the Speculation Inn, down near the southern tip of Wales. David is one-third (or maybe one-quarter) of the Haverfordwest SF, Helmet and Marching Society, and in Greg's words, remains "the greatest living Welsh science fiction writer still living in Wales."

Reed, Mary

Mary emigrated to the US in 1976. She now lives on the eastern coast and is co-author with her husband Eric Mayer of, among other things, two mystery series. These are the Inspector Dorj stories (modern day Mongolia) and the John the Eunuch historical mysteries, set in and around the sixth century Constantinople court of Justinian I. The fifth novel about John will be published in early 2004, and the sixth is already being researched

Rickard, Bob

Inspired in part by all the fun he had with *Speculation*, Bob began his own fanzine, *The News*, which gave full vent to his Fortean interests. Bob says, "I have always regarded those years as my apprenticeship. Under Peter's cruel gaze, I learned the craft of putting together a fanzine; to vary the tone of its different sections; to mix articles with reviews and reference material; the useful little editorial bits, like standfirst paragraphs, pull quotes, interjections and answers to letters and critics; and not forgetting illustrations. Not only did this give me the confidence to publish my own fanzine later, but it also showed me the techniques to use.

"The late 1960s was the heyday of so-called 'underground' mags and papers, and I used to devour each issue of *Oz, International Times (IT), Friendz,* and the like. Strange to think that *Oz* played a part in us meeting, then, in 1971, in *Oz* I saw a notice from the U.K. membership secretary of the American International Fortean Organisation (INFO), who wanted to find a successor and retire. I immediately volunteered and was sent a few boxes of the American publication and a handful of addresses. Over the next two years, I sent INFO so many news clippings on strange phenomena they had trouble using them. The editors—Ron and Paul Willis, who were also involved in H. P. Lovecraft fandom—suggested I do my own fanzine. As I mulled it over, I had additional encouragement from Paul Screeton, of Cumberland, who published a very professional fanzine of his own devoted to the New Age pursuit of ancient trackways, UFOs and 'ley hunting.' Another rousing voice came from my old friend Steve Moore, who went on to be one of the U.K.'s finest writers of imaginative adventures for modern comics and an *I Ching* scholar of renown.

"The first issue of *The News* came out in November 1973. The title referred to Samuel Butler's *News From Nowhere,* as the contents were a typical Fortean melange of strange phenomena, anomalous experiences, odd omens and peculiar portents, all culled from UK newspapers. I typed the stories, set the titles in Letraset, cut-and-pasted pictures from any relevant source and rushed off to the Xerox copy bureau to print and collate 100 copies. I was working nights in a printed circuit factory, having quit the loathsome profession of product design, and now saw publishing as my salvation.

"It was Peter's pursuit of quality in presentation and content that I remembered, and it inspired me to seek ever-better ways of producing my growing magazine. As its circulation increased, I moved from typing to typesetting to computer-setting on home PCs, from borrowed illustrations to commissioned artwork and proper filmset printing. Now called *Fortean Times (FT),* more pages were added, and better distribution obtained through New Age shops and mail-order subscriptions. I took on a co-editor, Paul Sieveking, and we worked very well in harness together.

"In 1998, Paul and I lost our employment (creating a microfilm version of the British Library Catalogue), and we put some of our redundancy money into making *FT* look positively professional and cast about for an independent publisher to take us on full-time. That's how we joined the stable of John Brown, the publisher of *Viz*, and we went from a 2000-circulation fanzine to 25,000 sales as a newsstand monthly. In time, *FT* passed to I Feel Good Ltd., and then to Dennis Publishing, and is still going strong.

"After 19 years in the hot-seat as editor of *FT,* I have now semi-retired. I'm still writing though, and working on other projects, such as the creation of a Fortean Encyclopedia, so necessary to separate the grains of fact from today's ocean of fiction. I moved to London in 1976 and married Sam, a Chinese lady who grew up on the same street I had lived on when I was a child in Malaysia. Our two wonderful children are now grown up and about to flee the nest.

"Inevitably, my adventures in publishing took me far from SF fandom, but strangely our paths cross often and unexpectedly, such as at the birthday party in Cardiff for Lionel Fanthorpe (known to the nation as host of Fortean TV), at which I again met Terry Pratchett, David Langford, Jack Cohen and Brian Stableford. *Fortean Times* also hosts an annual convention—which, in true fannish tradition, I caused to be named UnConvention—attended by many SF fans, old and new. It has to be said though that, despite the incestuous relationship between SF and Forteanism (did you know that Charles Fort coined the word *teleportation* and was deified as "Charles Hoy Jaunt" in Alfred Bester's *Tiger, Tiger?*), the overlaps in readership are rare enough to be interesting."

Roberts, Peter

After Seacon '79 Peter vanished from the scene, having moved to the remote town of Dawlish in Devon, where, as he says, he eventually found a proper job. "Back in 1980 I became a copywriter with the publishers David & Charles in Devon. This wasn't quite what I had in mind when I dreamed of being a full-time writer, but it was certainly better than being an out-of-work librarian. The only trouble was that, after sitting at a typewriter from nine till five, I didn't want to spend my spare time doing pretty much the same thing, so the Gestetner fell silent and the fanzines and correspondence piled up and gathered dust. Devon not being a hotbed of fannish activity, things kind of drifted, whilst I ended up doing even more writing by moving to an advertising agency."

"I also developed my interest in fungi, which would be an inconsequential side note if the advertising agency hadn't gone bust in the early 1990s. But by then, my interest had grown to such an extent that I applied for and got a post as a mycologist at the Royal Botanic Gardens, Kew. I even got the brain cells into gear and undertook a PhD in Mycology, so (as Roj Gilbert used to say) my first name is now Doctor. And that's where I remain today. I re-established some fannish contacts when I moved to Kew, even attended a Corflu, and still write the (very occasional) loc. Most years, I can be found at Fortean Unconventions reminiscing with Bob Rickard...but I'm afraid it's hardly crifanac. We'll see what happens in the future."

Rogers, Doreen

Doreen married Phil Rogers in 1972, an event apparently attended by most of British fandom, and settled down in Scunthorpe with daughter Trish, two cats, and a dog, finally leaving the BSFA committee in 1975 after many years as Company Secretary. She continued to work as a Legal Executive, then took Law Society exams to become a Solicitor. In 1984 the steelworks closed, Phil was made redundant and Doreen had a series of heart attacks which ended her legal career. They moved to Shropshire and continued to read SF and go to conventions until Phil's death in 1998. Doreen says, "I spend my time with my DAB digital radio, playing Bridge, reading SF (and mysteries), walking the dog, and e-mailing old friends, but not necessarily in that order." Doreen was Guest of Honour at the second Novacon in 1972.

Rogers, Phil

Phil died of a heart attack in 1998. PW comments, "Once I stopped being frightened of Phil's loud voice we became good friends, and we even managed to have that game of brag (at Jersey in 1989; he won). At the end, I was privileged to be asked by Doreen to deliver the Tribute at Phil's humanist funeral, which was a very moving experience."

Shaw, Bob

Bob died in February 1996, and as Dave Langford wrote, "the shockwaves of dismay that raced around the SF world signalled the hugeness of the loss." He had married his new wife, Nancy Tucker, in December, and had just returned to Manchester from the USA. (*Ansible* 194)

PW adds, "Bob's health had been poor for some years, and in 1993 Eileen and I made a surprise visit to his bedside when he was in hospital in Warrington, after major surgery. His bewilderment was quite touching. "But you've come over a hundred miles," he said, "just to see me?" Bob and Sadie were always kind, and immediately after Seacon '79 they invited my family to spend the following weekend with them in the Lake District, which greatly cheered us at a time when I was feeling low."

Shaw, Sadie

Sadie died with "shocking unexpectedness" (Langford again) in 1991, leaving Bob bereft and fandom the poorer for the loss of her sparkle and kindness.

Shippey, Tom

Tom moved from Oxford to become Chair of English Language and Medieval Literature at Leeds University, before emigrating to the United States in the early '90s, where he now holds a senior post at the University of St Louis. He wrote two excellent short stories for the Andromeda series (as Tom Allen), but then did little more fiction apart from his collaboration with Harry Harrison on the impressive "Hammer and Cross" trilogy, an alternate worlds series set in Viking times. Tom edited *The Oxford Book of Science Fiction* and *The Oxford Book of Fantasy*, and has become the major Tolkien authority with his best-selling books, *The Road to Middle Earth* and *JRR Tolkien: Author of the Century.*

He recollects, "I remember giving a talk at the Brighton WorldCon on the theme of the 'invisible man' in science fiction, which I related to the notion of technical revolution. That was a good one because several of the authors I was discussing—Poul Anderson and Bob Shaw, as I remember—were in the audience and prepared to talk about what they thought they were doing. That was a strange experience for an academic: being contradicted by your subject! Not that Poul and Bob did contradict, exactly, though I have known others do so—Greg Benford really torpedoed me on one occasion. But it is good for academics to be confronted, to prevent them contracting Teachers' Syndrome (the conviction that you know more about everything than everyone else).

"I remember a World SF conference in Dun Laoghaire, maybe about 1976—hearing a really rather tedious and SLOW academic decide to ask rhetorical questions from the podium. Unfortunately his audience were all much faster than he was, and answered them before he could. At one point he said portentously, something like: 'How can we tell? After all, what is the opposite of "civilisation"?' And a voice from the audience—it was Norman Spinrad—yelled out, in his New York accent: 'De opposite of civilisation? I'll tell ya what's de opposite of civilisation. Detroit, dat's de opposite of civilisation.' "

"The lecture never got back on track, and that was good. It was (I think) on the flight back from that conference—and by this time I was an Oxford Fellow and on the way to getting my own Chair and Department—that I found myself staring out of the window and thinking, with reference to the talks I'd heard on Tolkien (who had died in 1973), "Blimey, they were bad. The old fellow really wouldn't like to hear the kind of nonsense these academics are talking about him. Somebody really ought to put the record straight." At this point a cold realisation formed, which said, in effect, "Yes, *you*. And you're going to have to come out of the closet." Which I did, but not until I'd gone up one more rung of the academic ladder.

"So yes, those early conventions were very important to me. People will tell you things are all very different now, and there certainly are differences. But SF courses I've seen in universities remain terribly predictable, picking out the authors who 'fit the academic bill' (Orwell, Huxley, C. S. Lewis, Margaret Atwood). And academic interests in the humanities are nowadays centred on what I call 'victimology.' SF fans, writers, and techies generally are very obviously not a victim group, and it is impossible for humanities professors to patronise scientists convincingly, so it's still an academic fringe activity. But then academic writing has become more and more of a fringe activity. My very heavily researched book on *Beowulf*, ten years work, out in 1998, has sold its first run of 500 copies, wow! My recent book on Tolkien has been translated into three languages so far and sold, I don't know, heading for 100,000. The Oxford Books I edited reach about the same number between them, and the collaborations with Harry Harrison far more. So those conventions, whatever else one may say, were good business for me. And good fun."

Tom and his wife Catherine maintain homes in the United States and in Dorset, retreating to the latter in the summer for R&R, and to see old friends.

Shorrock, Ina

Ina won the "Doc Weir" Award in 1976 and continues to attend most conventions, where she invariably volunteers as a gopher and assists with the Art Show. She has made many of Norman's photographs available to contemporary fandom, including their album from the 1957 London worldcon, which are on the efanzine site.

Shorrock, Norman

Norman died in November 1999, at age 70. Ken Slater wrote, "Those of us who can still recall the high fannish years of the very late forties and the fifties will be aware that Norman had considerable influence on the development of British fandom. He and Ina, his wife, were founder members of the Liverpool SF Group in 1951; it was Norman who talked the society into buying a tape recorder, and making sound tape productions filled with fannish puns and fun. Later in the same decade he was instrumental in getting British fan film production started. Norman was also a fanzine publisher, a Knight of St Fantony from the order's inception, and one of the card-school who got coffee and drinks delivered to a bathroom in the Bull Hotel in Peterborough. At the same time, he was quiet and friendly, and helpful when help was needed. A fan's fan." (*Ansible* 149)

Slater, Ken

Despite his most unfannish interests in such activities as Hunter Trials and other horsey pursuits, Ken has continued to appear with his bookstall at almost every Eastercon up to the present day, plus Novacons and European conventions—he says his record was fourteen, in 1981! He was Guest of Honour at Novacon 4 and finally received his overdue recognition as Worldcon GoH at Conspiracy, in 1987. Joyce, wife and ever-loyal assistant, died in 1995, but Ken is indestructible, last year celebrating over *sixty years* in active fandom.

Stephenson, Andrew

Andrew was an electronics engineer until the demise of Plessey in 1976, when he became a full-time free-lance. He said, "I had two SF novels published, *Nightwatch* (1977) and *The Wall of Years* (1981), plus two short stories, but actually did more work of other kinds, including computer programming and computer reviewing. I dropped pro art (Ames) in 1978 when a big job went off the rails. Spent years trying to combine word/art interests, pushing comics projects at an indifferent world. My mid-'90s decision to give that up provoked the world to beat down my door with an offer to write a comics mini-series, 'Waterloo Sunset' (due to launch in July 2004). I am sometimes bemused by how alike SF and comics fandoms can be!"

Steward, John

As if one worldcon wasn't enough, John bravely allowed himself to be mobilised into becoming Treasurer of the successor convention, Conspiracy in 1987, which—alas!—did not enjoy quite such a smooth ride, financially. Since that trauma, John seems to have mysteriously disappeared from fandom. Wonder why!

Teague, Cliff

In the '70s Cliff met Jill, a non-fan, and had three sons, and for a time they ran a second-hand bookshop in central Birmingham. However, in 1984 he separated from his family in a cataclysmic upheaval during which he lost his shop and his Collection, and since then he has lived quietly in the suburbs, trading in a small way in books and comics. Sadly, he now appears to have very little memory of the events described in this book.

Thomson, Arthur

Arthur died in 1990, and his ATom cartoons were rarely seen in fanzines after 1980. He received a posthumous Rotsler memorial award in 2001.

Tubb, Ted

Ted Tubb seems to have slipped quietly away from fandom, and was probably last seen at Conspiracy, in 1987. His greatest success as a writer came relatively late in his career with the "Dumarest" series, commencing in 1967 and running to 32 titles. The *Encyclopaedia of SF* says, "The sequence stopped— perhaps at the behest of its publishers—at a somewhat inconclusive point. Though some of the late-middle titles seemed aimless, the author showed consistent skill at prolonging Dumarest's intense suspense about the outcome of his long quest. The final book appeared in France as *La Retour* (1992) and was published in the U.S. as *The Return* in 1997."

PW adds, "Ted wrote recently to wish me well with this book, saying, 'I hope you resist the temptation to squeeze it down. It could be an interesting window on a time now gone, and you can't have too much of a good thing.' Ted still lives with his wife Iris at their house in South-East London, though he has little contact with modern fandom."

Turner, Mike

After 1966, Mike sold off most of his collection to finance other hobbies, including railway modelling, photography, and folk music. He married in 1979, had a daughter in 1980, and in 1981 moved to the island of Mull, where he founded his computer software engineering business, Island Software. After the end of his first marriage he met Gill at a writers' group, and they married in 1995 and now have "two wonderful kids." Their extensive house (on yet another Scottish island) is gradually filling up with a new collection of SF, as Gill is also an enthusiast.

Some years ago, Rog Peyton was astounded to hear that Mike was a multimillionaire and had bought his Scottish island. This was not entirely true, and Mike says, "I'd better kill that rumour stone-dead. It comes from the *Sunday Times* front-page article in February 1983, in which my software publishers, ESI, estimated that the market for my 'Toolbox' products was worth £2m and I was on 10% royalties. All rubbish except the 10% bit. 'Toolbox' made me a total of £30,000 over about two years, which wasn't even enough to pay the bills."

Walsh, Tony

Tony and Simone separated in the mid-seventies and he left fandom behind, working for long periods in Saudi Arabia and the Middle East as a contract engineer. He died in 1998.

Webb, Gerry

According to the web-site of his company, Commercial Space Technologies, Gerry has now launched seven satellites using hardware provided by the former Soviet Union, which Gerry has been visiting since 1987 and where he now has a permanent Moscow base.

After a holiday from the fan-scene after Conspiracy, Gerry re-appeared at Blackpool in 1992, having swapped Spitfire for Rolls Royce, cravat for fashionable braces (= "suspenders"), and gained the tiny but beautiful Mali and son, Alan. To the general awe of fandom, Gerry then turned up in 1993 at Helicon in Jersey with a bevy of Russian girls and a couple of rocket engineers, and has attended most British Eastercons since then. The *2001* poster still graces the wall in his London dining room.

Williams, Kevin

Tynecon was Kevin's first con, and he attended all of the 'seventies Eastercons and most of the Novacons, also editing the fanzines *Durfed* and *Out of the Blue* (with Harry Bell). Kevin says, "I was lucky to be actively involved with the Gannets during their most productive period, in setting up the North East Science Fiction Group, running a long run of Silicons, and establishing the success of the fancon idea." In 1984 he was one of the prime movers of the first Mexicon (Tynecon II), chairing the event. However, a busy career with Procter & Gamble moved Kevin and Sue south in 1986. This, a family, and escalating workload caused them to drift away from fandom, and in 1992, work again moved them to the U.S.A. (initially to Connecticut and later Cincinnati, Ohio).

Kevin continues, "Though the job increasingly occupied more and more of my waking time and energy, and caused me to travel a great deal (U.S.; West & Eastern Europe; Japan and China), I had long planned to retire at age 55—and did so in July 2003. I am still adjusting to the retiree life and doing lots of travel, hiking, photography, running a walking club, and am on the Board of Surrey Young Enterprise—helping sixth formers understand the wonderful world of industry—while trying to catch up on old friends. Sue is doing a fine arts degree at Reading, and son Mike is in his A-Level year, intent on studying Media and Communication and leading a rock band. All is well!"

Willis, Walt

Walt Willis turned up unexpectedly at the 1976 Mancon, but never again came to a British convention, though he appeared as Guest of Honour at Magicon, the 1992 Worldcon. A last issue of *Hyphen* appeared in 1987, to celebrate forty years of Irish fandom. Walt died from a heart attack in October 1999 just before his eightieth birthday, after more than a year in hospital. (*Ansible* 149)

Winstone, Charlie

After 1966, Charlie had no contact with local fandom until he re-appeared briefly in 1971–1972 with the re-launch of the Birmingham group. He produced a final issue of *Nadir* in 1972 before leaving fandom completely. He died after a short illness in April 1984.

Winterman, Geoff

Leaving the dust of Birmingham behind in 1974, and by this time safely married to Rowena, Geoff moved to Haverfordwest, where he became headmaster of a large school. He retired recently and now lives very comfortably in a village, where he pursues various hobbies and is an adviser to the local education board. He has a daughter and two sons, and is still considering whether or not to become one-quarter of the Haverfordwest SF, Helmet and Marching Society.

Some Science-Fictional Speculation About Peter Weston
Appendix 2

In 2002, the British Eastercon was held in St Helier, on the island of Jersey, and was distinguished by the presence of Harry Turtledove as Guest of Honour. Accordingly, the whole of the convention's programme and publications were devoted to an exploration of the possibilities posed by that simple question, "What If?" and I was vastly flattered and amused when Mark Plummer chose to examine my fannish career from this perspective!

In common with the experiences of many others, there's more than a little serendipity in Peter's fannish career path; but it's all so mythic in nature—the way things are supposed to happen—that it's easy to forget that, once upon a time, things really *did* happen this way.

Back in 1963 the Birmingham SF Group—a forerunner of the current BSFG and temporarily re-branded as the Erdington SF Circle to secure coverage in a local newspaper—advertised its existence by seeding little slips of pink paper in the SF books in the rag market and the local libraries. The slips were primarily to establish the group's credentials and secure that eagerly-sought press publicity; the fact that they brought a 19-year-old Peter Weston to fandom in January 1963 was merely a spin-off benefit, although it kicked off a chain of consequences that arguably shaped the direction of British fandom in the 1960s and led ultimately to the 1979 British Worldcon.

"After six years of solitary reading it was the first indication that others like me existed. And I needed something like this. I knew that I had gone about as far as I could on my own. Six years hanging around the market twice per week and I'd nearly given up hope of finding *Galaxy* numbers 5, 6, 7, 36 and 52, issues I desperately needed to complete my index of authors and story-titles." ("Slice of Life," *Maya* 11, July 1976)

This is indeed how fans are supposed to discover fandom. And it's stories like this that cause me to read print references to *Galaxy* magazine with a faint underlying Birmingham accent (while *F&SF* exudes a combination of hair, glasses and Welshness for some reason that I just can't fathom).

The Birmingham group that Peter discovered included Rog Peyton, Charlie Winstone, and Cliff Teague, whose book and magazine collection did indeed contain those missing issues of *Galaxy* as well as a copy of Damon Knight's *In Search of Wonder*, a book that every science fiction fan should still seek out and read. But they had had no contact with greater fandom and when Teague told the others of a rumoured convention in Peterborough, they all ignored him. After all, Peterborough was a remote and exotic location that was about as accessible as Vladivostok or Mars. Still, Teague—fulfilling his role in the chain of consequences—hitch-hiked to the 1963 Eastercon, Bullcon, and after a weekend of freeloading returned with no tales of ten-foot-tall six-armed green Martians but a far more practical rucksack full of books including an autographed copy of Michael Moorcock's *Stormbringer*.

Indeed, were Harry Turtledove ever to write an alternate history of British science fiction fandom—which seems likely as given his current production rate he will eventually write an alternate history of absolutely everything—he might look to Cliff Teague to provide his "point of divergence." Because it was Teague again who hitch-hiked to London to check out one of the fan meetings at the Parker Penitentiary, Ella Parker's flat in Canterbury Road. Fortunately for our chain of consequences, if not for Teague, Ella had been re-housed in a nearby tower block and the old flat was boarded up and derelict.

Fandom, of course, does not make 'em like it used to; younger fans like myself, a mere 38 years old and brought up on word processors, thousands of science fiction books easily available, and dozens of conventions every year, would not know how to cope with this kind of set back. Teague, however, came from the era when they did still make 'em like they used to. He was undeterred by this seemingly insurmountable obstacle and did what any self-respecting early '60s fan would do in the face of such a complication: he broke in.

Actually, no. Everything I've read suggests that Teague was pretty much the *only* person who would have done this, which suggests that he was indeed the right man in the right place at the right time, placed on this earth for a Grand Purpose by the Fannish Elder Gods (and that's a phrase which I feel should probably have more "h"s in it but I really can't bring myself to do it, not even for Peter).

Inside, Cliff Teague found *Inside:* Jon White's *Inside,* that is, and Norm Metcalf's *New Frontiers,* fanzines which had been mailed to Parker and which had obviously arrived after she left and never been forwarded. Instantly discerning their Cosmic Significance, Teague took them with him when he fled the flat in the early hours of the morning after having been startled by a tramp. (And just think, if that tramp had arrived just a little earlier, then *he* might have found those fanzines and been converted to the fannish true way. Or he might have used them for firelighters, but one way or another the chain of consequences would have been broken. Harry Turtledove, are you getting all this?)

When he got back to Birmingham, after spending the night in a public lavatory in Kilburn (ah, the glamour of the '60s Travelling Jiant fan existence), Teague showed his haul to Peter. Parenthetically here, back in 1997 I remember watching two baffled Young Conservatives—who were sharing hotel space with "Attitude: The Convention"—puzzling over a single-page one-shot fanzine by then fourteen-year-old Felix Cohen (about Gestetner duplicators), and a "Year of the Wombat" flyer. What cosmic leaps of imagination would they have had to make to extrapolate from this basic starting point to the stage where they could deduce the implied existence of Stephen Baxter, *Plokta* and Alison Freebairn?

Although I've never seen either the White or Metcalf fanzines in question, I suspect Peter had a better jumping-off place than our 1997 Young Conservatives—even hardened fans like John Harvey were struggling with the "Year of the Wombat" flyer and the strap-line, "If it had been tails it would have been badger"—but all the same it can't have been a great deal to go on. And crucially, *Inside* and *New Frontiers* were resolutely sercon fanzines: they talked about science fiction.

This may seem hardly worth pointing out, because of course all SF fanzines talk about SF, don't they? I mean, what would be the point otherwise? Yes, yes, I know that *we* all know that this isn't the case—although the myth that arises from it, that fanzine editors and writers have *no* interest in SF, is just that: a myth—but there have always been SF fanzines that do pretty much what a neutral outside observer would expect SF fanzines to do, and as it so happens it was a couple of these that shaped the young Peter's (excuse me while I temporarily relish the opportunity to refer to him as "young Peter") perceptions of what a fanzine is and what it does. Well, no, there was one other influence: a copy of *Les Spinge,* produced by local BNF Ken Cheslin, but:

"... quite honestly it made little impression in itself. It was too thoroughly alien, with green paper, erratic lines of type and weird, in-group humour. Now

I suspect Ken's peculiar blend of chatter and insane layout would have bewildered a far more experienced fan than I was. But it did make me realise that quite ordinary-looking people could aspire to bring out a magazine, while *Inside* and *New Frontiers* gave me a target to aim for." ("Slice of Life," *Maya* 11, July 1976)

In October 1963, Peter Weston published the first issue of his fanzine. It was called *Zenith*, a title allegedly chosen—at least in part—because the letters in the word, when written in capitals, consist of straight lines, which makes it easier to draw the heading. It was, of course, also a title that had been previously used by Harry Turner in the 1940s and '50s, although given the circumstances I guess it's kinda unsurprising that Peter didn't know that. It was a half-foolscap production, spirit-duplicated in purple ink, which included some Charlie Winstone poetry, Rog Peyton's checklist of Digit books, and Peter's rave review of Jack Vance's *Big Planet*. Nothing by Cliff Teague; but he had already played his part in the chain of consequences.

At this point I should really send you off to Greg Pickersgill's Memory Hole fanzine library to see if you can beg a copy for yourself. However, you won't find a copy of that first issue of *Zenith*, as Greg doesn't even have one himself. The print run was a whole 30 copies, and I suspect few have survived into the twenty-first century.

A second issue of *Zenith* appeared in December 1963 (38 duplicated quarto pages), followed by five 40–50-page issues in 1964 and a change of title in December '64 (number 7) to *Zenith-Speculation*. Another title change came with number 14 (October 1966): thereafter the fanzine went by the name of *Speculation*.

Looking at those later *Speculations*—the fanzine saw 20 issues under that title, running through to issue 33, dated 1973 but distributed as a rider with *Maya* 11 in July 1976—you can see something that clearly represents this notion to which I referred earlier: what an outside observer might expect of a science fiction fanzine, namely a publication that discusses science fiction with a fan's sensibilities. Writing on the Memory Hole e-list in 1999, Greg Pickersgill listed his ten favourite fanzines of the '60s, which included:

"*Speculation*—edited by Peter Weston. Quite simply one of the best fanzines about science fiction ever, and one that I find bears endless re-reading. It's all just endlessly interesting...full of useful knowledge and commentary. A very British version of [Dick] Geis's magazines, without the strange professional fannishness that flourished in them, but much more orderly and readable than anything Geis ever did."

It's the prevalence of these professional contributors that seems surprising to a modern reader. Looking at issue 25 for instance, dated January/February 1970, you'll see letters from James Blish, John Foyster, Bruce Gillespie, Sam Moskowitz, Ted White, Robert Coulson, Dan Morgan, Piers Anthony, Brian

Aldiss and M. John Harrison, and reviews by Blish, Pamela Bulmer, and Brian Stableford. As noted, some writers got their first breaks within the fanzine: it introduced *Interzone* editor David Pringle to fandom, as well as Bob Rickard—later co-editor of *Fortean Times,* who contributed articles and artwork.

Looking back on *Speculation* in Rob Jackson's *Maya,* Peter wrote:

"[It] long ago cast me as an editor rather than as a writer, and I sometimes wonder if things might have been different if I'd never started that fanzine. Writing has never been easy or natural for me; I've had to work at it, and editing is too easy, too much of a cop-out. It doesn't force one to develop any real facility with words, and so although I entered fanzine fandom in 1963 it wasn't until quite recently that I started to do very much more than re-type other people's words for public consumption." ("Slice of Life," *Maya* 9, November 1975)

So, once again, we're looking back to what might have been; back to the Erdington SF Circle again, those pink slips of paper, and Cliff Teague's breaking and entering; to the alternate history of British fandom where *Speculation* never came into being. What would have been the consequences of a British fandom without it? Well—and here's our chain of consequences again—it was within the pages of *Speculation* that the idea of a British Worldcon bid "sometime during the 1970s" was floated (Editorial, number 27, September 1970). Malcolm Edwards was later to take up and run with the idea in *Magic Pudding* (November 1973), which is ironic given that, for all that *this* Malcolm Edwards is a real person, the name had previously been used as a pseudonym by Peter for fanzine reviews in the BSFA's *Vector.*

And of course, Britain did get its Worldcon, just about squeezed in within the projected timescale and with Peter as chairman; over 3,000 people attended, making it by far the largest convention held in the U.K. up to that point. It is a long road from Erdington to St Helier; from 1963 to 2002. But what's it all about, really; all those stages on the road from pink slips in Birmingham to fannish celebrity in Jersey? Well:

"I feel that fandom has achieved amazingly much for a small scattered group of people with no commercial backing. A lot of people in this country complain about fandom; they ought to stop and look for any other amateur group that has done more, for its size, so far as good writing, intelligent discussion and thoughtful interest in its subject matter is concerned. I'm rather proud to be involved with fandom."

(Editorial, *Speculation* 25, January/February 1970)

Erdington Science Fiction Circle—front page of the *Erdington News,*
4th January 1963. Rog Peyton (standing), Jack Pickering, Cliff Teague, Dave
Casey. *(Rog Peyton album)*

First Birmingham S F Group badge 1949 *(Rog Peyton)*

Pro-panel at Brumcon 1965; Ted Tubb, Mike Moorcock, Brian Aldiss, Harry Harrison, James White *(Norman Shorrock)*

British Science Fiction Convention
Drawn by Eddie Jones—used for 3 years
(Peter Weston)

Bob Shaw & Peter Weston, at the first "Speculation" conference,
June 1970 *(Peter Weston album)*

"Like identical twin undertakers, dressed in dark suits and short back-&-side
haircut."
Rear: Jim Marshall, Peter Weston
Front: Graham Charnock, Chris Priest
Bristol 1967 *(Harry Bell)*

St Fantony Ceremony, Eastercon 22—Eddie Jones, Phil Rogers, Dave Kyle, Ramsey Campbell, Michael Rosenblum, Ethel Lindsay, and candidate Bob Shaw *(Peter Weston album)*

The Brum Group meets King Kong—Autumn, 1972! Charlie Winstone on left, next to Rowena Winterman, Stan Eling, Hazel Reynolds, Vernon Brown. Eileen Weston holding baby Alison. *(Peter Weston album)*

Mike Moorcock with whisky bottle, with Phil Rogers and Rog
Peyton at Sci-con
(*Bill Burns*)

Setting off for his TAFF trip! Peter Weston leaves home,
August 1974 (*Peter Weston album*)

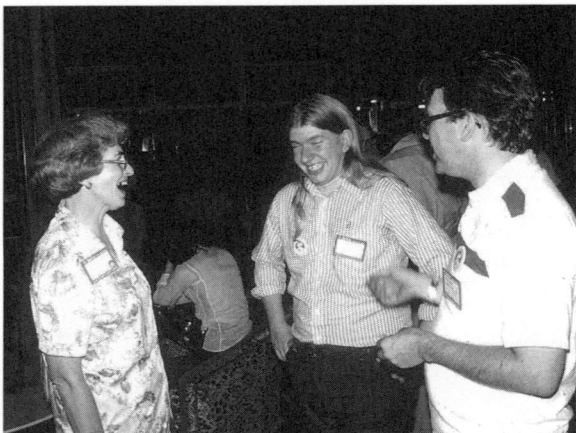

Lee Hoffman, Terry Hughes & Tom Perry, Suncon 1977
(Rob Jackson)

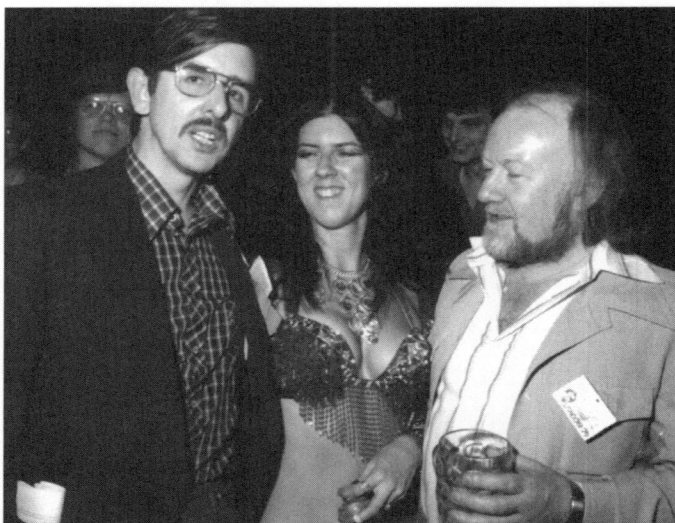

Fun in the Fan Room! Peter Weston with Kathy Sanders
& Rog Peyton, Seacon (Peter Weston album)

Peter Weston directs building the Tower of
Beer-cans to the Moon at the Gopher Party
*(Kevin Williams album, with assistance
from Catherine Pickersgill)*

Bob Shaw gets his Hugo from Bob Tucker at Seacon
(Peter Weston album)

The Shield of Umor—outside The Speculation Inn, Pembrokeshire
(*Peter Weston album, with assistance from Catherine Pickersgill*)

Harry Harrison, Peter Weston, Dave Langford,
Novacon 33, 2003 (*Peter Weston album*)

Name Index

A

B